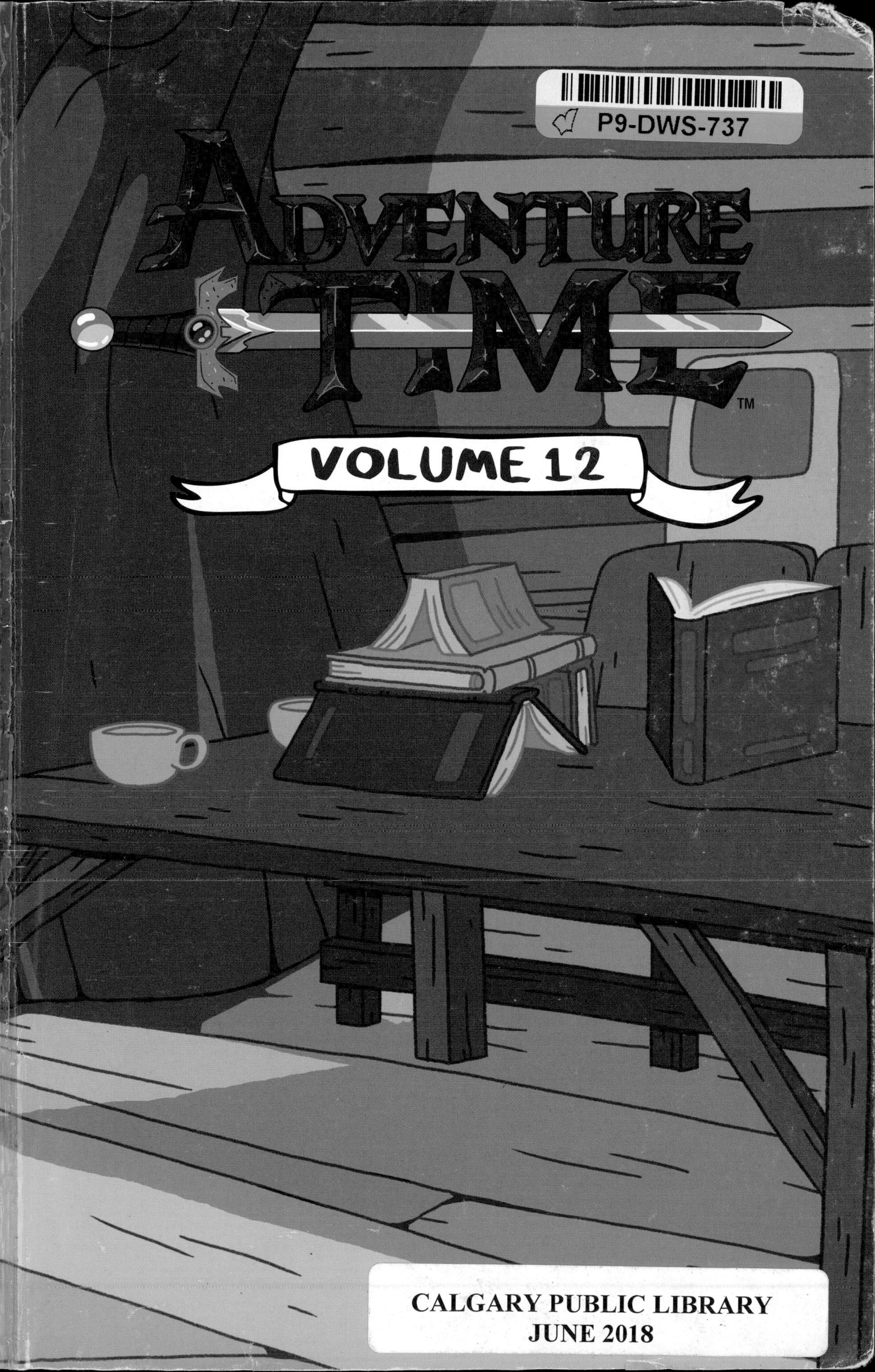
ADVENTURE TIME
TM
VOLUME 12

ROSS RICHIE CEO & Founder • MATT GAGNON Editor-in-Chief • FILIP SABLIK President of Publishing & Marketing • STEPHEN CHRISTY President of Development • LANCE KREITER VP of Licensing & Merchandising
PHIL BARBARO VP of Finance • ARUNE SINGH VP of Marketing • BRYCE CARLSON Managing Editor • MEL CAYLO Marketing Manager • SCOTT NEWMAN Production Design Manager • KATE HENNING Operations Manager
SIERRA HAHN Senior Editor • DAFNA PLEBAN Editor, Talent Development • SHANNON WATTERS Editor • ERIC HARBURN Editor • WHITNEY LEOPARD Editor • JASMINE AMIRI Editor • CHRIS ROSA Associate Editor
ALEX GALER Associate Editor • CAMERON CHITTOCK Associate Editor • MATTHEW LEVINE Assistant Editor • SOPHIE PHILIPS-ROBERTS Assistant Editor • KELSEY DIETERICH Designer • JILLIAN CRAB Production Designer
MICHELLE ANKLEY Production Designer • KARA LEOPARD Production Designer • GRACE PARK Production Design Assistant • ELIZABETH LOUGHRIDGE Accounting Coordinator • STEPHANIE HOCUTT Social Media Coordinator
JOSÉ MEZA Event Coordinator • JAMES ARRIOLA Mailroom Assistant • HOLLY AITCHISON Operations Assistant • MEGAN CHRISTOPHER Operations Assistant • AMBER PARKER Administrative Assistant

ADVENTURE TIME Volume Twelve, August 2017. Published by KaBOOM!, a division of Boom Entertainment, Inc. ADVENTURE TIME, CARTOON NETWORK, the
logos, and all related characters and elements are trademarks of and © Cartoon Network. (S17) Originally published in single magazine form as ADVENTURE TIME No.
54-57. © Cartoon Network. (S16) All rights reserved. KaBOOM!™ and the KaBOOM! logo are trademarks of Boom Entertainment, Inc., registered in various countries and
categories. All characters, events, and institutions depicted herein are fictional. Any similarity between any of the names, characters, persons, events, and/or institutions in
this publication to actual names, characters, and persons, whether living or dead, events, and/or institutions is unintended and purely coincidental. KaBOOM! does not read
or accept unsolicited submissions of ideas, stories, or artwork.

BOOM! Studios, 5670 Wilshire Boulevard, Suite 450, Los Angeles, CA 90036-5679. Printed in China. First Printing.

ISBN: 978-1-68415-005-2, eISBN: 978-1-61398-676-9

CREATED BY
# Pendleton Ward

WRITTEN BY
# Christopher Hastings

ILLUSTRATED BY
# Ian McGinty

COLORS BY
# Maarta Laiho

ISSUE #54 LETTERS BY
# Steve Wands

ISSUES #55-57 LETTERS BY
# Mike Fiorentino

COVER BY
# Ian McGinty

DESIGNER
**Grace Park**

ASSOCIATE EDITOR
**Alex Galer**

EDITOR
**Whitney Leopard**

With Special Thanks to Marisa Marionakis, Janet No, Curtis Lelash, Conrad Montgomery, Meghan Bradley, Kelly Crews, Scott Malchus, Adam Muto and the wonderful folks at Cartoon Network.

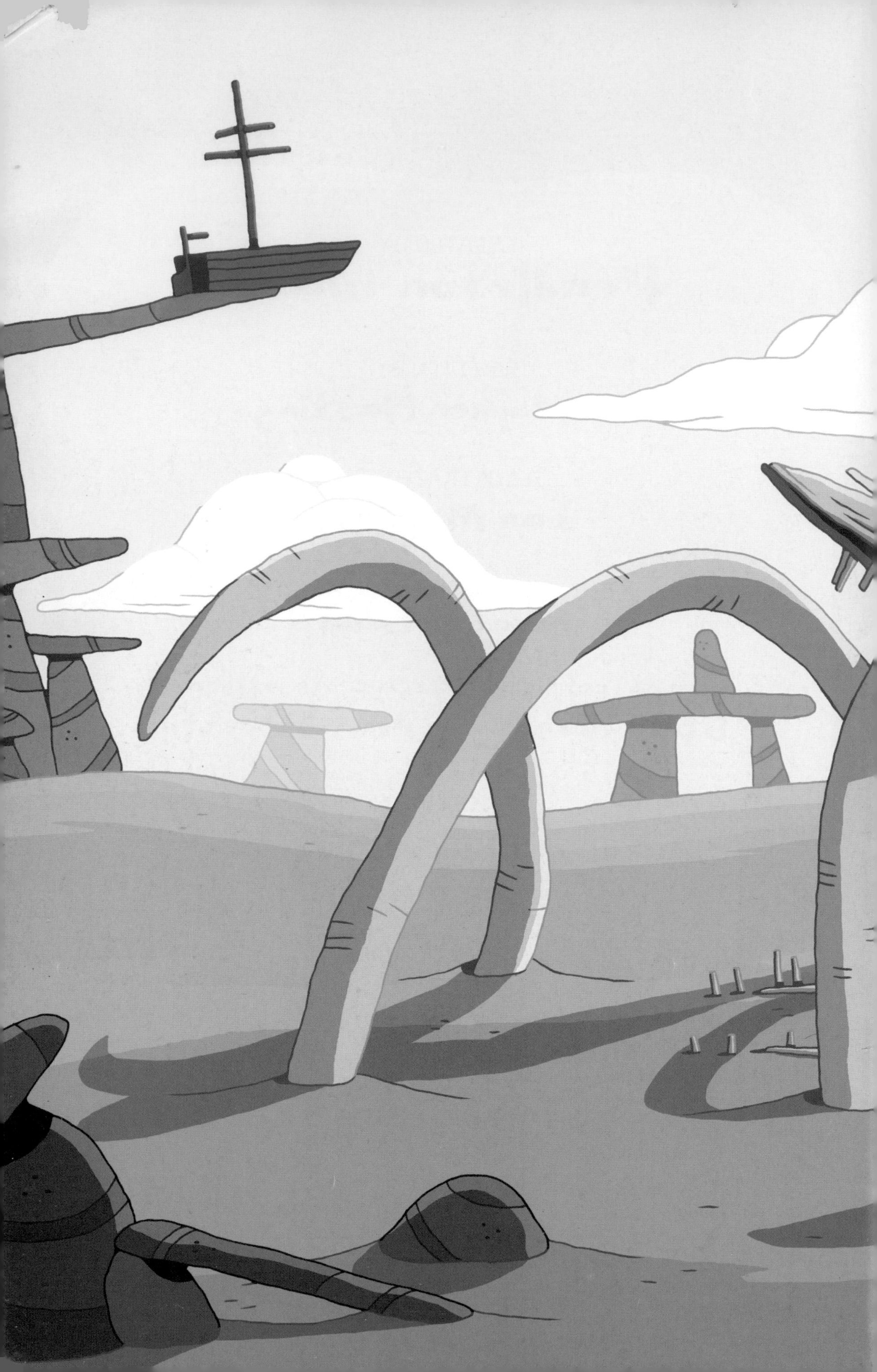

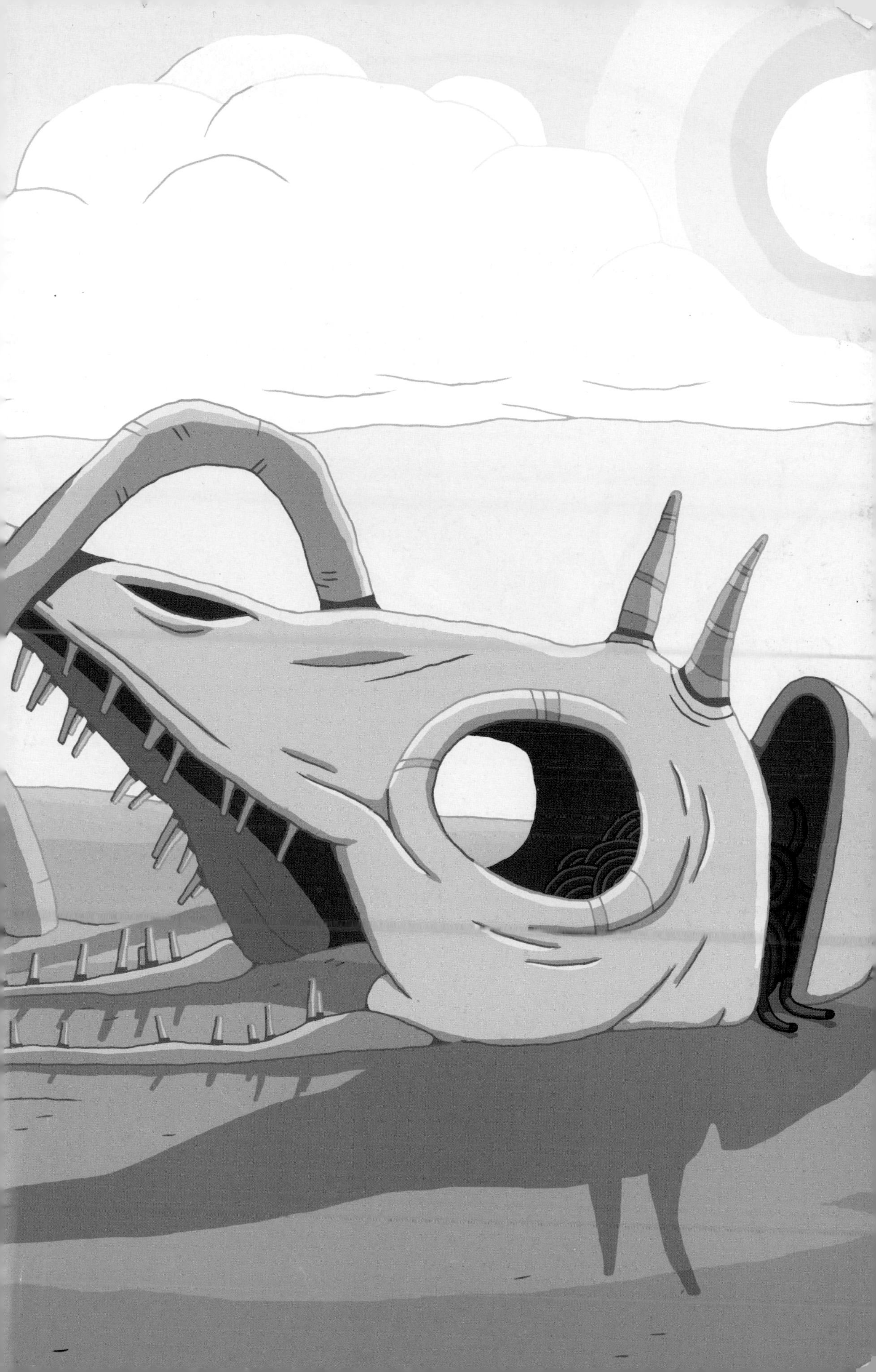

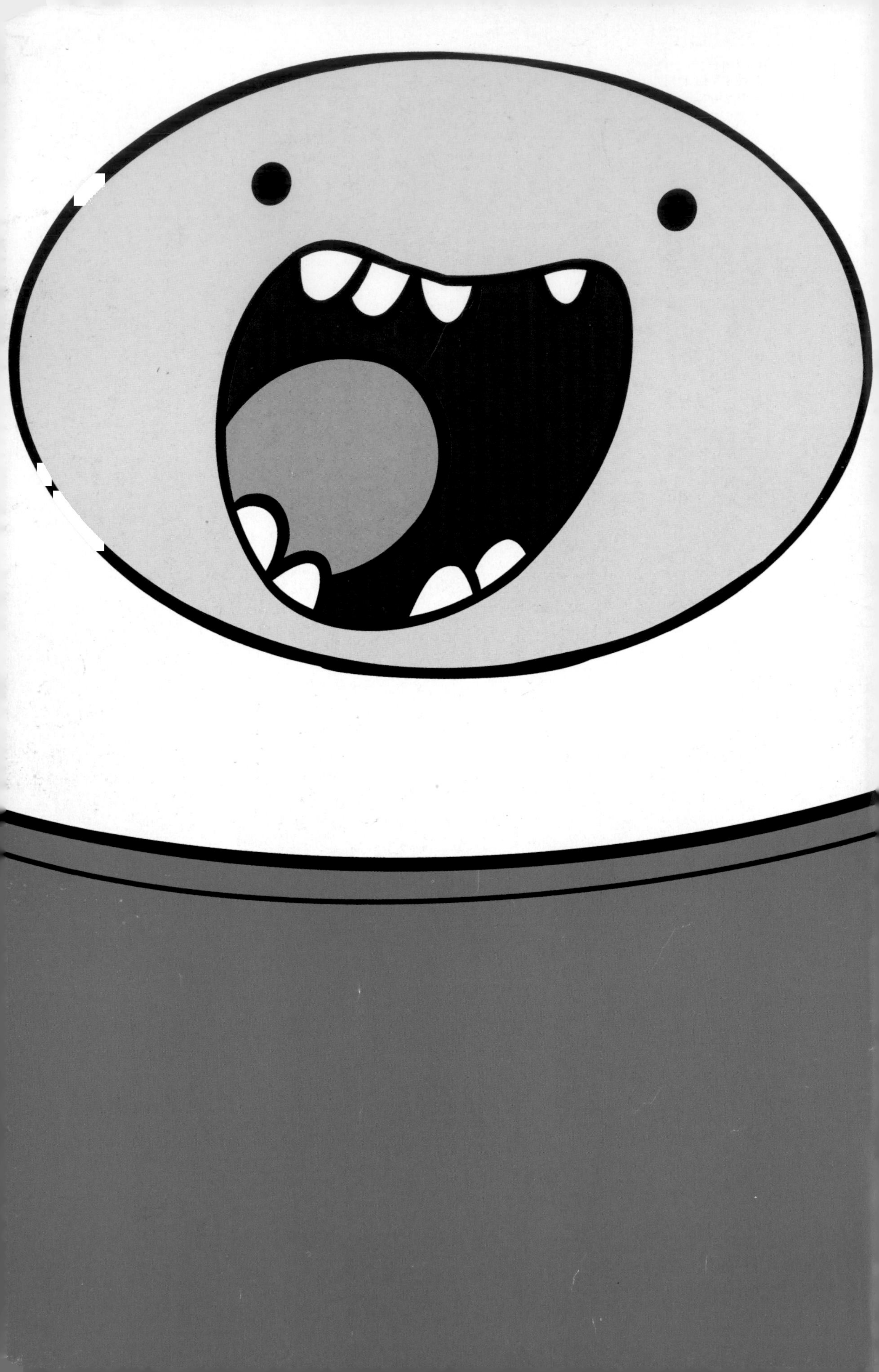

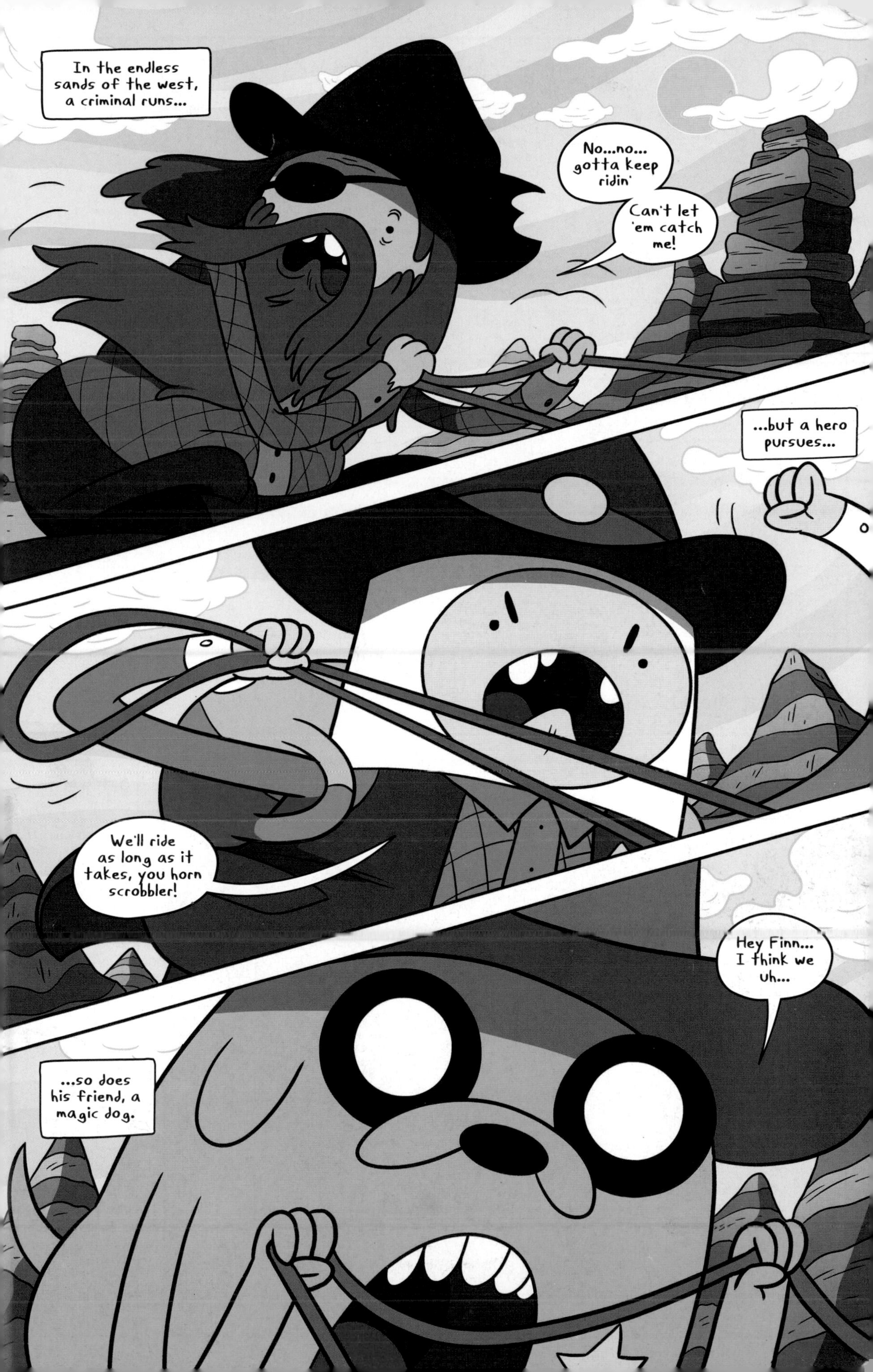
In the endless sands of the west, a criminal runs...
No...no... gotta keep ridin'
Can't let 'em catch me!
...but a hero pursues...
We'll ride as long as it takes, you horn scrobbler!
Hey Finn... I think we uh...
...so does his friend, a magic dog.

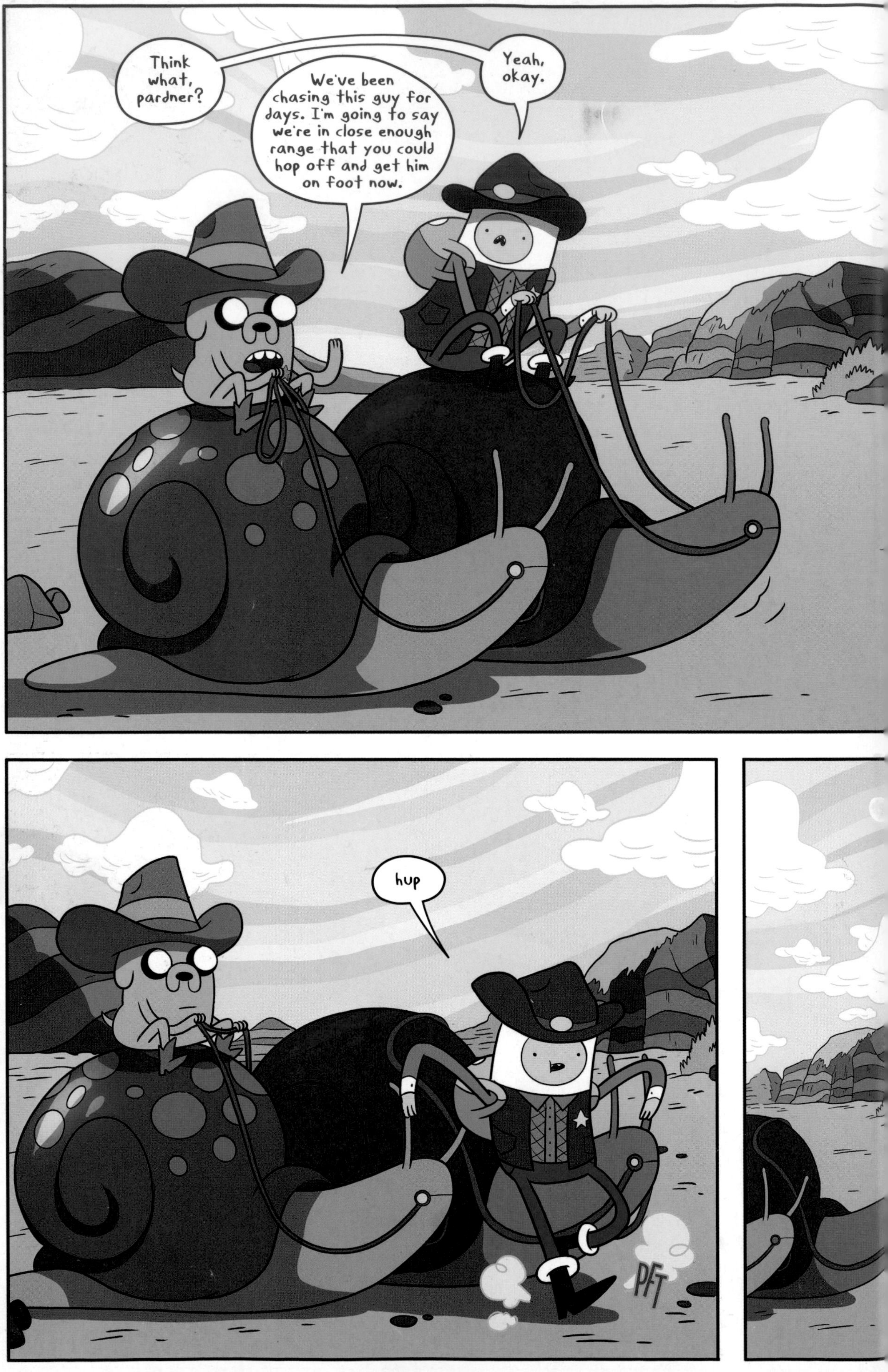
Think what, pardner?
We've been chasing this guy for days. I'm going to say we're in close enough range that you could hop off and get him on foot now.
Yeah, okay.
hup
PFT

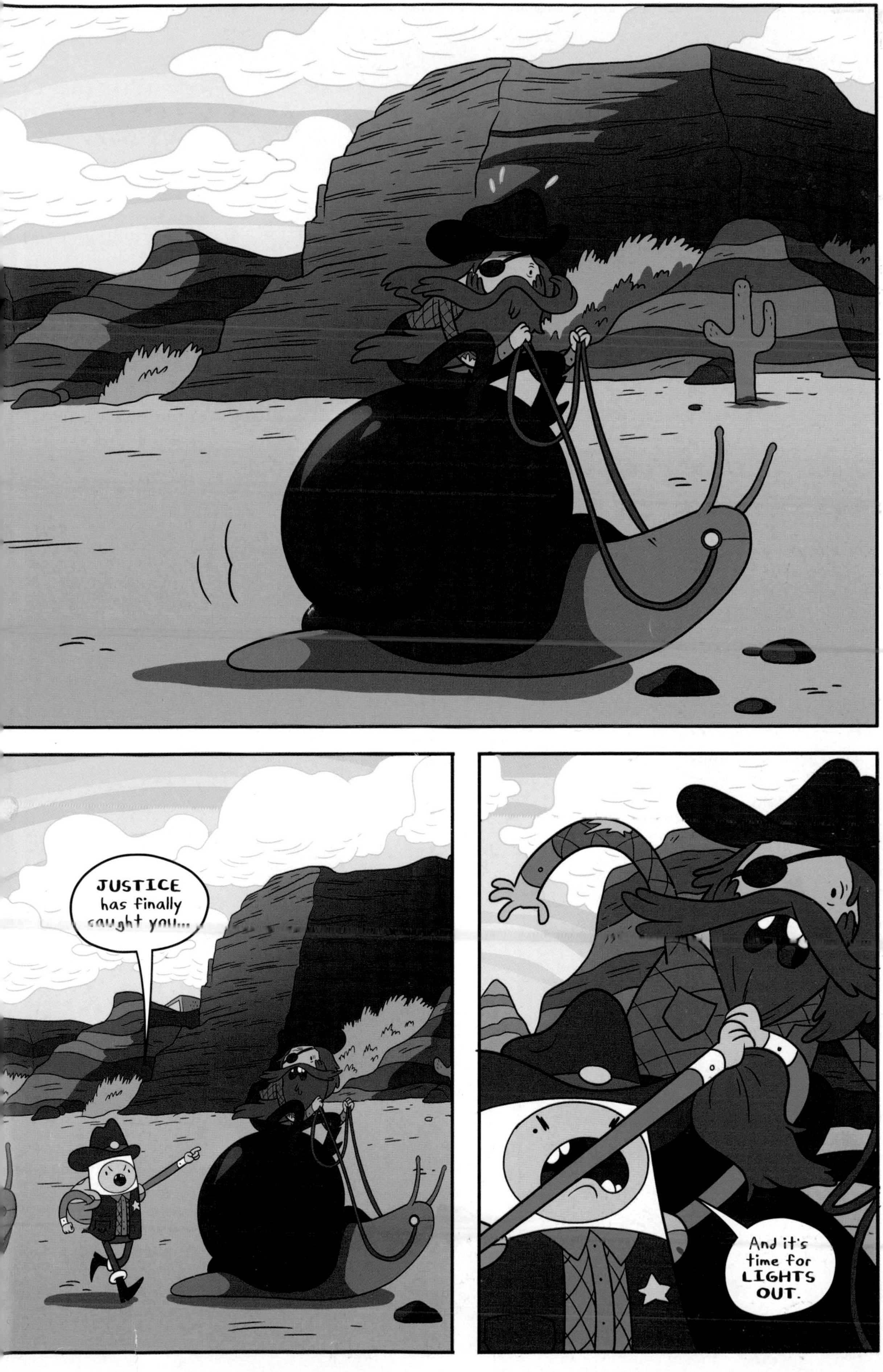
JUSTICE has finally caught you...
And it's time for LIGHTS OUT.

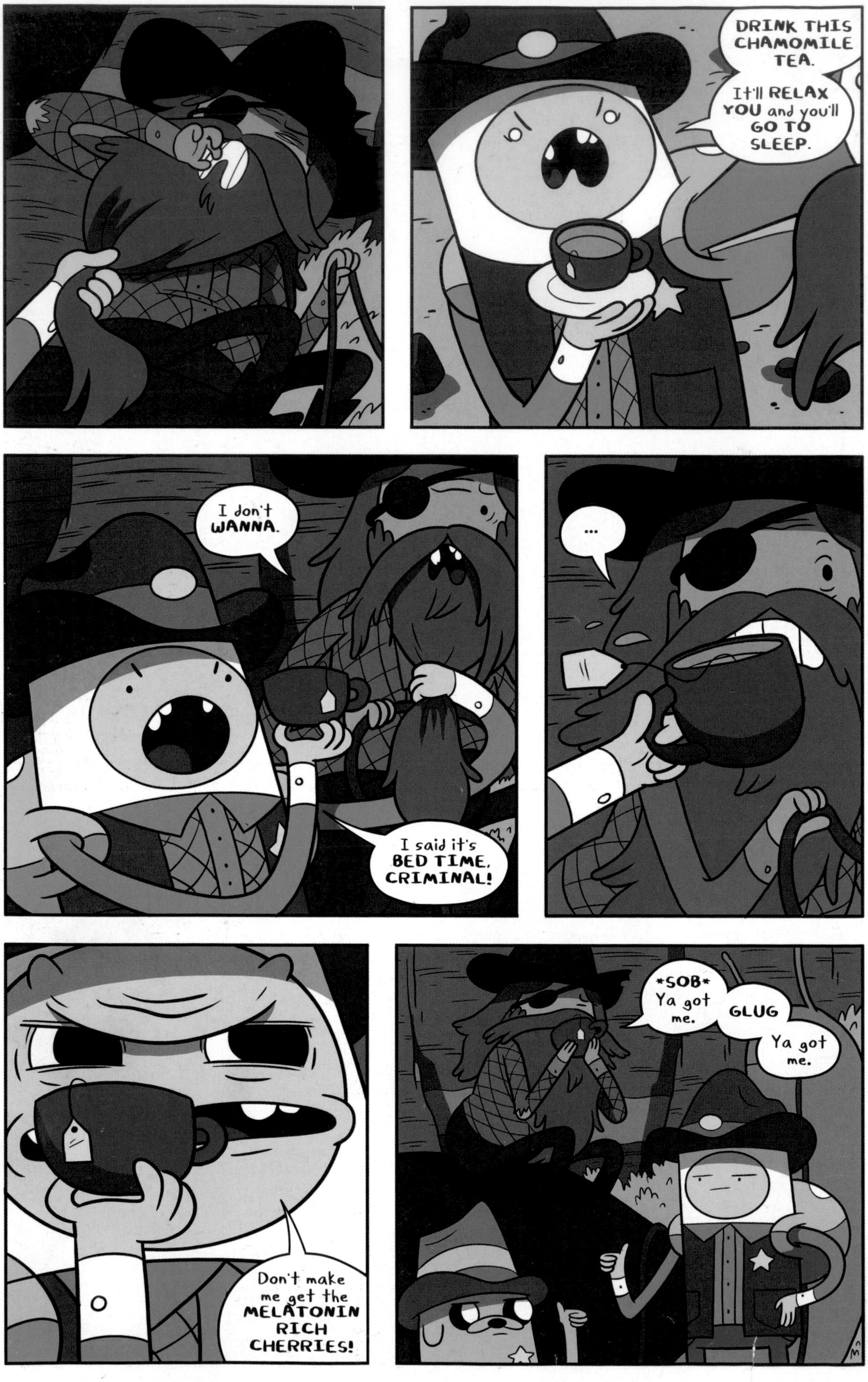

DRINK THIS CHAMOMILE TEA.
It'll RELAX YOU and you'll GO TO SLEEP.
I don't WANNA.
I said it's BED TIME, CRIMINAL!
...
Don't make me get the MELATONIN RICH CHERRIES!
*SOB* Ya got me.
GLUG
Ya got me.

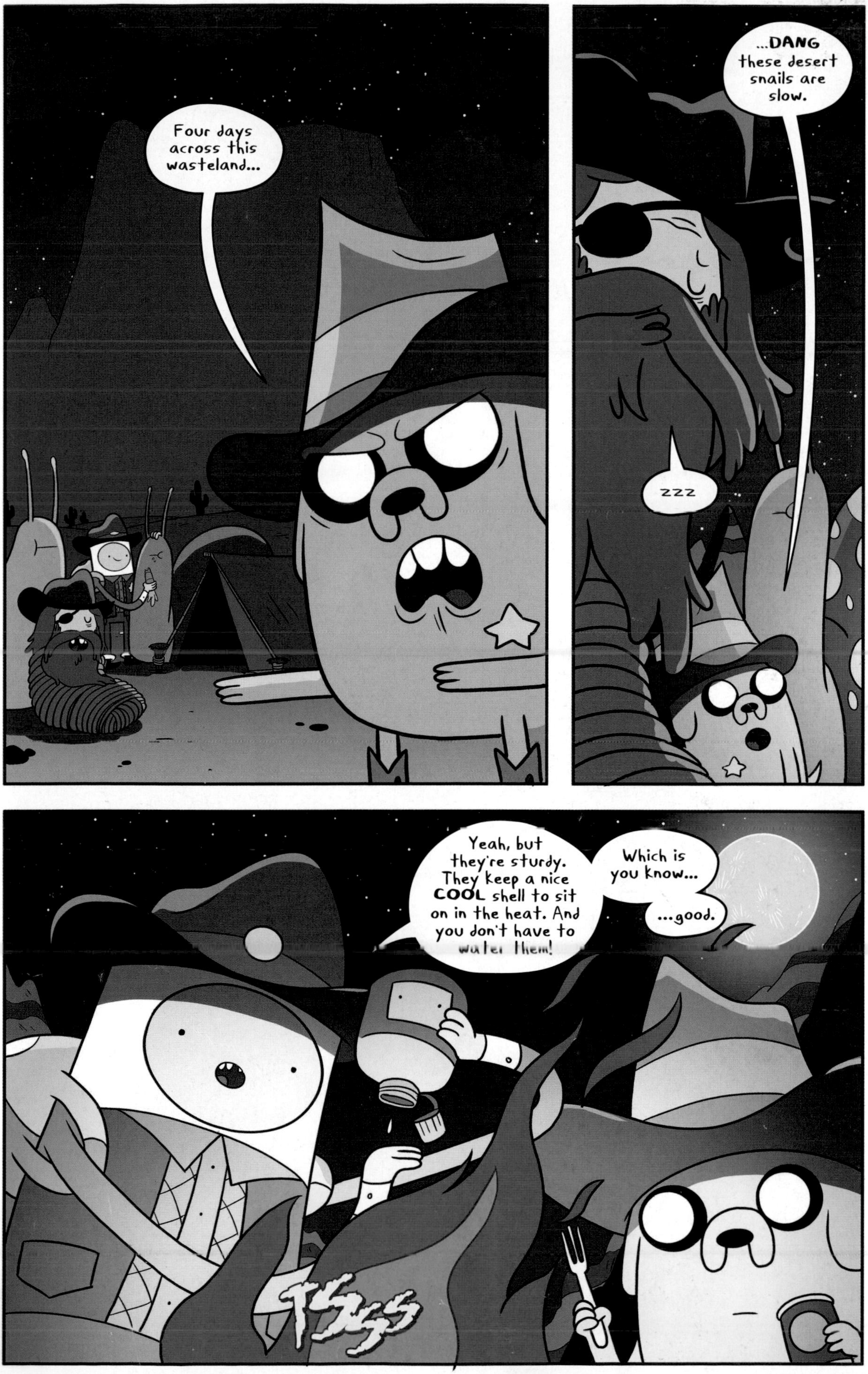
Four days across this wasteland...
...DANG these desert snails are slow.
zzz
Yeah, but they're sturdy. They keep a nice COOL shell to sit on in the heat. And you don't have to water them!
Which is you know...
...good.
TSSSS

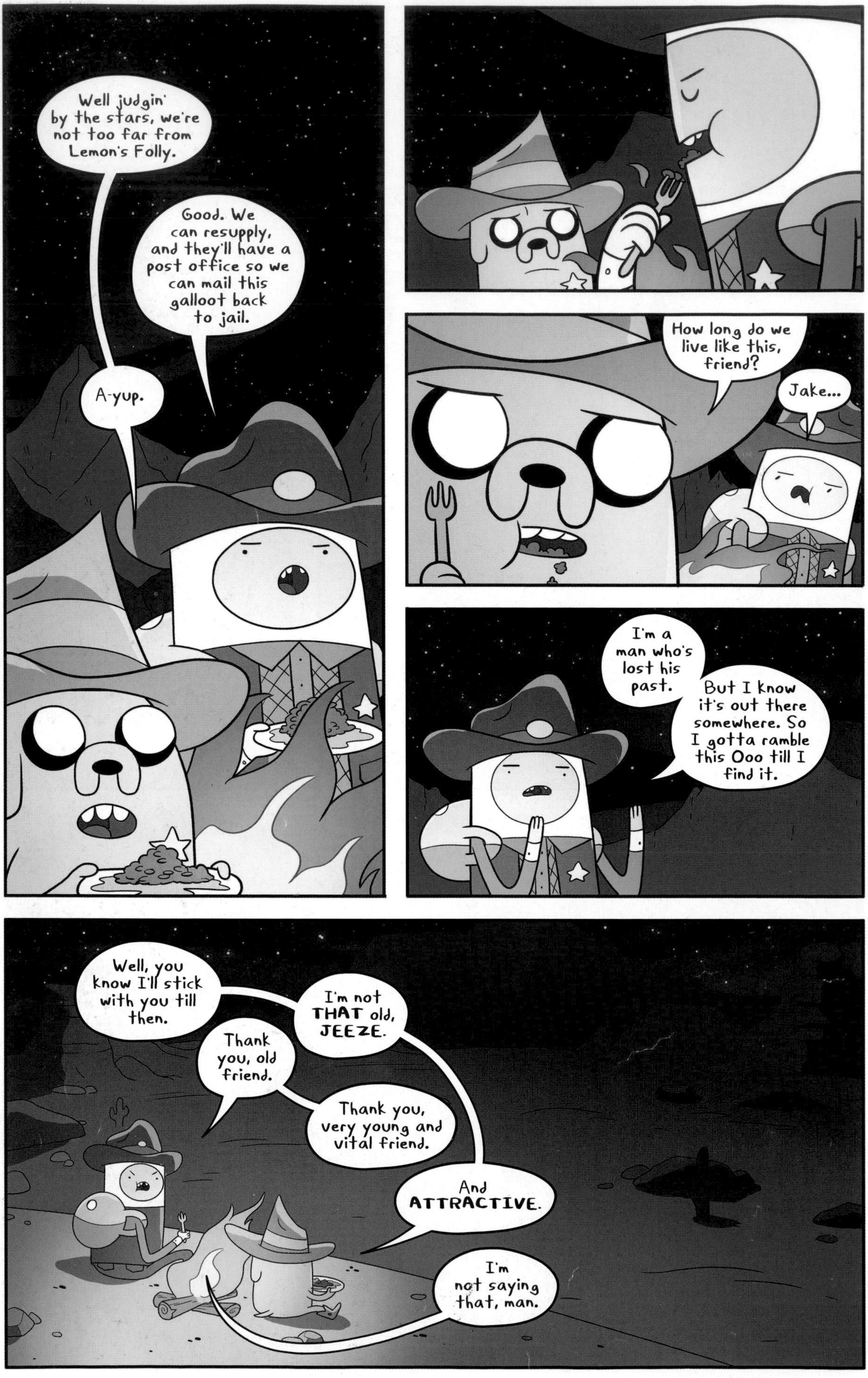
Well judgin' by the stars, we're not too far from Lemon's Folly.
Good. We can resupply, and they'll have a post office so we can mail this galloot back to jail.
A-yup.
How long do we live like this, friend?
Jake...
I'm a man who's lost his past.
But I know it's out there somewhere. So I gotta ramble this Ooo till I find it.
Well, you know I'll stick with you till then.
Thank you, old friend.
I'm not THAT old, JEEZE.
Thank you, very young and vital friend.
And ATTRACTIVE.
I'm not saying that, man.

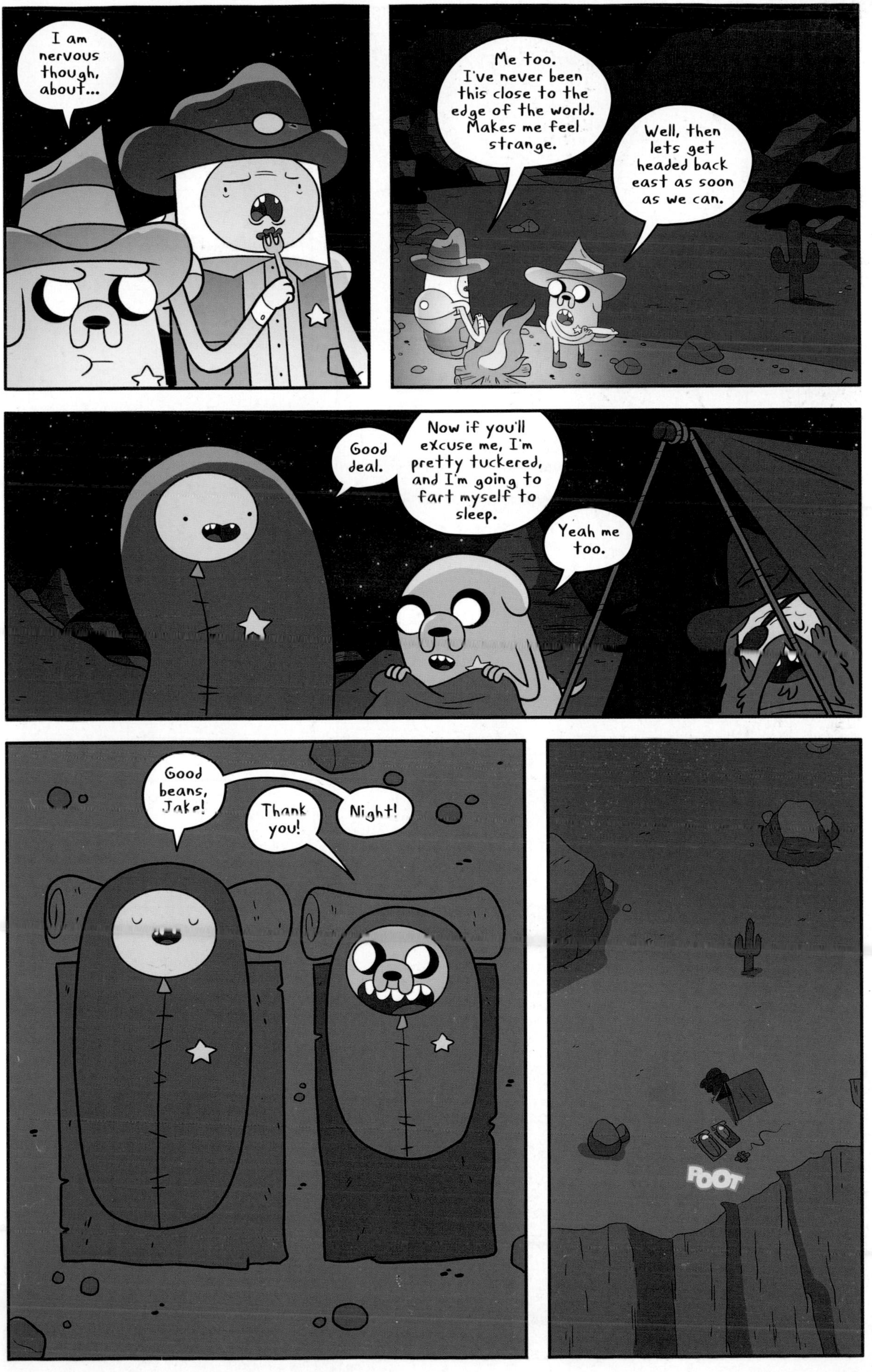
I am nervous though, about...
Me too. I've never been this close to the edge of the world. Makes me feel strange.
Well, then lets get headed back east as soon as we can.
Good deal.
Now if you'll excuse me, I'm pretty tuckered, and I'm going to fart myself to sleep.
Yeah me too.
Good beans, Jake!
Thank you!
Night!
POOT

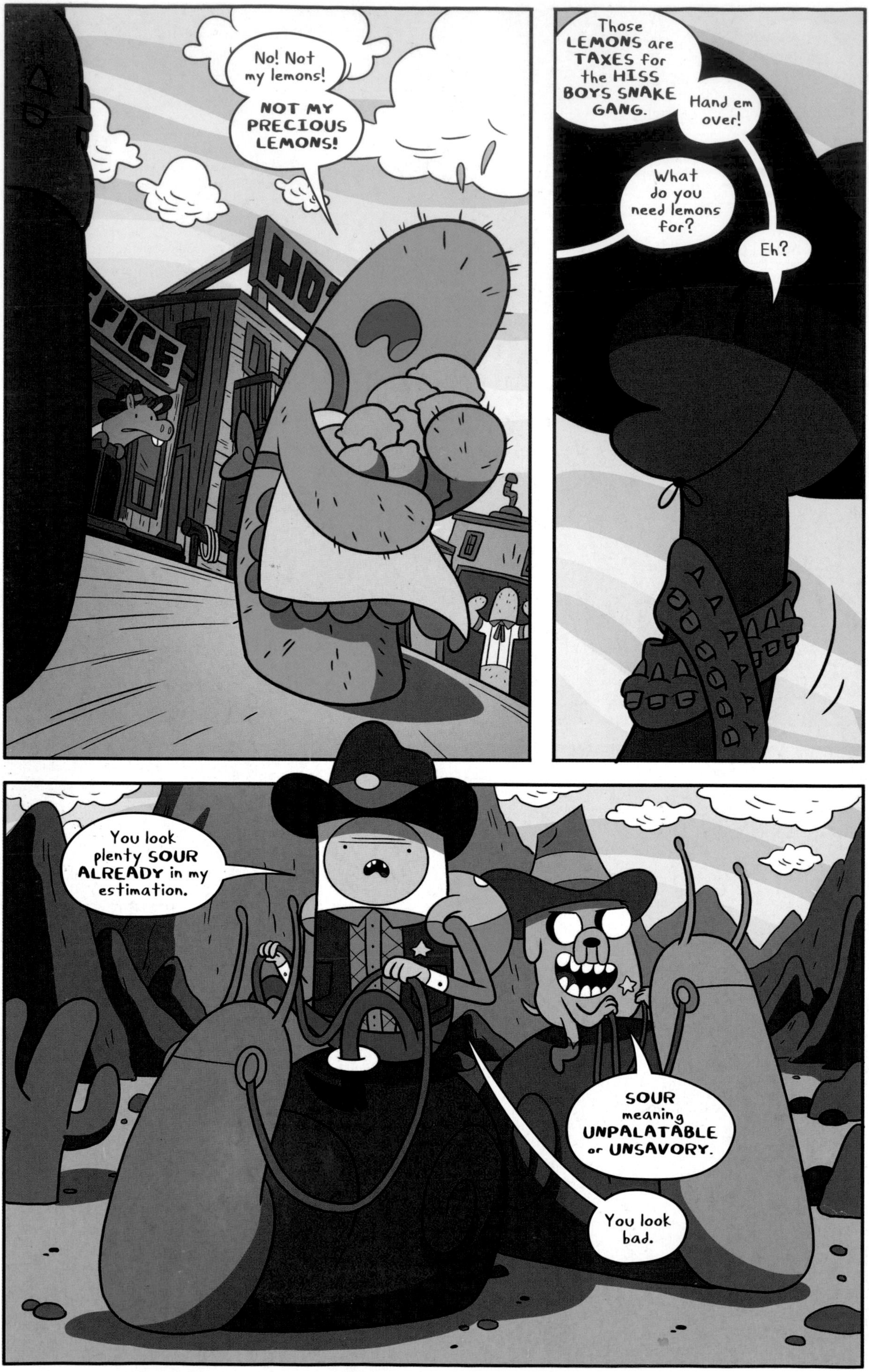
No! Not my lemons!
NOT MY PRECIOUS LEMONS!
Those LEMONS are TAXES for the HISS BOYS SNAKE GANG.
Hand em over!
What do you need lemons for?
Eh?
You look plenty SOUR ALREADY in my estimation.
SOUR meaning UNPALATABLE or UNSAVORY.
You look bad.

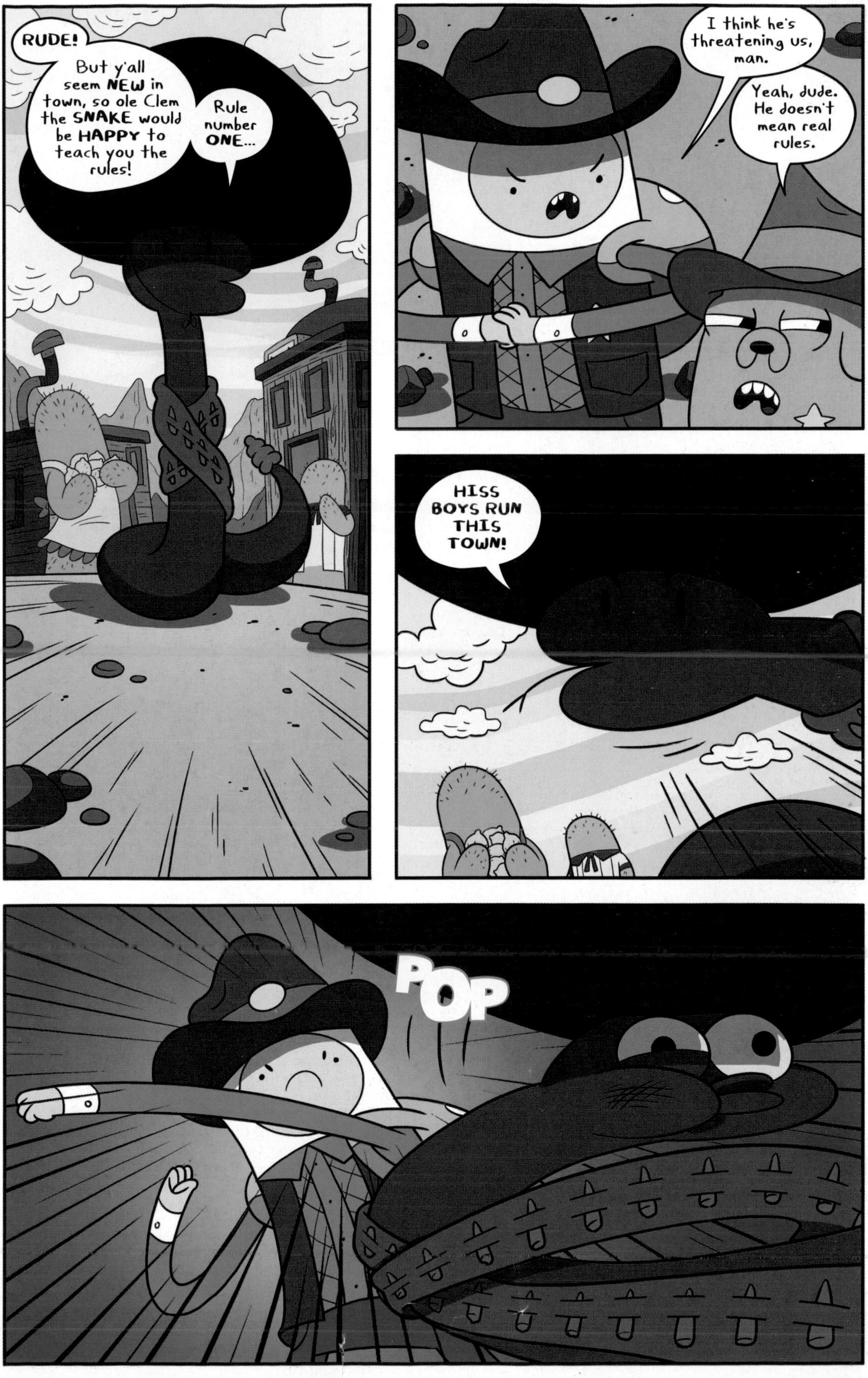
RUDE!
But y'all seem NEW in town, so ole Clem the SNAKE would be HAPPY to teach you the rules!
Rule number ONE...
I think he's threatening us, man.
Yeah, dude. He doesn't mean real rules.
HISS BOYS RUN THIS TOWN!
POP

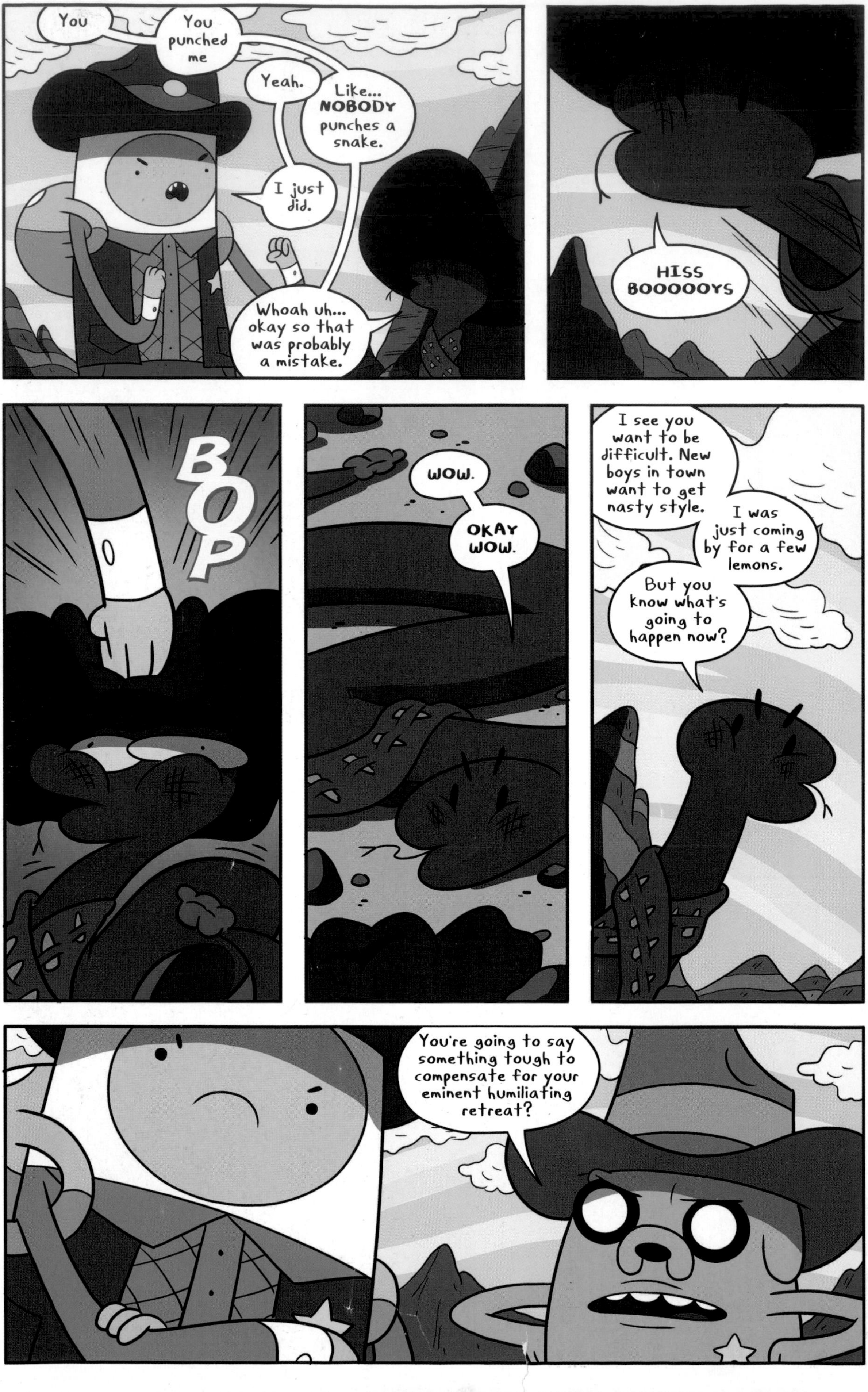
You
You punched me
Yeah.
Like... NOBODY punches a snake.
I just did.
Whoah uh... okay so that was probably a mistake.
HISS BOOOOOYS
BOP
WOW.
OKAY WOW.
I see you want to be difficult. New boys in town want to get nasty style.
I was just coming by for a few lemons.
But you know what's going to happen now?
You're going to say something tough to compensate for your eminent humiliating retreat?

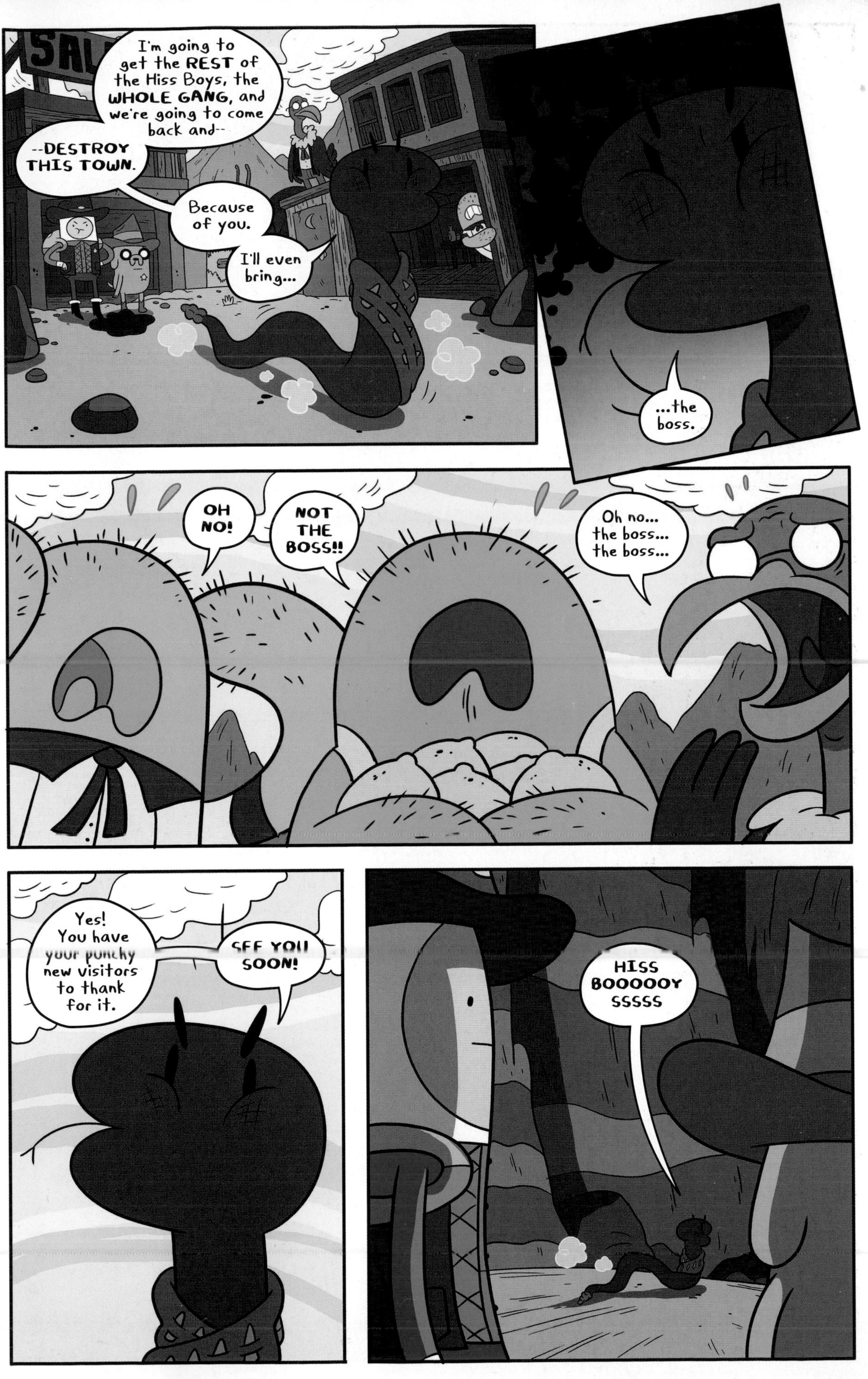
I'm going to get the REST of the Hiss Boys, the WHOLE GANG, and we're going to come back and--
--DESTROY THIS TOWN.
Because of you.
I'll even bring...
...the boss.
OH NO!
NOT THE BOSS!!
Oh no... the boss... the boss...
Yes! You have your punchy new visitors to thank for it.
SEE YOU SOON!
HISS BOOOOOY SSSSS

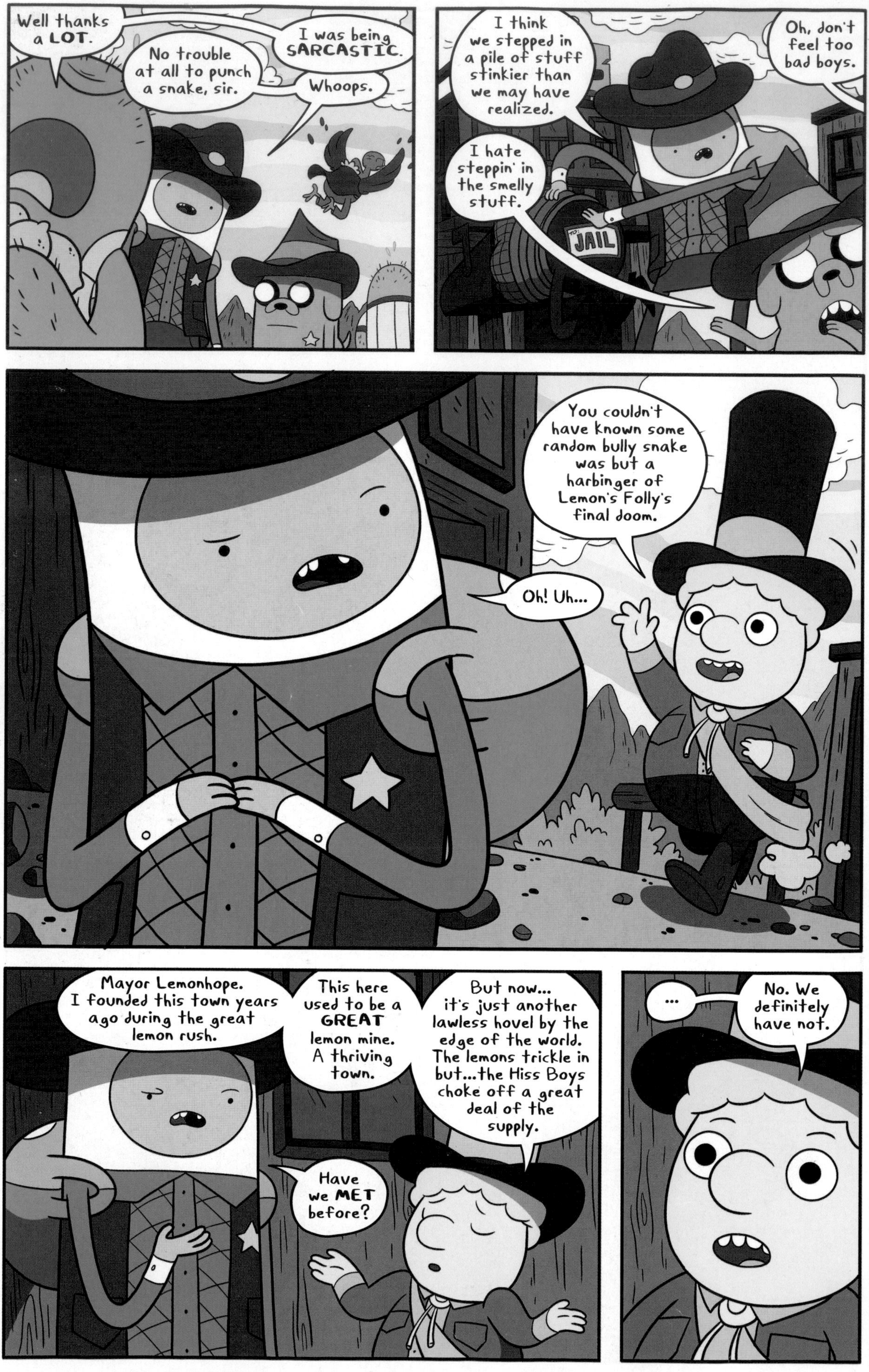

Well thanks a LOT.
No trouble at all to punch a snake, sir.
I was being SARCASTIC.
Whoops.
I think we stepped in a pile of stuff stinkier than we may have realized.
I hate steppin' in the smelly stuff.
JAIL
Oh, don't feel too bad boys.
You couldn't have known some random bully snake was but a harbinger of Lemon's Folly's final doom.
Oh! Uh...
Mayor Lemonhope. I founded this town years ago during the great lemon rush.
This here used to be a GREAT lemon mine. A thriving town.
But now... it's just another lawless hovel by the edge of the world. The lemons trickle in but...the Hiss Boys choke off a great deal of the supply.
Have we MET before?
...
No. We definitely have not.

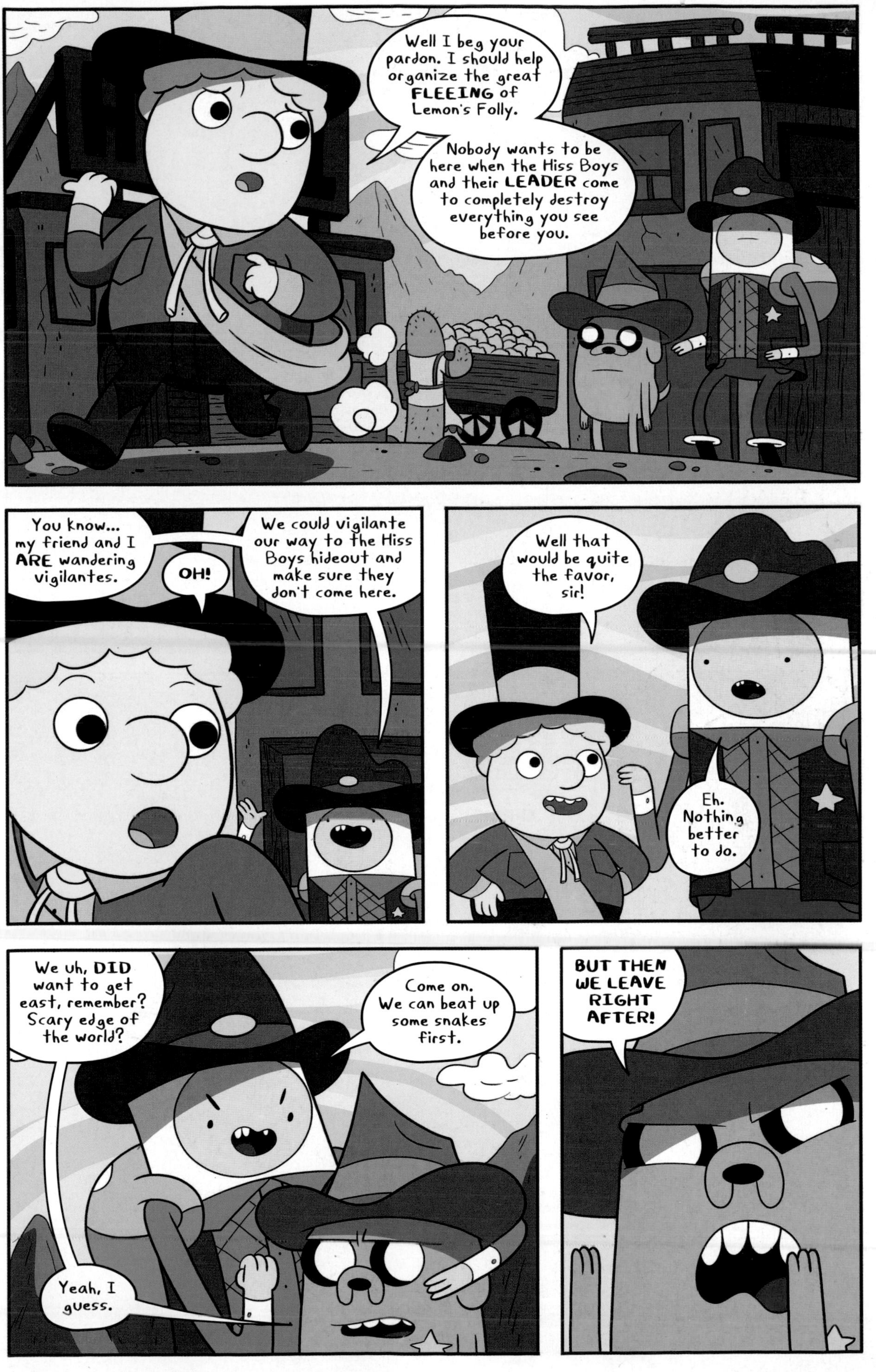
Well I beg your pardon. I should help organize the great **FLEEING** of Lemon's Folly.
Nobody wants to be here when the Hiss Boys and their **LEADER** come to completely destroy everything you see before you.
You know... my friend and I **ARE** wandering vigilantes.
OH!
We could vigilante our way to the Hiss Boys hideout and make sure they don't come here.
Well that would be quite the favor, sir!
Eh. Nothing better to do.
We uh, **DID** want to get east, remember? Scary edge of the world?
Come on. We can beat up some snakes first.
Yeah, I guess.
**BUT THEN WE LEAVE RIGHT AFTER!**

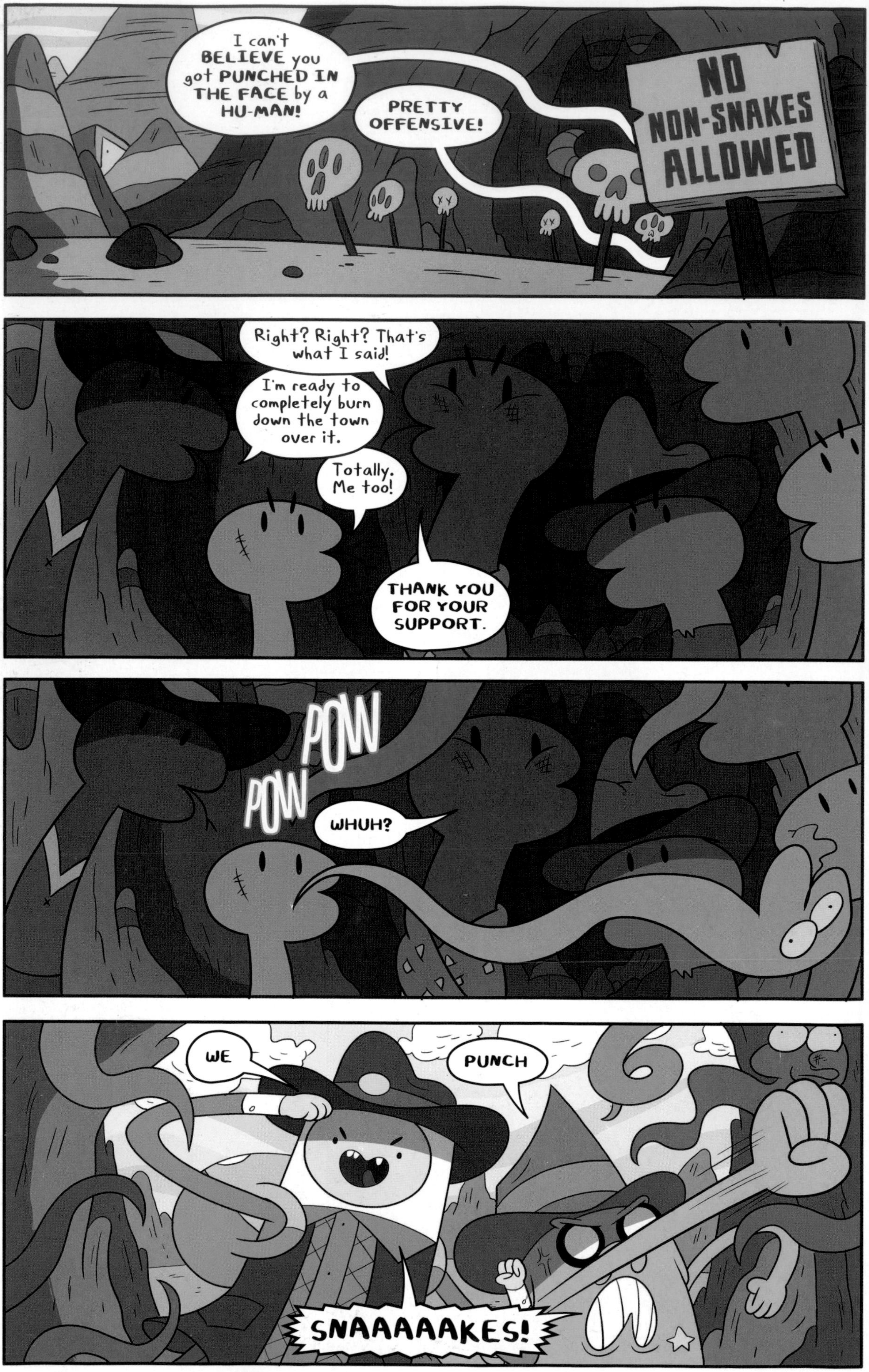
I can't BELIEVE you got PUNCHED IN THE FACE by a HU-MAN!
PRETTY OFFENSIVE!
NO NON-SNAKES ALLOWED
Right? Right? That's what I said!
I'm ready to completely burn down the town over it.
Totally. Me too!
THANK YOU FOR YOUR SUPPORT.
POW
POW
WHUH?
WE
PUNCH
SNAAAAAKES!

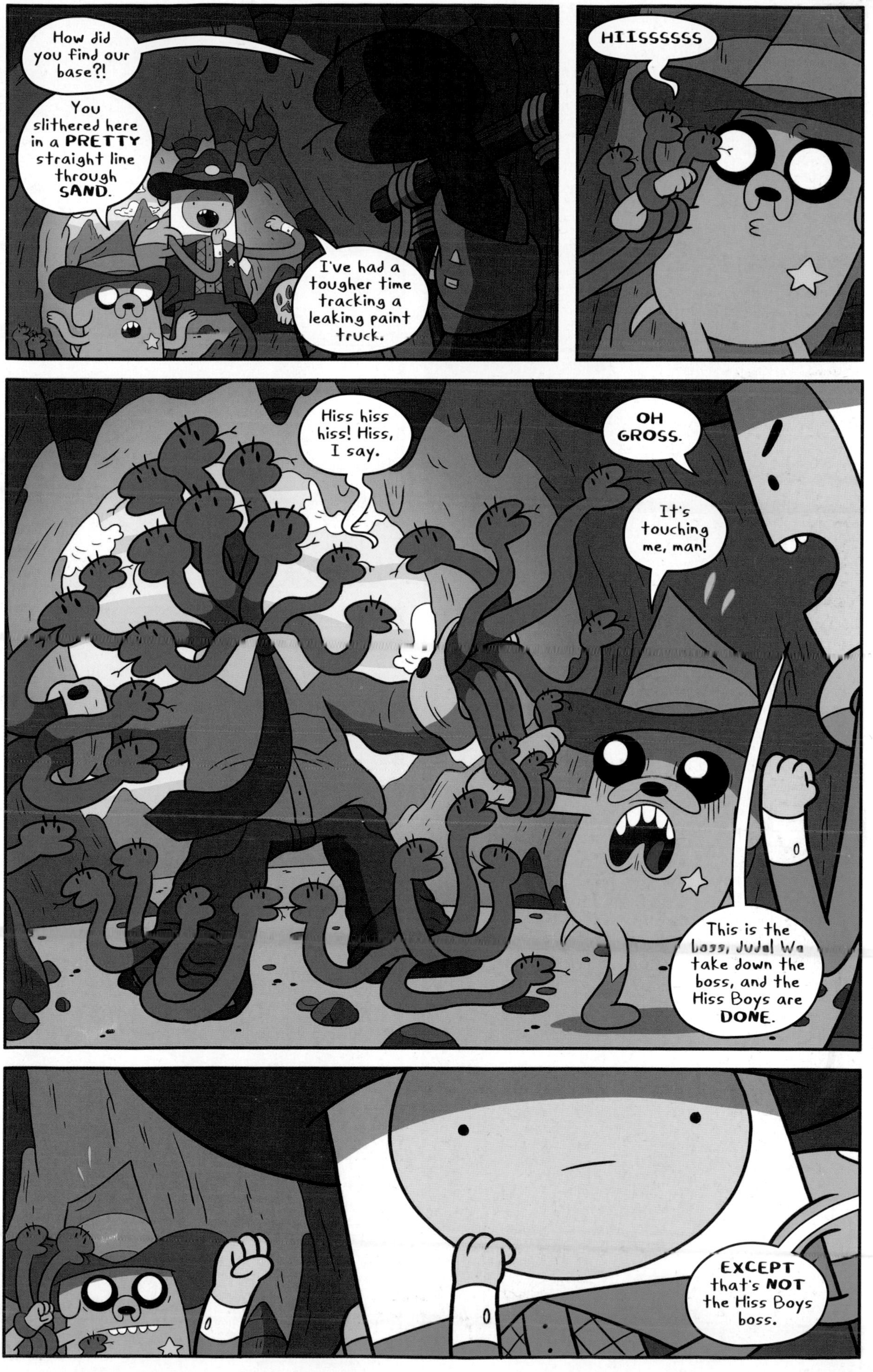
How did you find our base?!
You slithered here in a PRETTY straight line through SAND.
I've had a tougher time tracking a leaking paint truck.
HIISSSSSS
Hiss hiss hiss! Hiss, I say.
OH GROSS.
It's touching me, man!
This is the boss, Jude! We take down the boss, and the Hiss Boys are DONE.
EXCEPT that's NOT the Hiss Boys boss.

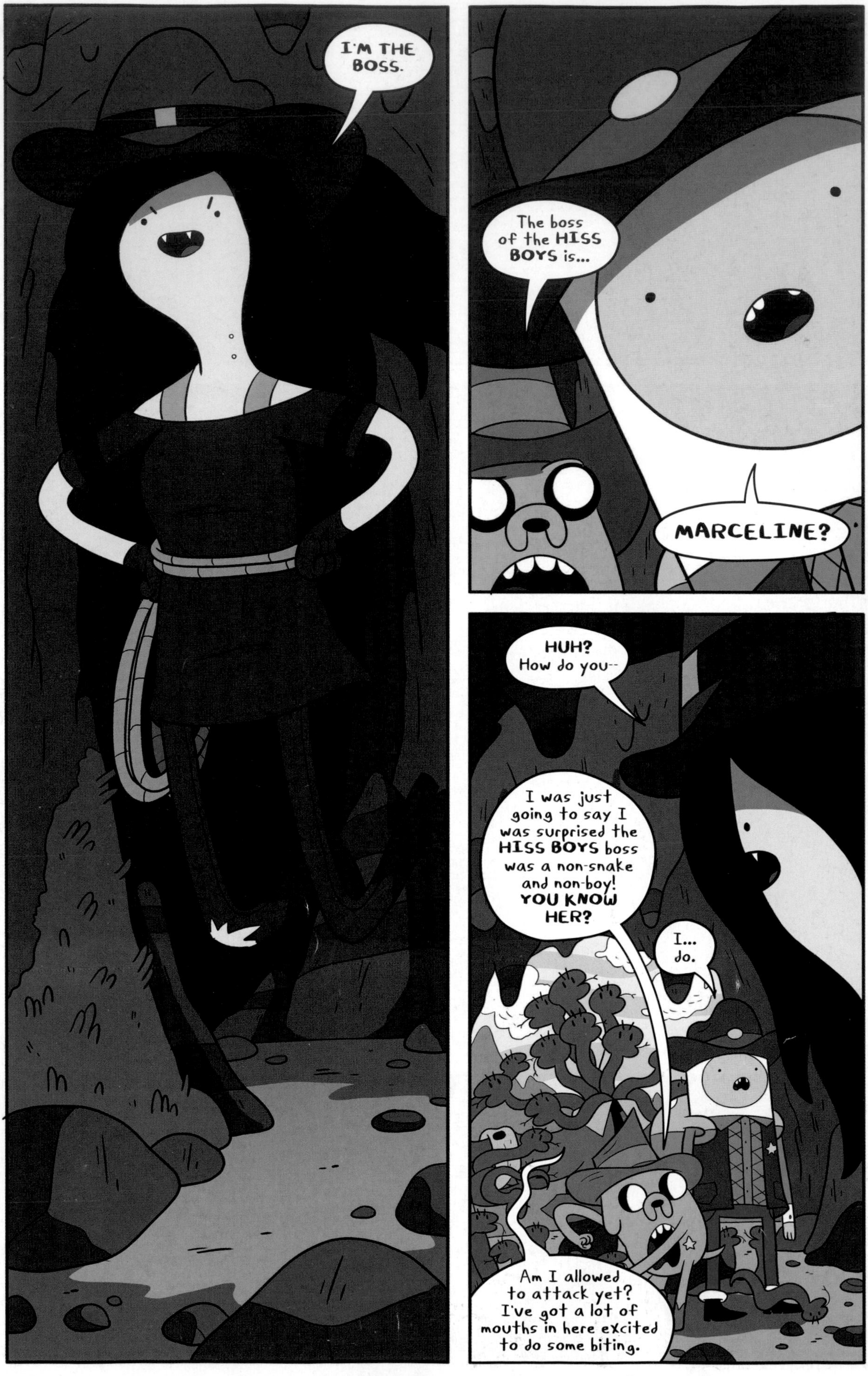

I'M THE BOSS.
The boss of the HISS BOYS is...
MARCELINE?
HUH? How do you--
I was just going to say I was surprised the HISS BOYS boss was a non-snake and non-boy! YOU KNOW HER?
I... do.
Am I allowed to attack yet? I've got a lot of mouths in here excited to do some biting.

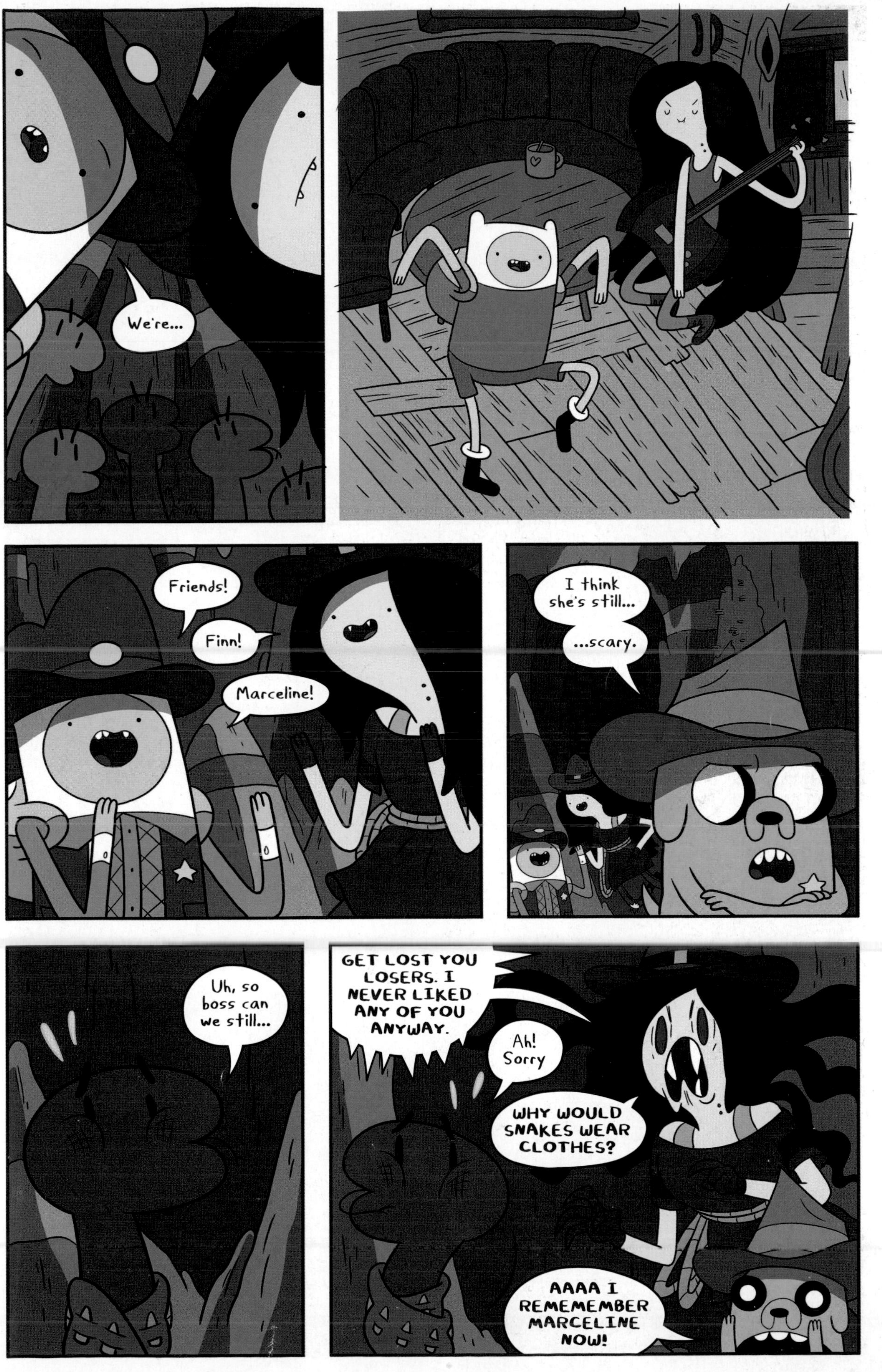
We're...
Friends!
Finn!
Marceline!
I think she's still...
...scary.
Uh, so boss can we still...
GET LOST YOU LOSERS. I NEVER LIKED ANY OF YOU ANYWAY.
Ah! Sorry
WHY WOULD SNAKES WEAR CLOTHES?
AAAA I REMEMBER MARCELINE NOW!

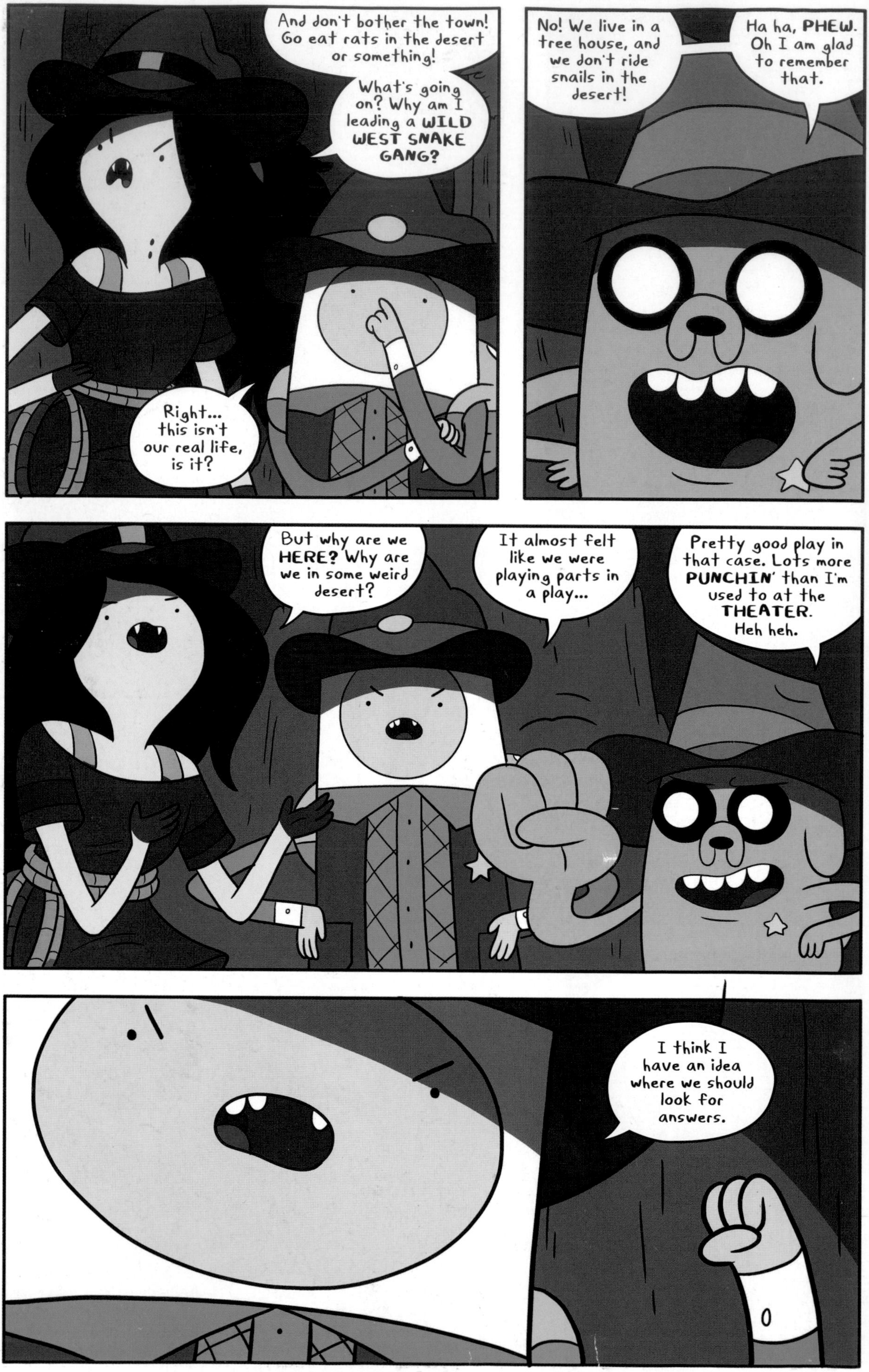
And don't bother the town! Go eat rats in the desert or something!
What's going on? Why am I leading a **WILD WEST SNAKE GANG?**
Right... this isn't our real life, is it?
No! We live in a tree house, and we don't ride snails in the desert!
Ha ha, **PHEW.** Oh I am glad to remember that.
But why are we **HERE?** Why are we in some weird desert?
It almost felt like we were playing parts in a play...
Pretty good play in that case. Lots more **PUNCHIN'** than I'm used to at the **THEATER**. Heh heh.
I think I have an idea where we should look for answers.

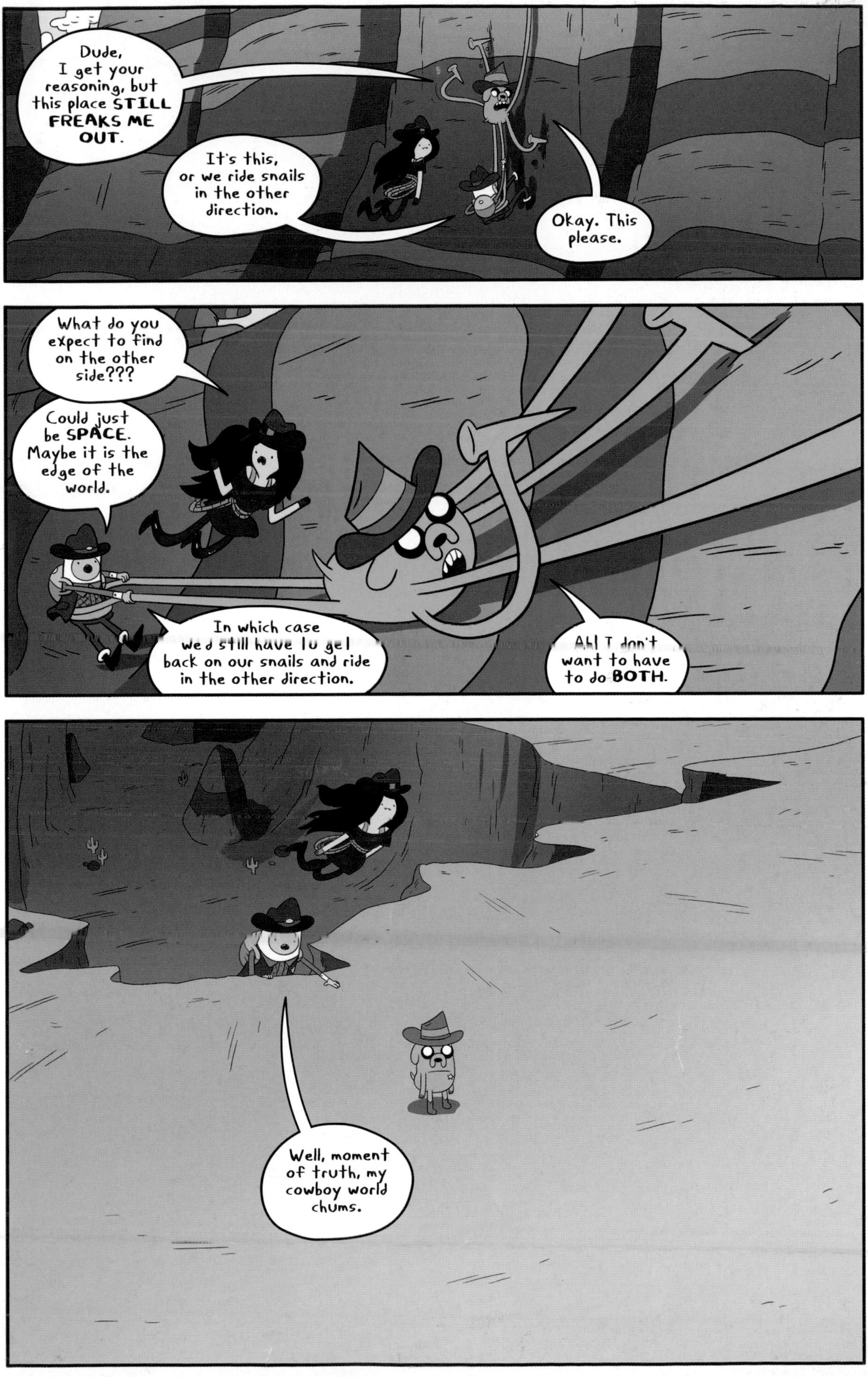
Dude, I get your reasoning, but this place STILL FREAKS ME OUT.
It's this, or we ride snails in the other direction.
Okay. This please.
What do you expect to find on the other side???
Could just be SPACE. Maybe it is the edge of the world.
In which case we'd still have to get back on our snails and ride in the other direction.
Ah! I don't want to have to do BOTH.
Well, moment of truth, my cowboy world chums.

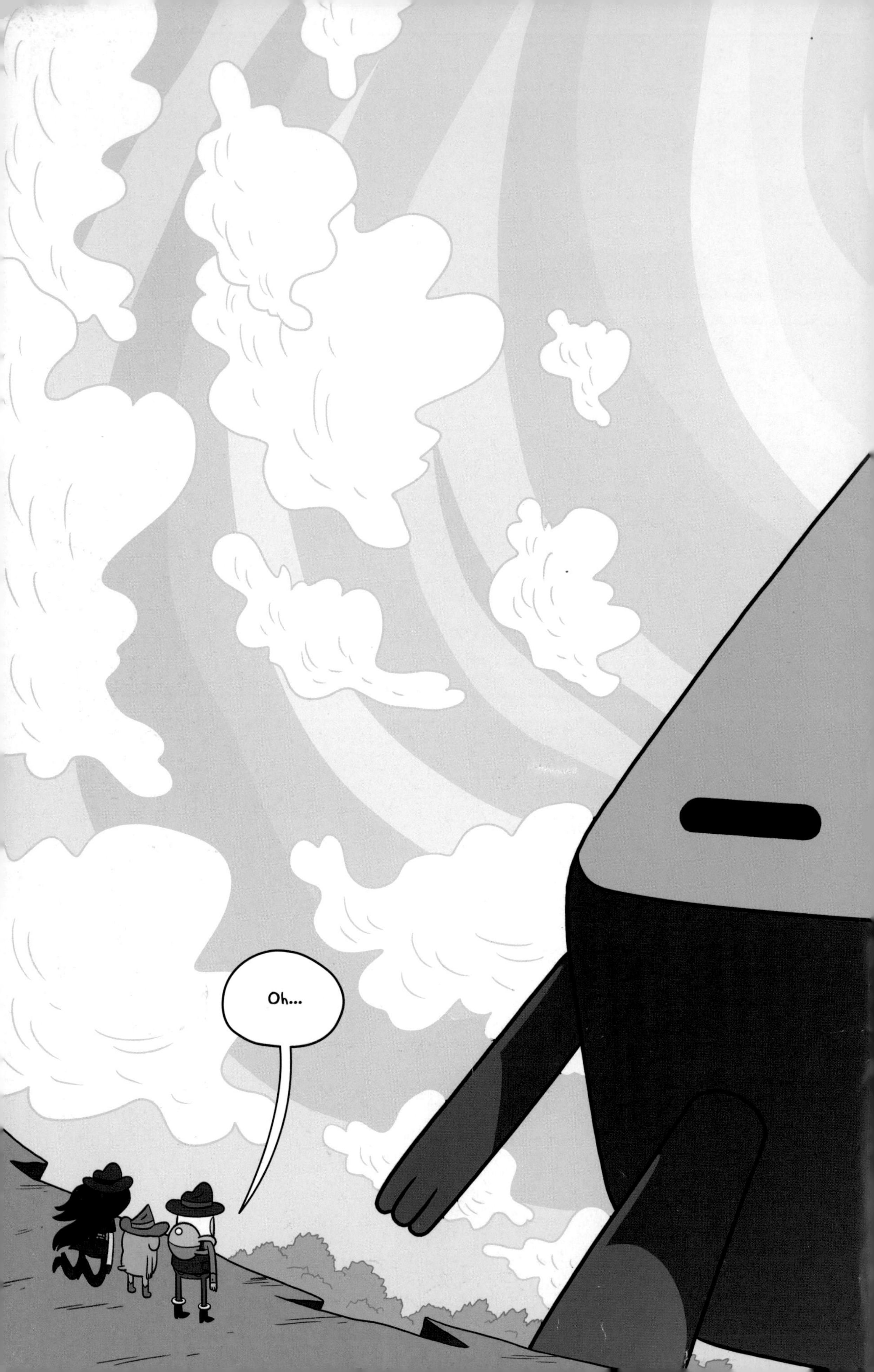
Oh...

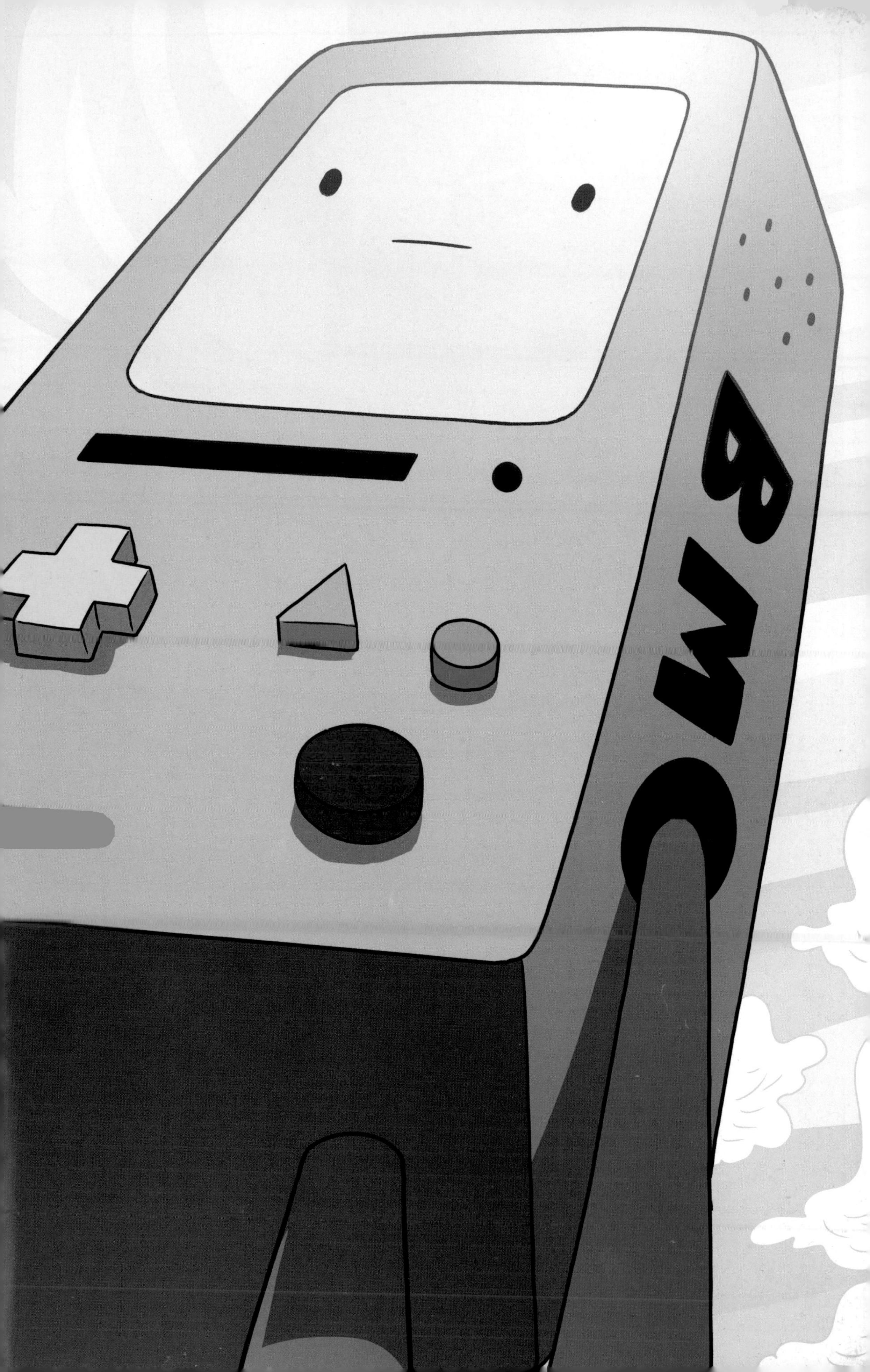
BMO

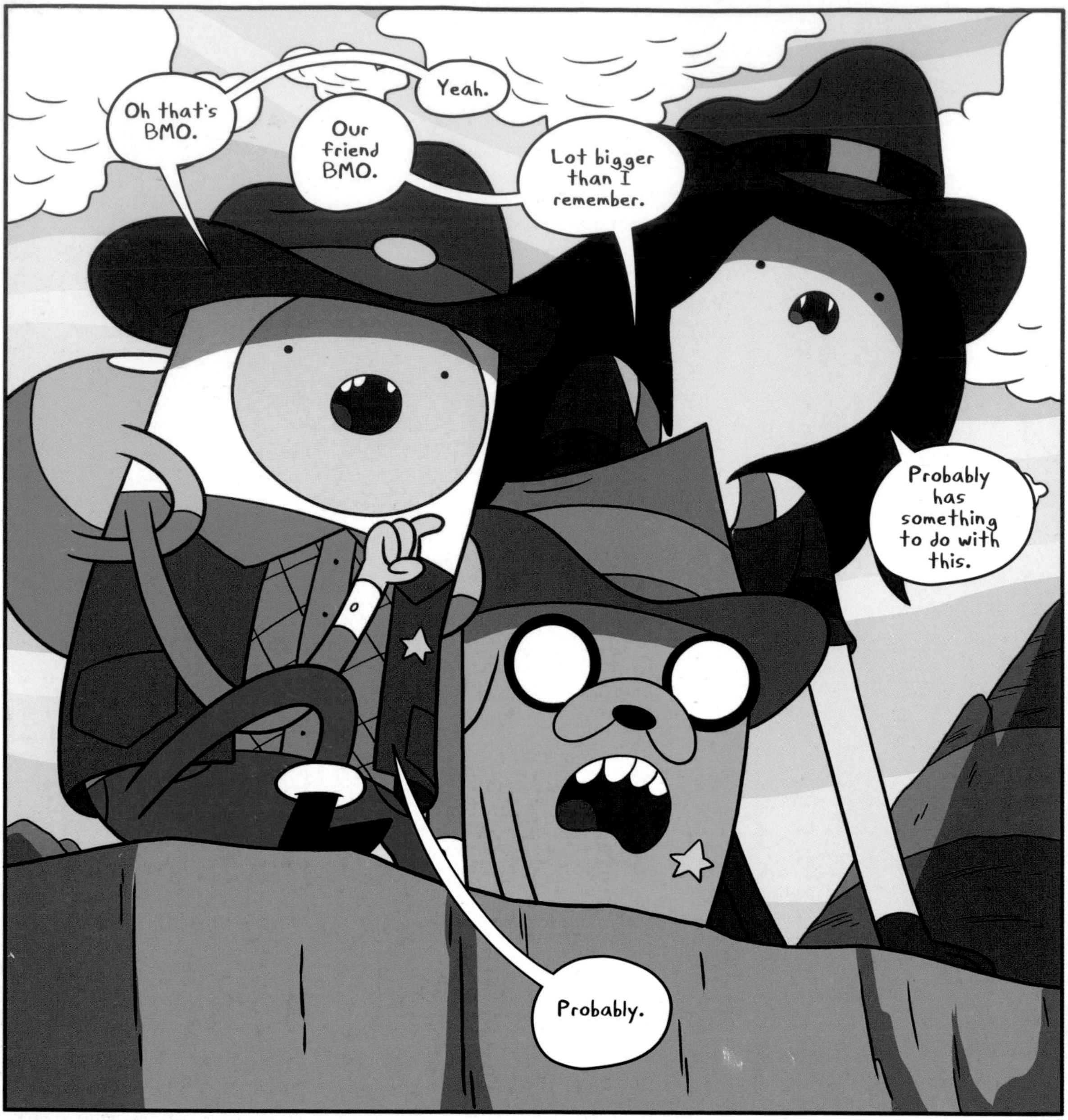
Oh that's BMO.
Yeah.
Our friend BMO.
Lot bigger than I remember.
Probably has something to do with this.
Probably.

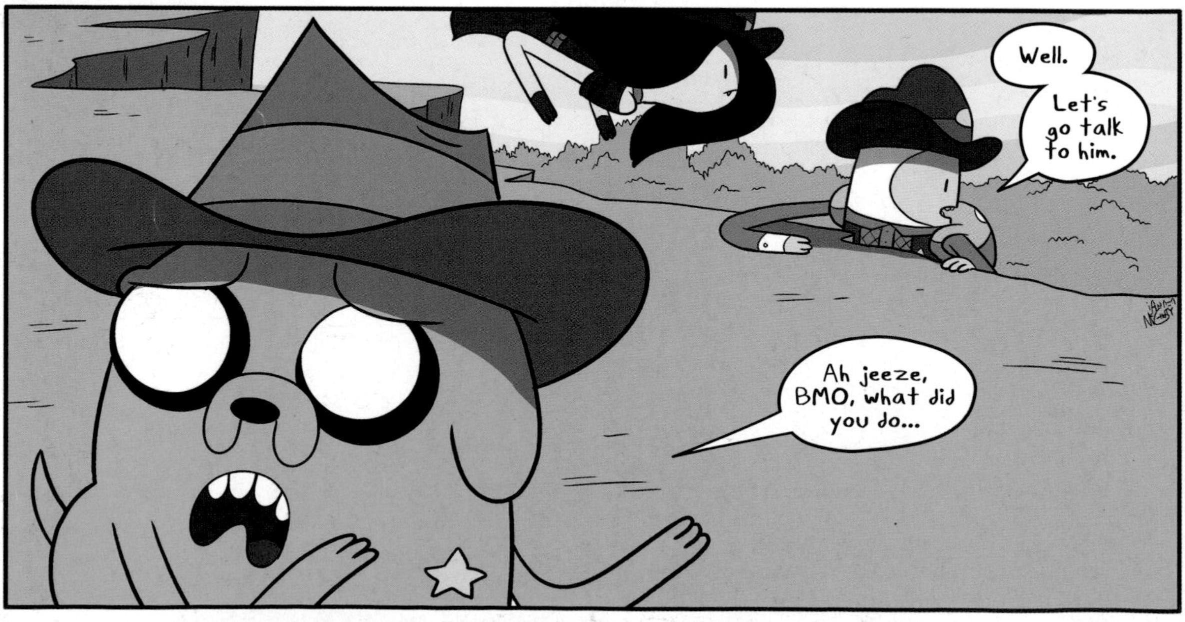
Well.
Let's go talk to him.
Ah jeeze, BMO, what did you do...

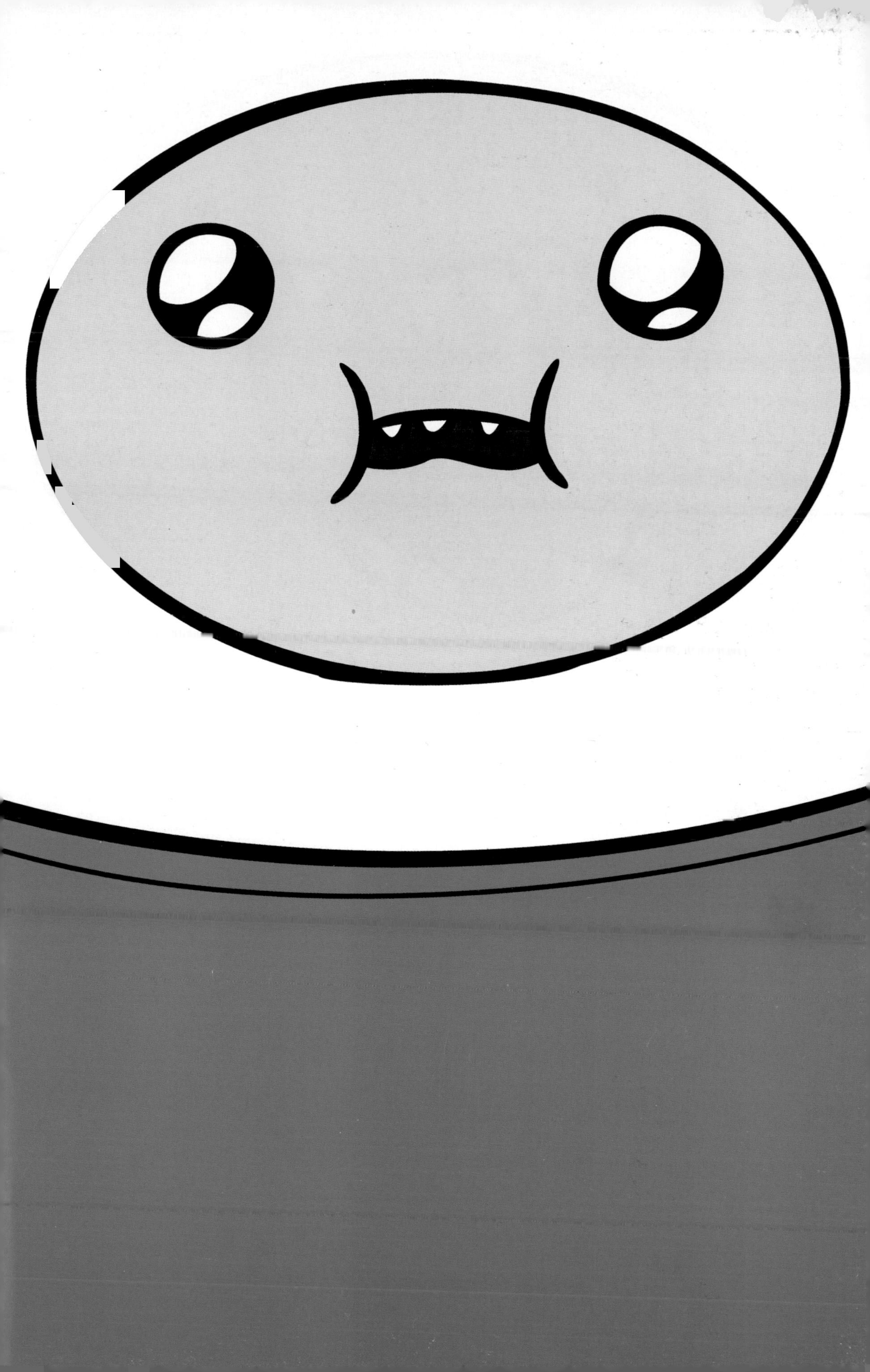

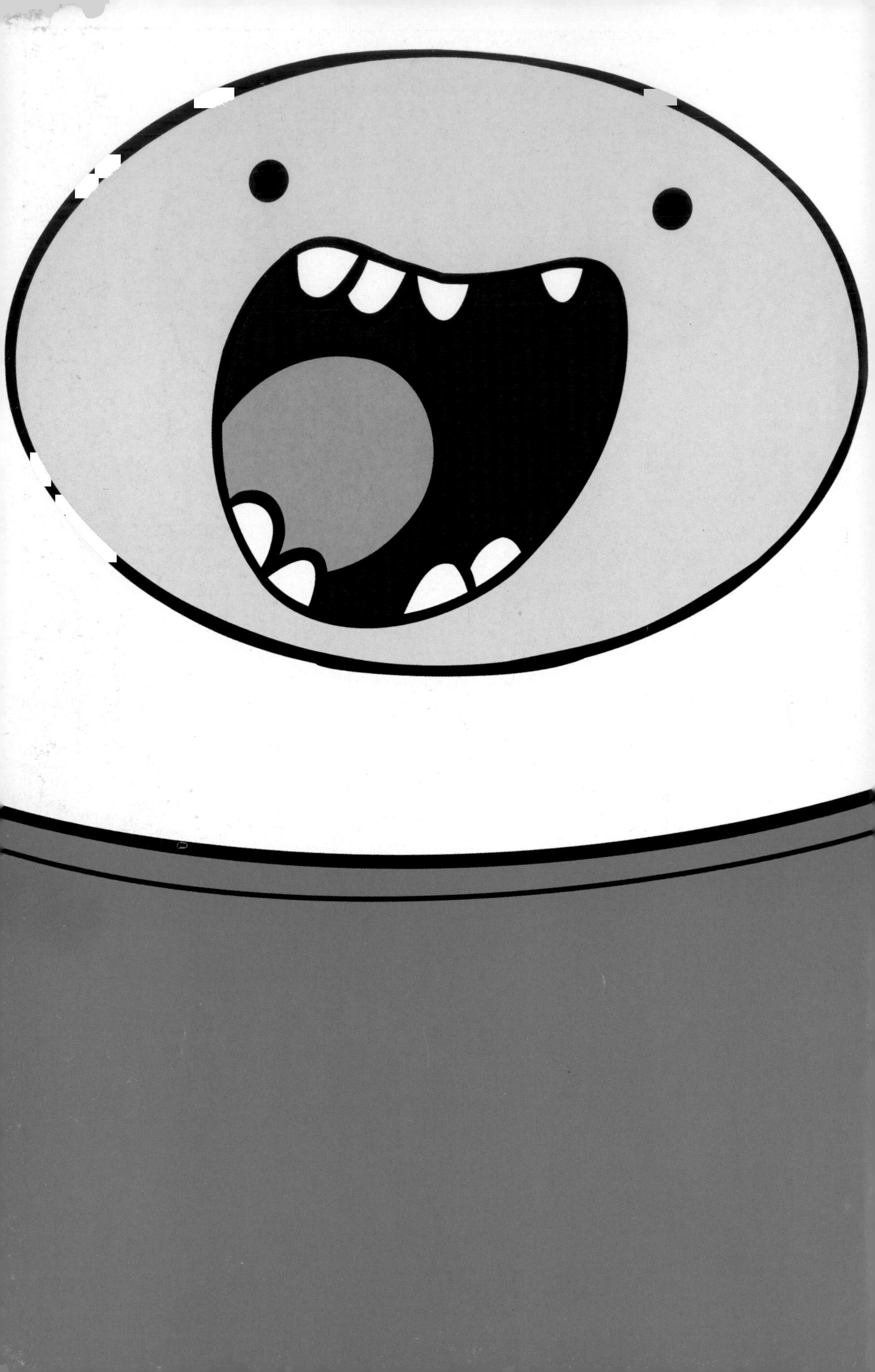

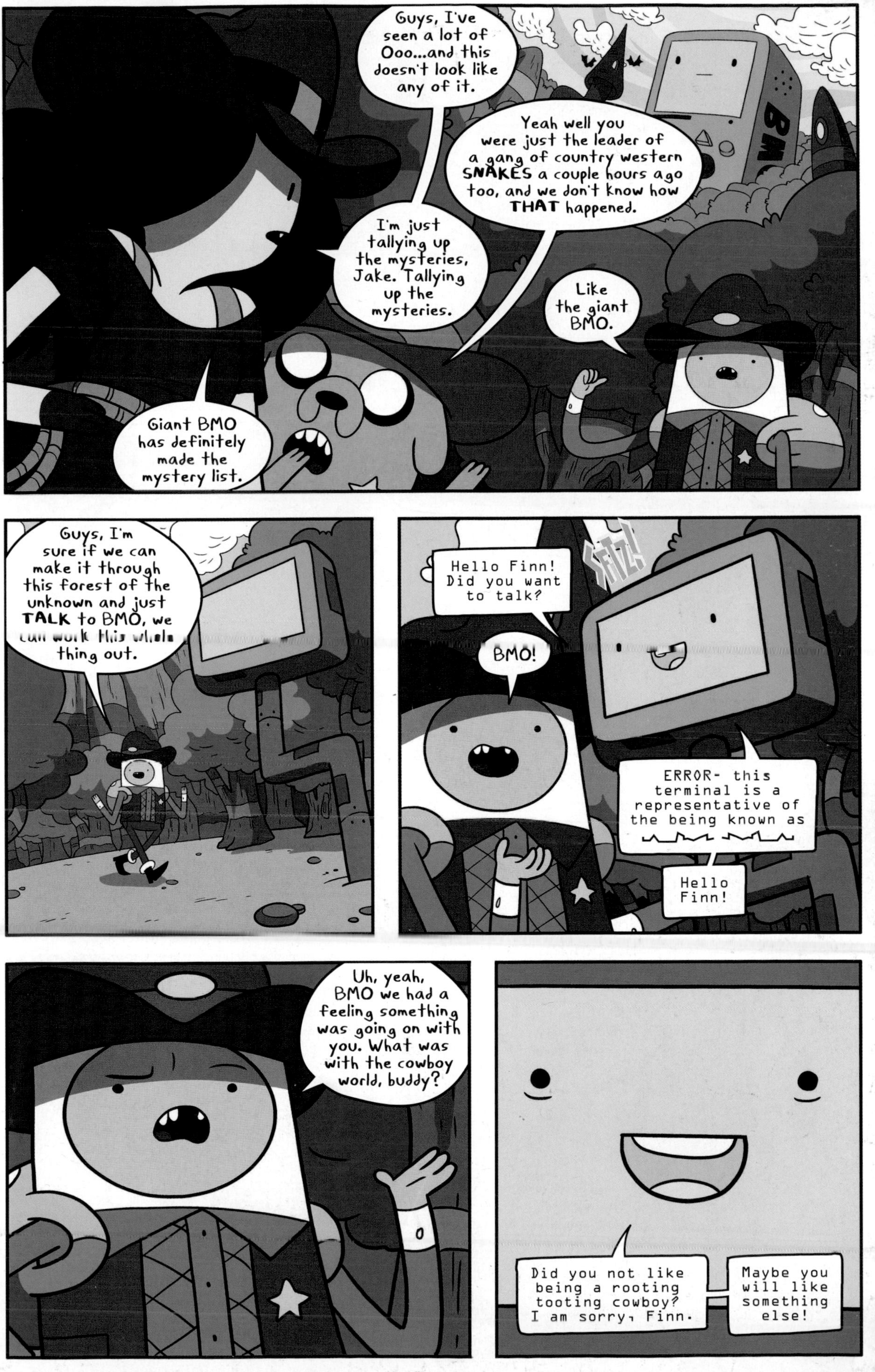
Guys, I've seen a lot of Ooo...and this doesn't look like any of it.
I'm just tallying up the mysteries, Jake. Tallying up the mysteries.
Yeah well you were just the leader of a gang of country western SNAKES a couple hours ago too, and we don't know how THAT happened.
Like the giant BMO.
Giant BMO has definitely made the mystery list.
BMO
Guys, I'm sure if we can make it through this forest of the unknown and just TALK to BMO, we can work this whole thing out.
SFIZZ!
Hello Finn! Did you want to talk?
BMO!
ERROR- this terminal is a representative of the being known as
Hello Finn!
Uh, yeah, BMO we had a feeling something was going on with you. What was with the cowboy world, buddy?
Did you not like being a rooting tooting cowboy? I am sorry, Finn.
Maybe you will like something else!

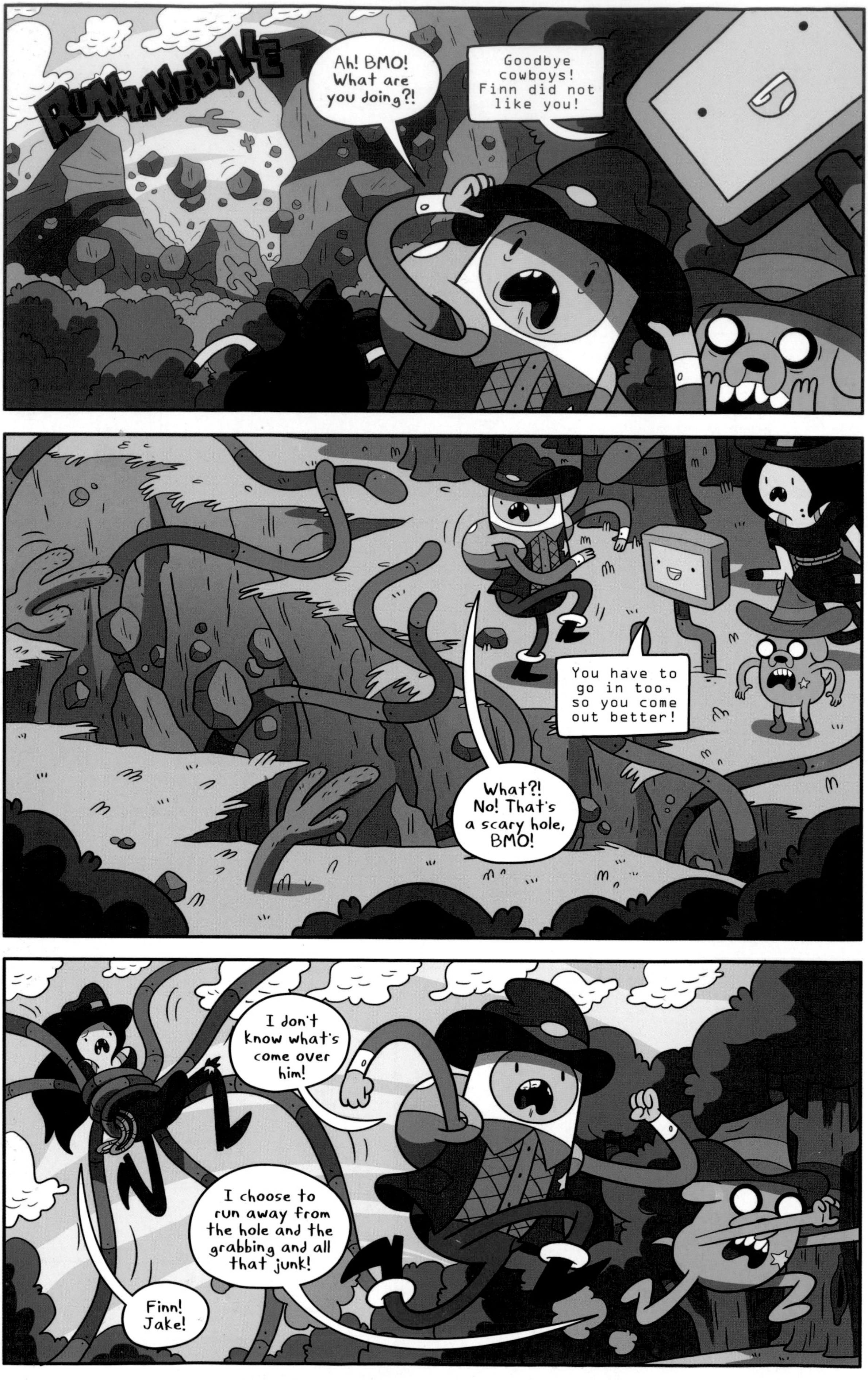
RUMMMBBLLE
Ah! BMO! What are you doing?!
Goodbye cowboys! Finn did not like you!
You have to go in too, so you come out better!
What?! No! That's a scary hole, BMO!
I don't know what's come over him!
I choose to run away from the hole and the grabbing and all that junk!
Finn! Jake!

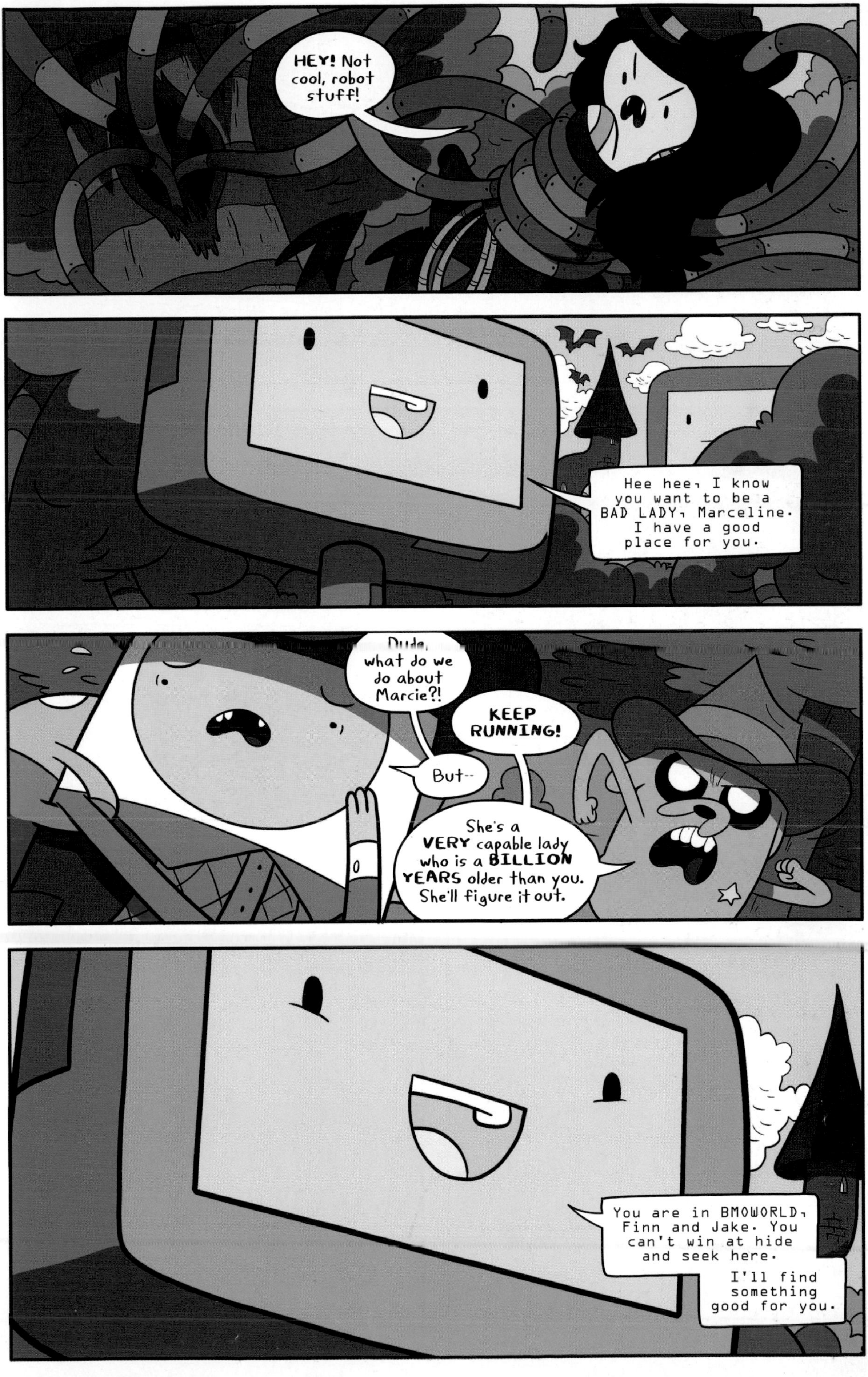
HEY! Not cool, robot stuff!
Hee hee, I know you want to be a BAD LADY, Marceline. I have a good place for you.
Dude, what do we do about Marcie?!
KEEP RUNNING!
But--
She's a VERY capable lady who is a BILLION YEARS older than you. She'll figure it out.
You are in BMOWORLD, Finn and Jake. You can't win at hide and seek here.
I'll find something good for you.

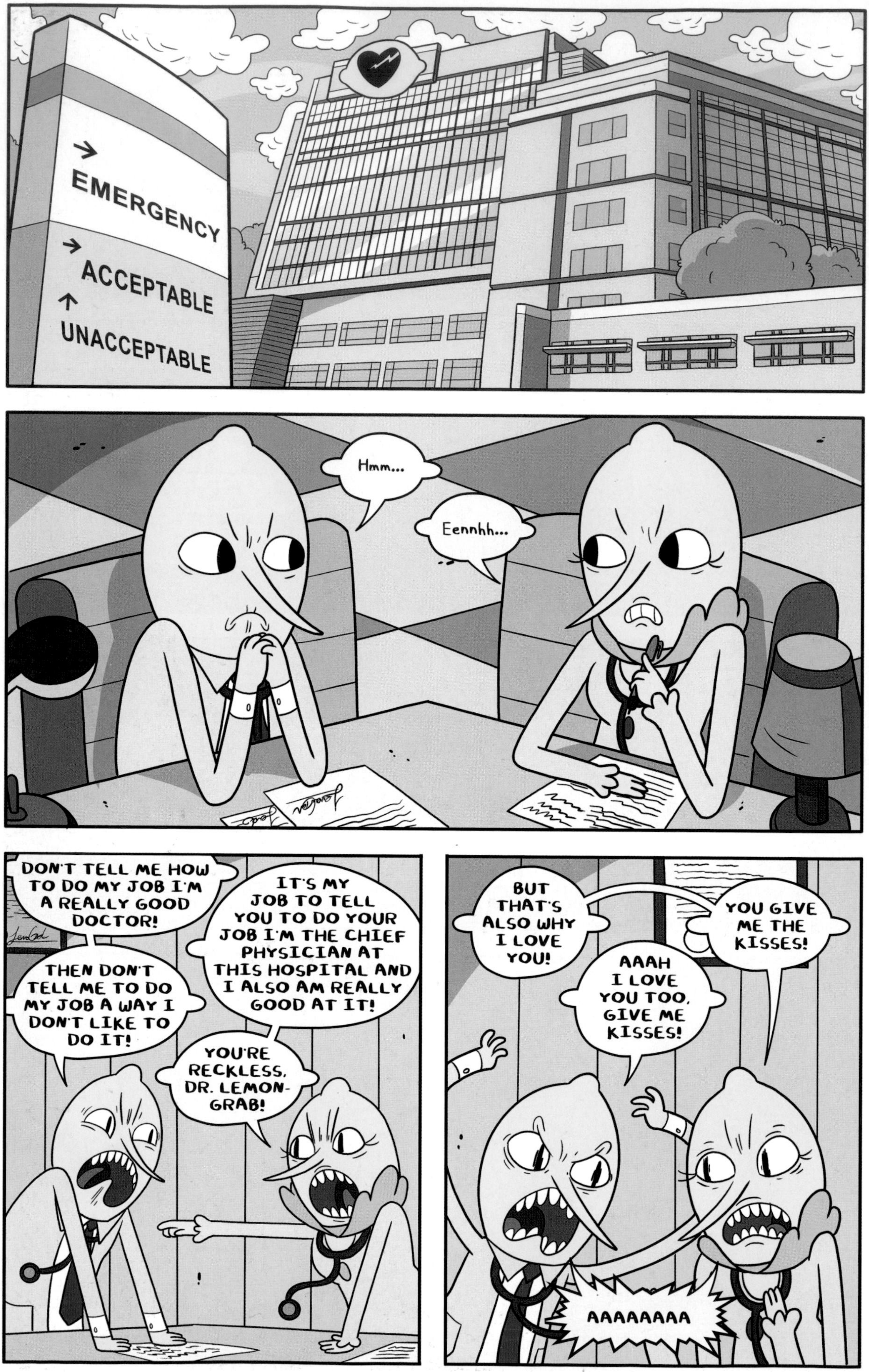
EMERGENCY
ACCEPTABLE
UNACCEPTABLE
Hmm...
Eennhh...
DON'T TELL ME HOW TO DO MY JOB I'M A REALLY GOOD DOCTOR!
THEN DON'T TELL ME TO DO MY JOB A WAY I DON'T LIKE TO DO IT!
IT'S MY JOB TO TELL YOU TO DO YOUR JOB I'M THE CHIEF PHYSICIAN AT THIS HOSPITAL AND I ALSO AM REALLY GOOD AT IT!
YOU'RE RECKLESS, DR. LEMON-GRAB!
BUT THAT'S ALSO WHY I LOVE YOU!
YOU GIVE ME THE KISSES!
AAAH I LOVE YOU TOO, GIVE ME KISSES!
AAAAAAAA

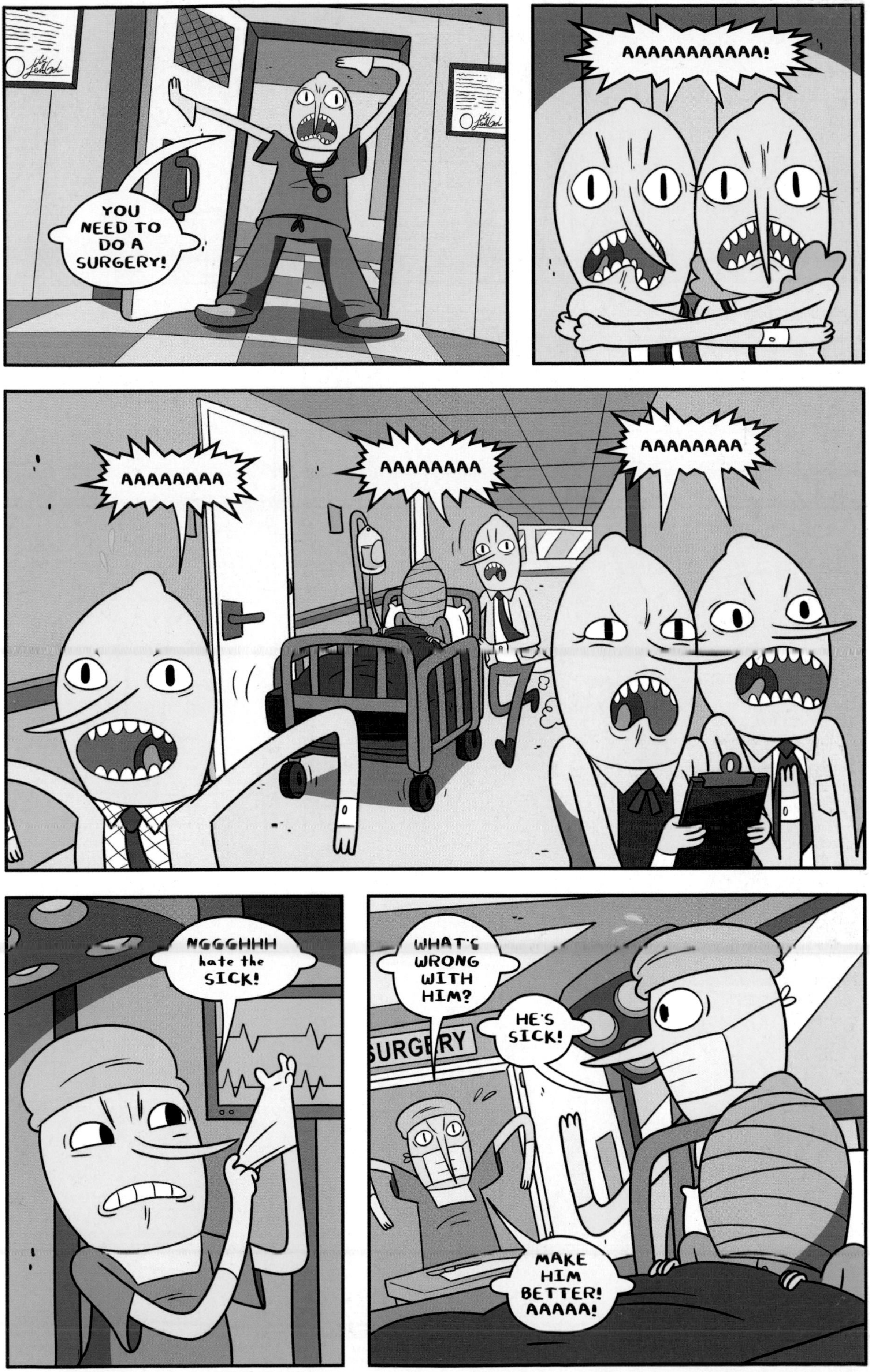
YOU NEED TO DO A SURGERY!
AAAAAAAAAAA!
AAAAAAAA
AAAAAAAA
AAAAAAAA
NGGGHHH hate the SICK!
WHAT'S WRONG WITH HIM?
SURGERY
HE'S SICK!
MAKE HIM BETTER! AAAAA!

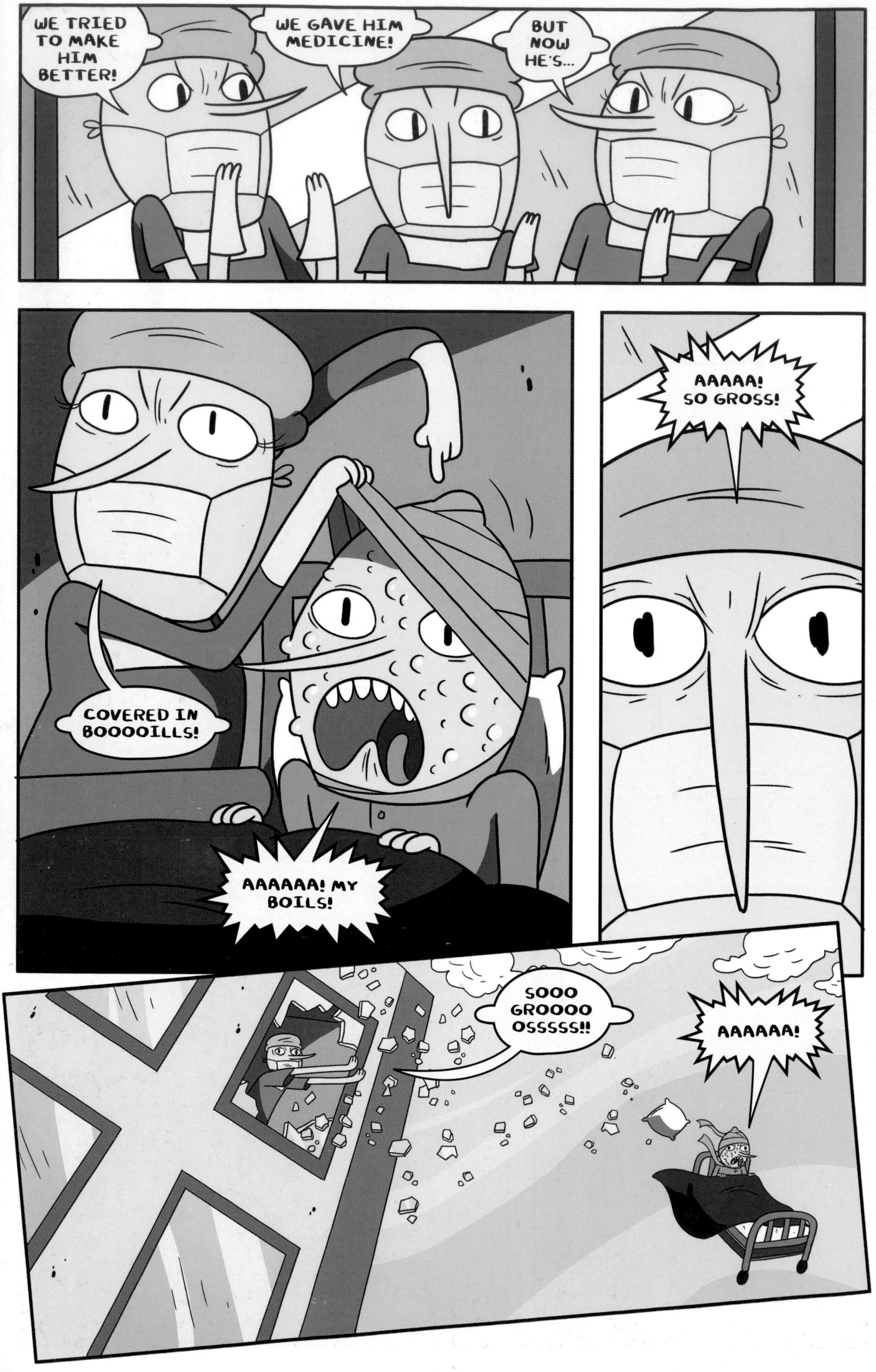
WE TRIED TO MAKE HIM BETTER!
WE GAVE HIM MEDICINE!
BUT NOW HE'S...
COVERED IN BOOOOILLS!
AAAAAA! MY BOILS!
AAAAA! SO GROSS!
SOOO GROOOO OSSSSS!!
AAAAAA!

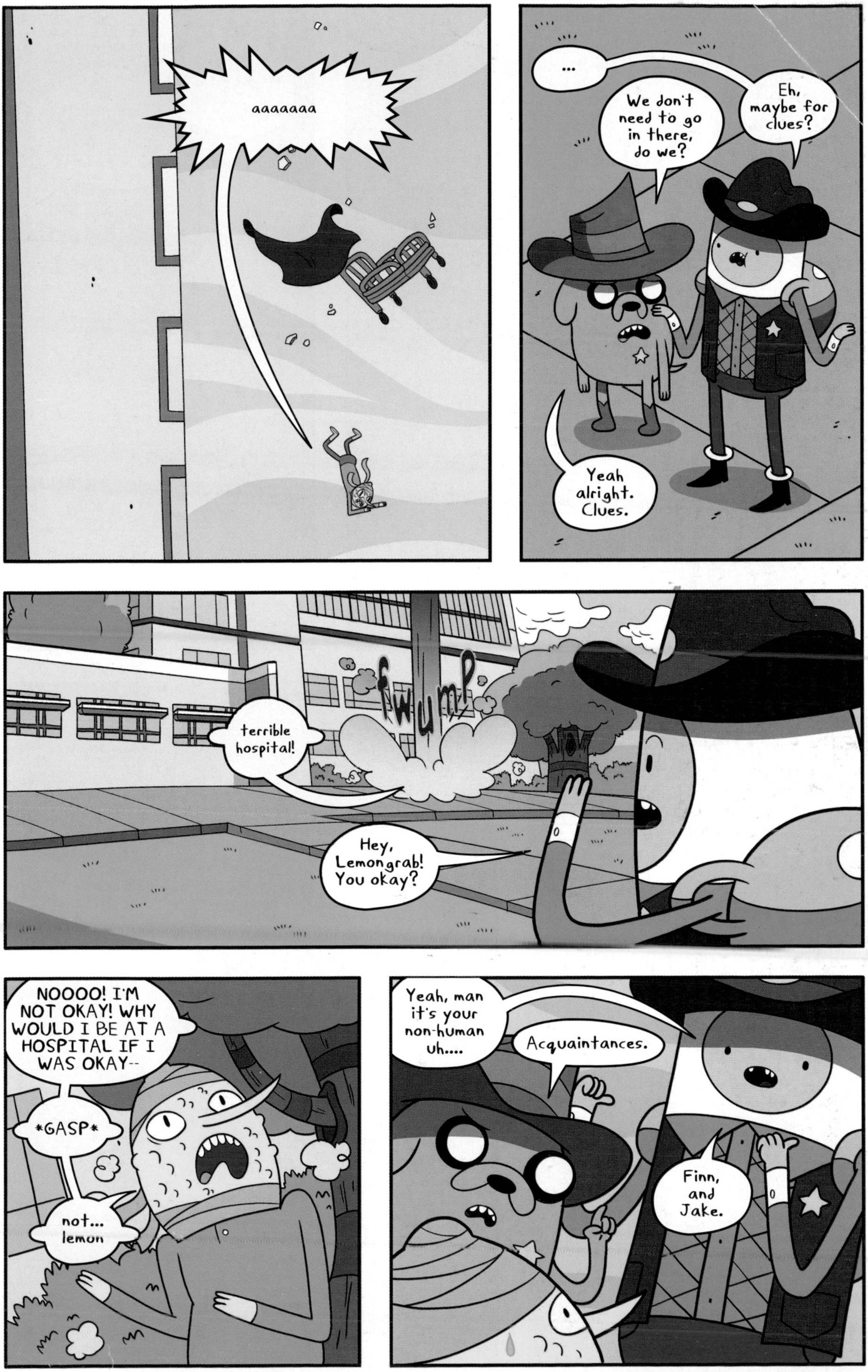
aaaaaaa
...
We don't need to go in there, do we?
Eh, maybe for clues?
Yeah alright. Clues.
fwump
terrible hospital!
Hey, Lemongrab! You okay?
NOOOO! I'M NOT OKAY! WHY WOULD I BE AT A HOSPITAL IF I WAS OKAY--
*GASP*
not... lemon
Yeah, man it's your non-human uh....
Acquaintances.
Finn, and Jake.

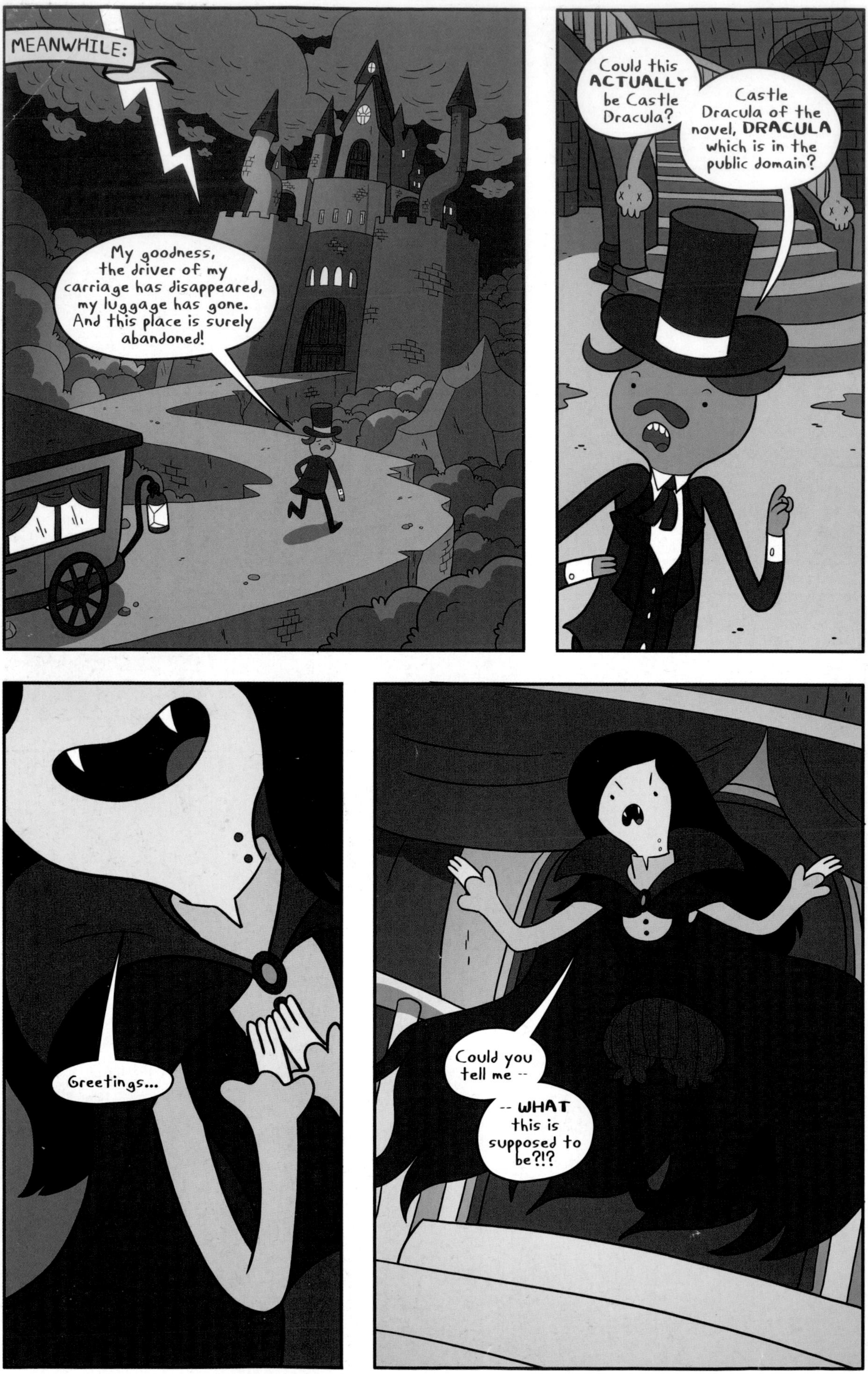
MEANWHILE:
My goodness, the driver of my carriage has disappeared, my luggage has gone. And this place is surely abandoned!
Could this ACTUALLY be Castle Dracula?
Castle Dracula of the novel, DRACULA which is in the public domain?
Greetings...
Could you tell me --
-- WHAT this is supposed to be?!?

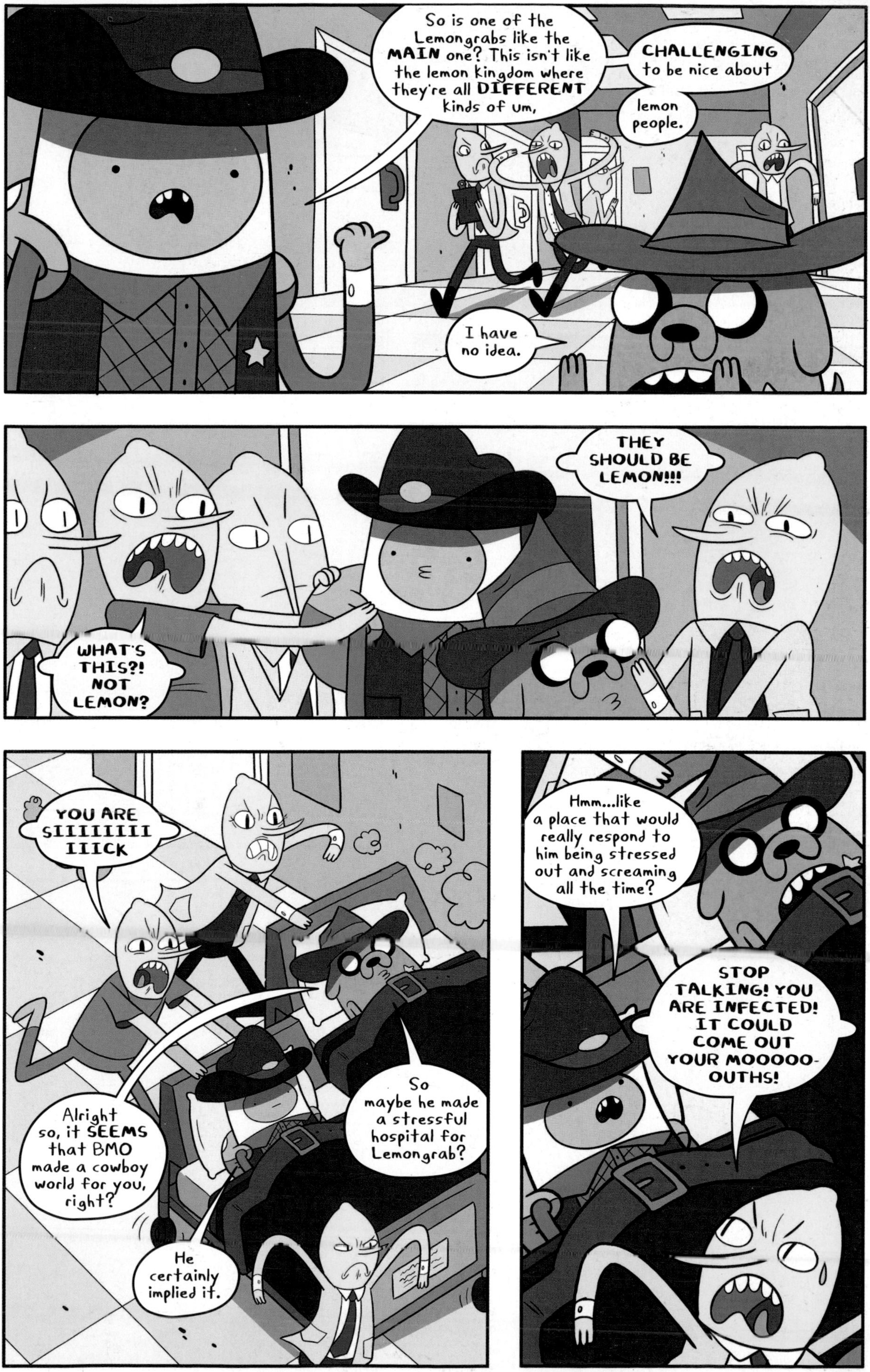
So is one of the Lemongrabs like the MAIN one? This isn't like the lemon kingdom where they're all DIFFERENT kinds of um,
CHALLENGING to be nice about
lemon people.
I have no idea.
THEY SHOULD BE LEMON!!!
WHAT'S THIS?! NOT LEMON?
YOU ARE SIIIIIIII IIICK
Alright so, it SEEMS that BMO made a cowboy world for you, right?
He certainly implied it.
So maybe he made a stressful hospital for Lemongrab?
Hmm...like a place that would really respond to him being stressed out and screaming all the time?
STOP TALKING! YOU ARE INFECTED! IT COULD COME OUT YOUR MOOOOO-OUTHS!

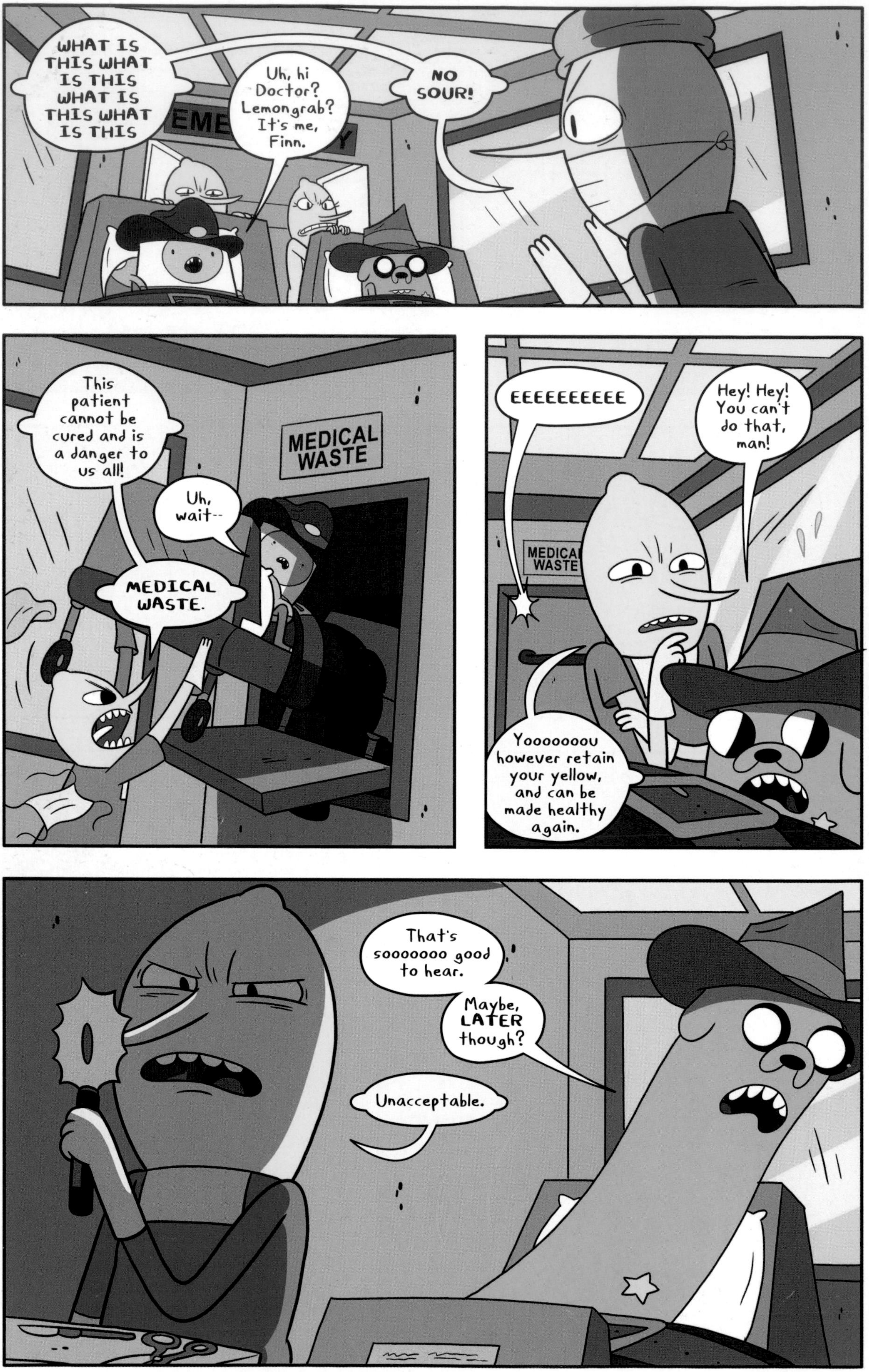

WHAT IS THIS WHAT IS THIS WHAT IS THIS WHAT IS THIS
Uh, hi Doctor? Lemongrab? It's me, Finn.
NO SOUR!
EME
This patient cannot be cured and is a danger to us all!
MEDICAL WASTE
Uh, wait--
MEDICAL WASTE.
EEEEEEEEEE
Hey! Hey! You can't do that, man!
MEDICAL WASTE
Yoooooooou however retain your yellow, and can be made healthy again.
That's soooooooo good to hear.
Maybe, LATER though?
Unacceptable.

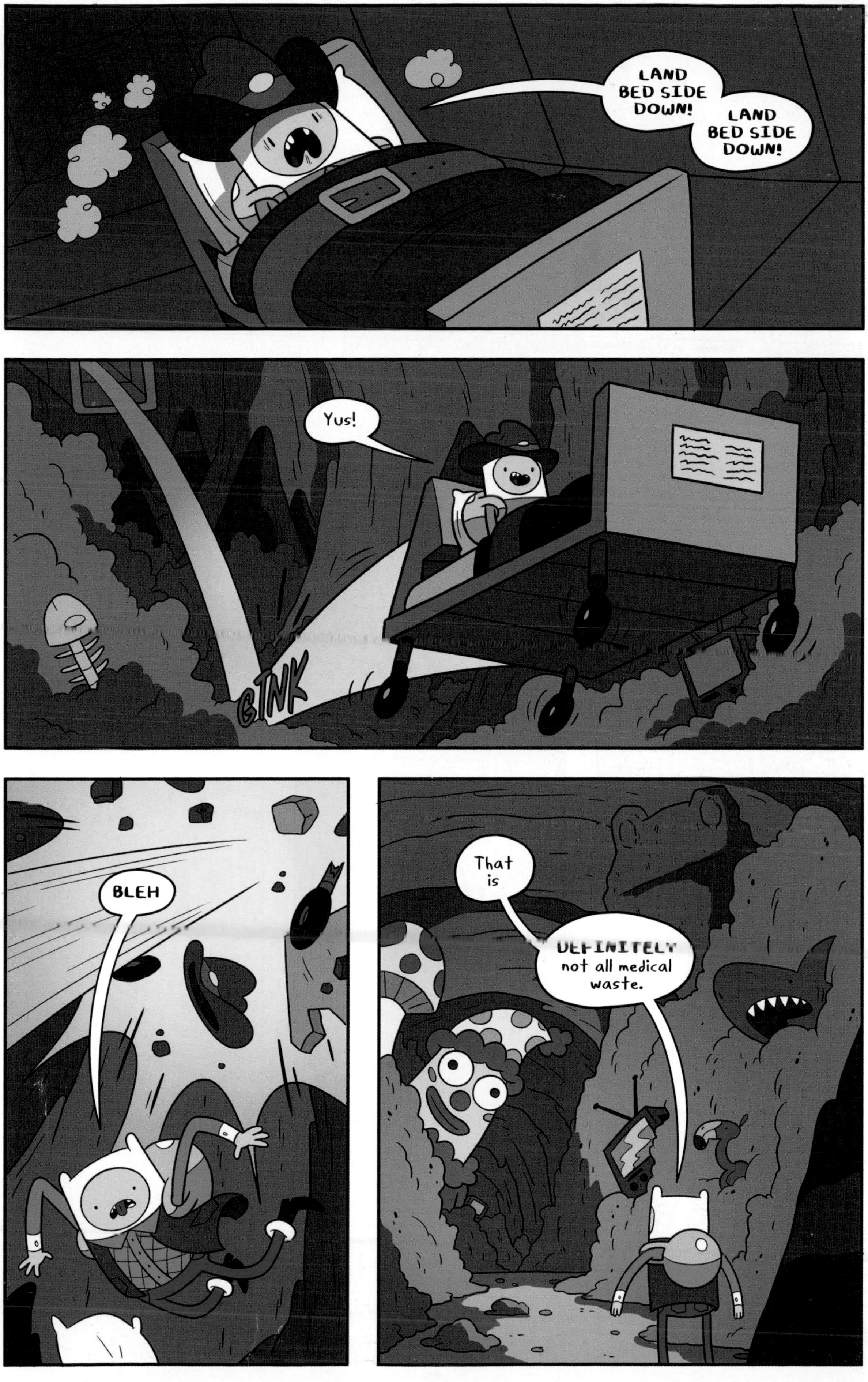
LAND BED SIDE DOWN!
LAND BED SIDE DOWN!
Yus!
GINK
BLEH
That is
DEFINITELY not all medical waste.

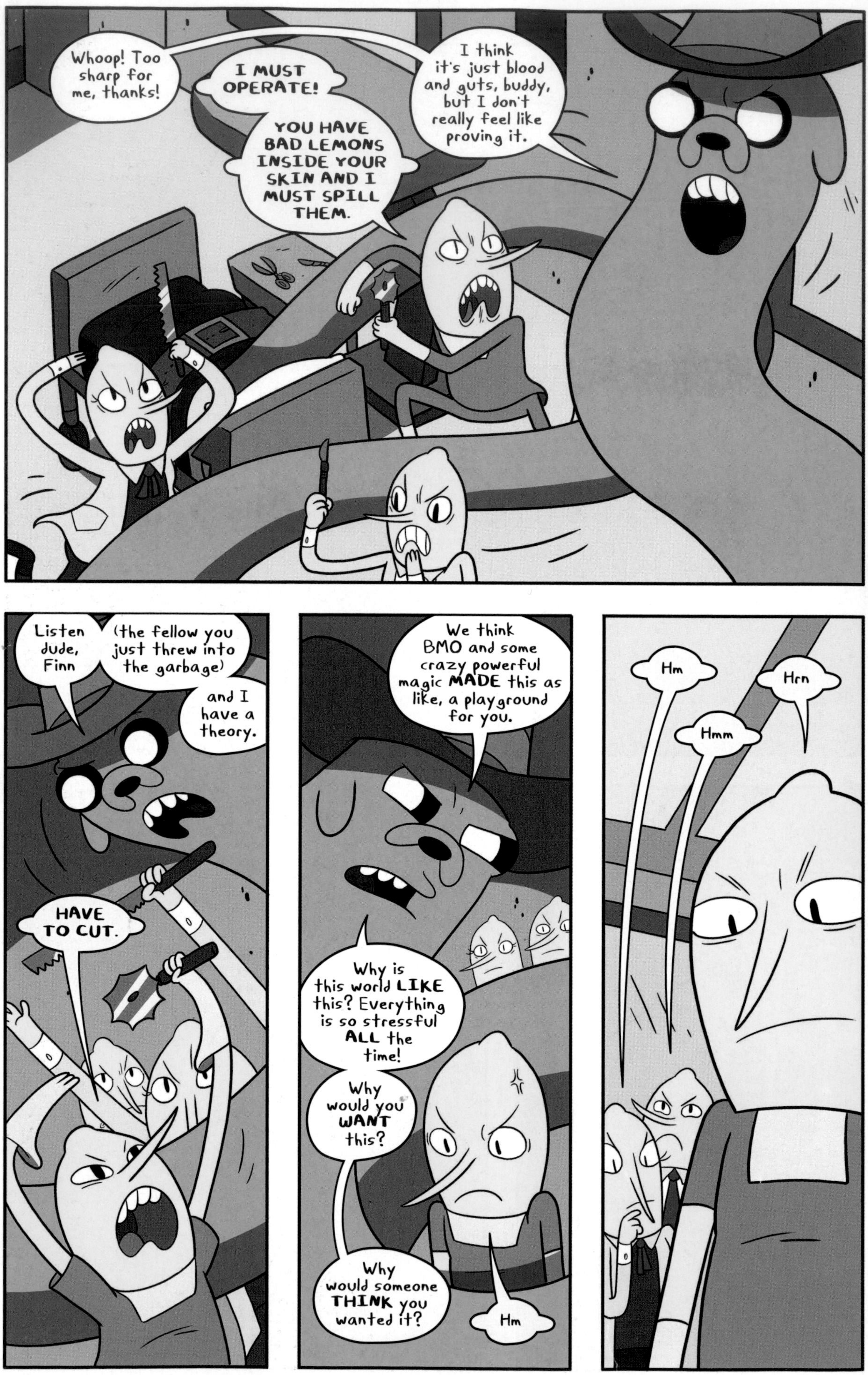
Whoop! Too sharp for me, thanks!
I MUST OPERATE!
YOU HAVE BAD LEMONS INSIDE YOUR SKIN AND I MUST SPILL THEM.
I think it's just blood and guts, buddy, but I don't really feel like proving it.
Listen dude, Finn
(the fellow you just threw into the garbage)
and I have a theory.
HAVE TO CUT.
We think BMO and some crazy powerful magic MADE this as like, a playground for you.
Why is this world LIKE this? Everything is so stressful ALL the time!
Why would you WANT this?
Why would someone THINK you wanted it?
Hm
Hm
Hmm
Hrn

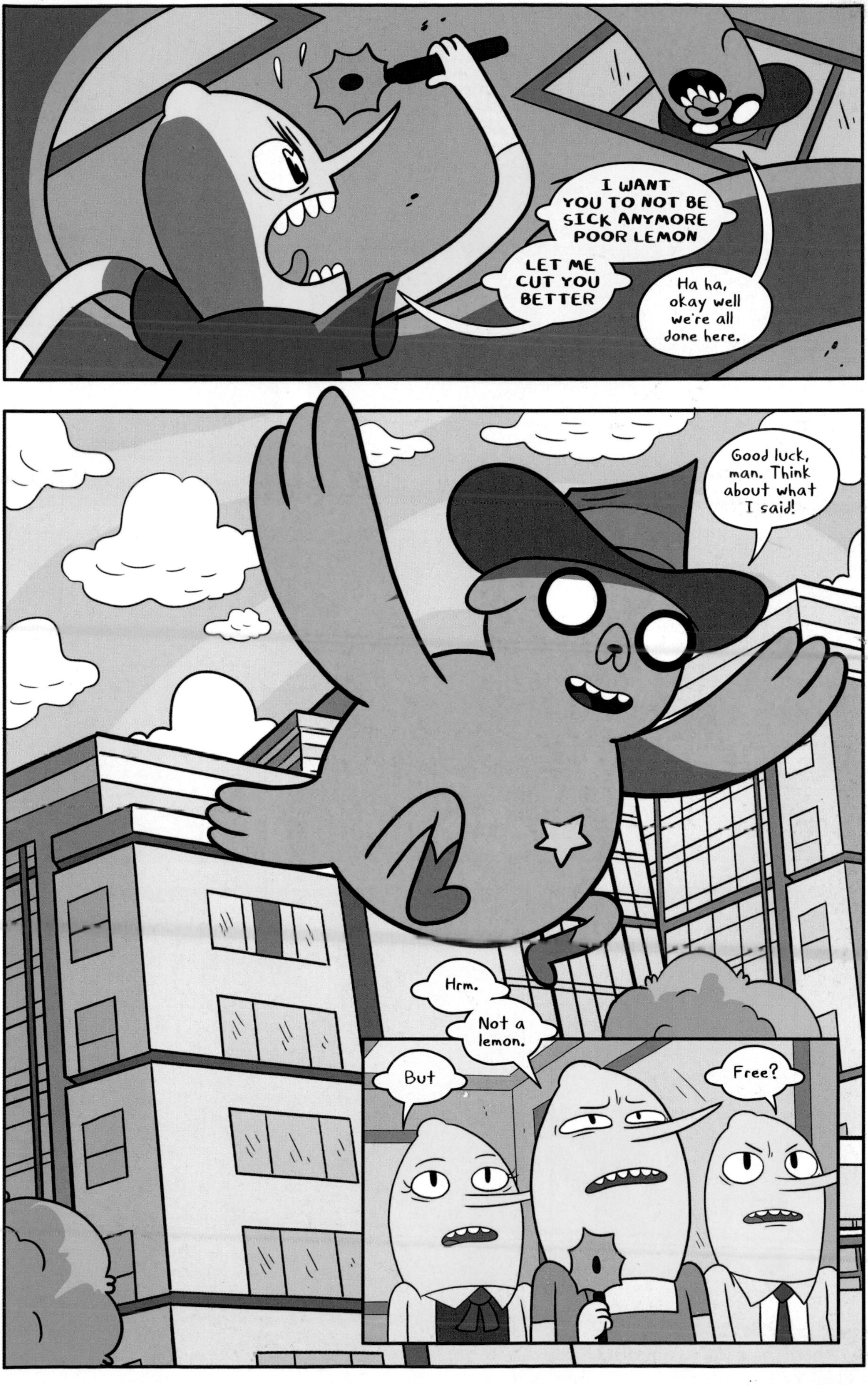
I WANT YOU TO NOT BE SICK ANYMORE POOR LEMON
LET ME CUT YOU BETTER
Ha ha, okay well we're all done here.
Good luck, man. Think about what I said!
Hrm.
Not a lemon.
But
Free?

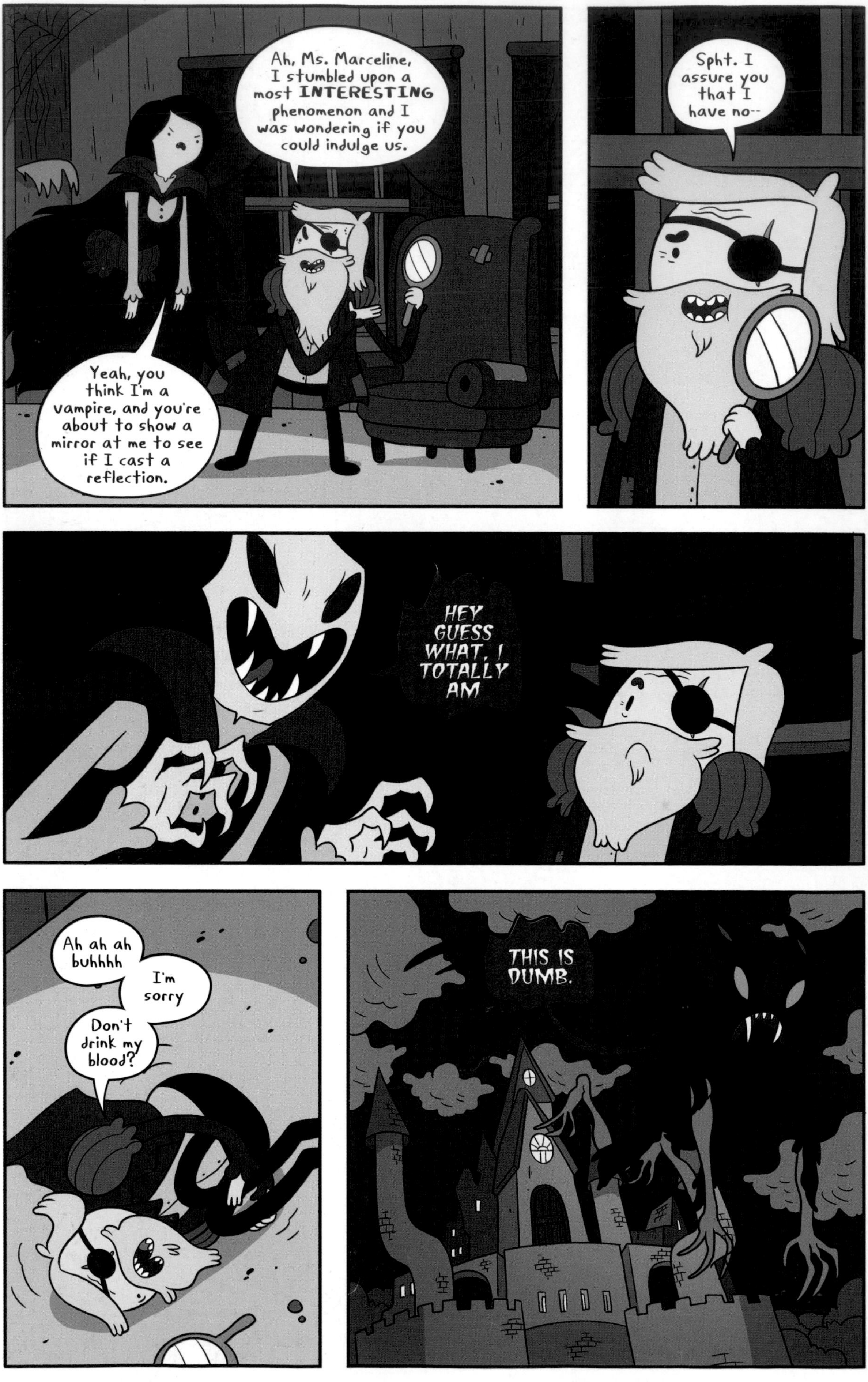
Ah, Ms. Marceline, I stumbled upon a most INTERESTING phenomenon and I was wondering if you could indulge us.
Yeah, you think I'm a vampire, and you're about to show a mirror at me to see if I cast a reflection.
Spht. I assure you that I have no--
HEY GUESS WHAT, I TOTALLY AM
Ah ah ah buhhhh
I'm sorry
Don't drink my blood?
THIS IS DUMB.

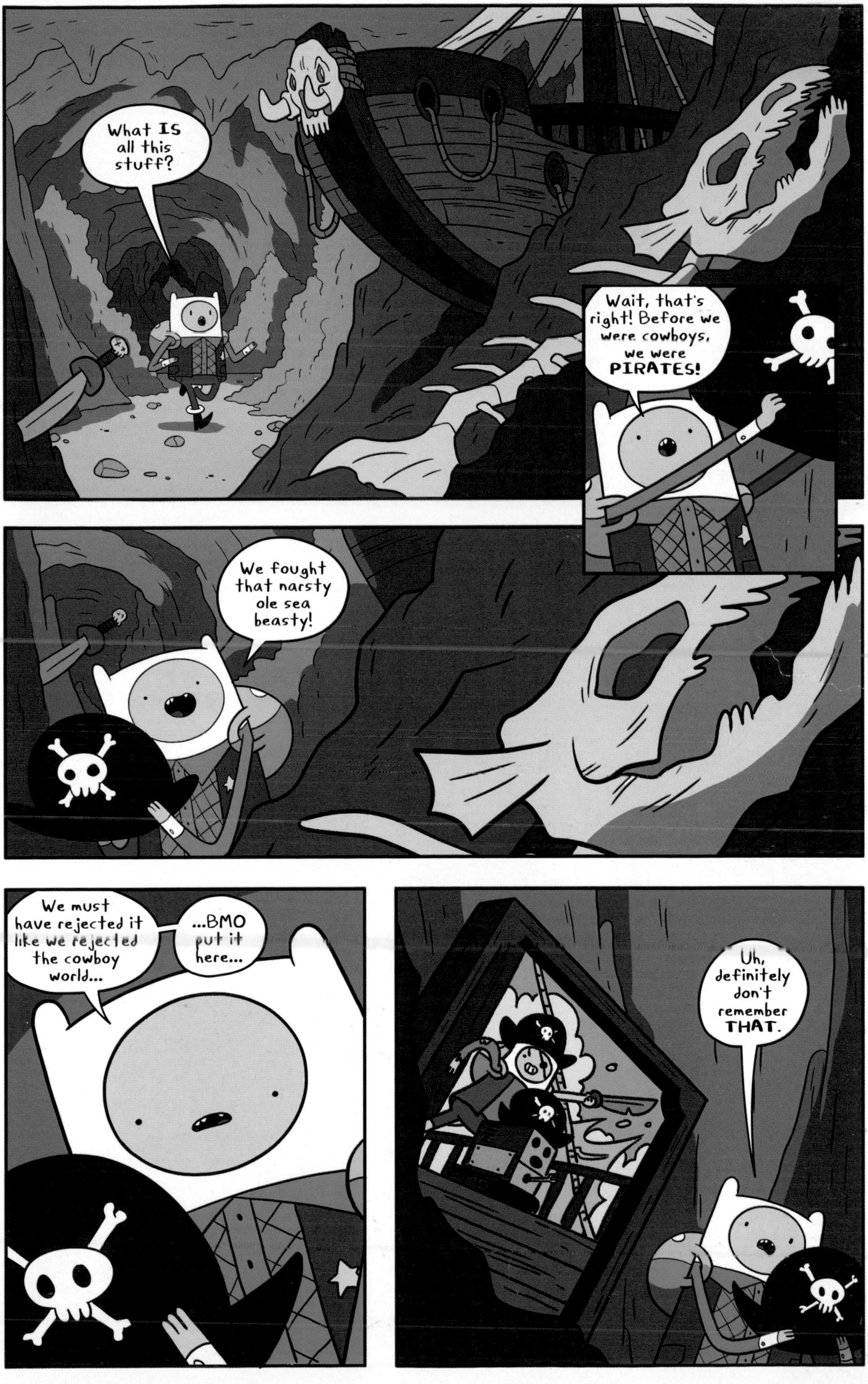
What IS all this stuff?
Wait, that's right! Before we were cowboys, we were PIRATES!
We fought that narsty ole sea beasty!
We must have rejected it like we rejected the cowboy world...
...BMO put it here...
Uh, definitely don't remember THAT.

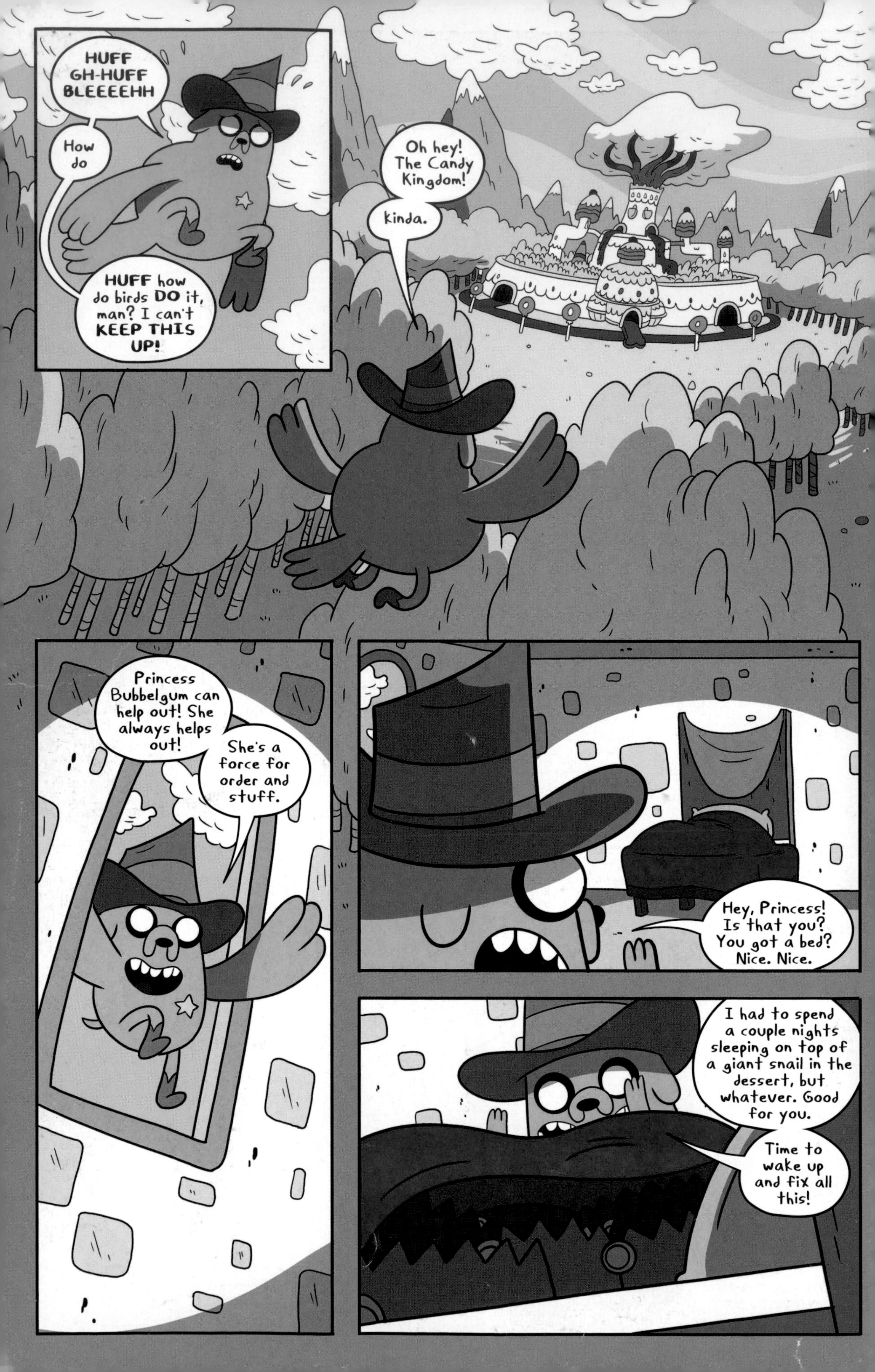

HUFF GH-HUFF BLEEEEHH
How do
HUFF how do birds DO it, man? I can't KEEP THIS UP!
Oh hey! The Candy Kingdom!
kinda.
Princess Bubbelgum can help out! She always helps out!
She's a force for order and stuff.
Hey, Princess! Is that you? You got a bed? Nice. Nice.
I had to spend a couple nights sleeping on top of a giant snail in the dessert, but whatever. Good for you.
Time to wake up and fix all this!

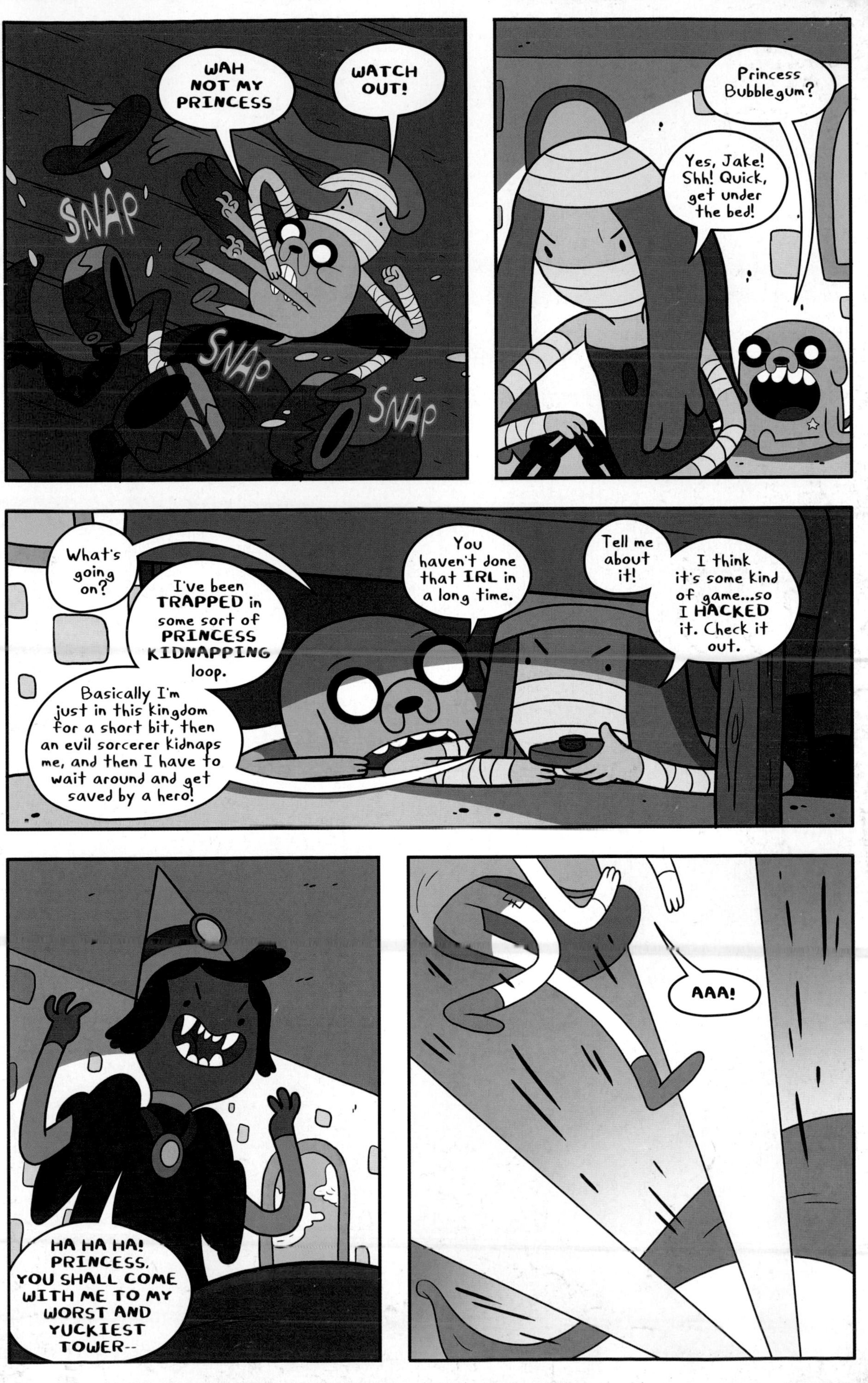
WAH NOT MY PRINCESS
WATCH OUT!
SNAP
SNAP
SNAP
Princess Bubblegum?
Yes, Jake! Shh! Quick, get under the bed!
What's going on?
I've been TRAPPED in some sort of PRINCESS KIDNAPPING loop.
Basically I'm just in this kingdom for a short bit, then an evil sorcerer kidnaps me, and then I have to wait around and get saved by a hero!
You haven't done that IRL in a long time.
Tell me about it!
I think it's some kind of game...so I HACKED it. Check it out.
HA HA HA! PRINCESS, YOU SHALL COME WITH ME TO MY WORST AND YUCKIEST TOWER--
AAA!

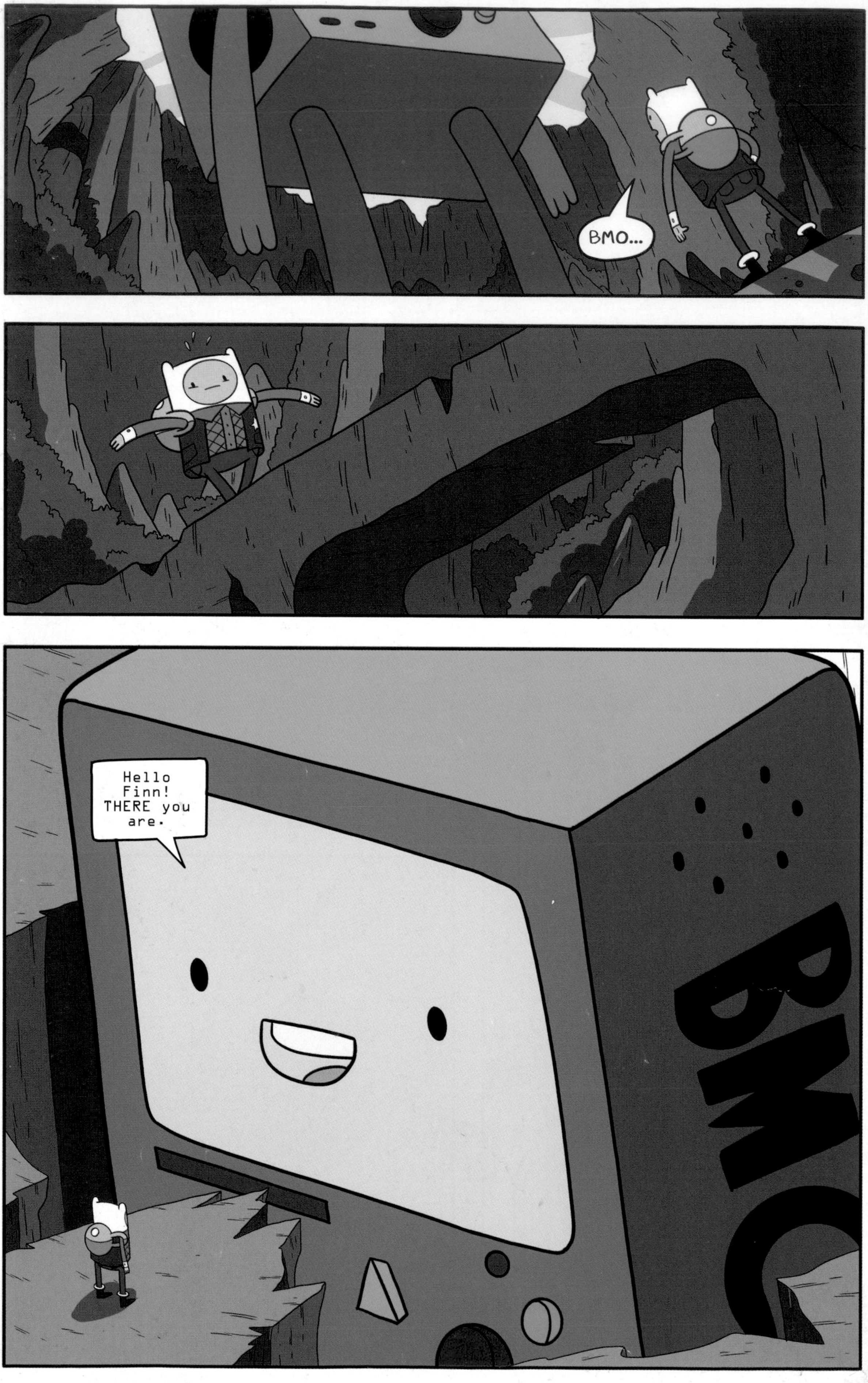
BMO...
Hello Finn! THERE you are.

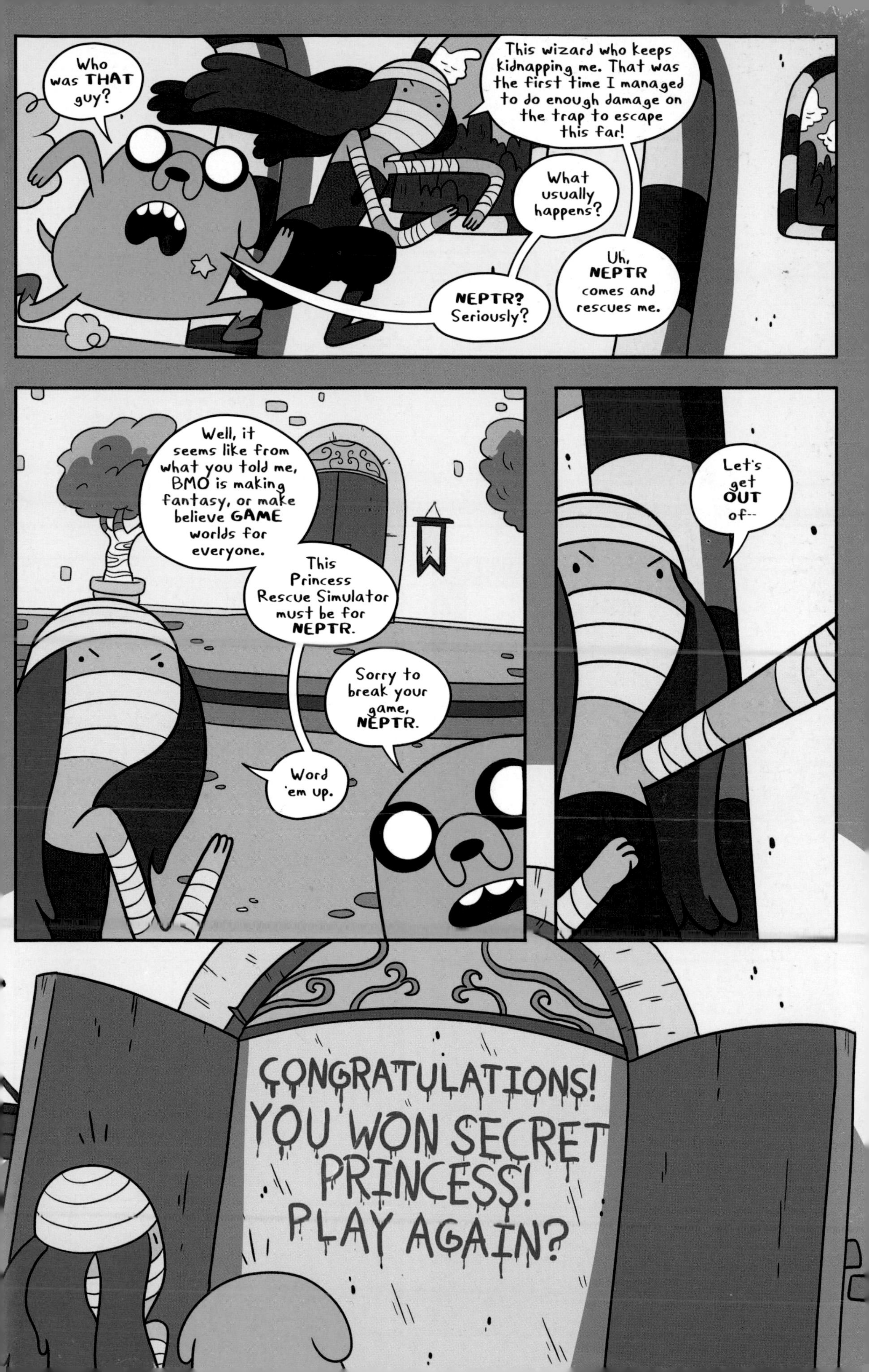

Who was THAT guy?
This wizard who keeps kidnapping me. That was the first time I managed to do enough damage on the trap to escape this far!
What usually happens?
Uh, NEPTR comes and rescues me.
NEPTR? Seriously?
Well, it seems like from what you told me, BMO is making fantasy, or make believe GAME worlds for everyone.
This Princess Rescue Simulator must be for NEPTR.
Word 'em up.
Sorry to break your game, NEPTR.
Let's get OUT of--
CONGRATULATIONS! YOU WON SECRET PRINCESS! PLAY AGAIN?

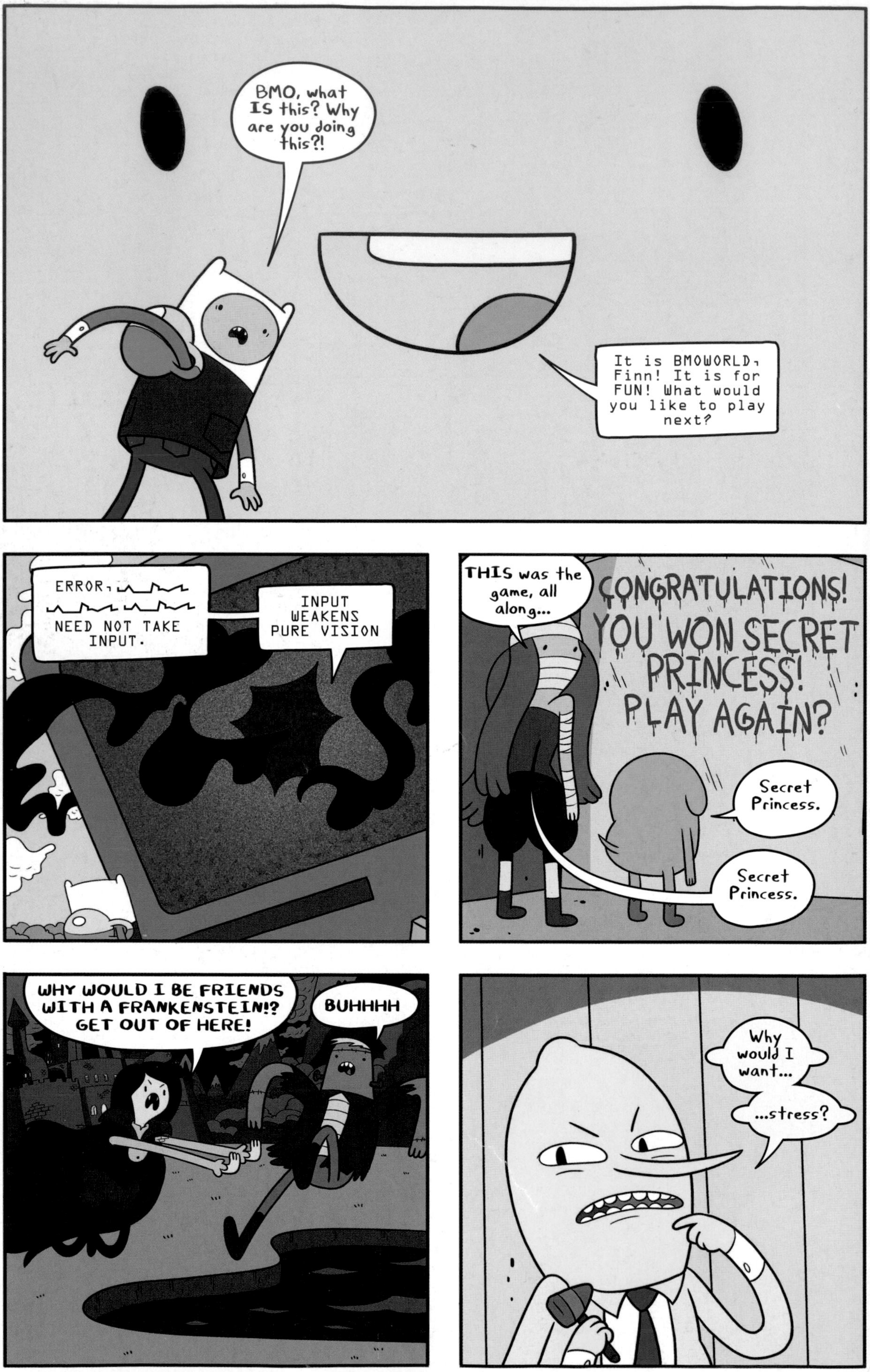

BMO, what IS this? Why are you doing this?!
It is BMOWORLD, Finn! It is for FUN! What would you like to play next?
ERROR,
NEED NOT TAKE INPUT.
INPUT WEAKENS PURE VISION
THIS was the game, all along...
CONGRATULATIONS! YOU WON SECRET PRINCESS! PLAY AGAIN?
Secret Princess.
Secret Princess.
WHY WOULD I BE FRIENDS WITH A FRANKENSTEIN!? GET OUT OF HERE!
BUHHHH
Why would I want...
...stress?

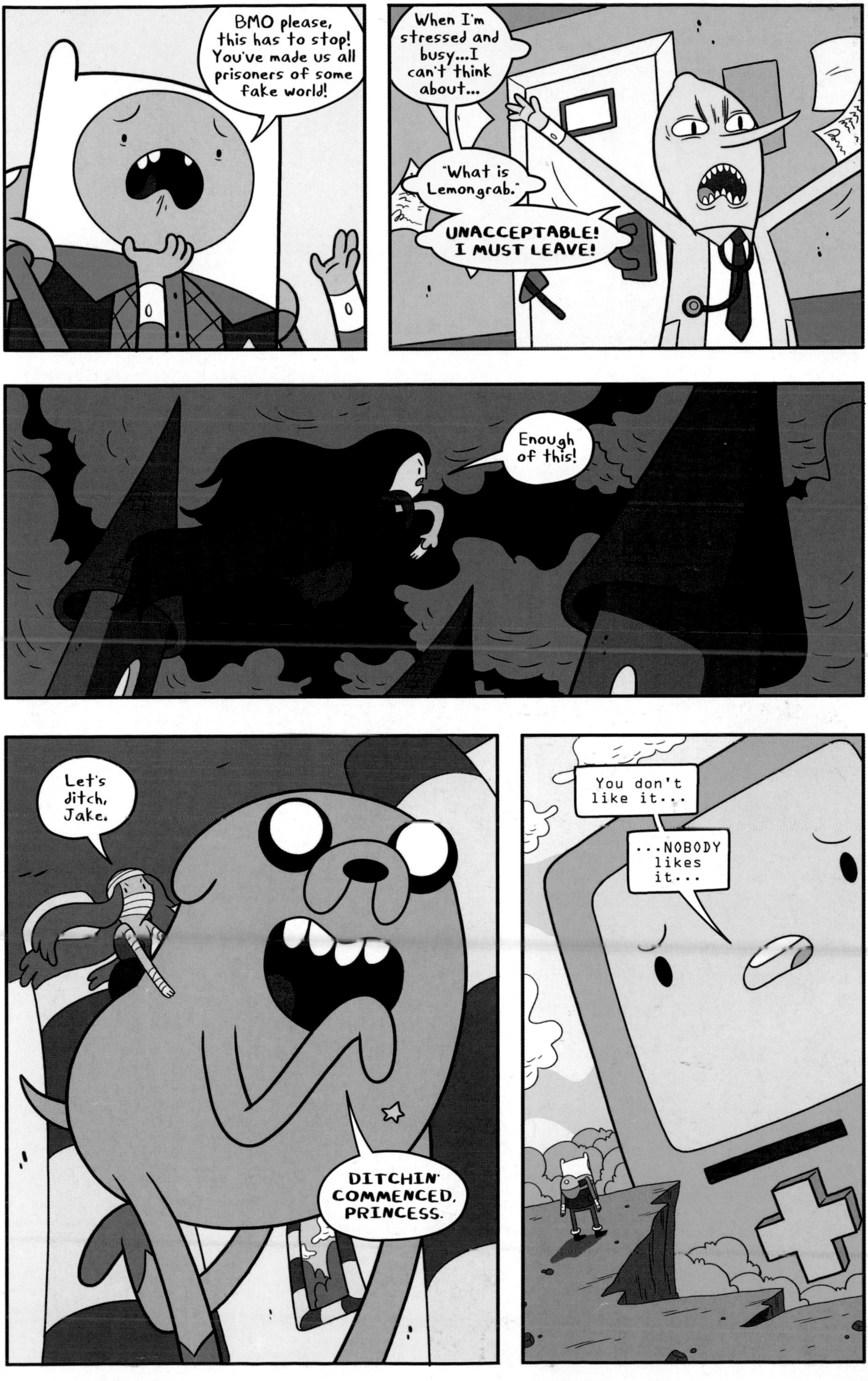
BMO please, this has to stop! You've made us all prisoners of some fake world!
When I'm stressed and busy...I can't think about...
"What is Lemongrab."
UNACCEPTABLE! I MUST LEAVE!
Enough of this!
Let's ditch, Jake.
DITCHIN' COMMENCED, PRINCESS.
You don't like it...
...NOBODY likes it...

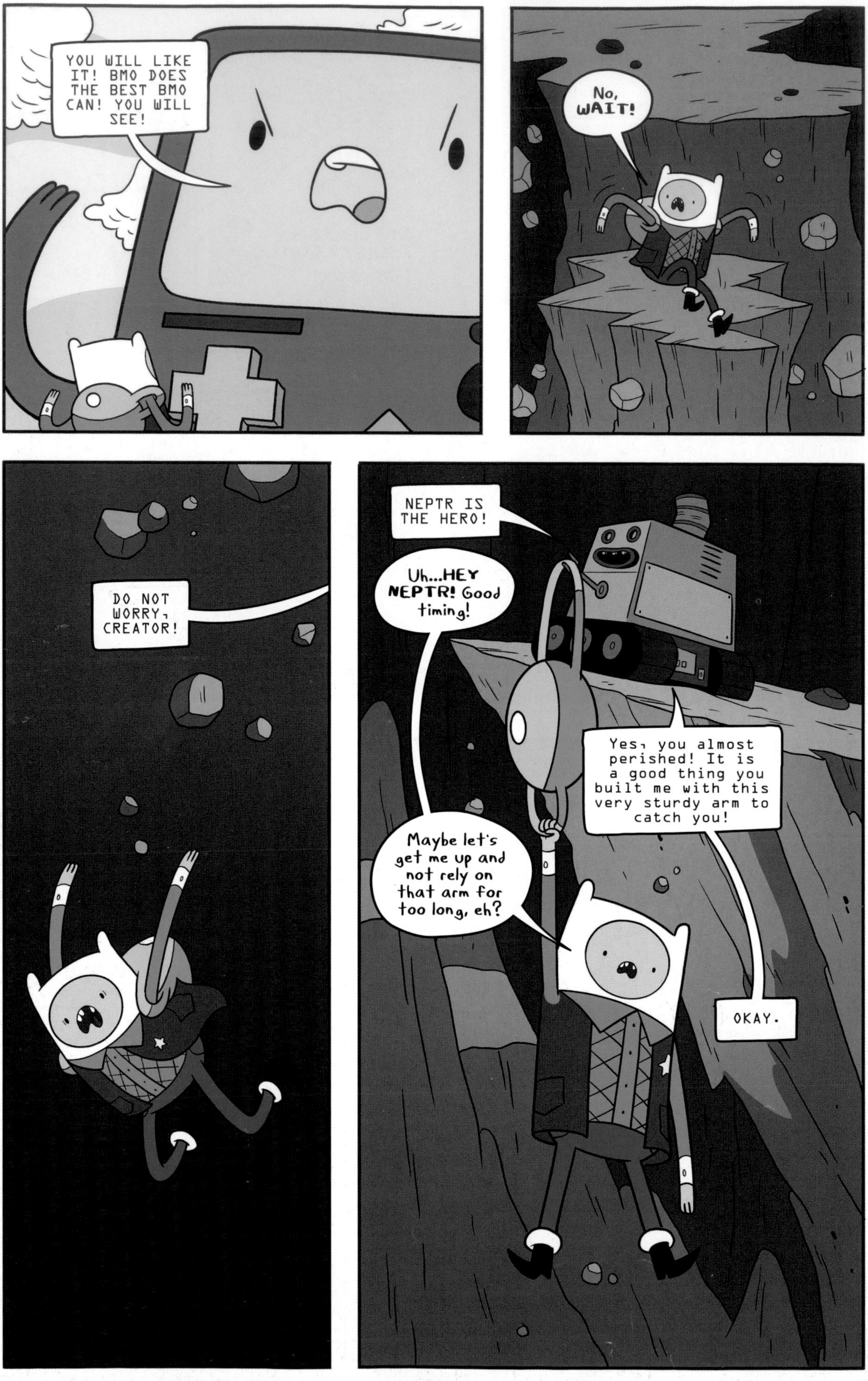
YOU WILL LIKE IT! BMO DOES THE BEST BMO CAN! YOU WILL SEE!
No, WAIT!
DO NOT WORRY, CREATOR!
NEPTR IS THE HERO!
Uh...HEY NEPTR! Good timing!
Yes, you almost perished! It is a good thing you built me with this very sturdy arm to catch you!
Maybe let's get me up and not rely on that arm for too long, eh?
OKAY.

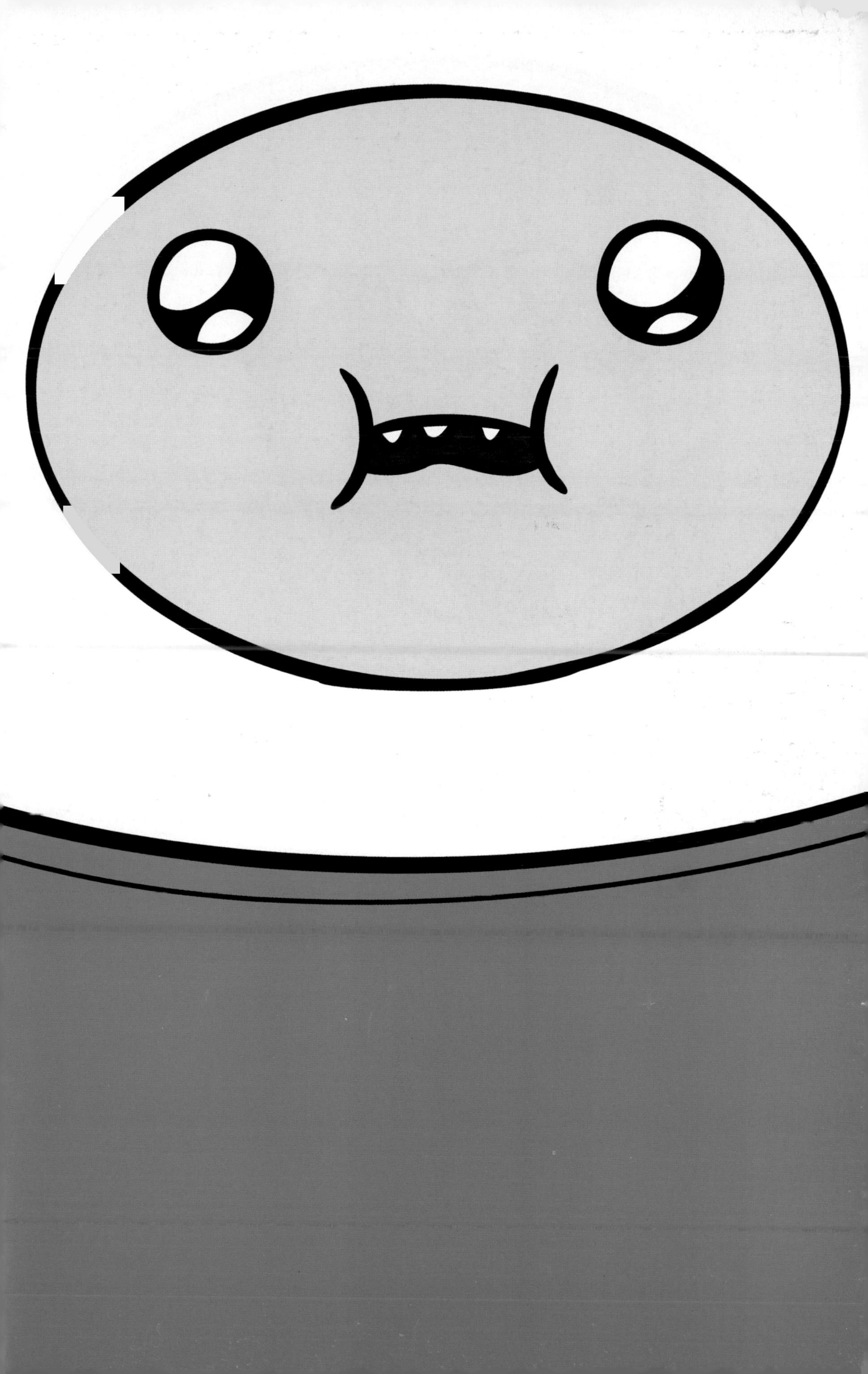

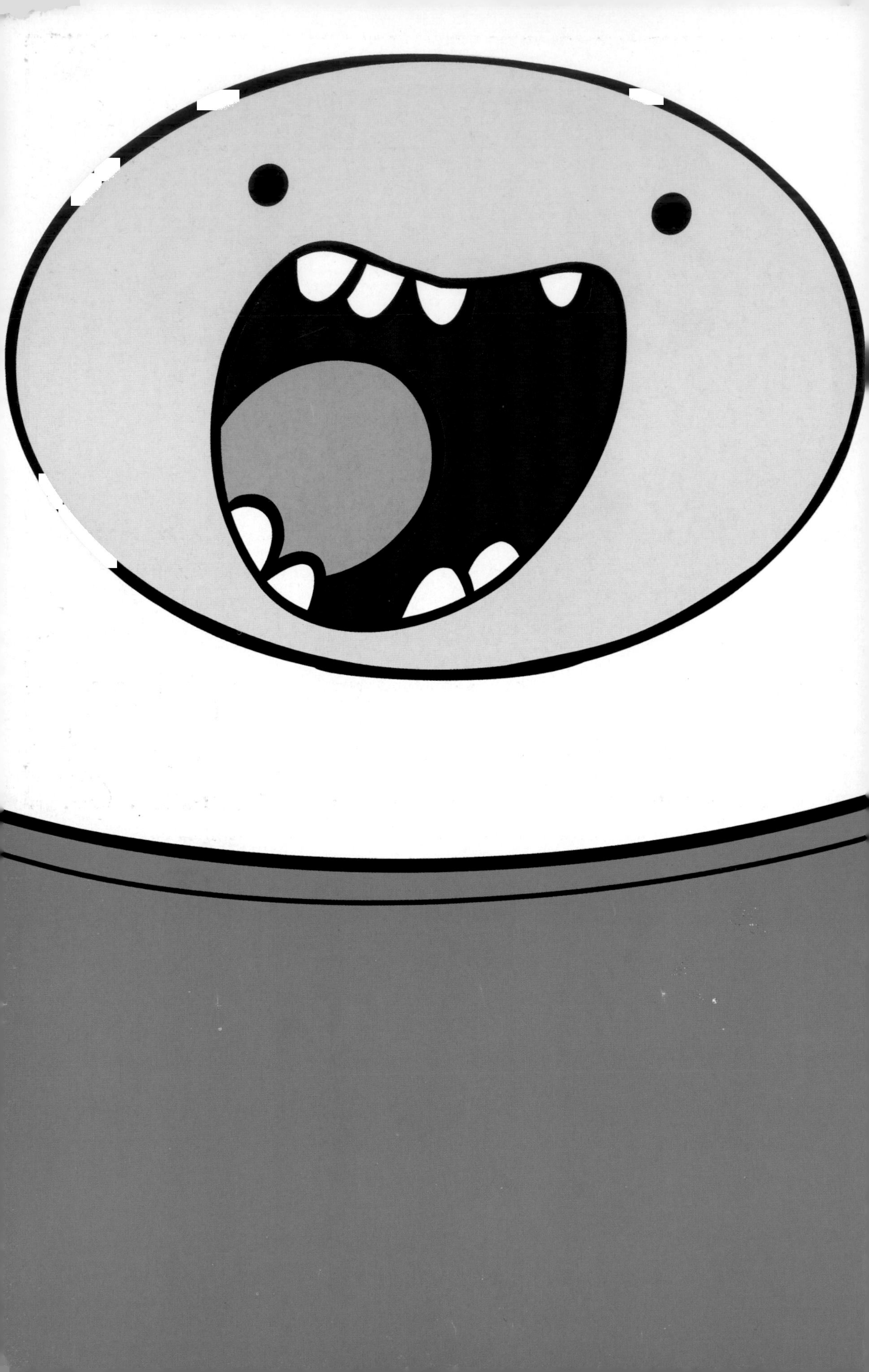

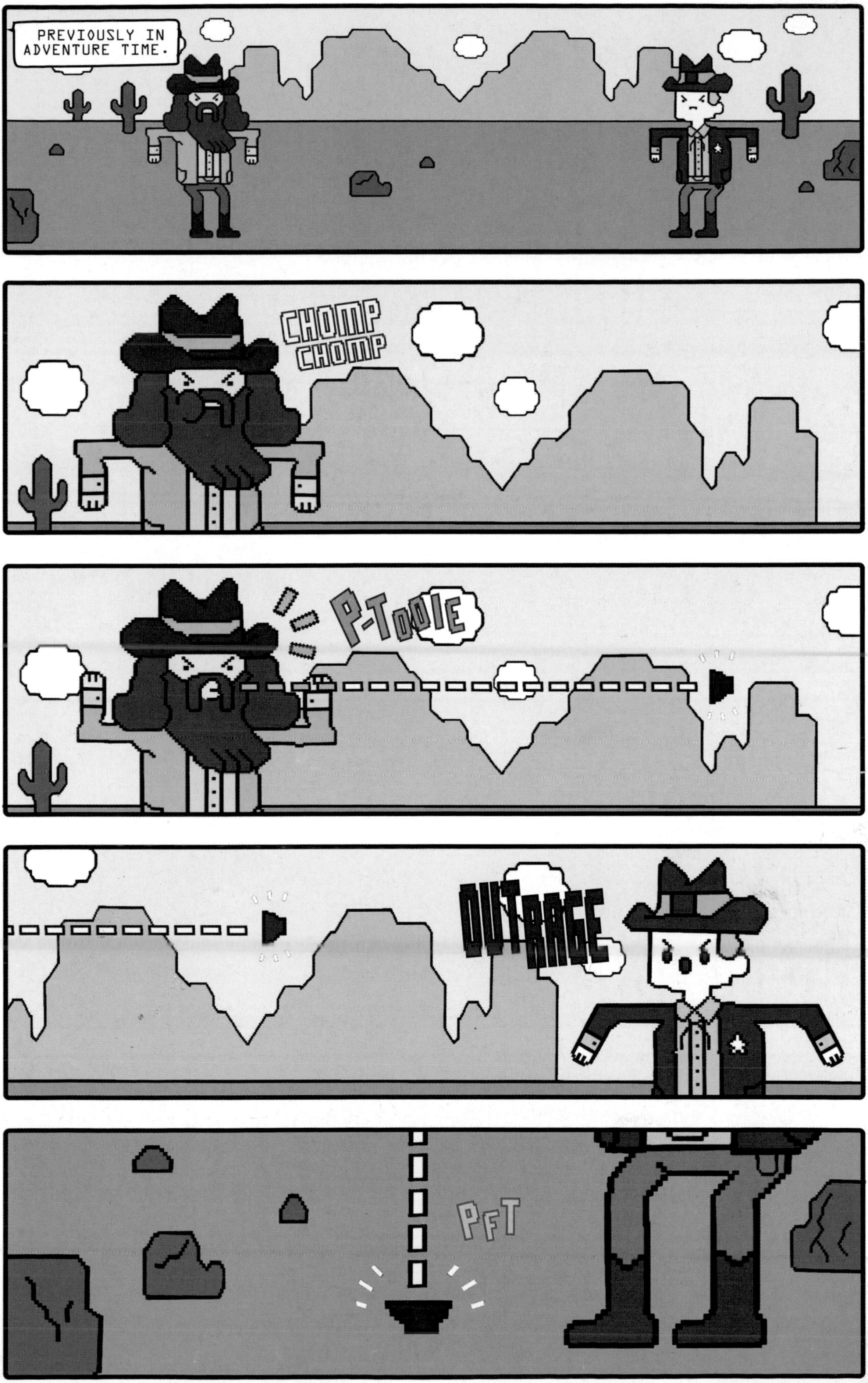
PREVIOUSLY IN ADVENTURE TIME.
CHOMP CHOMP
P-TOOIE
OUTRAGE
PFT

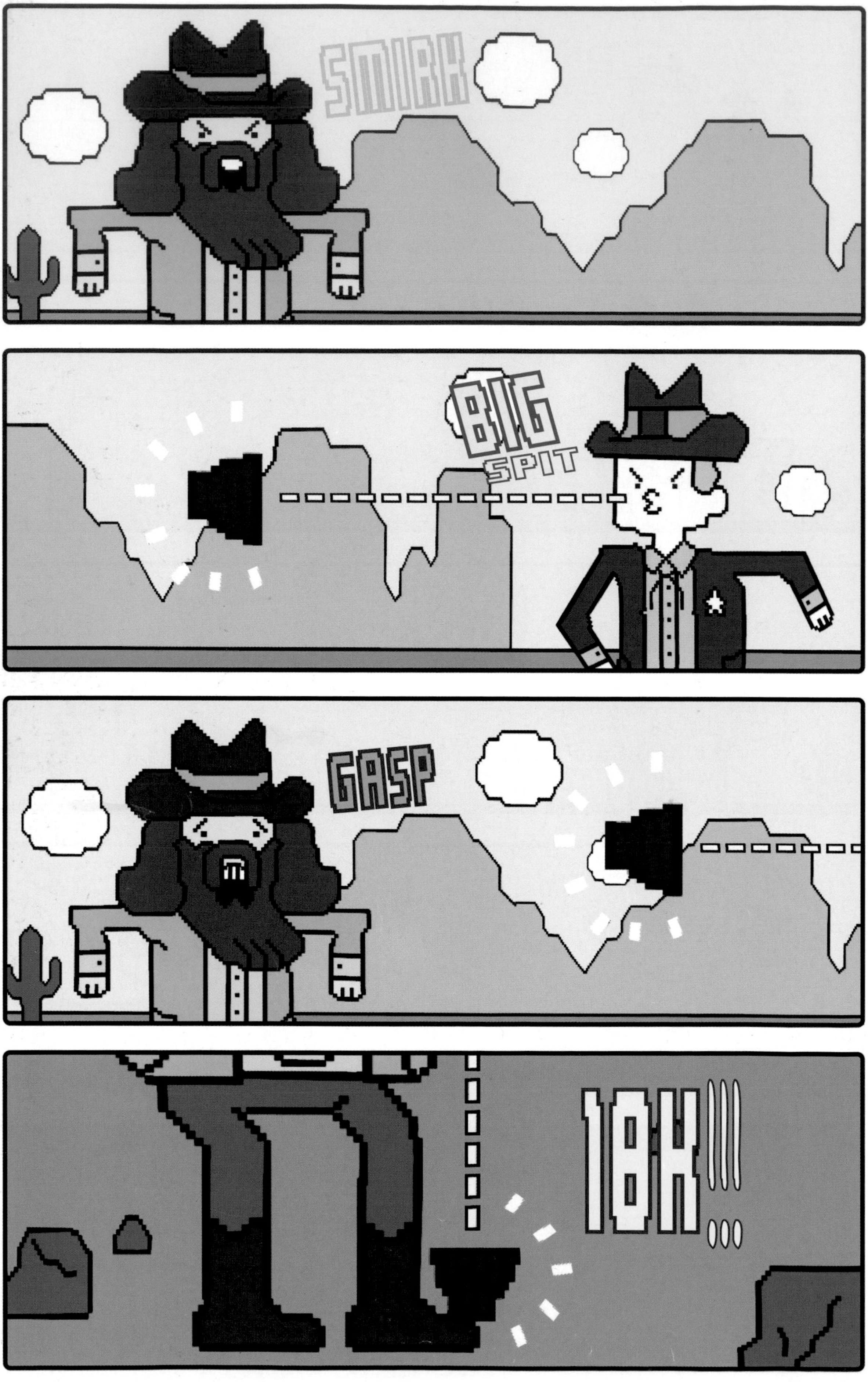
SMIRK
BIG
SPIT
GASP
1BK!!!

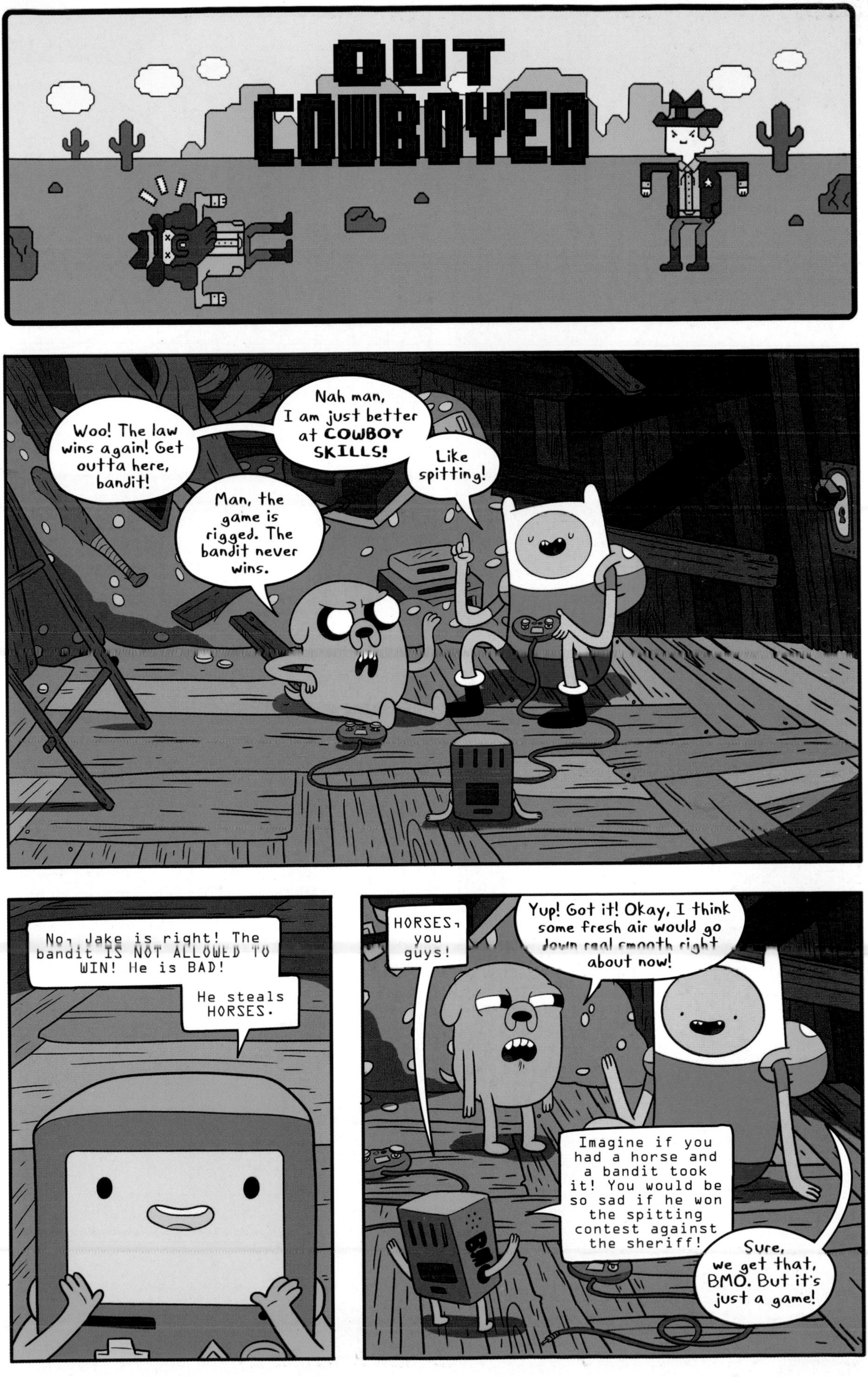
OUT COWBOYED
Woo! The law wins again! Get outta here, bandit!
Nah man, I am just better at **COWBOY SKILLS!**
Like spitting!
Man, the game is rigged. The bandit never wins.
No, Jake is right! The bandit IS NOT ALLOWED TO WIN! He is BAD!
He steals HORSES.
HORSES, you guys!
Yup! Got it! Okay, I think some fresh air would go down real smooth right about now!
Imagine if you had a horse and a bandit took it! You would be so sad if he won the spitting contest against the sheriff!
Sure, we get that, BMO. But it's just a game!
BMO

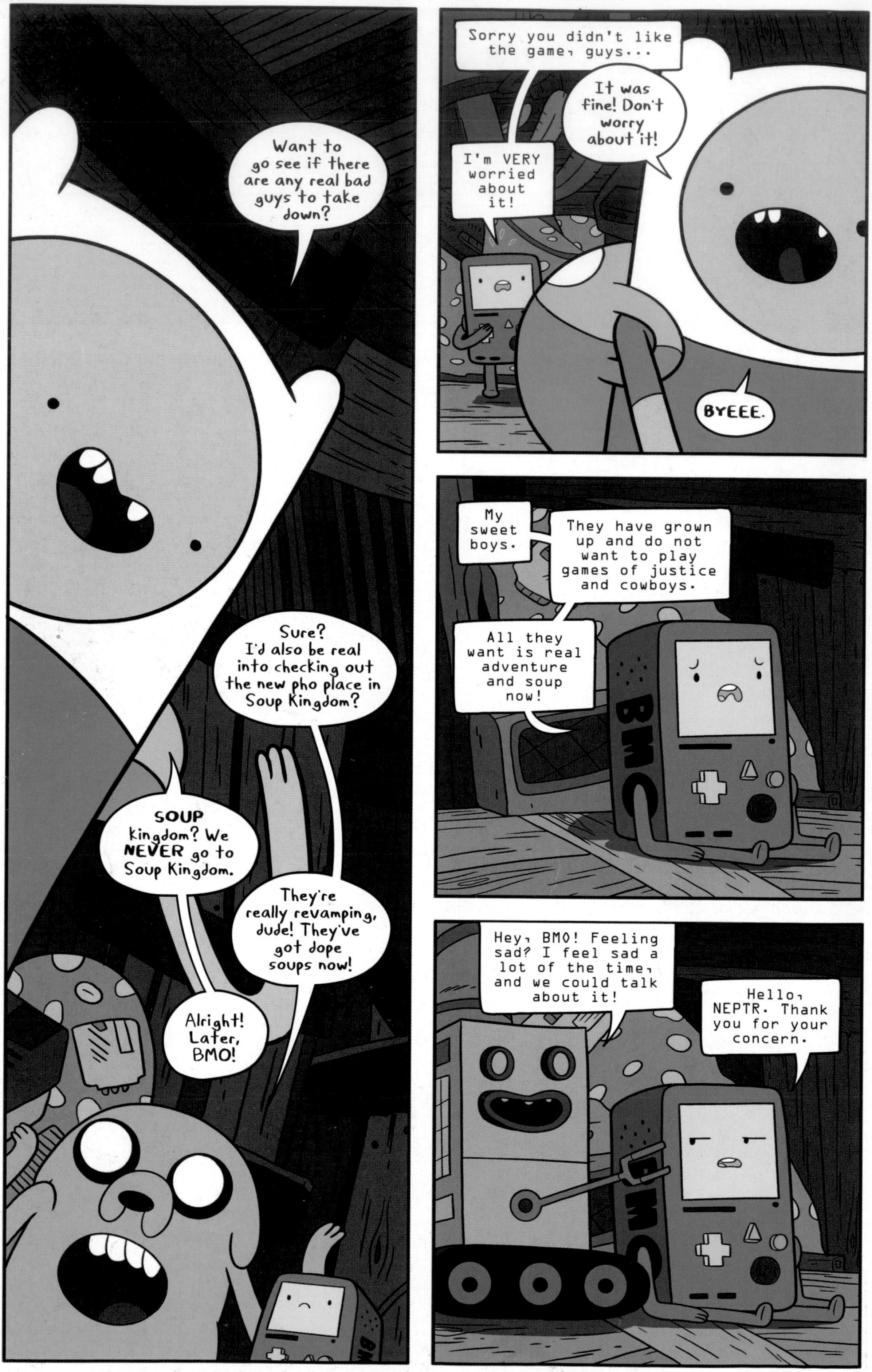
Want to go see if there are any real bad guys to take down?
Sure? I'd also be real into checking out the new pho place in Soup Kingdom?
SOUP kingdom? We NEVER go to Soup Kingdom.
They're really revamping, dude! They've got dope soups now!
Alright! Later, BMO!
Sorry you didn't like the game, guys...
It was fine! Don't worry about it!
I'm VERY worried about it!
BYEEE.
My sweet boys.
They have grown up and do not want to play games of justice and cowboys.
All they want is real adventure and soup now!
Hey, BMO! Feeling sad? I feel sad a lot of the time, and we could talk about it!
Hello, NEPTR. Thank you for your concern.

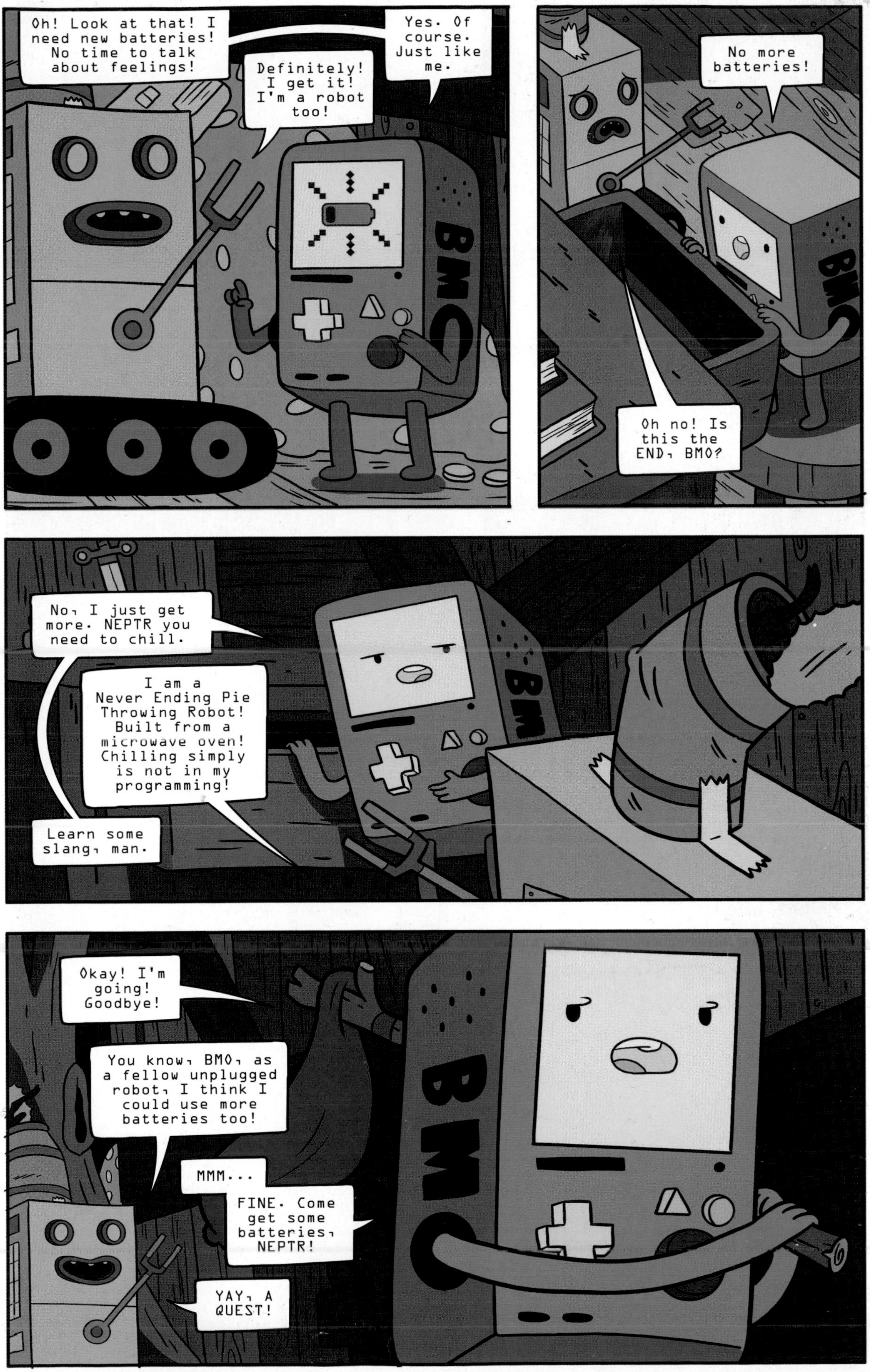
Oh! Look at that! I need new batteries! No time to talk about feelings!
Yes. Of course. Just like me.
Definitely! I get it! I'm a robot too!
No more batteries!
Oh no! Is this the END, BMO?
No, I just get more. NEPTR you need to chill.
I am a Never Ending Pie Throwing Robot! Built from a microwave oven! Chilling simply is not in my programming!
Learn some slang, man.
Okay! I'm going! Goodbye!
You know, BMO, as a fellow unplugged robot, I think I could use more batteries too!
MMM...
FINE. Come get some batteries, NEPTR!
YAY, A QUEST!

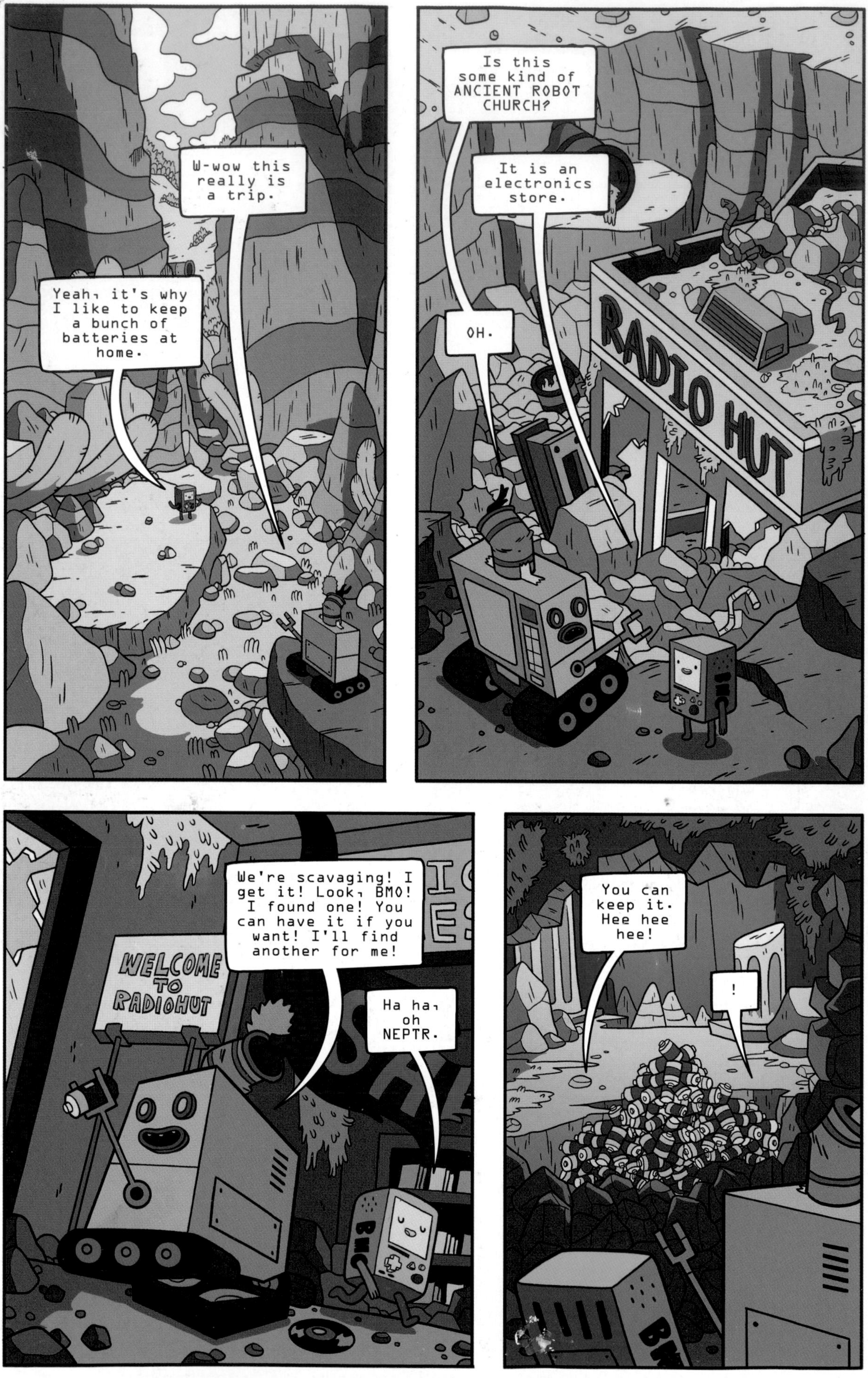
W-wow this really is a trip.
Yeah, it's why I like to keep a bunch of batteries at home.
Is this some kind of ANCIENT ROBOT CHURCH?
It is an electronics store.
OH.
RADIO HUT
WELCOME TO RADIOHUT
We're scavaging! I get it! Look, BMO! I found one! You can have it if you want! I'll find another for me!
Ha ha, oh NEPTR.
You can keep it. Hee hee hee!
!

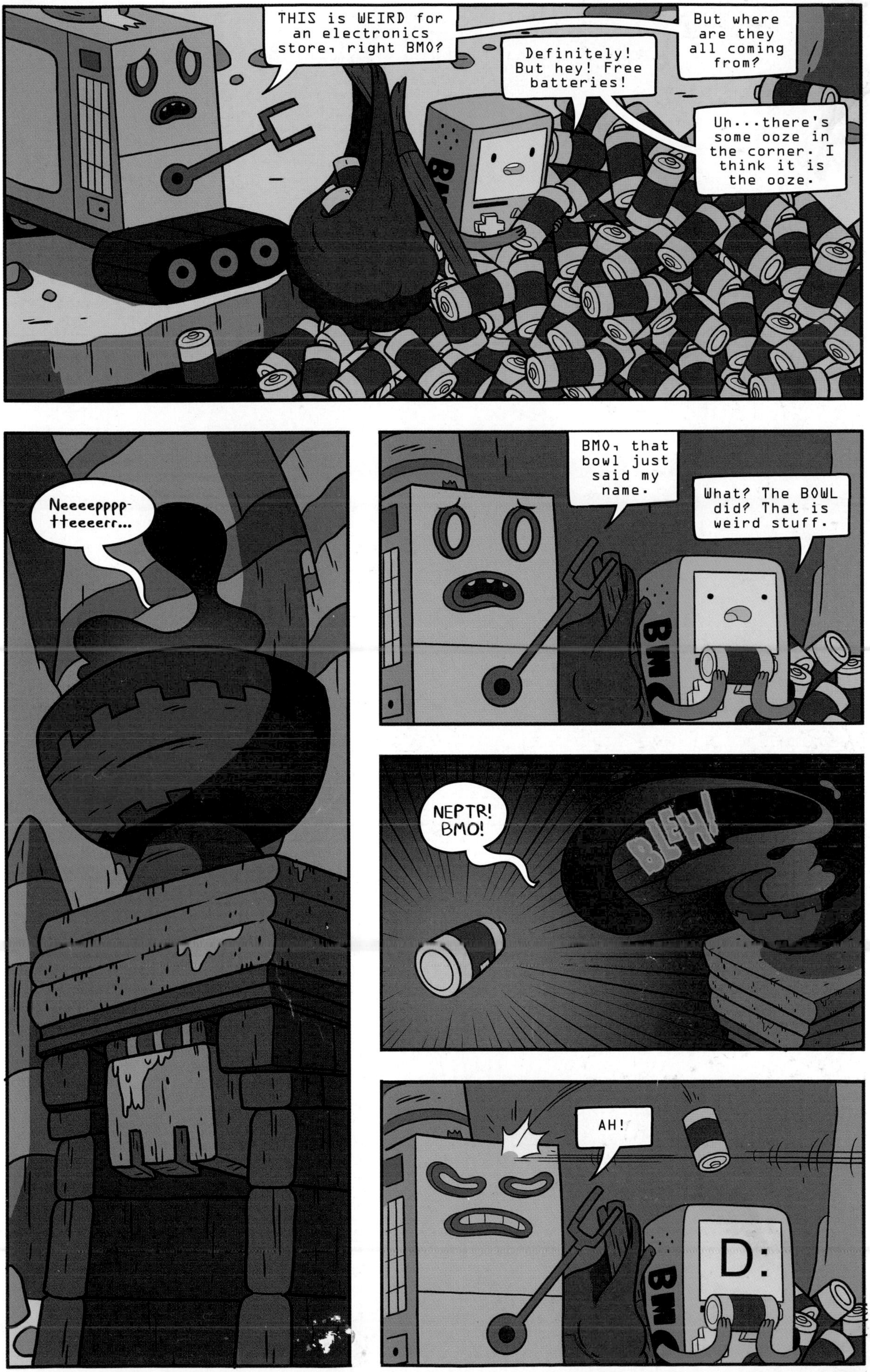
THIS is WEIRD for an electronics store, right BMO?
Definitely! But hey! Free batteries!
But where are they all coming from?
Uh...there's some ooze in the corner. I think it is the ooze.
Neeeepppp-tteeeerr...
BMO, that bowl just said my name.
What? The BOWL did? That is weird stuff.
NEPTR! BMO!
BLEH!
AH!
D:

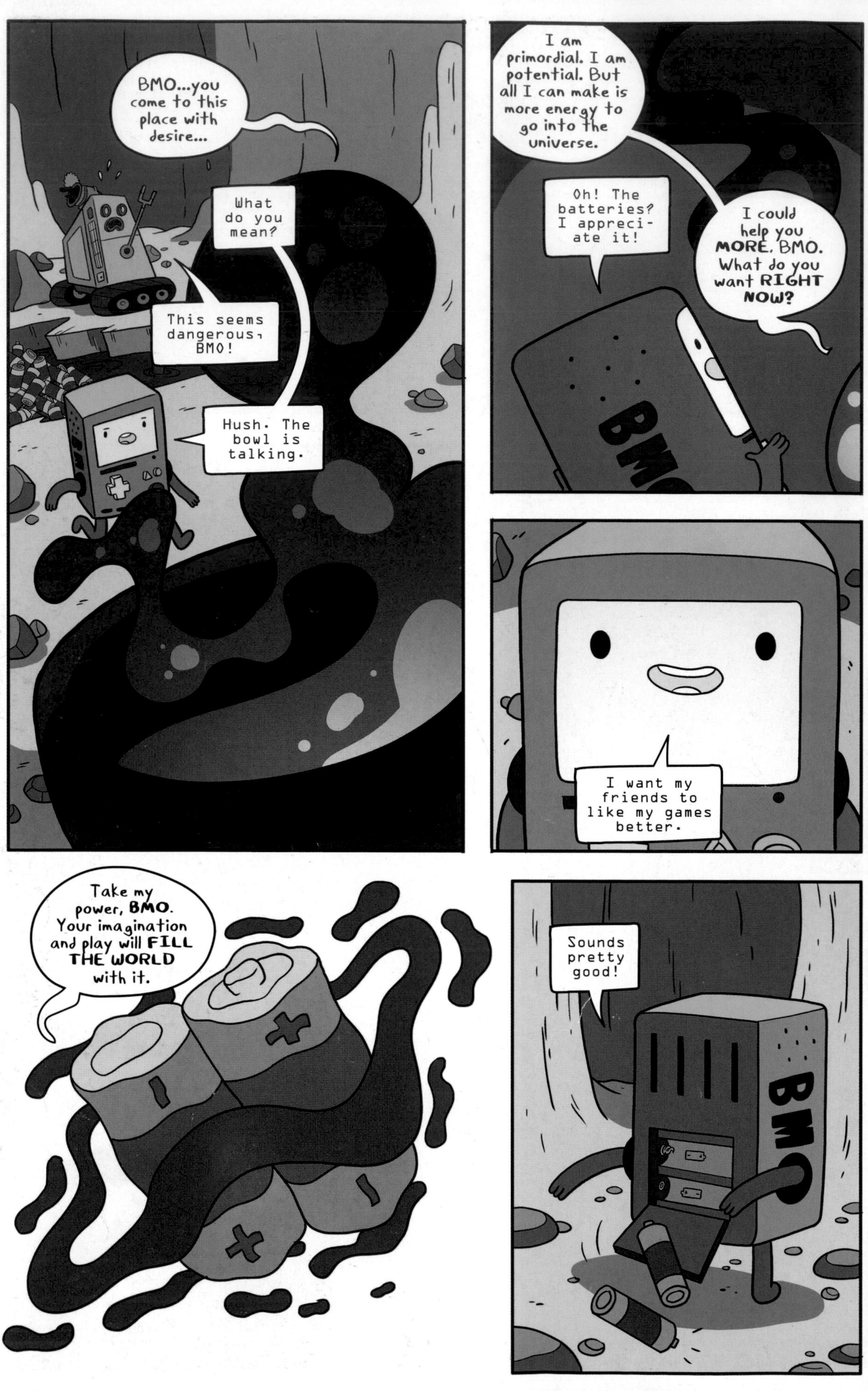
BMO...you come to this place with desire...
What do you mean?
This seems dangerous, BMO!
Hush. The bowl is talking.
I am primordial. I am potential. But all I can make is more energy to go into the universe.
Oh! The batteries? I appreciate it!
I could help you **MORE**, BMO. What do you want **RIGHT NOW?**
I want my friends to like my games better.
Take my power, **BMO**. Your imagination and play will **FILL THE WORLD** with it.
Sounds pretty good!

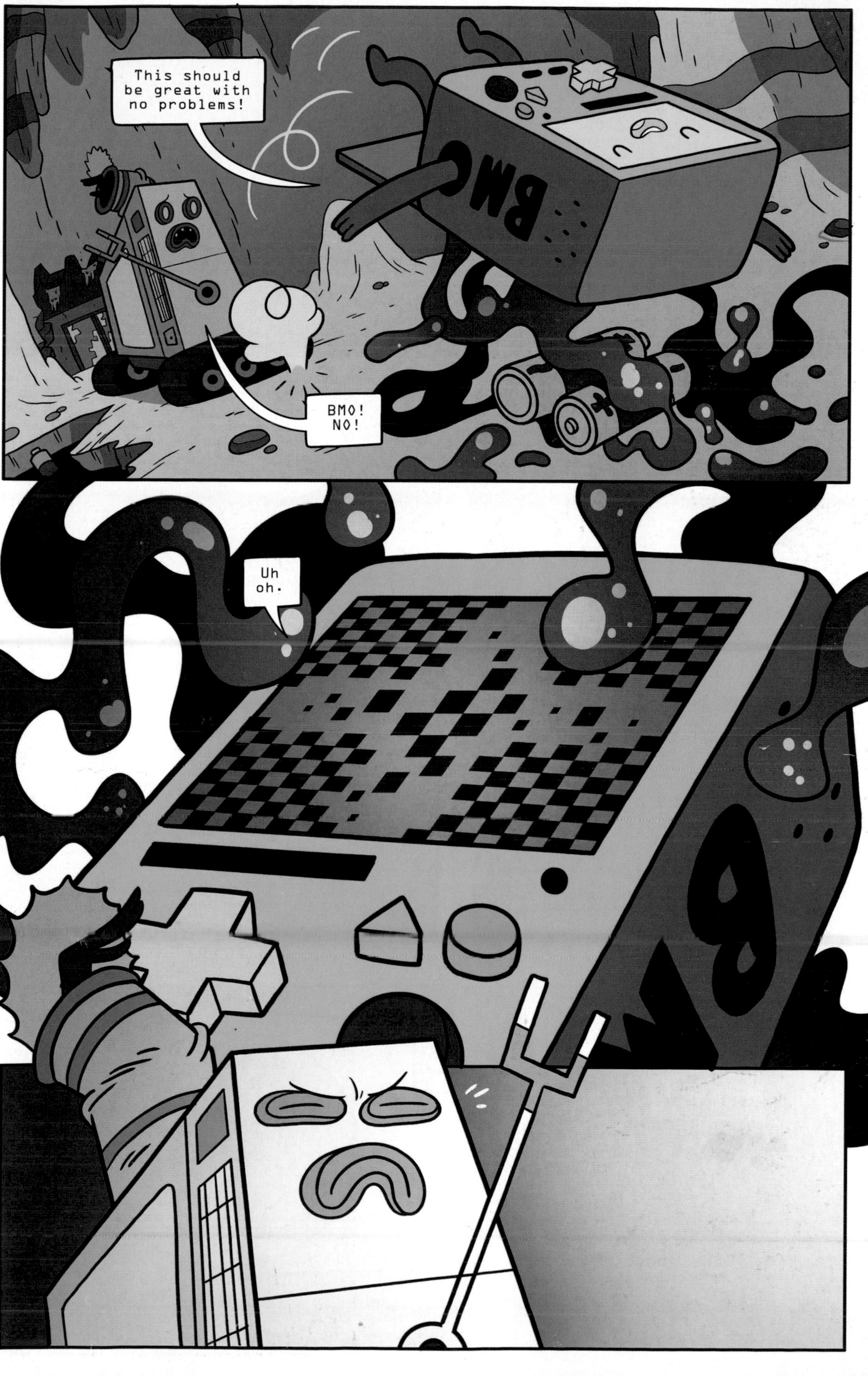
This should be great with no problems!
BMO! NO!
Uh oh.

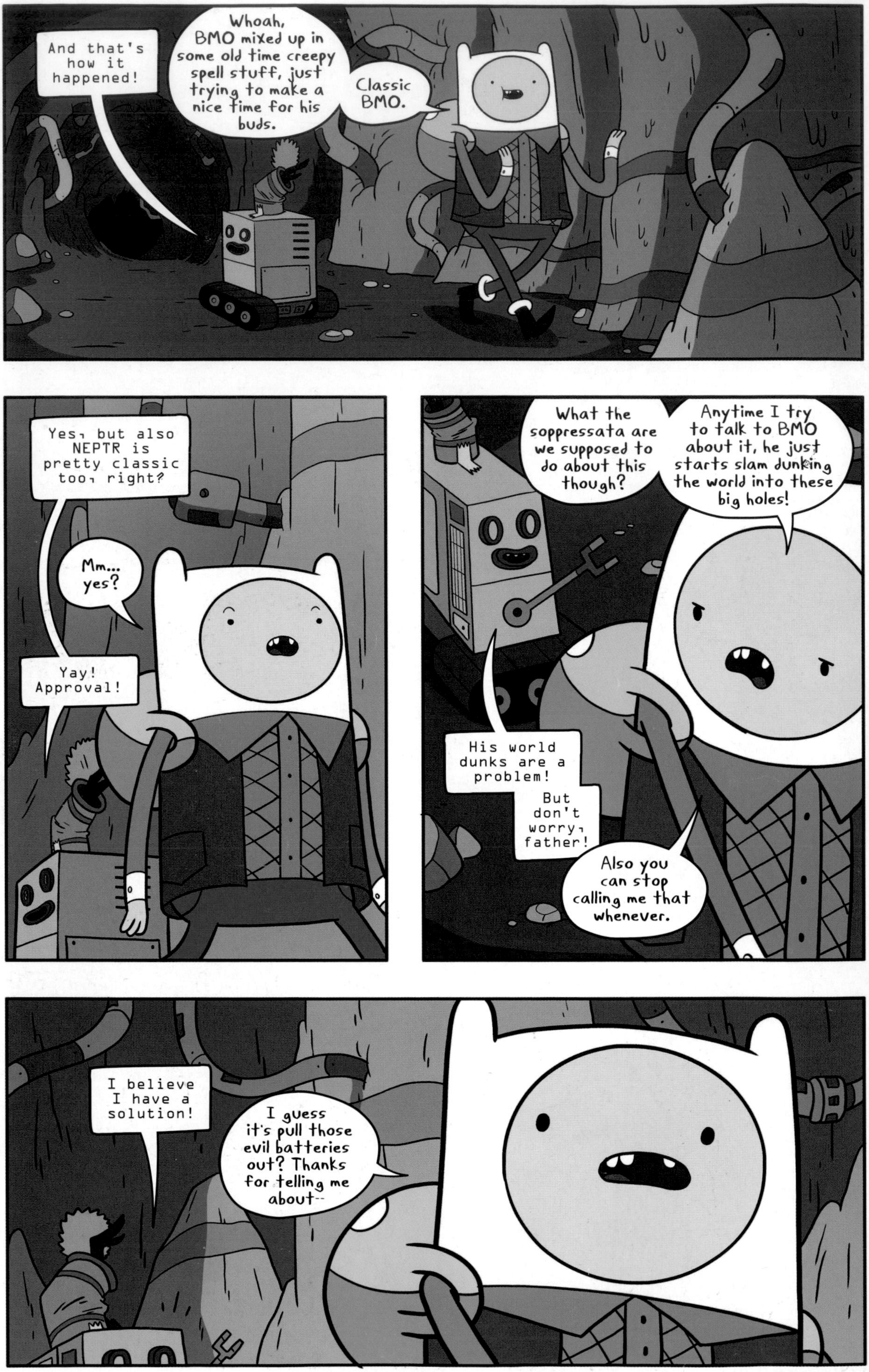
And that's how it happened!
Whoah, BMO mixed up in some old time creepy spell stuff, just trying to make a nice time for his buds.
Classic BMO.
Yes, but also NEPTR is pretty classic too, right?
Mm... yes?
Yay! Approval!
What the soppressata are we supposed to do about this though?
Anytime I try to talk to BMO about it, he just starts slam dunking the world into these big holes!
His world dunks are a problem!
But don't worry, father!
Also you can stop calling me that whenever.
I believe I have a solution!
I guess it's pull those evil batteries out? Thanks for telling me about--

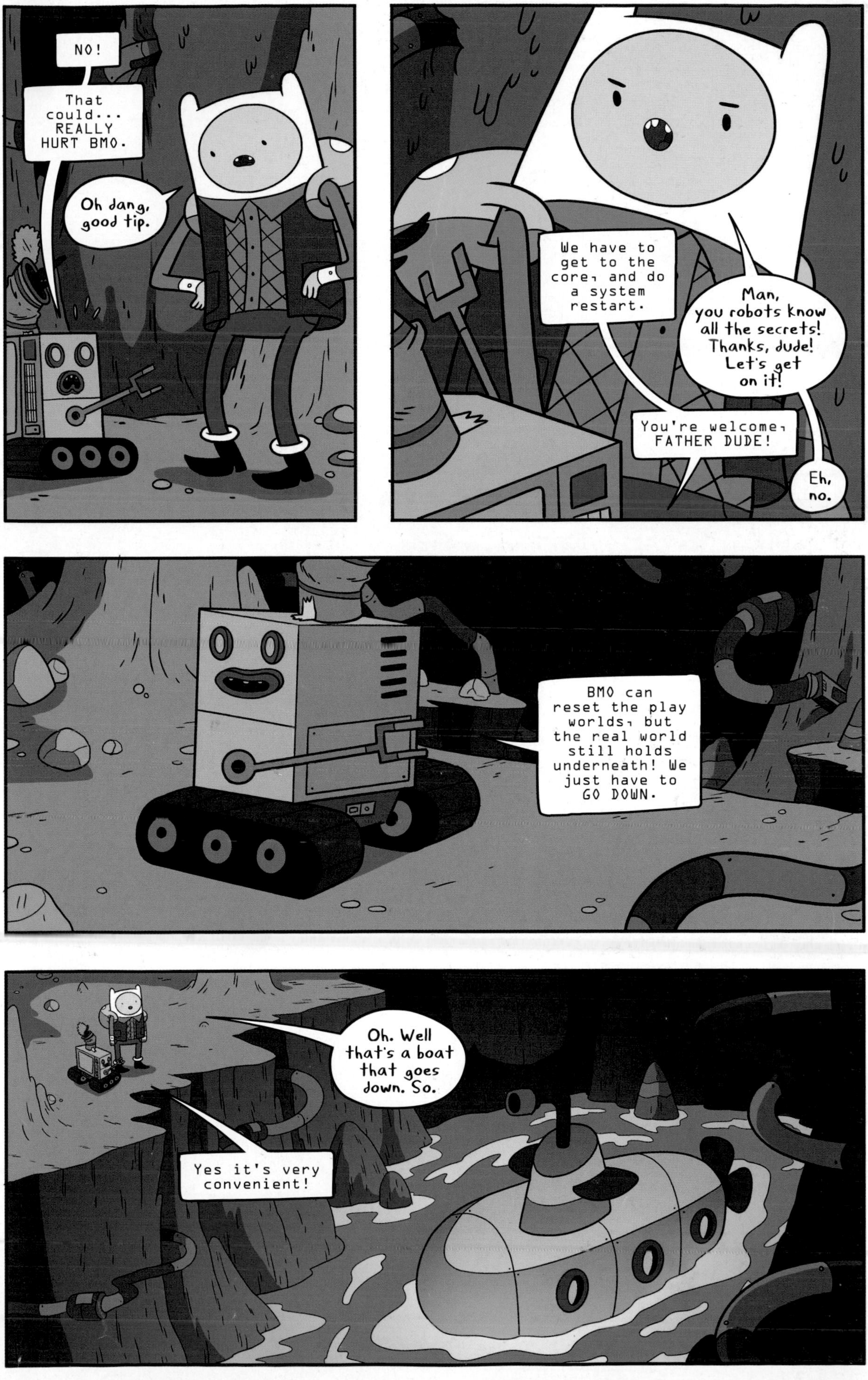
NO!
That could... REALLY HURT BMO.
Oh dang, good tip.
We have to get to the core, and do a system restart.
Man, you robots know all the secrets! Thanks, dude! Let's get on it!
You're welcome, FATHER DUDE!
Eh, no.
BMO can reset the play worlds, but the real world still holds underneath! We just have to GO DOWN.
Oh. Well that's a boat that goes down. So.
Yes it's very convenient!

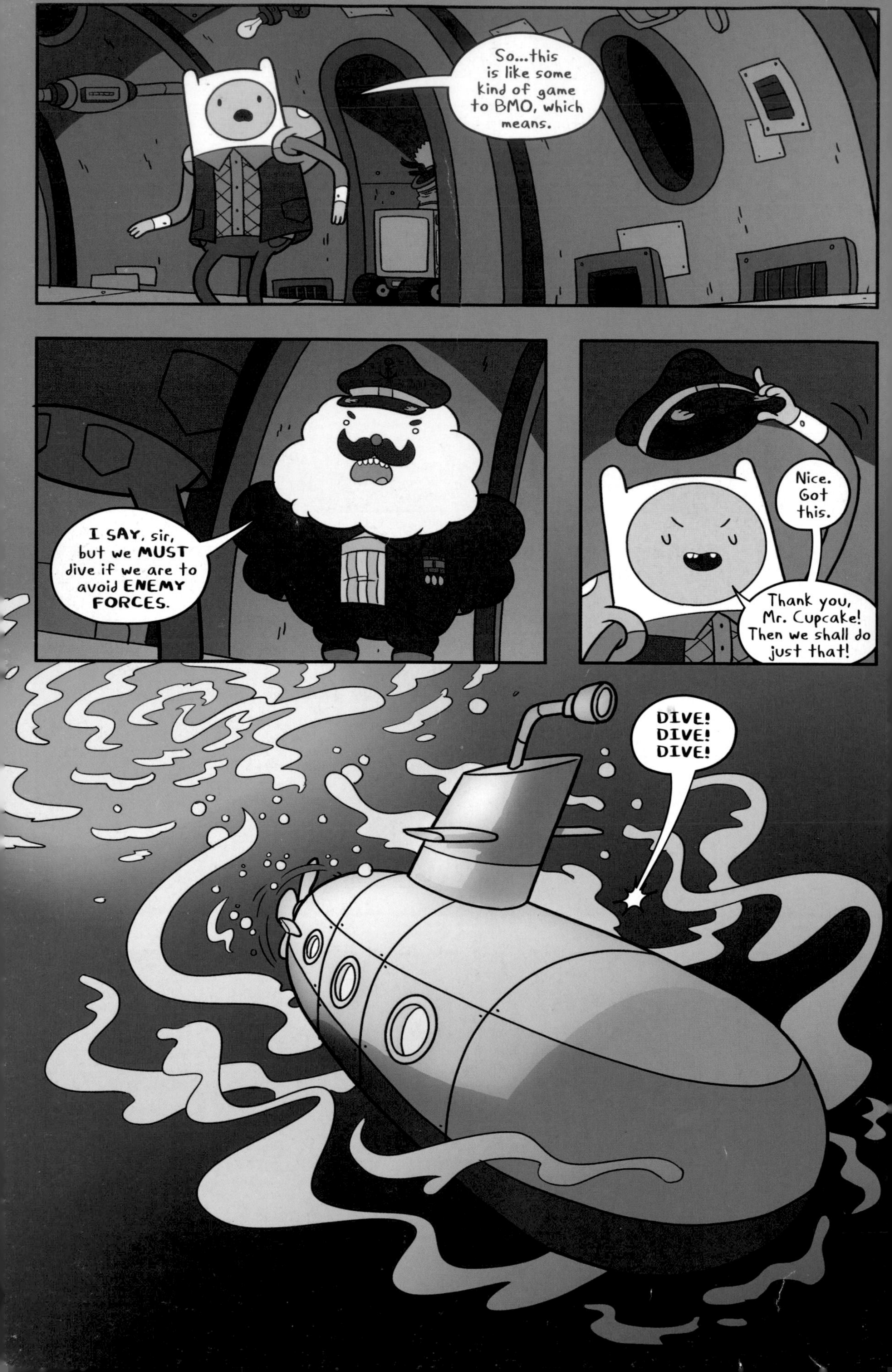
So...this is like some kind of game to BMO, which means.
I SAY, sir, but we MUST dive if we are to avoid ENEMY FORCES.
Nice. Got this.
Thank you, Mr. Cupcake! Then we shall do just that!
DIVE! DIVE! DIVE!

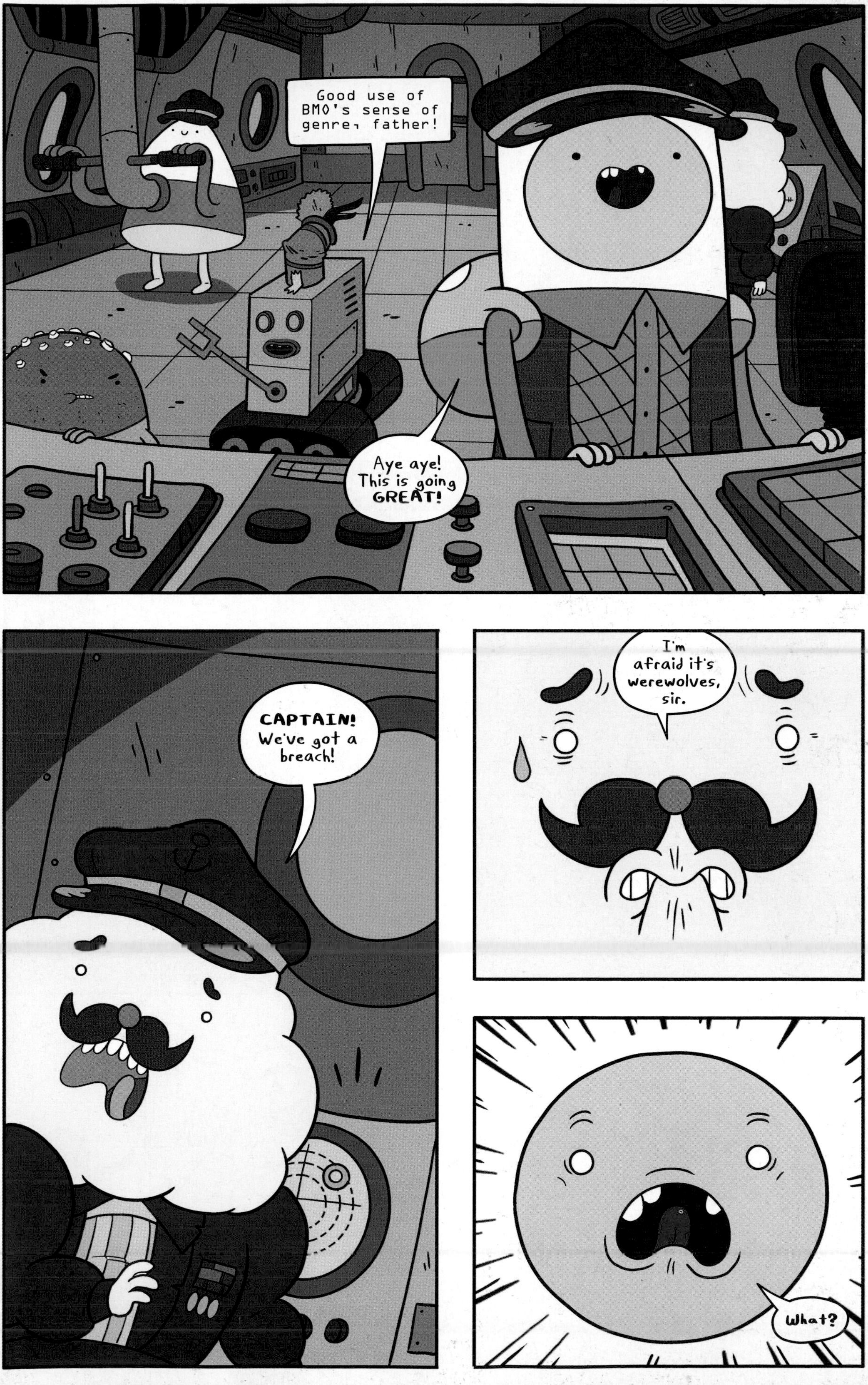

Good use of BMO's sense of genre, father!
Aye aye! This is going **GREAT!**
**CAPTAIN!** We've got a breach!
I'm afraid it's werewolves, sir.
What?

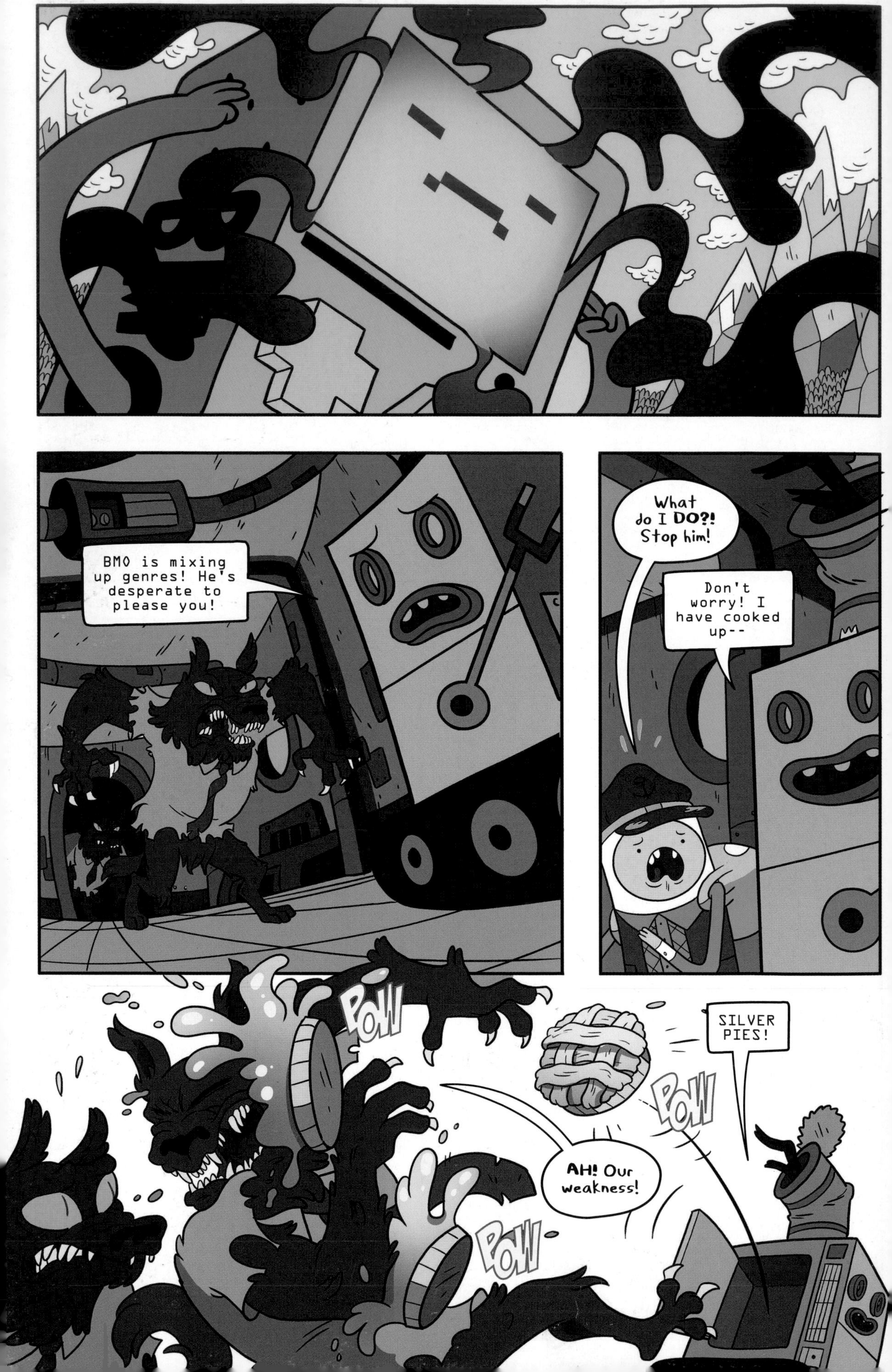
BMO is mixing up genres! He's desperate to please you!
What do I DO?! Stop him!
Don't worry! I have cooked up--
POW
SILVER PIES!
POW
AH! Our weakness!
POW

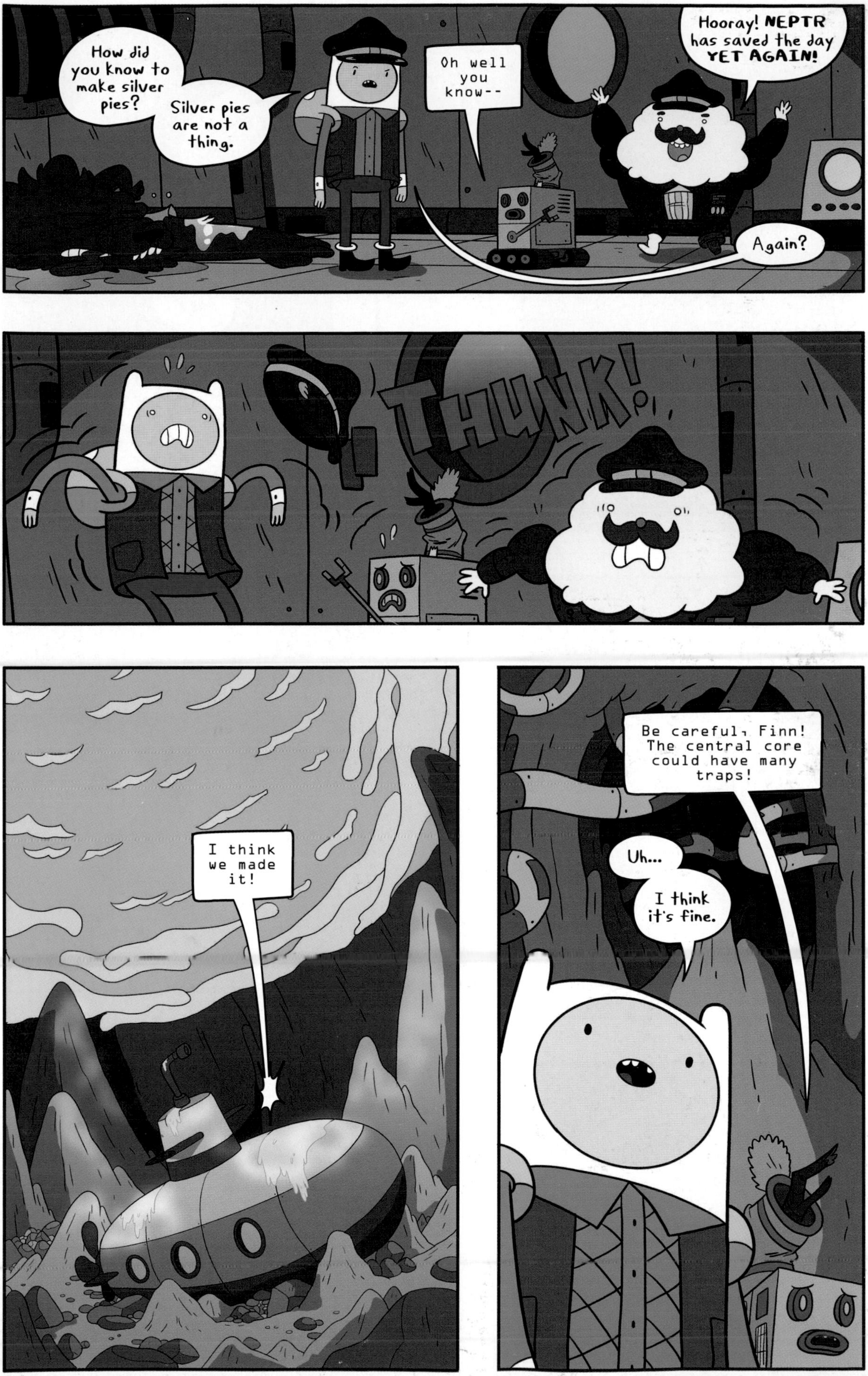
How did you know to make silver pies?
Silver pies are not a thing.
Oh well you know--
Hooray! NEPTR has saved the day YET AGAIN!
Again?
THUNK!
I think we made it!
Be careful, Finn! The central core could have many traps!
Uh...
I think it's fine.

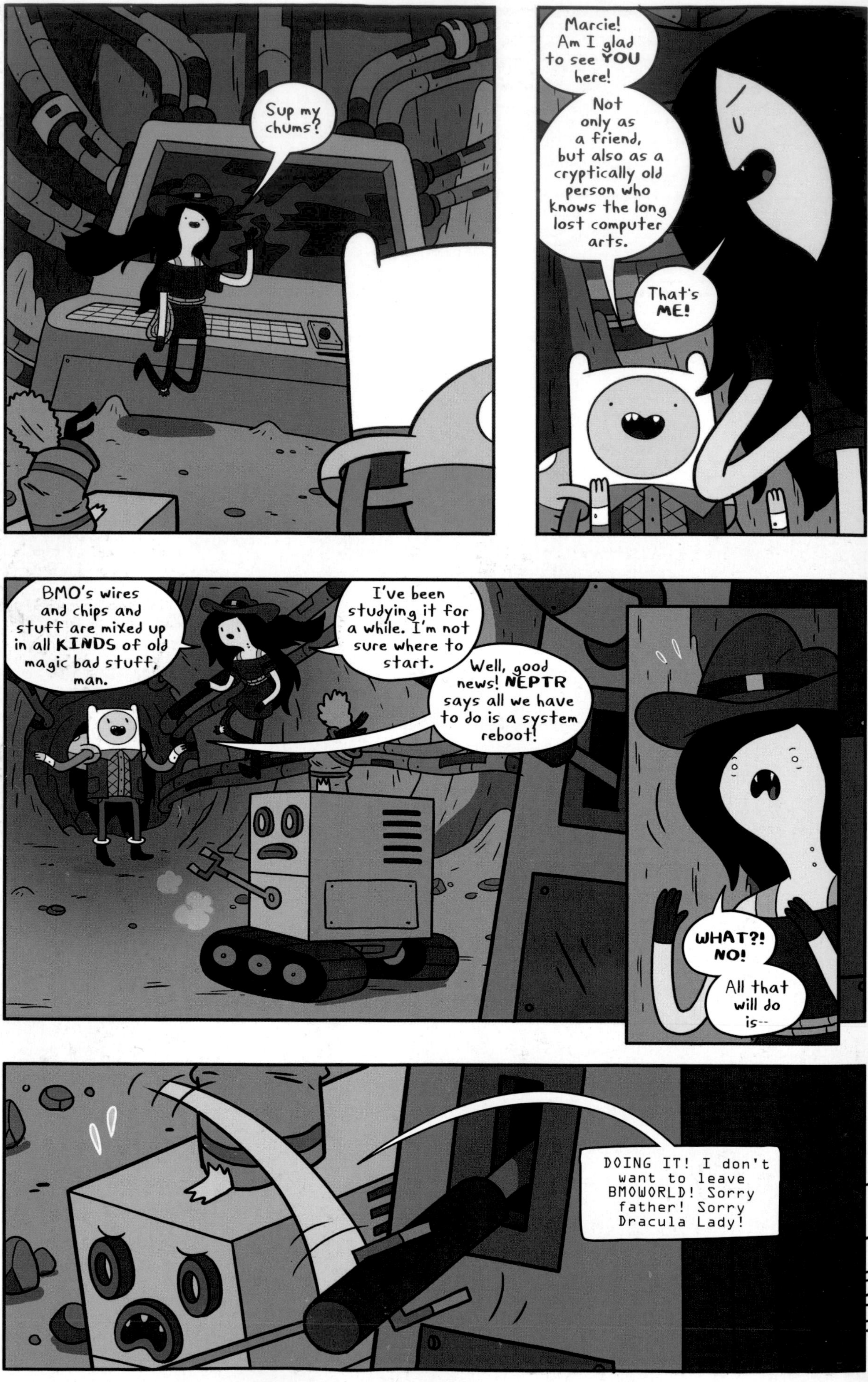
Sup my chums?
Marcie! Am I glad to see YOU here!
Not only as a friend, but also as a cryptically old person who knows the long lost computer arts.
That's ME!
BMO's wires and chips and stuff are mixed up in all KINDS of old magic bad stuff, man.
I've been studying it for a while. I'm not sure where to start.
Well, good news! NEPTR says all we have to do is a system reboot!
WHAT?! NO!
All that will do is--
DOING IT! I don't want to leave BMOWORLD! Sorry father! Sorry Dracula Lady!

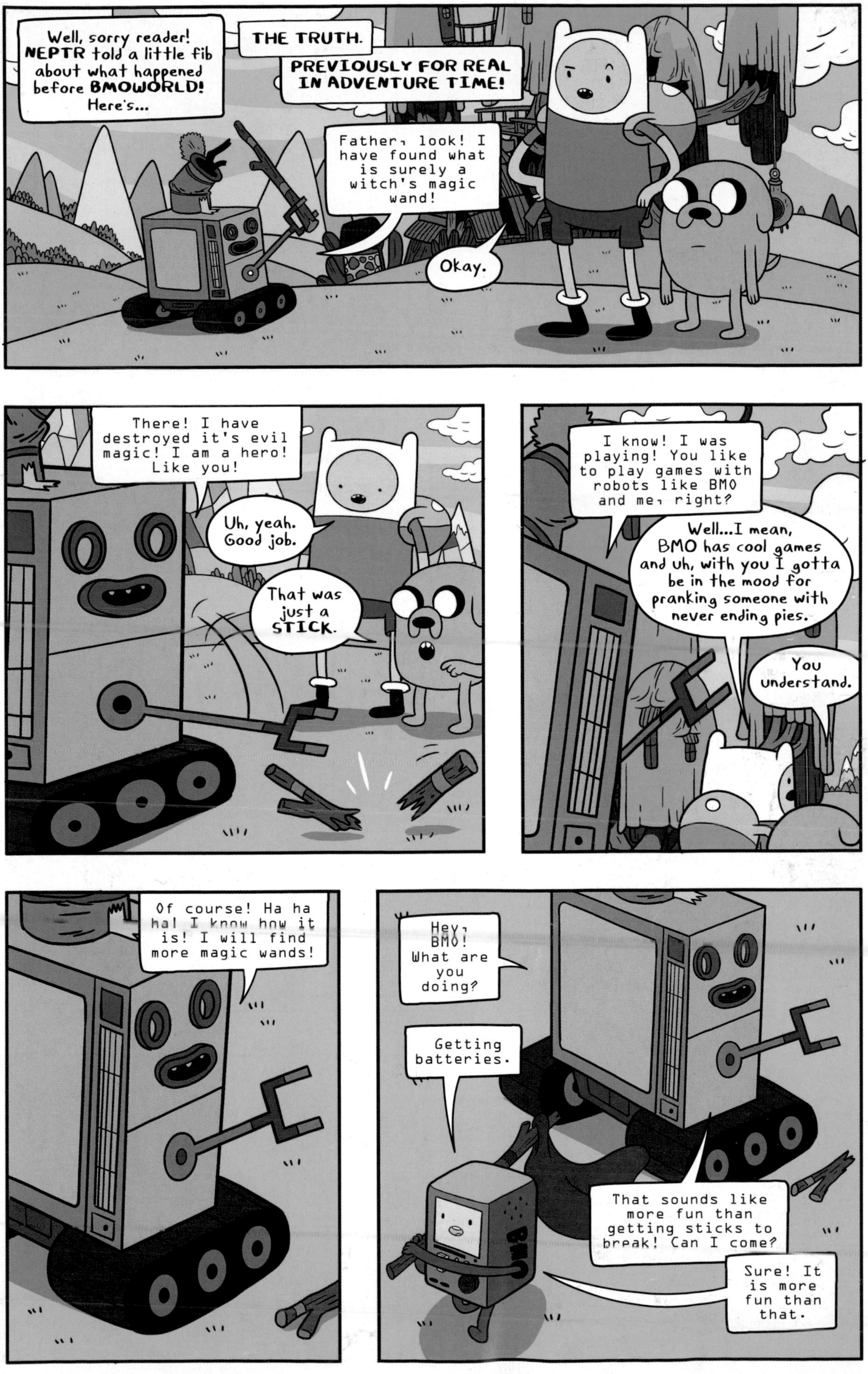
Well, sorry reader! NEPTR told a little fib about what happened before BMOWORLD! Here's...
THE TRUTH.
PREVIOUSLY FOR REAL IN ADVENTURE TIME!
Father, look! I have found what is surely a witch's magic wand!
Okay.
There! I have destroyed it's evil magic! I am a hero! Like you!
Uh, yeah. Good job.
That was just a STICK.
I know! I was playing! You like to play games with robots like BMO and me, right?
Well...I mean, BMO has cool games and uh, with you I gotta be in the mood for pranking someone with never ending pies.
You understand.
Of course! Ha ha ha! I know how it is! I will find more magic wands!
Hey, BMO! What are you doing?
Getting batteries.
That sounds like more fun than getting sticks to break! Can I come?
Sure! It is more fun than that.

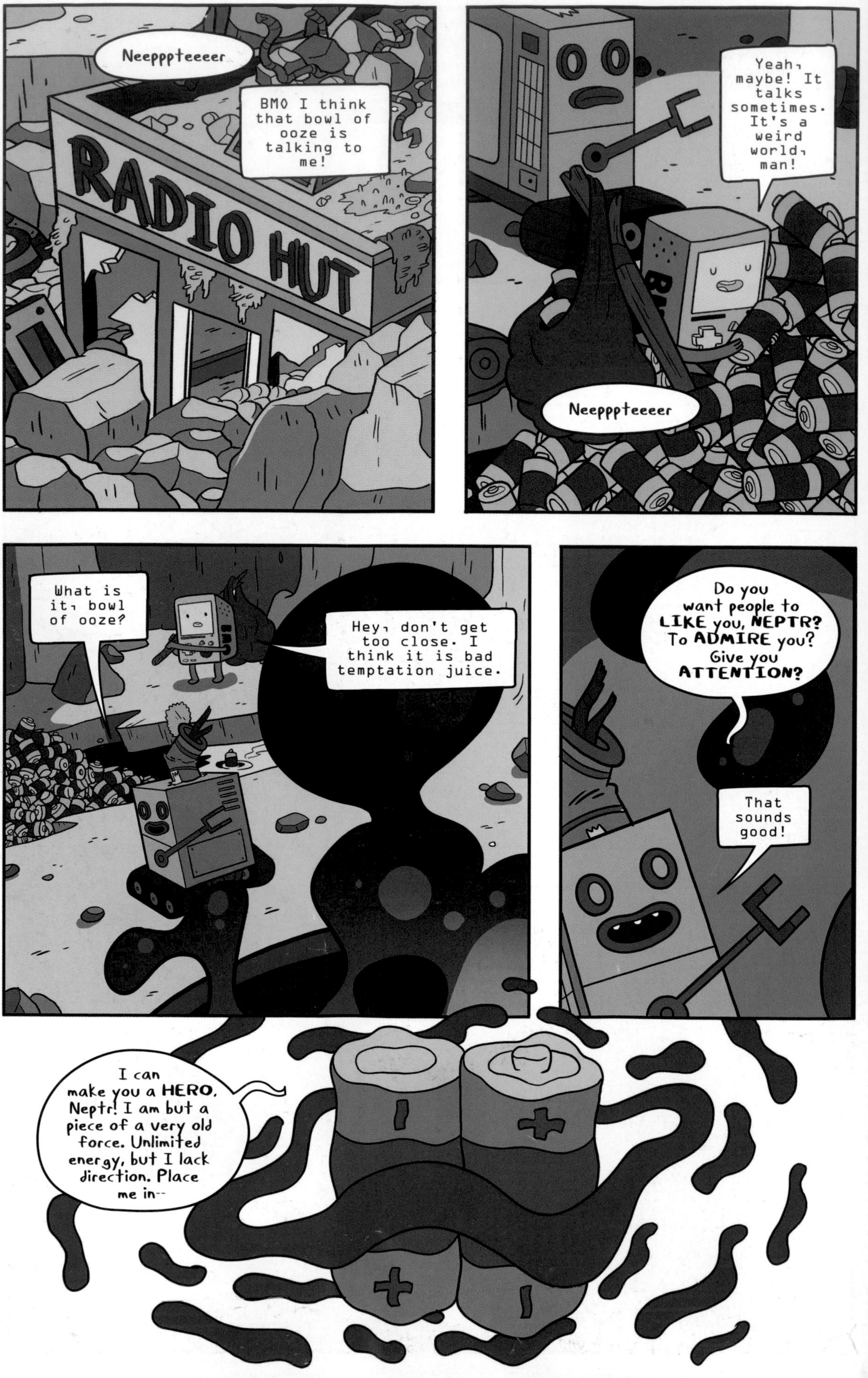

Neepppteeeer
BMO I think that bowl of ooze is talking to me!
RADIO HUT
Yeah, maybe! It talks sometimes. It's a weird world, man!
Neepppteeeer
What is it, bowl of ooze?
Hey, don't get too close. I think it is bad temptation juice.
Do you want people to LIKE you, NEPTR? To ADMIRE you? Give you ATTENTION?
That sounds good!
I can make you a HERO, Neptr! I am but a piece of a very old force. Unlimited energy, but I lack direction. Place me in--

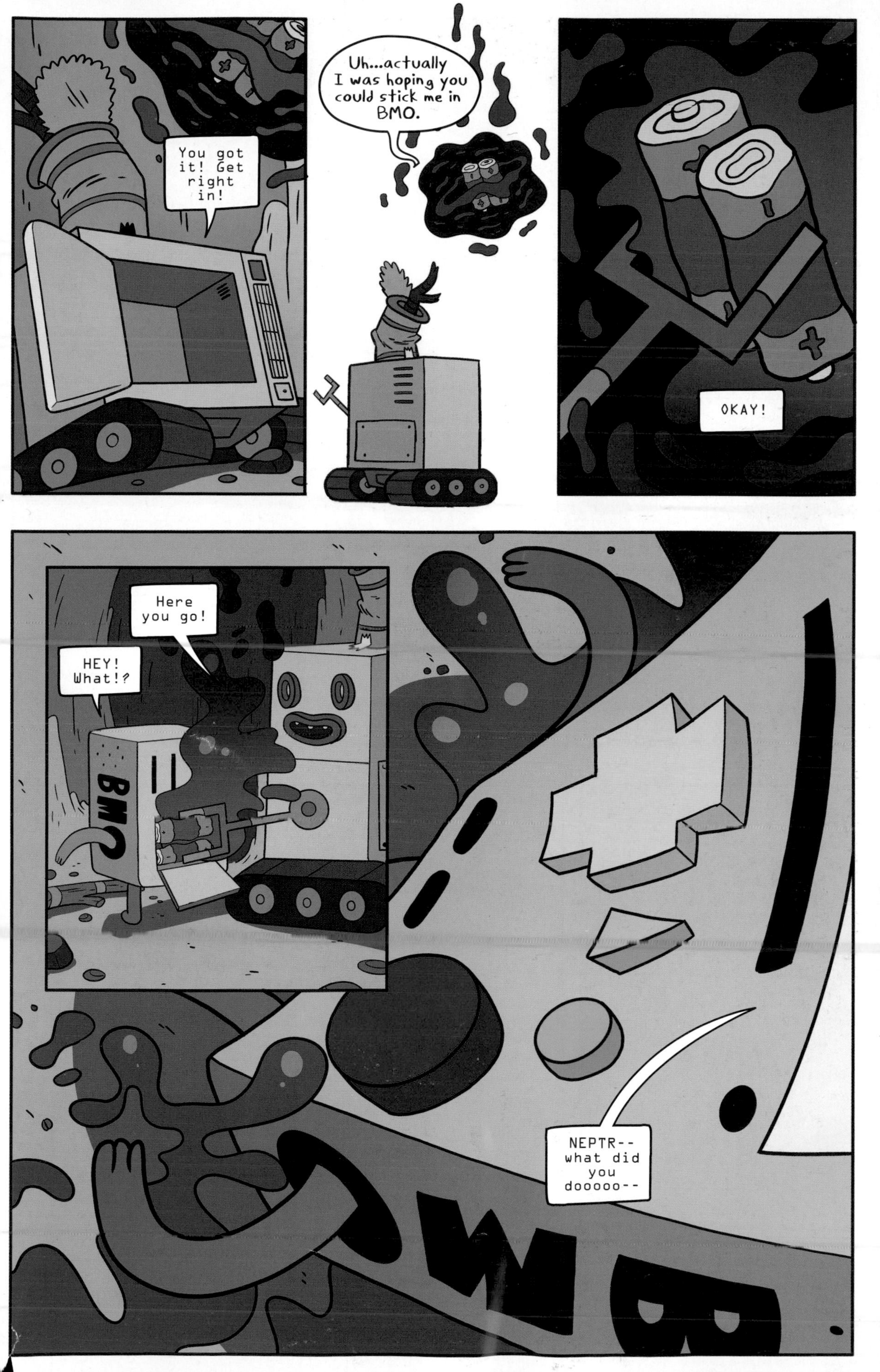
You got it! Get right in!
Uh...actually I was hoping you could stick me in BMO.
OKAY!
HEY! What!?
Here you go!
NEPTR-- what did you dooooo--

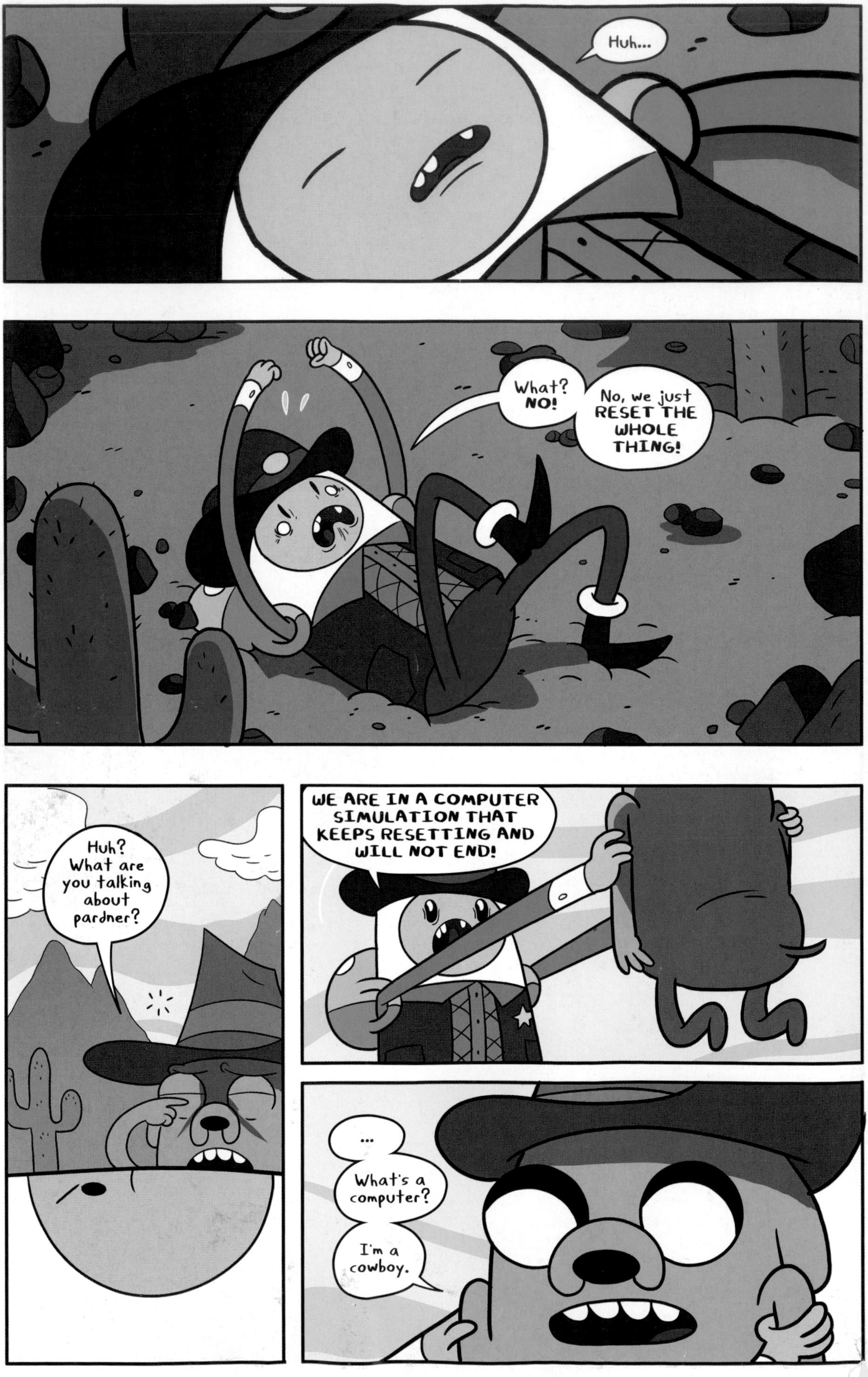
Huh...
What? NO!
No, we just RESET THE WHOLE THING!
Huh? What are you talking about pardner?
WE ARE IN A COMPUTER SIMULATION THAT KEEPS RESETTING AND WILL NOT END!
...
What's a computer?
I'm a cowboy.

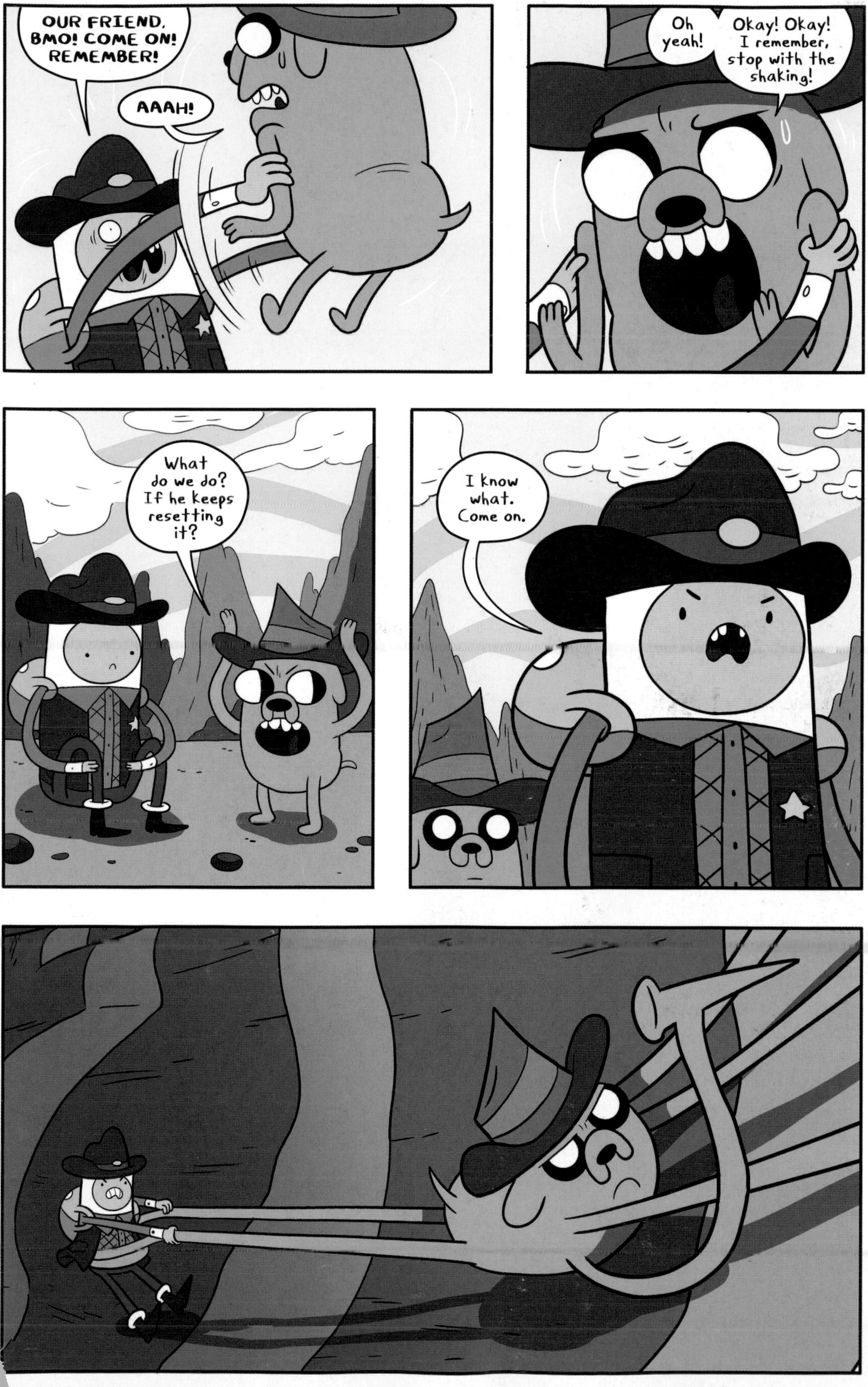
OUR FRIEND, BMO! COME ON! REMEMBER!
AAAH!
Oh yeah!
Okay! Okay! I remember, stop with the shaking!
What do we do? If he keeps resetting it?
I know what. Come on.

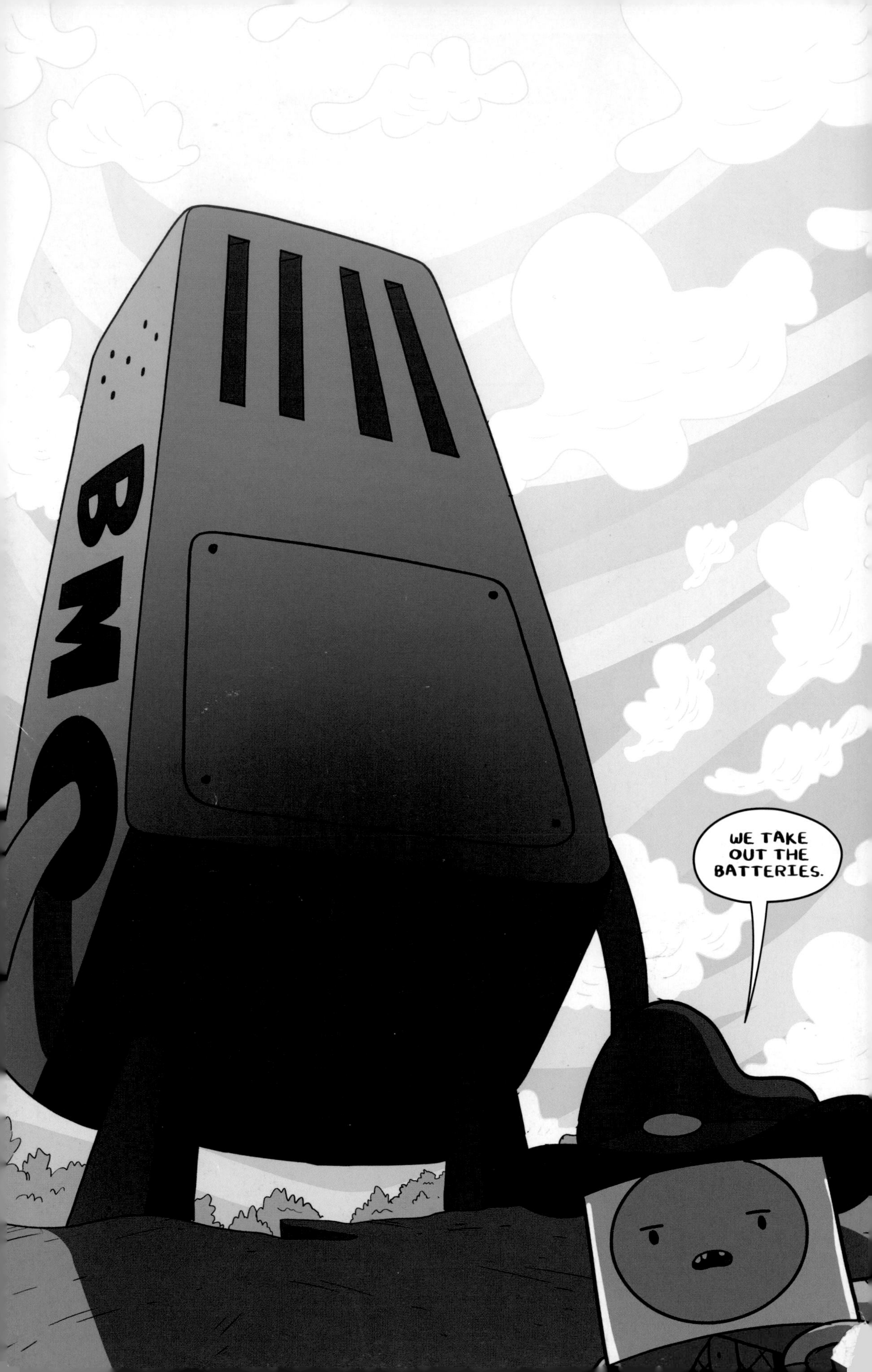
BMO
WE TAKE OUT THE BATTERIES.

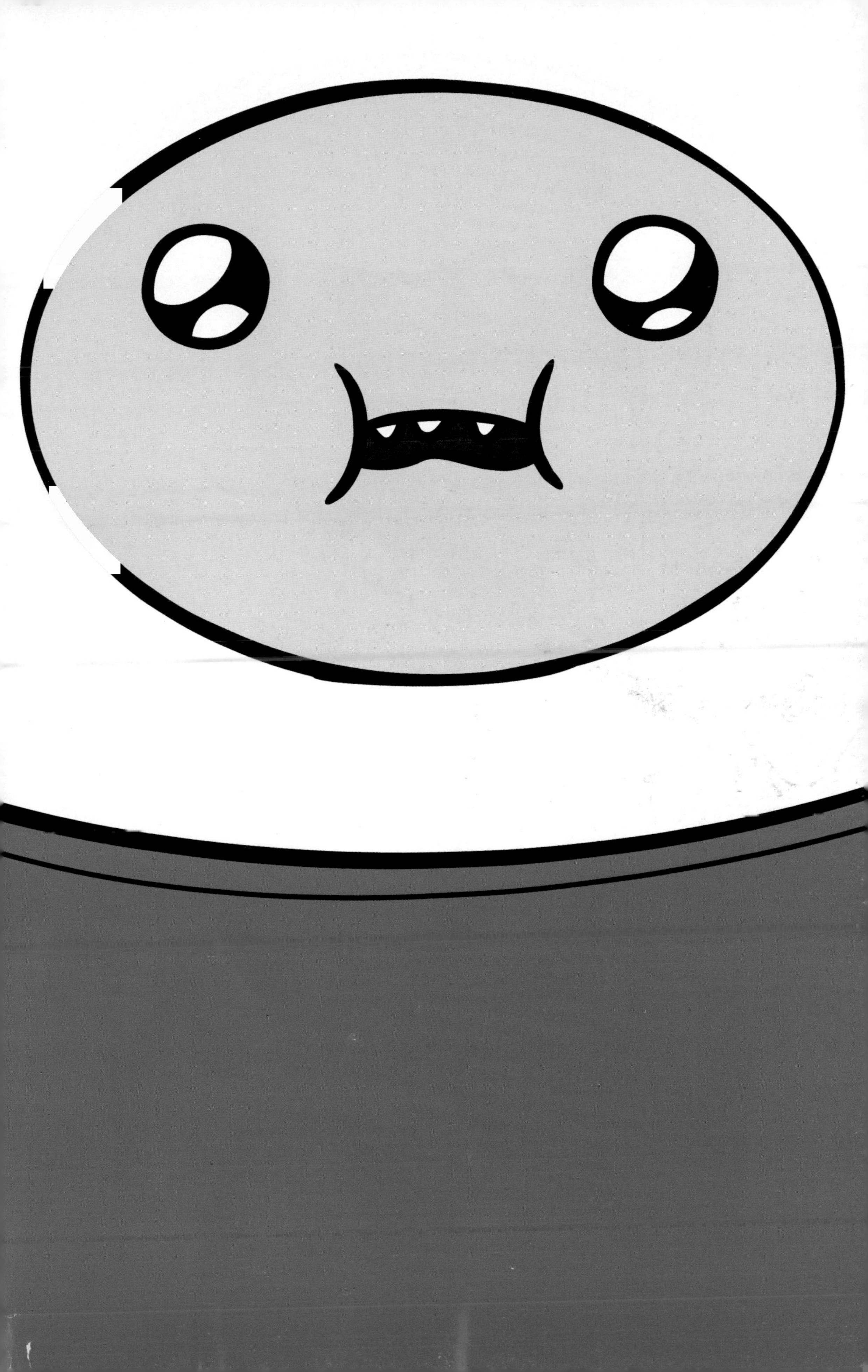

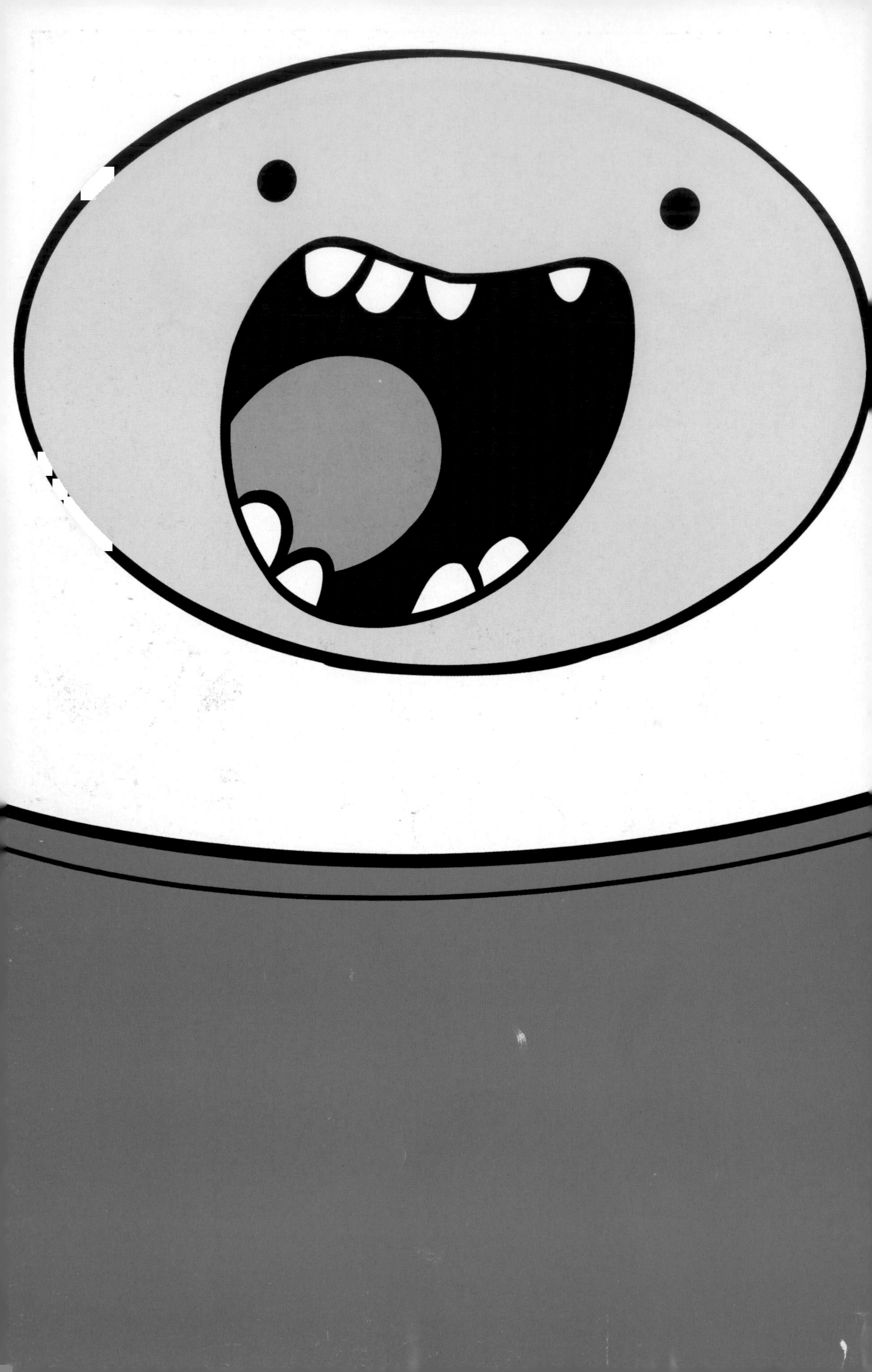

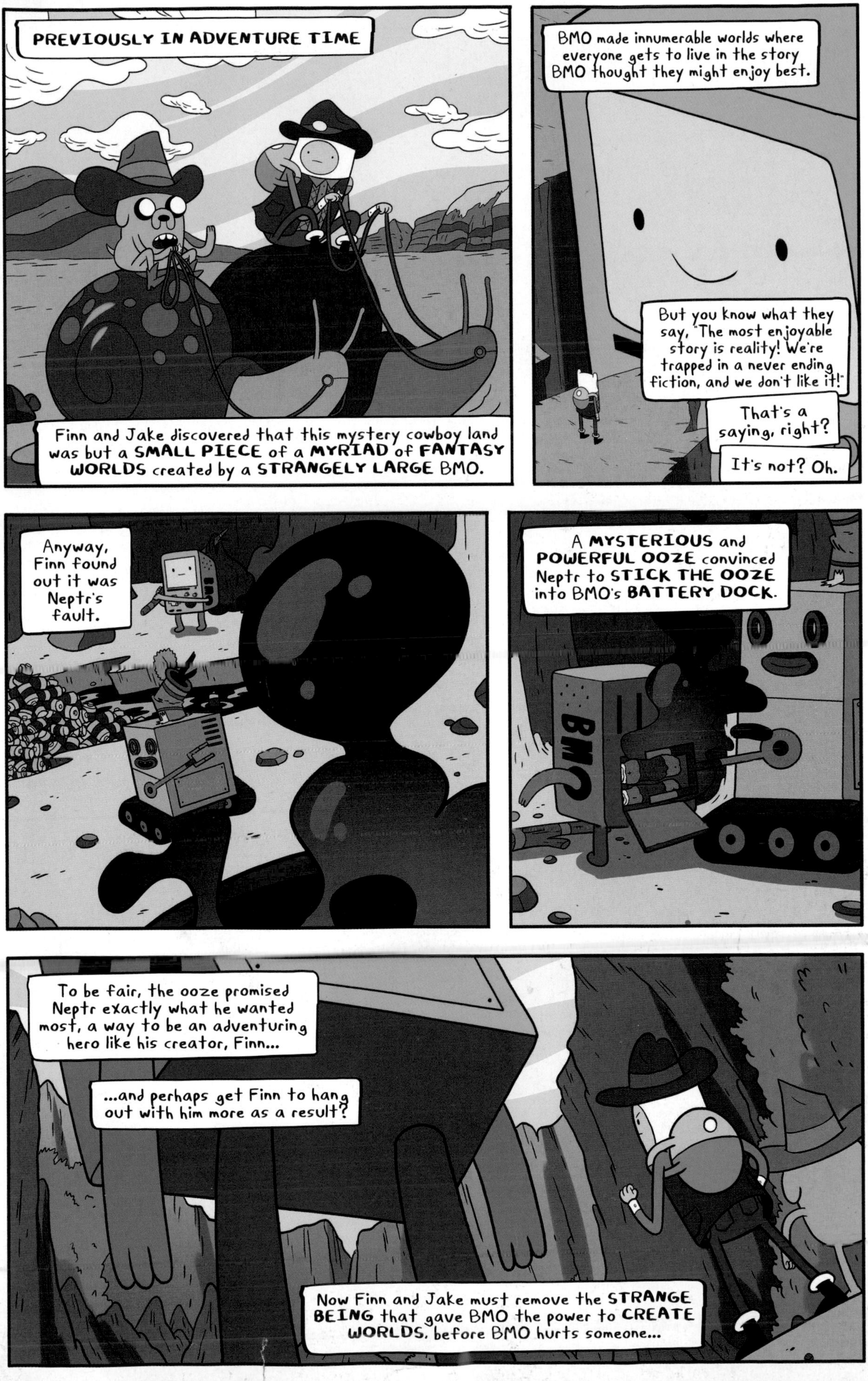
PREVIOUSLY IN ADVENTURE TIME
Finn and Jake discovered that this mystery cowboy land was but a SMALL PIECE of a MYRIAD of FANTASY WORLDS created by a STRANGELY LARGE BMO.
BMO made innumerable worlds where everyone gets to live in the story BMO thought they might enjoy best.
But you know what they say, "The most enjoyable story is reality! We're trapped in a never ending fiction, and we don't like it!"
That's a saying, right?
It's not? Oh.
Anyway, Finn found out it was Neptr's fault.
A MYSTERIOUS and POWERFUL OOZE convinced Neptr to STICK THE OOZE into BMO's BATTERY DOCK.
BMO
To be fair, the ooze promised Neptr exactly what he wanted most, a way to be an adventuring hero like his creator, Finn...
...and perhaps get Finn to hang out with him more as a result?
Now Finn and Jake must remove the STRANGE BEING that gave BMO the power to CREATE WORLDS, before BMO hurts someone...

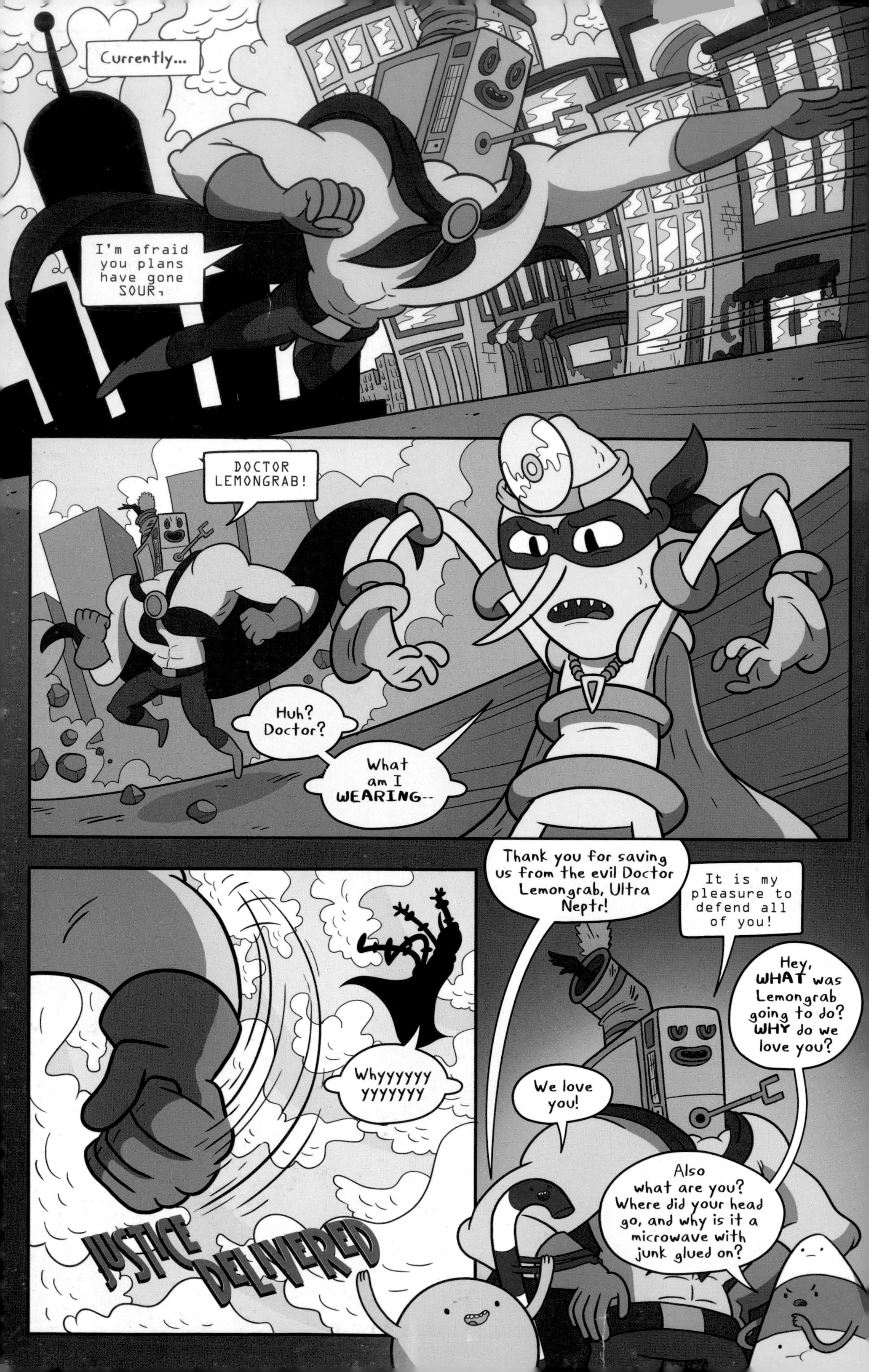

Currently...
I'm afraid you plans have gone SOUR,
DOCTOR LEMONGRAB!
Huh? Doctor?
What am I WEARING--
JUSTICE DELIVERED
Whyyyyyy yyyyyyy
Thank you for saving us from the evil Doctor Lemongrab, Ultra Neptr!
It is my pleasure to defend all of you!
Hey, WHAT was Lemongrab going to do? WHY do we love you?
We love you!
Also what are you? Where did your head go, and why is it a microwave with junk glued on?

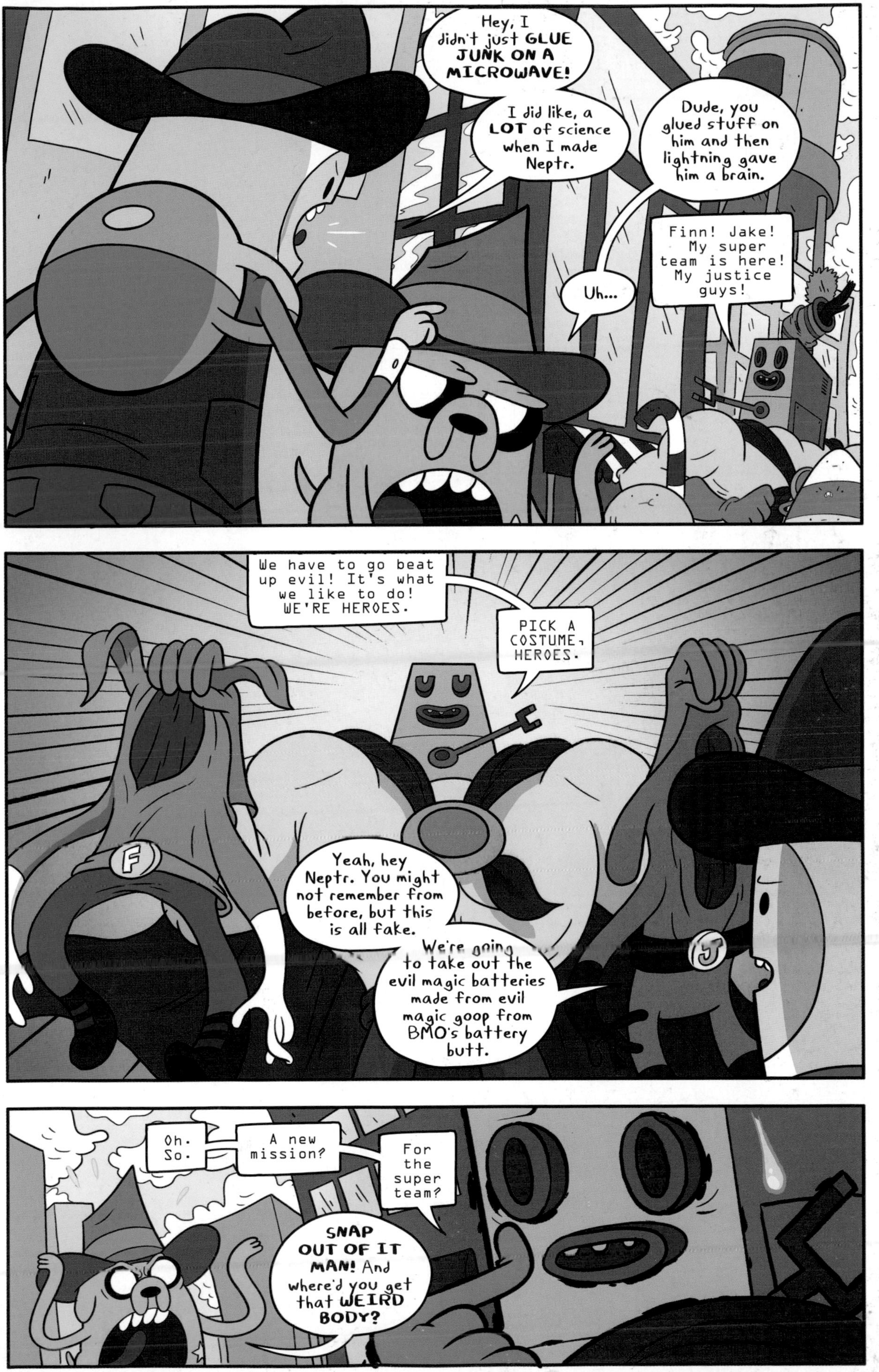
Hey, I didn't just GLUE JUNK ON A MICROWAVE!
I did like, a LOT of science when I made Neptr.
Dude, you glued stuff on him and then lightning gave him a brain.
Uh...
Finn! Jake! My super team is here! My justice guys!
We have to go beat up evil! It's what we like to do! WE'RE HEROES.
PICK A COSTUME, HEROES.
Yeah, hey Neptr. You might not remember from before, but this is all fake.
We're going to take out the evil magic batteries made from evil magic goop from BMO's battery butt.
Oh. So.
A new mission?
For the super team?
SNAP OUT OF IT MAN! And where'd you get that WEIRD BODY?

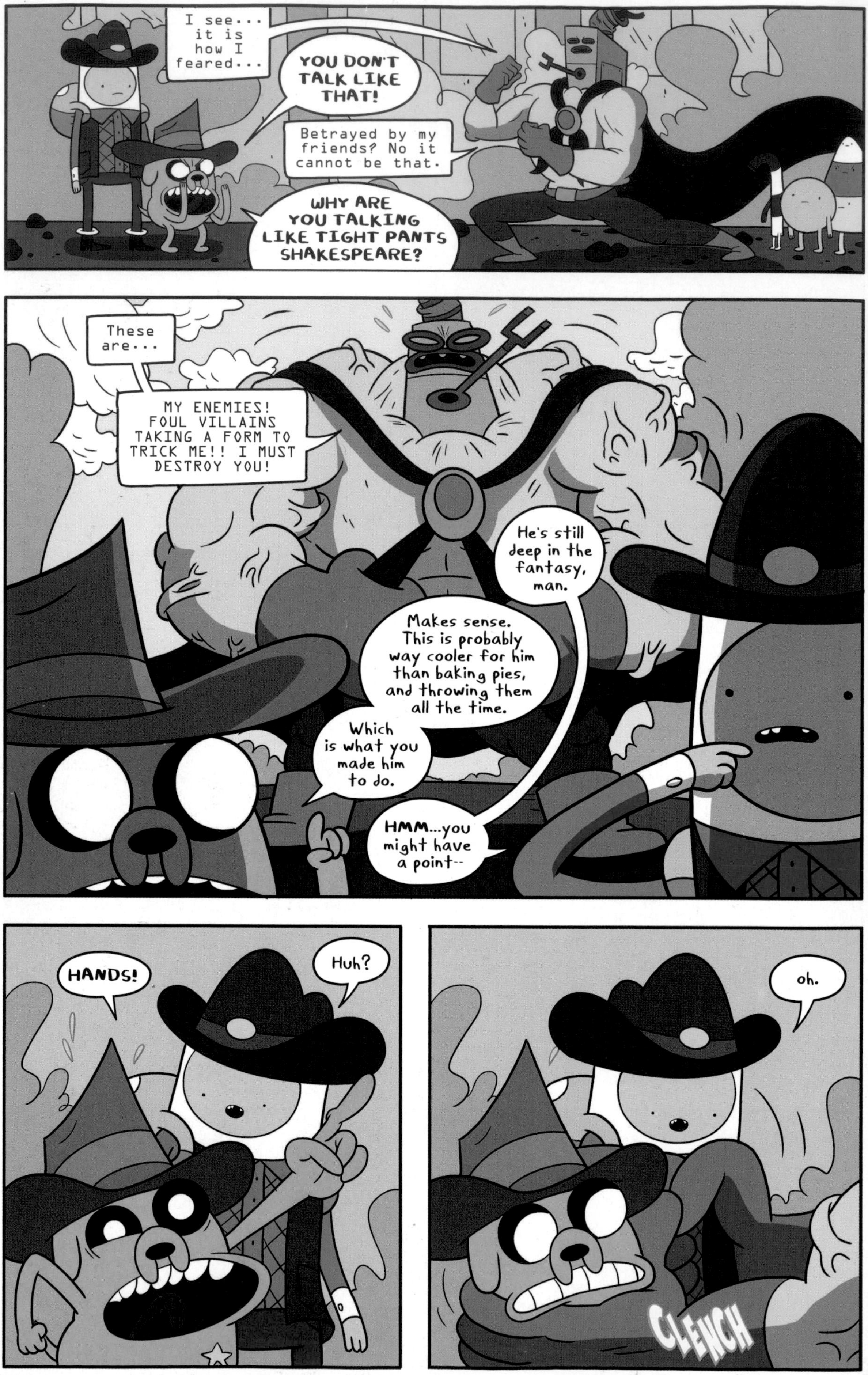
I see... it is how I feared...
YOU DON'T TALK LIKE THAT!
Betrayed by my friends? No it cannot be that.
WHY ARE YOU TALKING LIKE TIGHT PANTS SHAKESPEARE?
These are...
MY ENEMIES! FOUL VILLAINS TAKING A FORM TO TRICK ME!! I MUST DESTROY YOU!
He's still deep in the fantasy, man.
Makes sense. This is probably way cooler for him than baking pies, and throwing them all the time.
Which is what you made him to do.
HMM...you might have a point--
HANDS!
Huh?
oh.
CLENCH

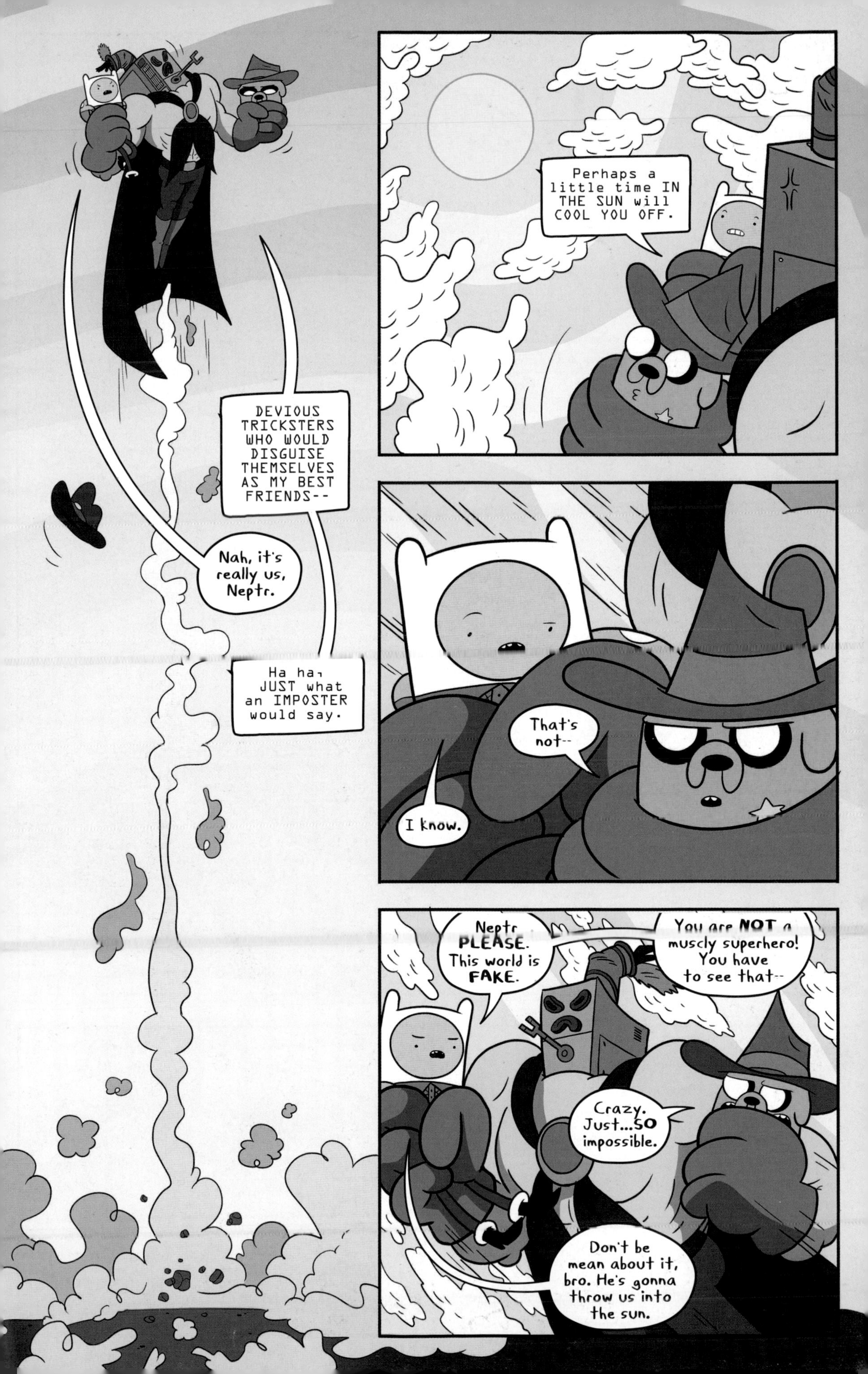
DEVIOUS TRICKSTERS WHO WOULD DISGUISE THEMSELVES AS MY BEST FRIENDS--
Nah, it's really us, Neptr.
Ha ha, JUST what an IMPOSTER would say.
Perhaps a little time IN THE SUN will COOL YOU OFF.
That's not--
I know.
Neptr PLEASE. This world is FAKE.
You are NOT a muscly superhero! You have to see that--
Crazy. Just...SO impossible.
Don't be mean about it, bro. He's gonna throw us into the sun.

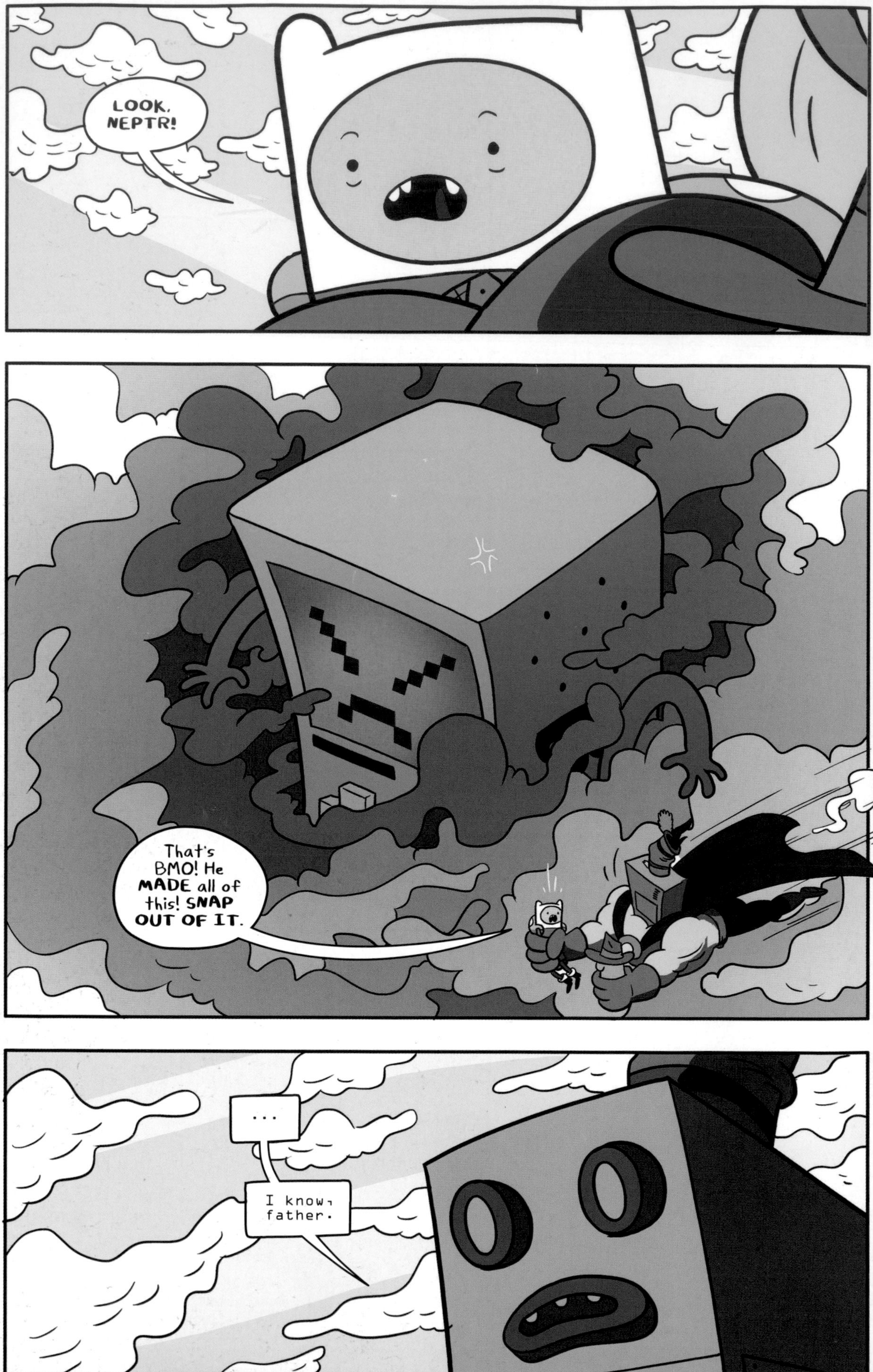
LOOK, NEPTR!
That's BMO! He MADE all of this! SNAP OUT OF IT.
...
I know, father.

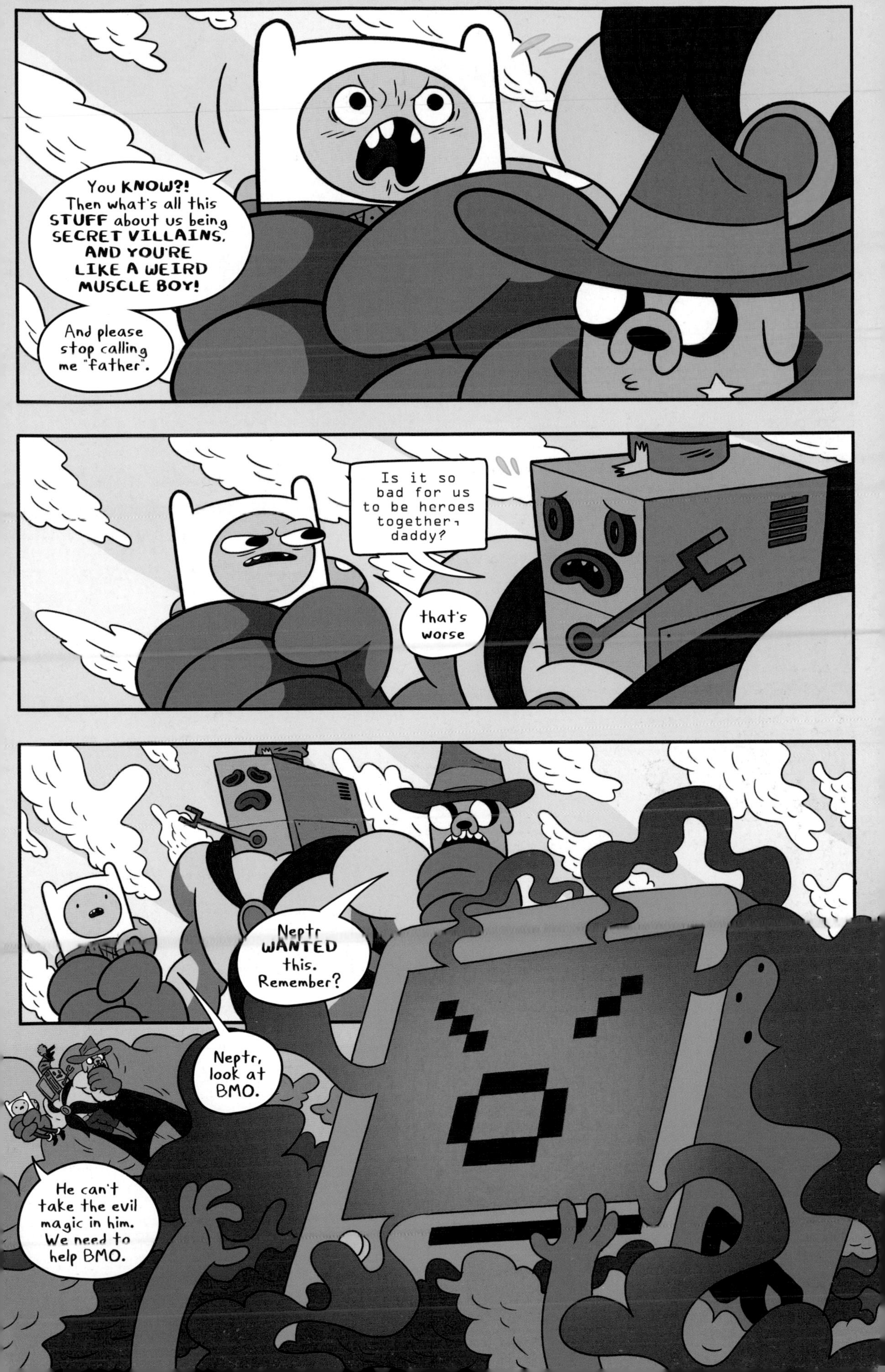

You KNOW?! Then what's all this STUFF about us being SECRET VILLAINS, AND YOU'RE LIKE A WEIRD MUSCLE BOY!
And please stop calling me "father".
Is it so bad for us to be heroes together, daddy?
that's worse
Neptr WANTED this. Remember?
Neptr, look at BMO.
He can't take the evil magic in him. We need to help BMO.

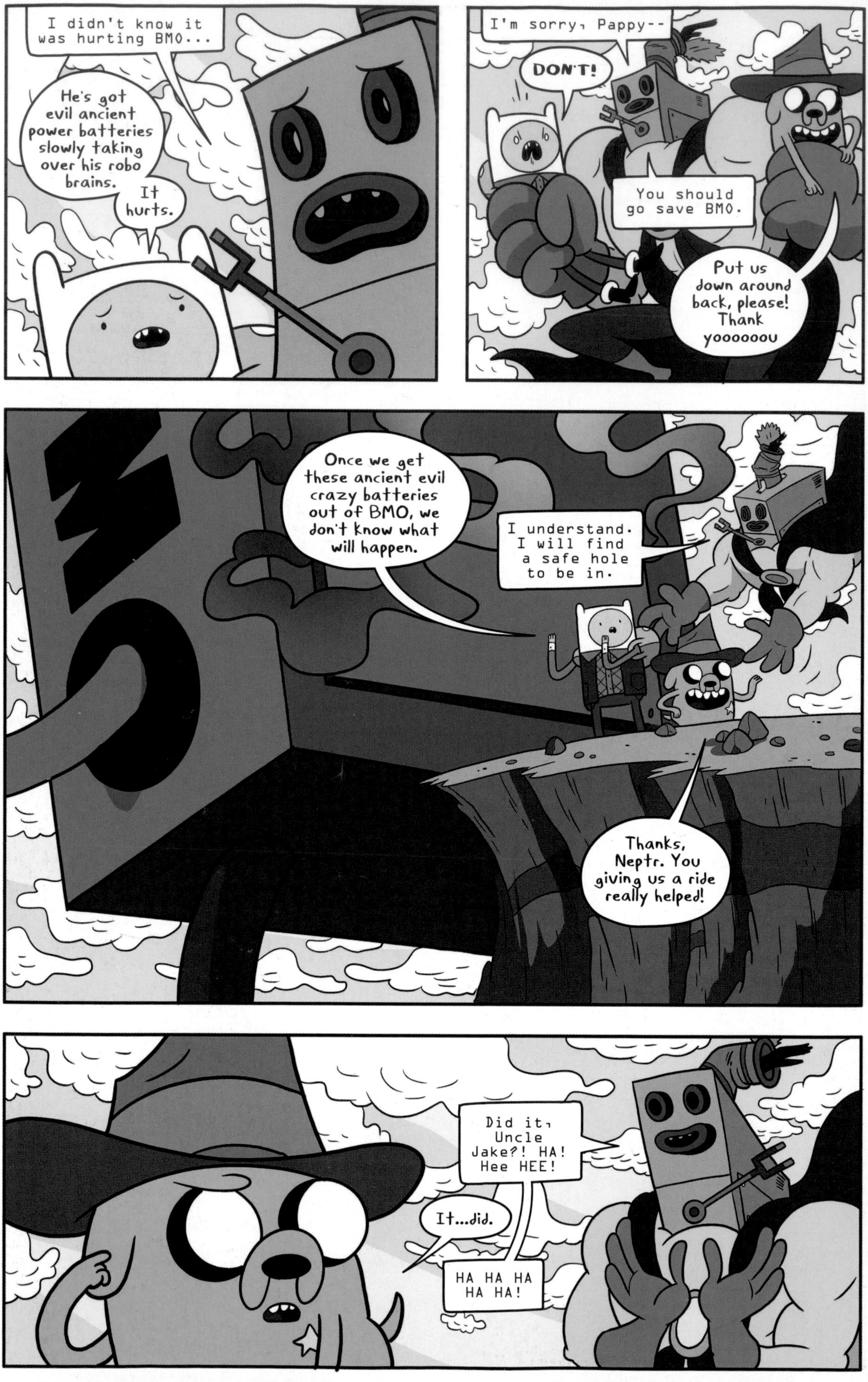
I didn't know it was hurting BMO...
He's got evil ancient power batteries slowly taking over his robo brains.
It hurts.
I'm sorry, Pappy--
DON'T!
You should go save BMO.
Put us down around back, please! Thank yoooooou
Once we get these ancient evil crazy batteries out of BMO, we don't know what will happen.
I understand. I will find a safe hole to be in.
Thanks, Neptr. You giving us a ride really helped!
Did it, Uncle Jake?! HA! Hee HEE!
It...did.
HA HA HA HA HA!

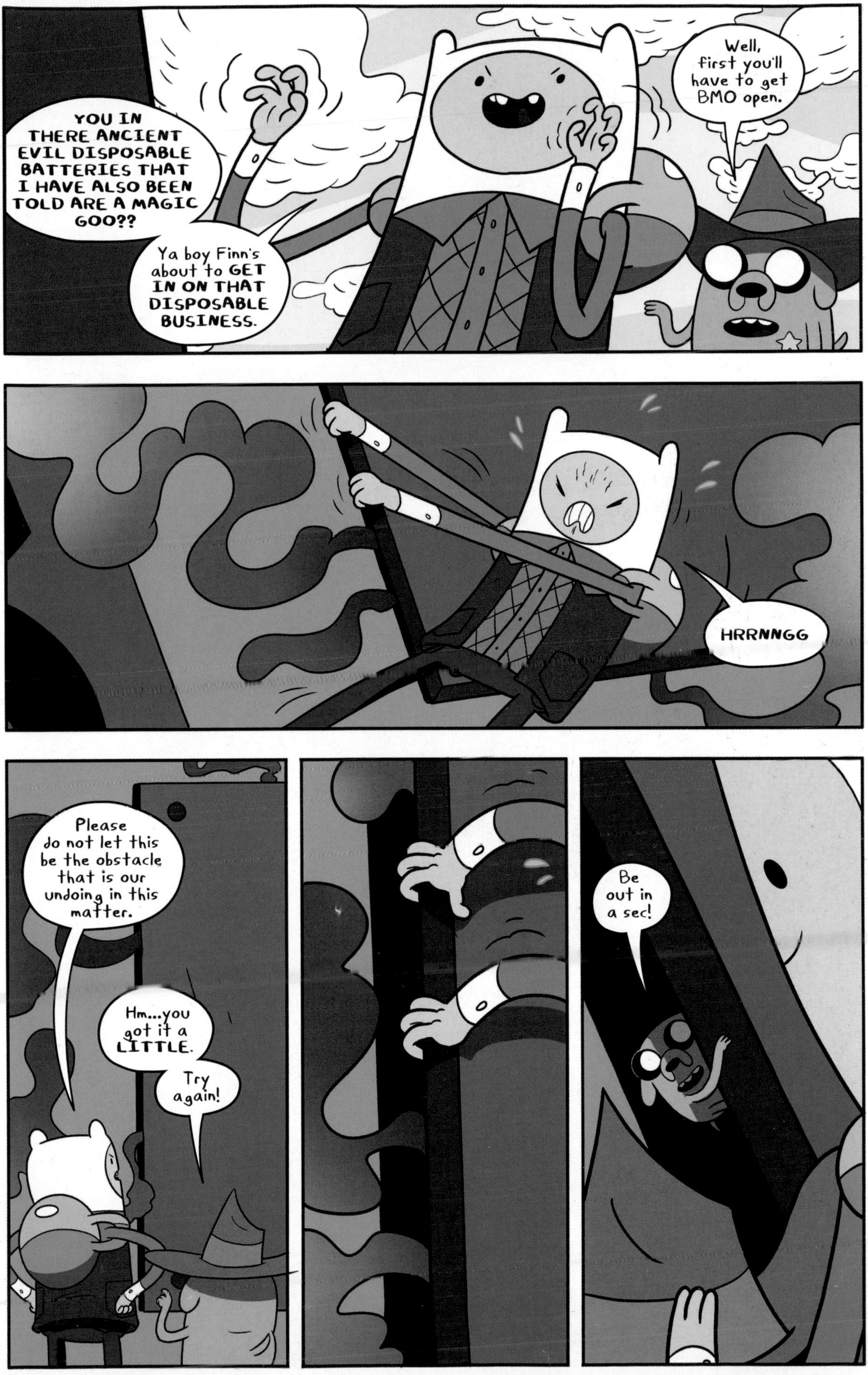
YOU IN THERE ANCIENT EVIL DISPOSABLE BATTERIES THAT I HAVE ALSO BEEN TOLD ARE A MAGIC GOO??
Ya boy Finn's about to GET IN ON THAT DISPOSABLE BUSINESS.
Well, first you'll have to get BMO open.
HRRNNGG
Please do not let this be the obstacle that is our undoing in this matter.
Hm...you got it a LITTLE.
Try again!
Be out in a sec!

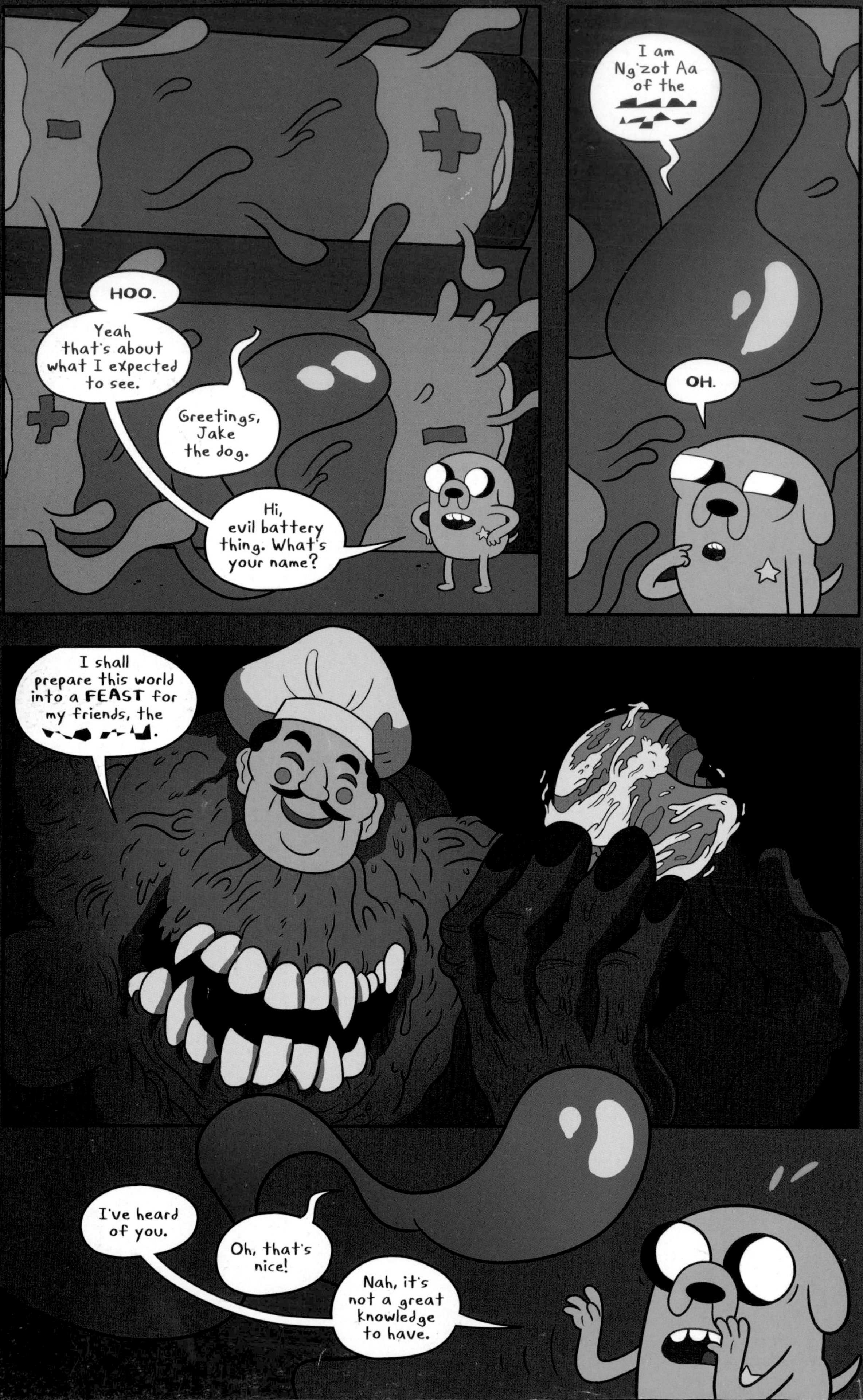

HOO.
Yeah that's about what I expected to see.
Greetings, Jake the dog.
Hi, evil battery thing. What's your name?
I am Ng'zot Aa of the
OH.
I shall prepare this world into a FEAST for my friends, the
I've heard of you.
Oh, that's nice!
Nah, it's not a great knowledge to have.

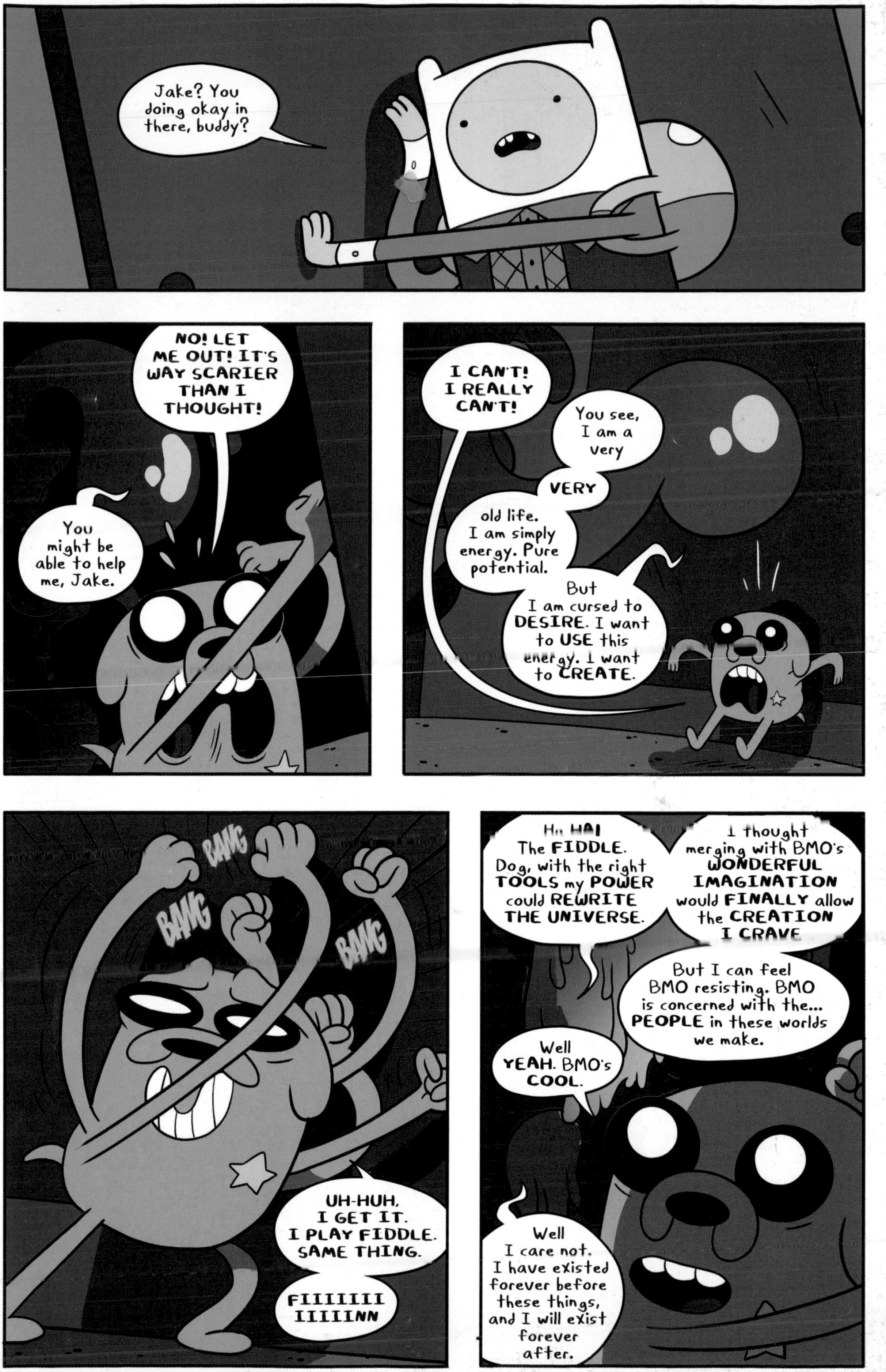
Jake? You doing okay in there, buddy?
NO! LET ME OUT! IT'S WAY SCARIER THAN I THOUGHT!
You might be able to help me, Jake.
I CAN'T! I REALLY CAN'T!
You see, I am a very
VERY
old life. I am simply energy. Pure potential.
But I am cursed to DESIRE. I want to USE this energy. I want to CREATE.
BANG
BANG
BANG
UH-HUH, I GET IT. I PLAY FIDDLE. SAME THING.
FIIIIIII IIIIIINN
H.. HA!
The FIDDLE. Dog, with the right TOOLS my POWER could REWRITE THE UNIVERSE.
I thought merging with BMO's WONDERFUL IMAGINATION would FINALLY allow the CREATION I CRAVE
But I can feel BMO resisting. BMO is concerned with the... PEOPLE in these worlds we make.
Well YEAH. BMO's COOL.
Well I care not. I have existed forever before these things, and I will exist forever after.

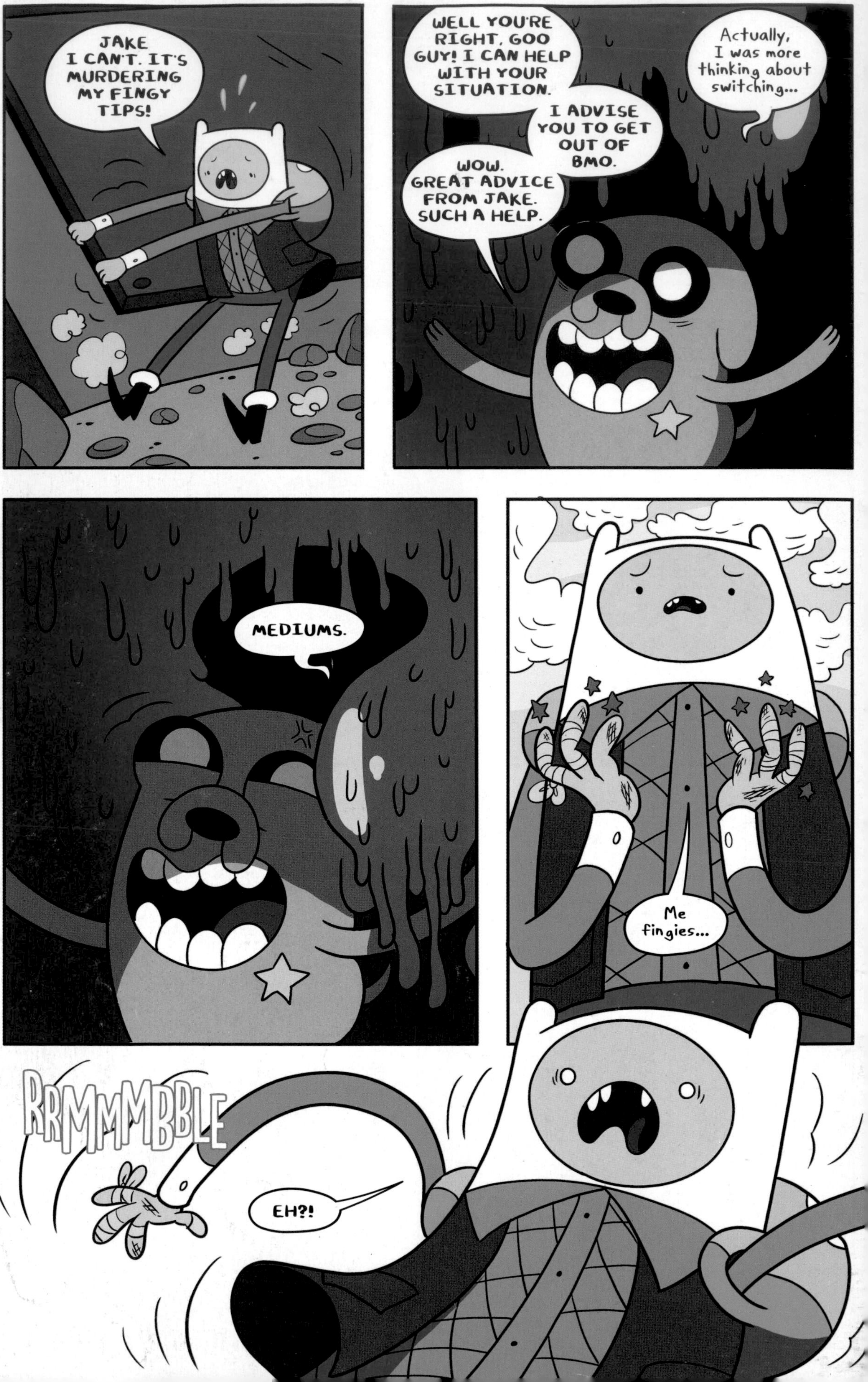
JAKE I CAN'T. IT'S MURDERING MY FINGY TIPS!
WELL YOU'RE RIGHT, GOO GUY! I CAN HELP WITH YOUR SITUATION.
I ADVISE YOU TO GET OUT OF BMO.
WOW. GREAT ADVICE FROM JAKE. SUCH A HELP.
Actually, I was more thinking about switching...
MEDIUMS.
Me fingies...
RRMMMBBLE
EH?!

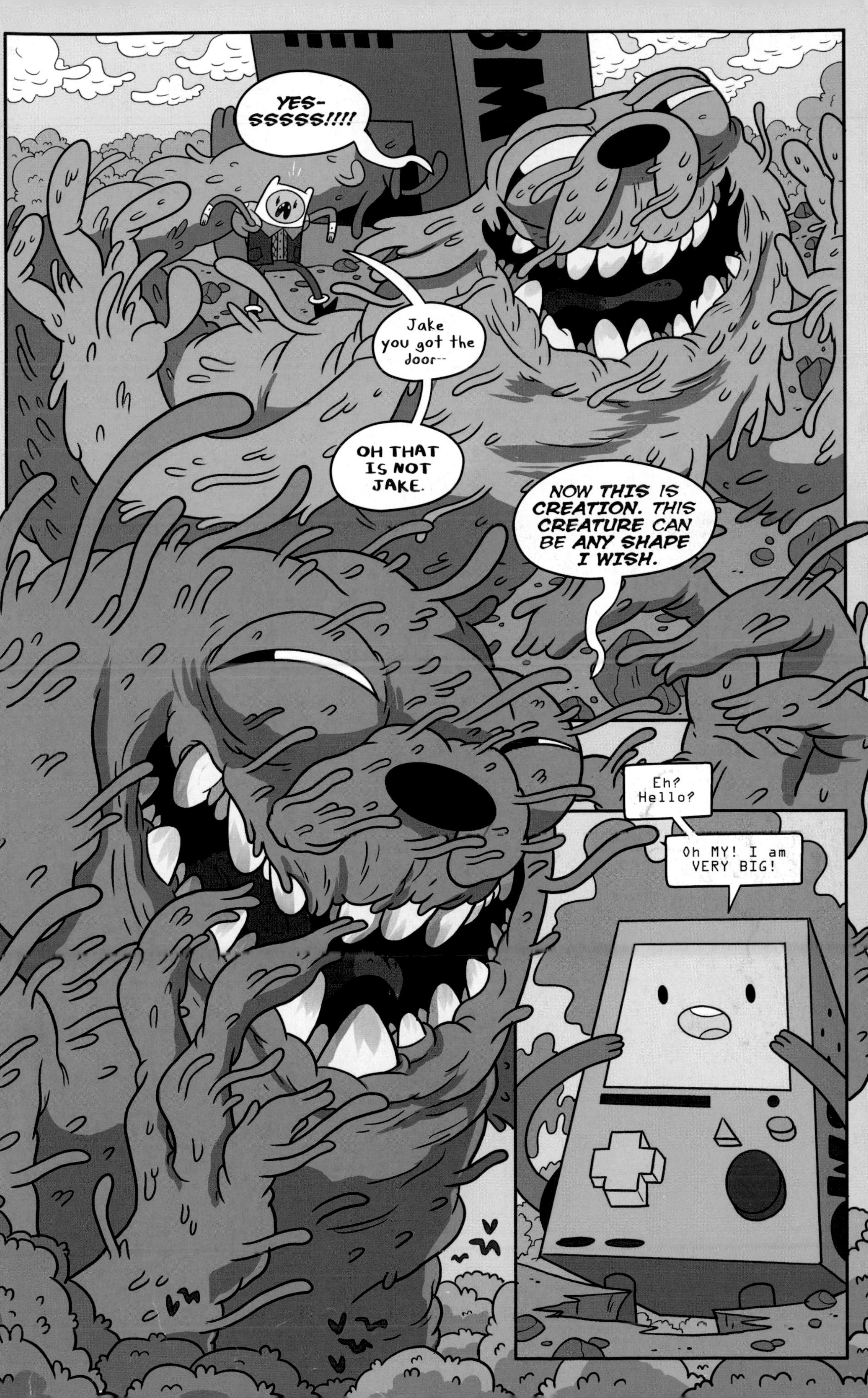
YES-SSSSS!!!!
Jake you got the door--
OH THAT IS NOT JAKE.
NOW THIS IS CREATION. THIS CREATURE CAN BE ANY SHAPE I WISH.
Eh? Hello?
Oh MY! I am VERY BIG!

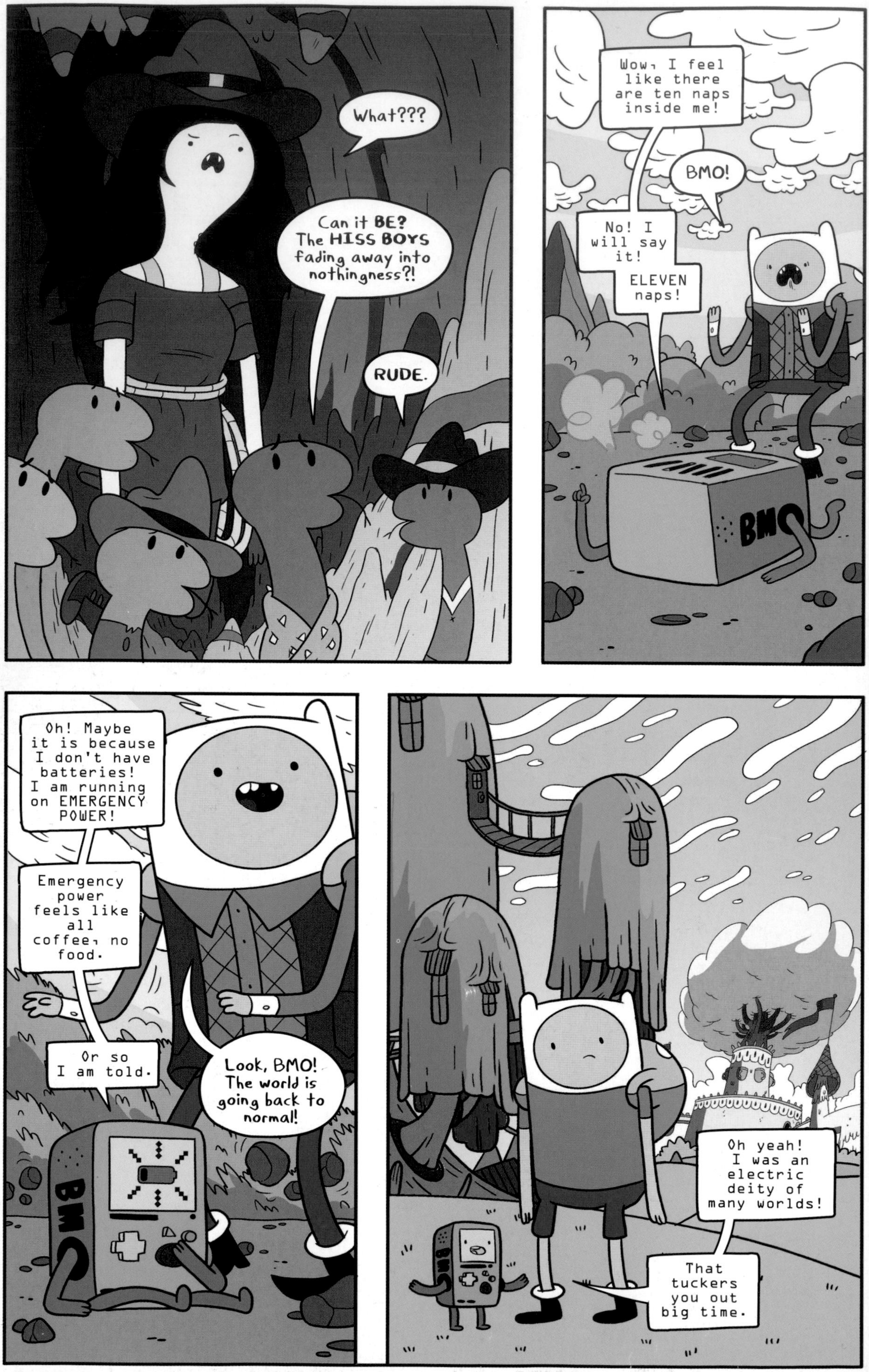
What???
Can it BE? The HISS BOYS fading away into nothingness?!
RUDE.
Wow, I feel like there are ten naps inside me!
BMO!
No! I will say it!
ELEVEN naps!
Oh! Maybe it is because I don't have batteries! I am running on EMERGENCY POWER!
Emergency power feels like all coffee, no food.
Or so I am told.
Look, BMO! The world is going back to normal!
Oh yeah! I was an electric deity of many worlds!
That tuckers you out big time.

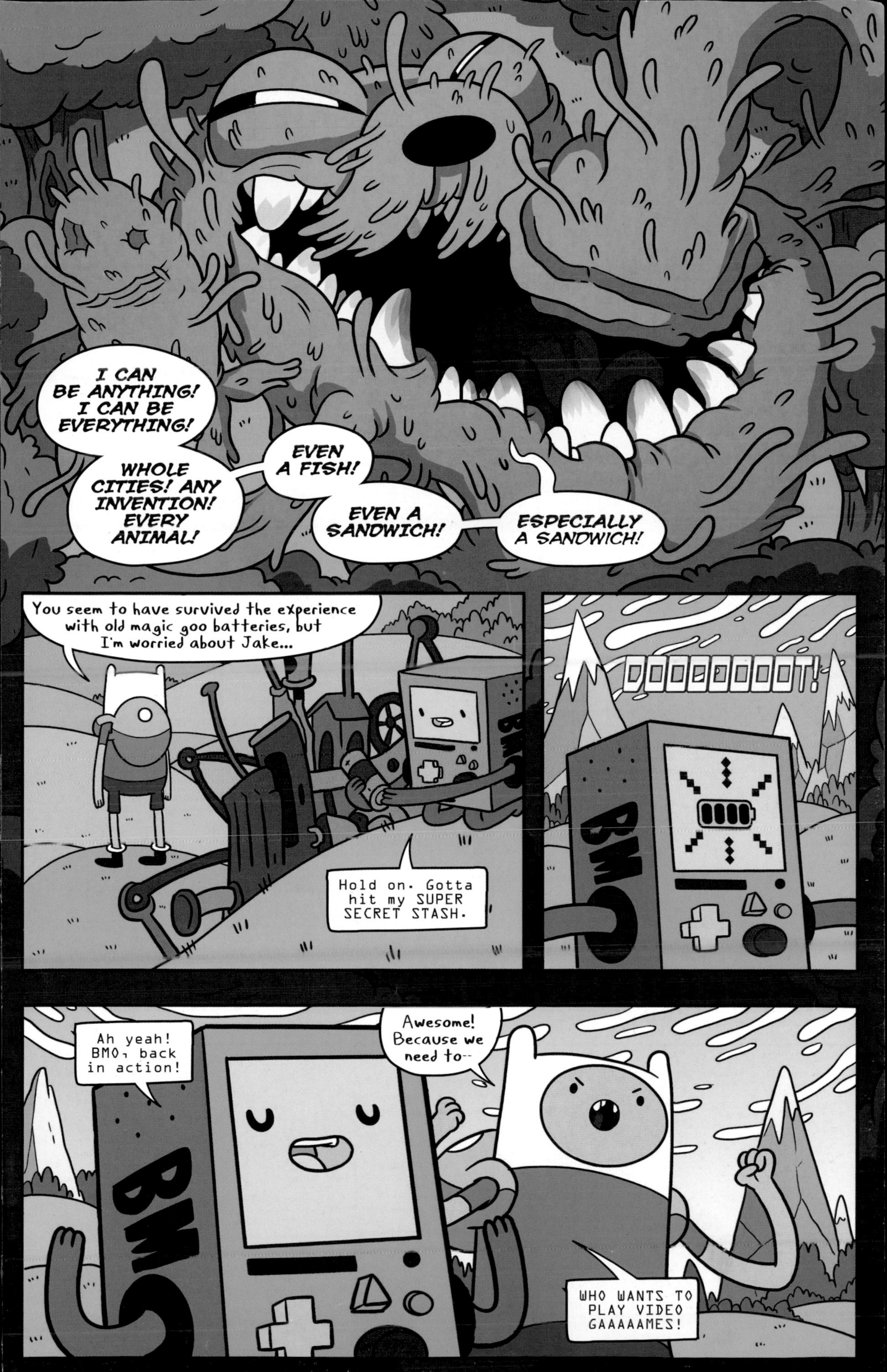

I CAN BE ANYTHING! I CAN BE EVERYTHING!
WHOLE CITIES! ANY INVENTION! EVERY ANIMAL!
EVEN A FISH!
EVEN A SANDWICH!
ESPECIALLY A SANDWICH!
You seem to have survived the experience with old magic goo batteries, but I'm worried about Jake...
Hold on. Gotta hit my SUPER SECRET STASH.
DOOOOOOOOT!
Ah yeah! BMO, back in action!
Awesome! Because we need to--
WHO WANTS TO PLAY VIDEO GAAAAAMES!

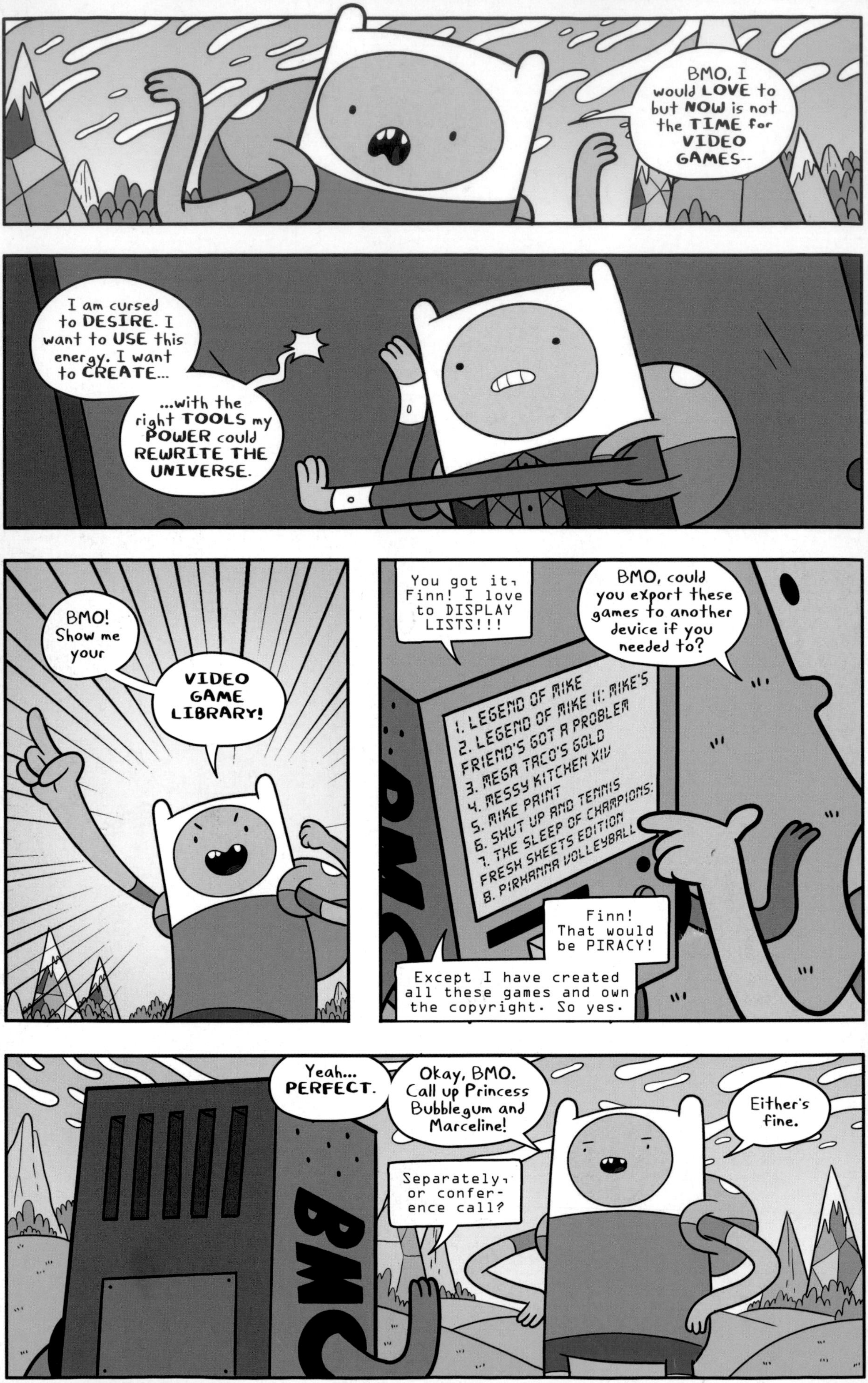
BMO, I would LOVE to but NOW is not the TIME for VIDEO GAMES--
I am cursed to DESIRE. I want to USE this energy. I want to CREATE...
...with the right TOOLS my POWER could REWRITE THE UNIVERSE.
BMO! Show me your
VIDEO GAME LIBRARY!
You got it, Finn! I love to DISPLAY LISTS!!!
BMO, could you export these games to another device if you needed to?
1. LEGEND OF MIKE
2. LEGEND OF MIKE II: MIKE'S FRIEND'S GOT A PROBLEM
3. MEGA TACO'S GOLD
4. MESSY KITCHEN XIV
5. MIKE PRINT
6. SHUT UP AND TENNIS
7. THE SLEEP OF CHAMPIONS: FRESH SHEETS EDITION
8. PIRHANNA VOLLEYBALL
Finn! That would be PIRACY!
Except I have created all these games and own the copyright. So yes.
Yeah... PERFECT.
Okay, BMO. Call up Princess Bubblegum and Marceline!
Separately, or confer-ence call?
Either's fine.

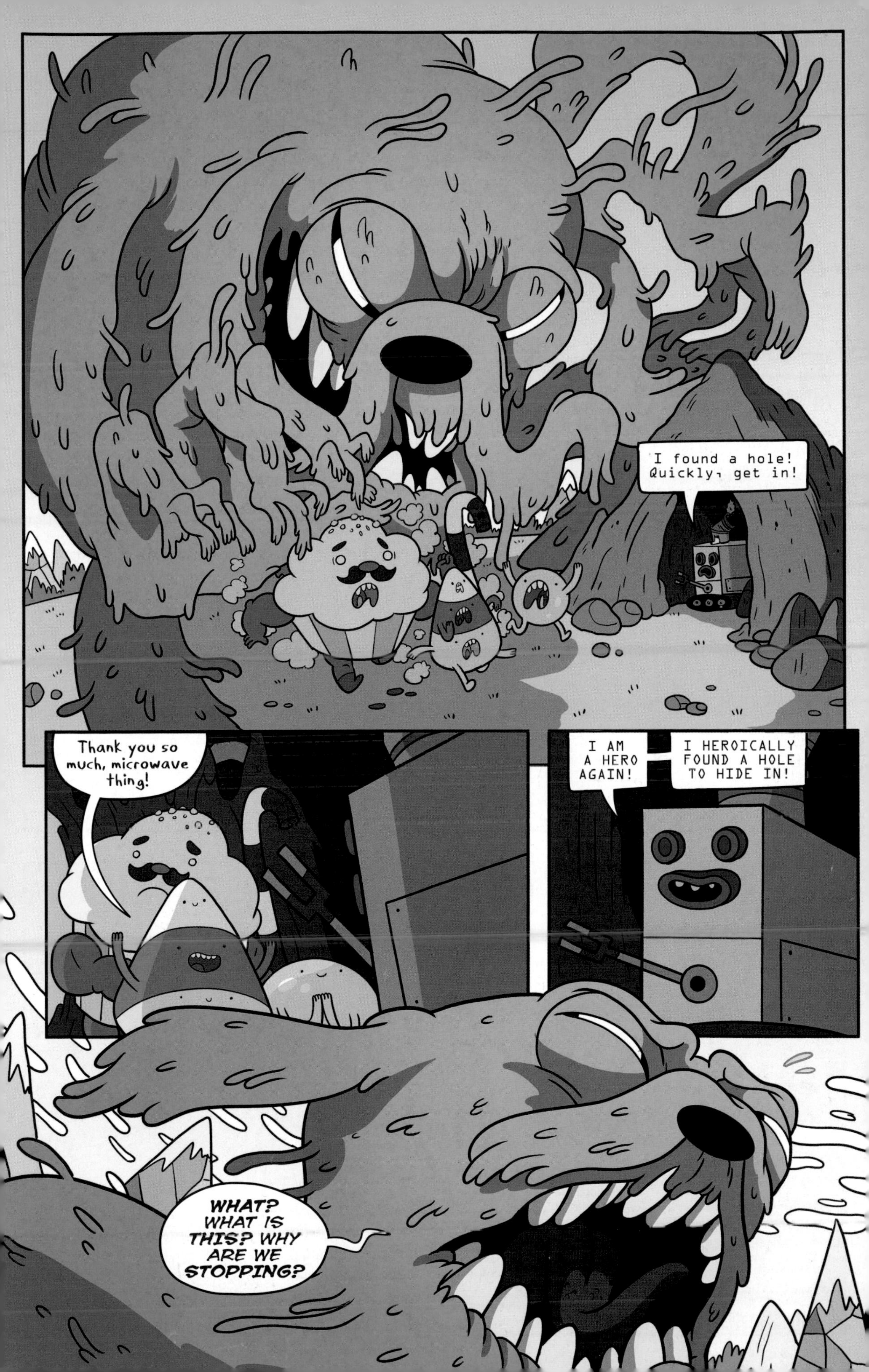

I found a hole! Quickly, get in!
Thank you so much, microwave thing!
I AM A HERO AGAIN!
I HEROICALLY FOUND A HOLE TO HIDE IN!
WHAT? WHAT IS THIS? WHY ARE WE STOPPING?

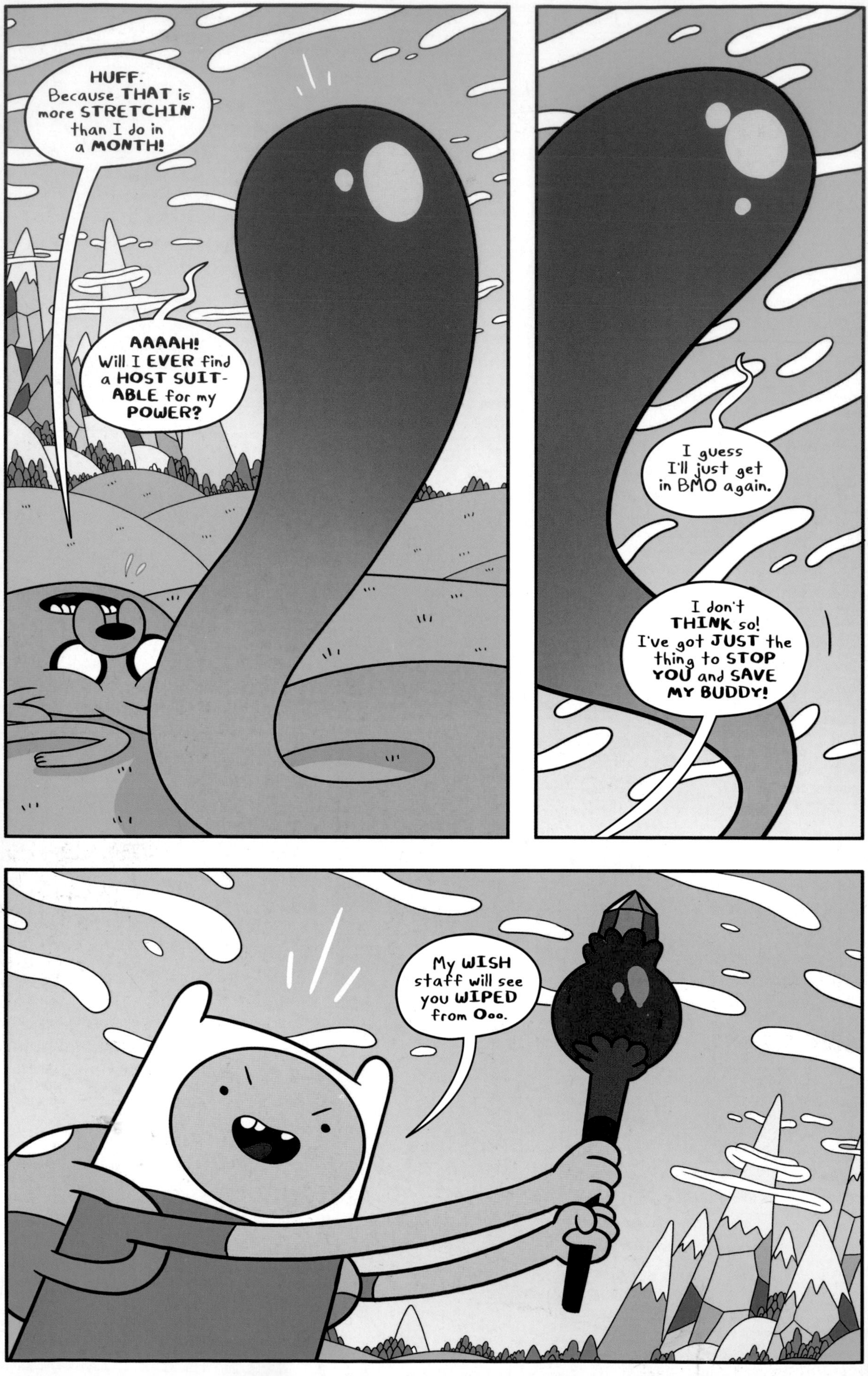
HUFF. Because THAT is more STRETCHIN' than I do in a MONTH!
AAAAH! Will I EVER find a HOST SUIT-ABLE for my POWER?
I guess I'll just get in BMO again.
I don't THINK so! I've got JUST the thing to STOP YOU and SAVE MY BUDDY!
My WISH staff will see you WIPED from Ooo.

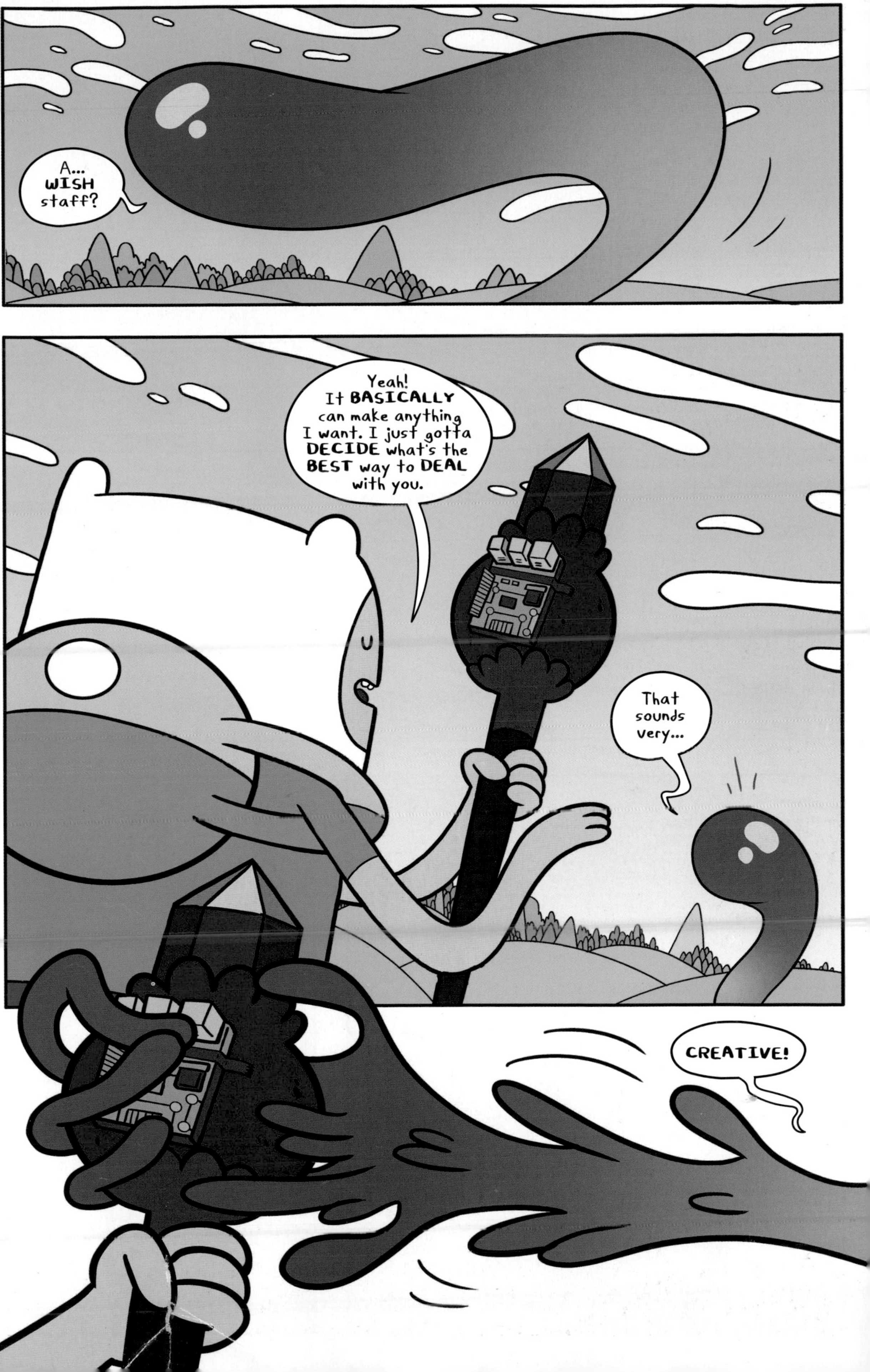
A... WISH staff?
Yeah! It BASICALLY can make anything I want. I just gotta DECIDE what's the BEST way to DEAL with you.
That sounds very...
CREATIVE!

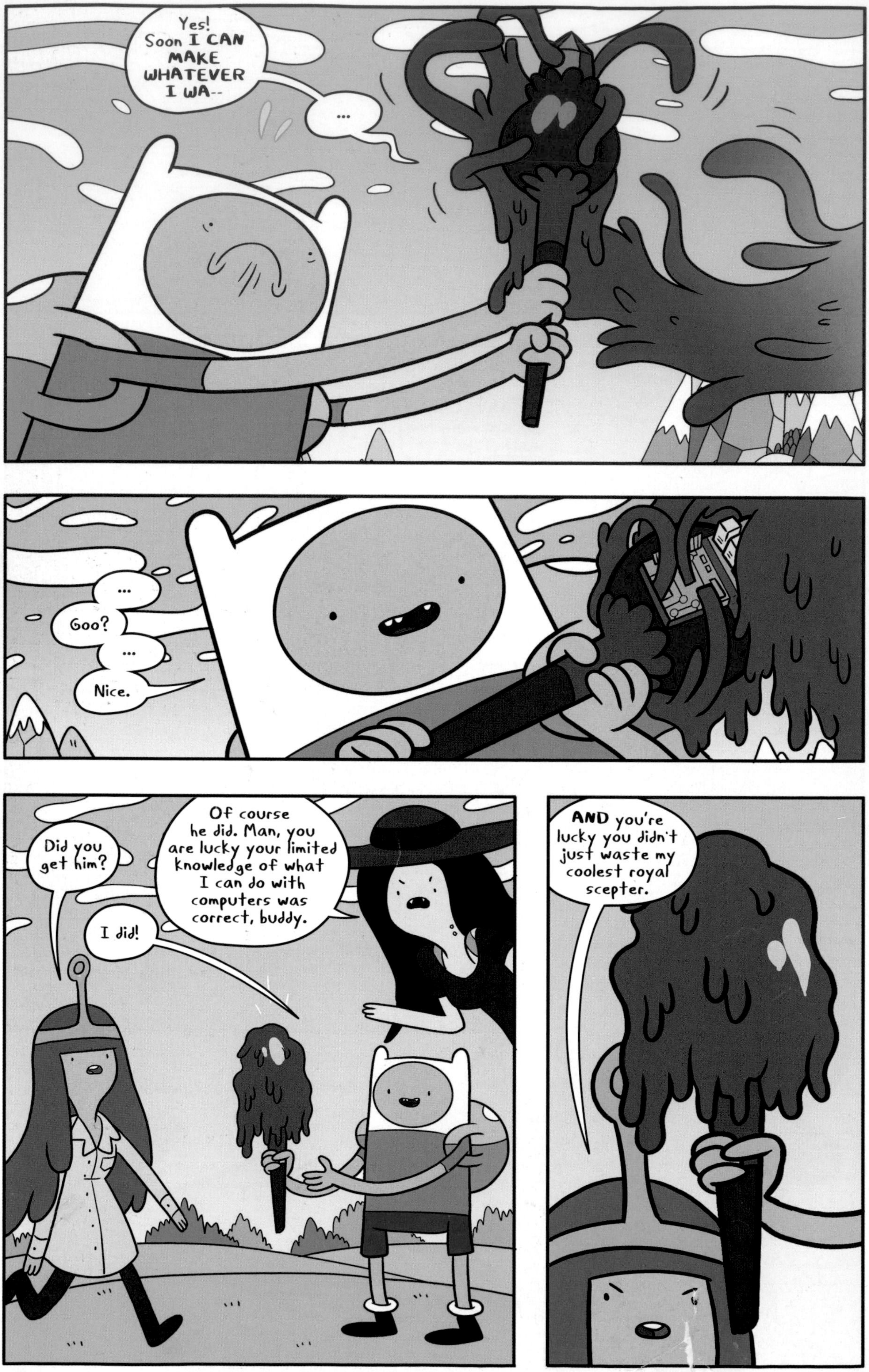
Yes! Soon I CAN MAKE WHATEVER I WA--
...
...
Goo?
...
Nice.
Did you get him?
Of course he did. Man, you are lucky your limited knowledge of what I can do with computers was correct, buddy.
I did!
AND you're lucky you didn't just waste my coolest royal scepter.

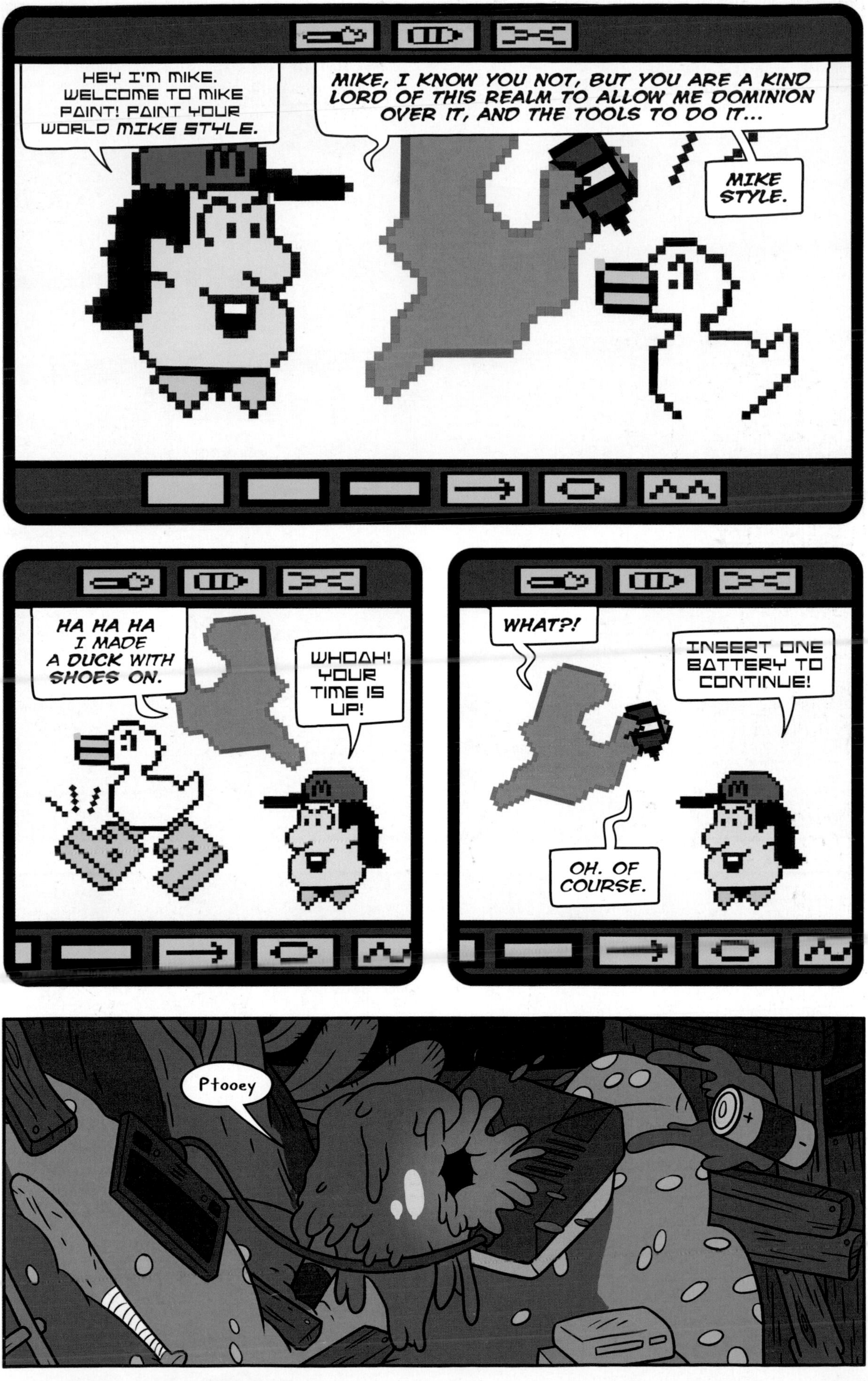
HEY I'M MIKE. WELCOME TO MIKE PAINT! PAINT YOUR WORLD MIKE STYLE.
MIKE, I KNOW YOU NOT, BUT YOU ARE A KIND LORD OF THIS REALM TO ALLOW ME DOMINION OVER IT, AND THE TOOLS TO DO IT...
MIKE STYLE.
HA HA HA I MADE A DUCK WITH SHOES ON.
WHOAH! YOUR TIME IS UP!
WHAT?!
INSERT ONE BATTERY TO CONTINUE!
OH. OF COURSE.
Ptooey

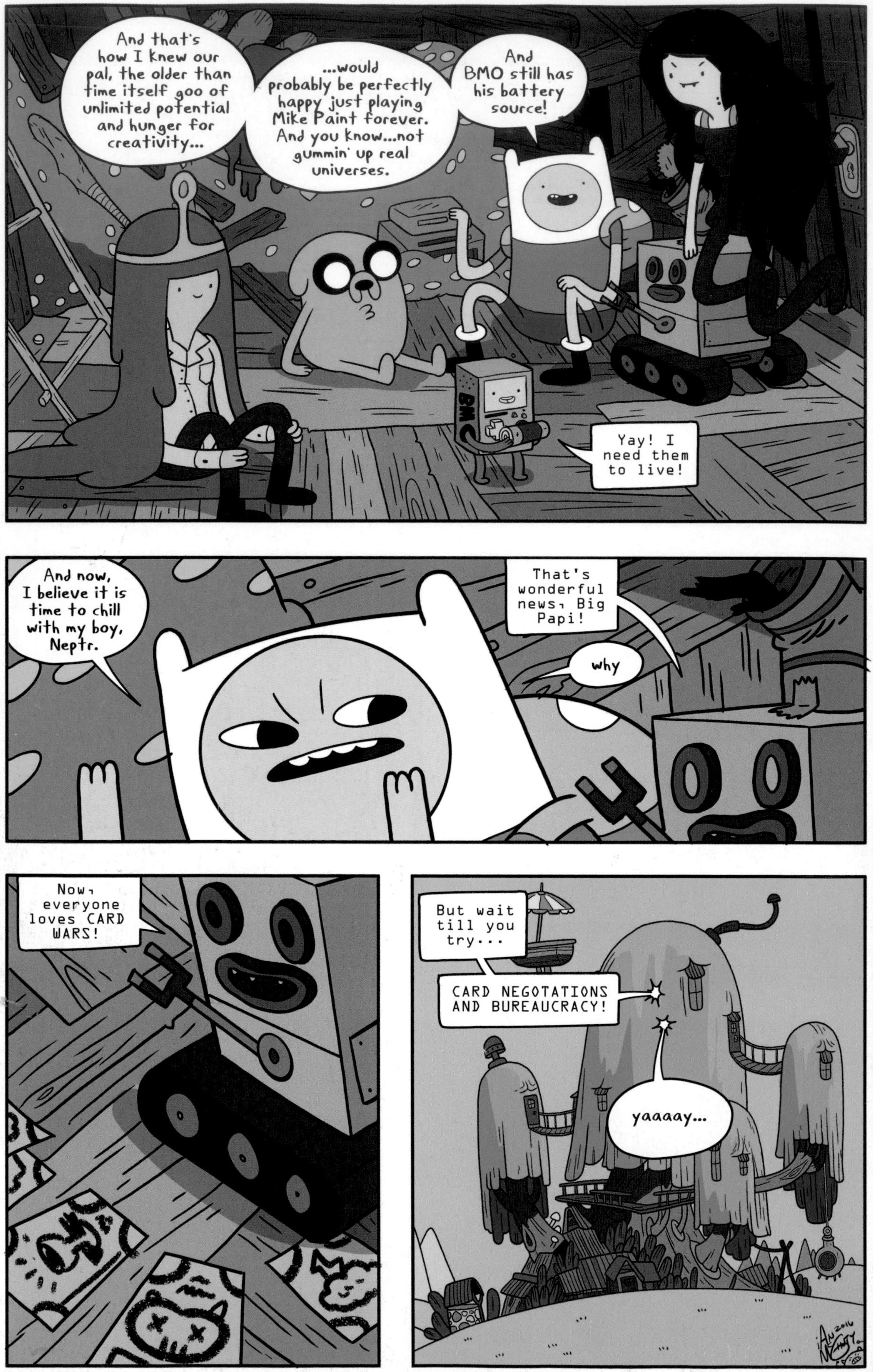
And that's how I knew our pal, the older than time itself goo of unlimited potential and hunger for creativity...
...would probably be perfectly happy just playing Mike Paint forever. And you know...not gummin' up real universes.
And BMO still has his battery source!
Yay! I need them to live!
And now, I believe it is time to chill with my boy, Neptr.
That's wonderful news, Big Papi!
why
Now, everyone loves CARD WARS!
But wait till you try...
CARD NEGOTATIONS AND BUREAUCRACY!
yaaaay...

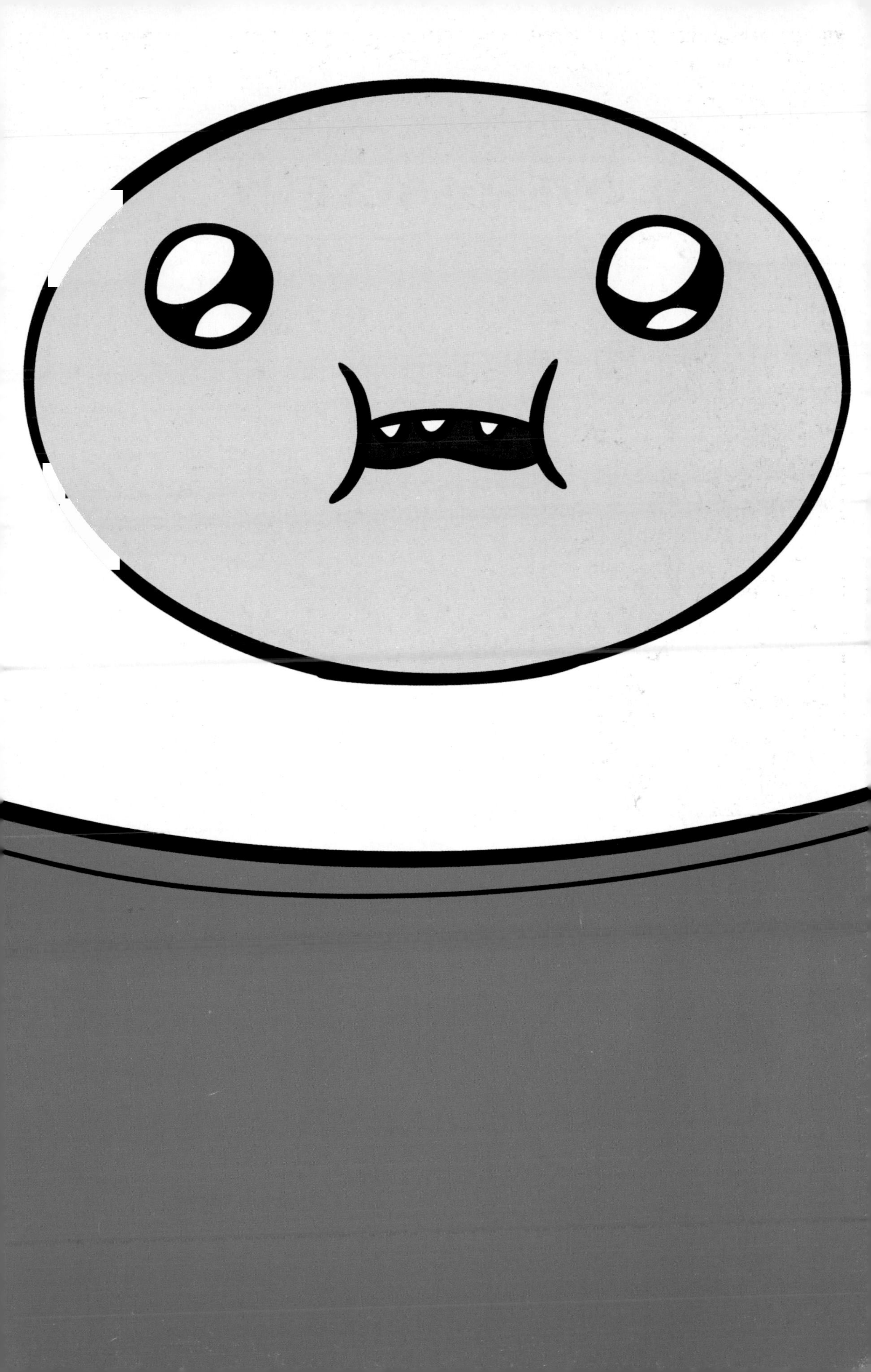

# COVER GALLERY

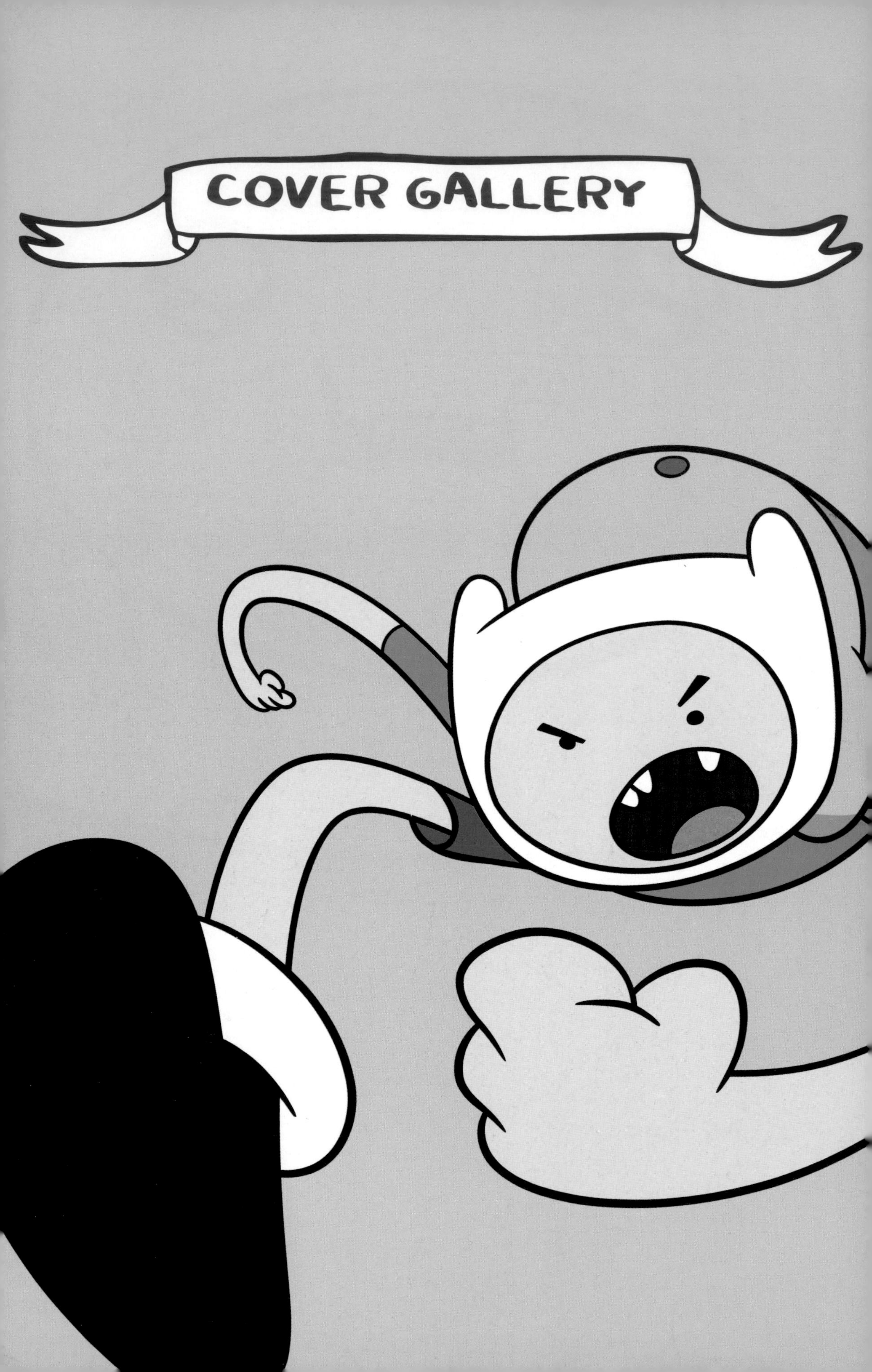

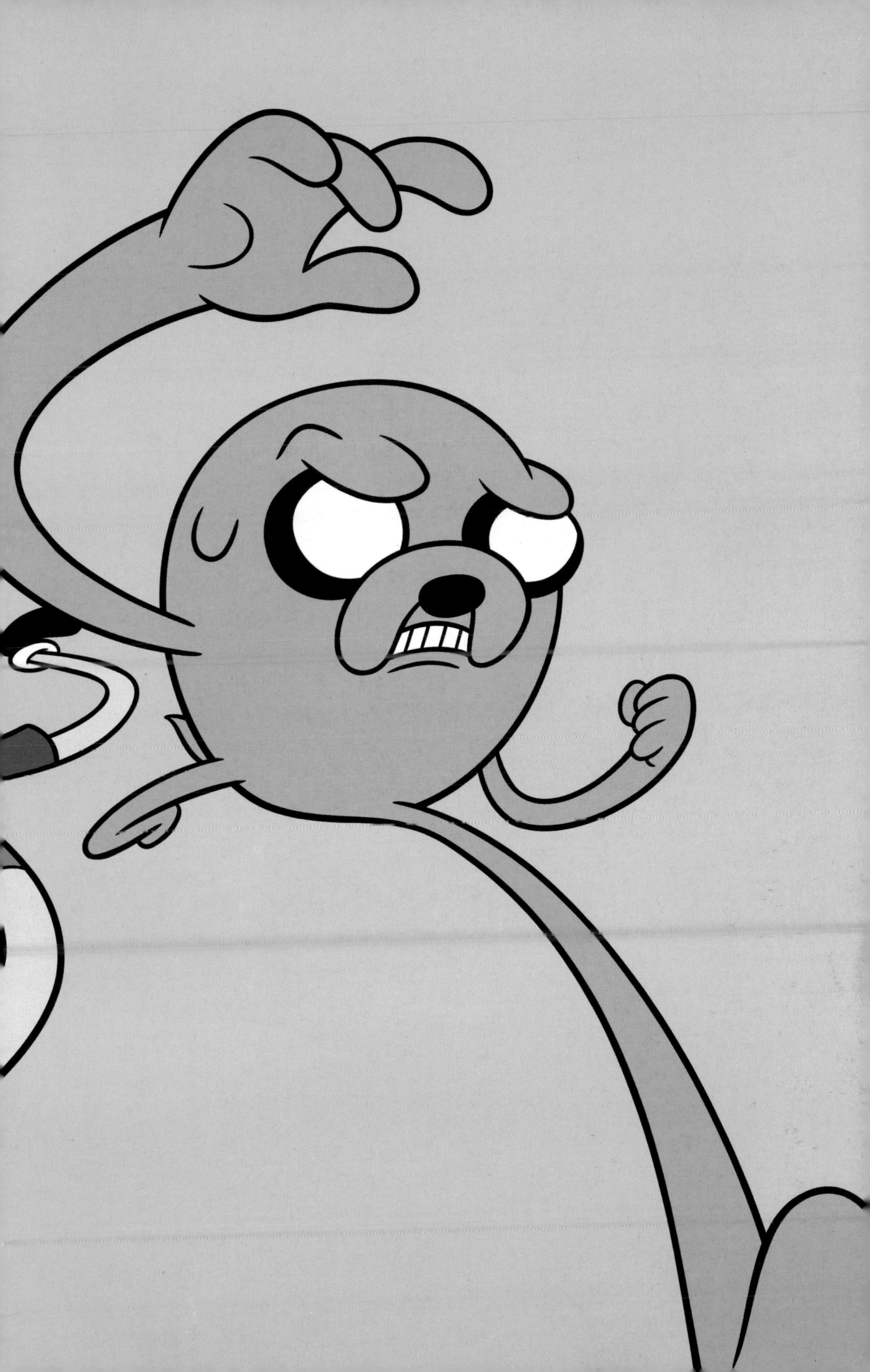

Issue 54 Cover:
Jackie Ferrentino

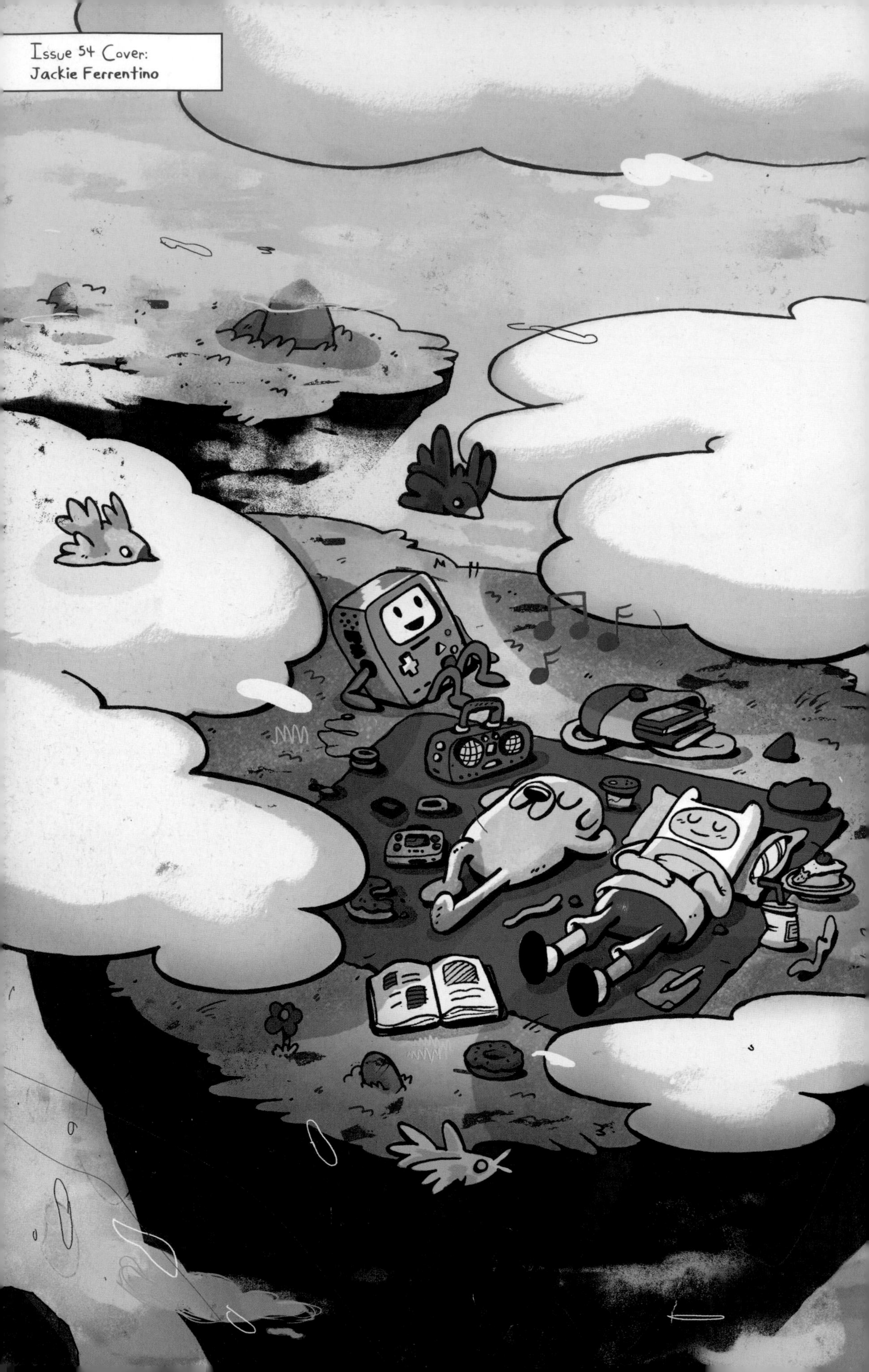

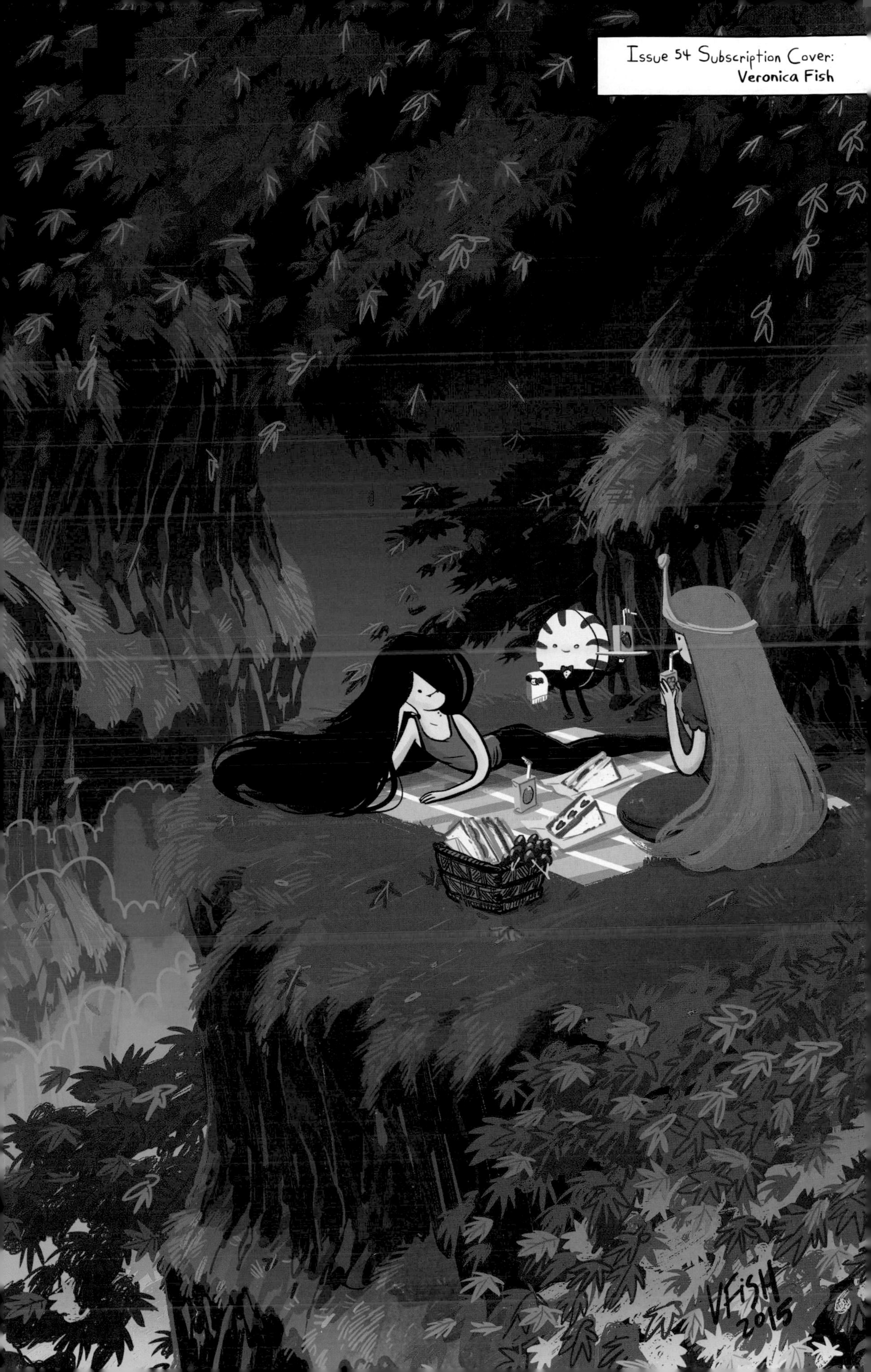
VFISH
2015

Issue 54 Subscription Cover:
**Veronica Fish**

Issue 55 Cover:
Myra Hild

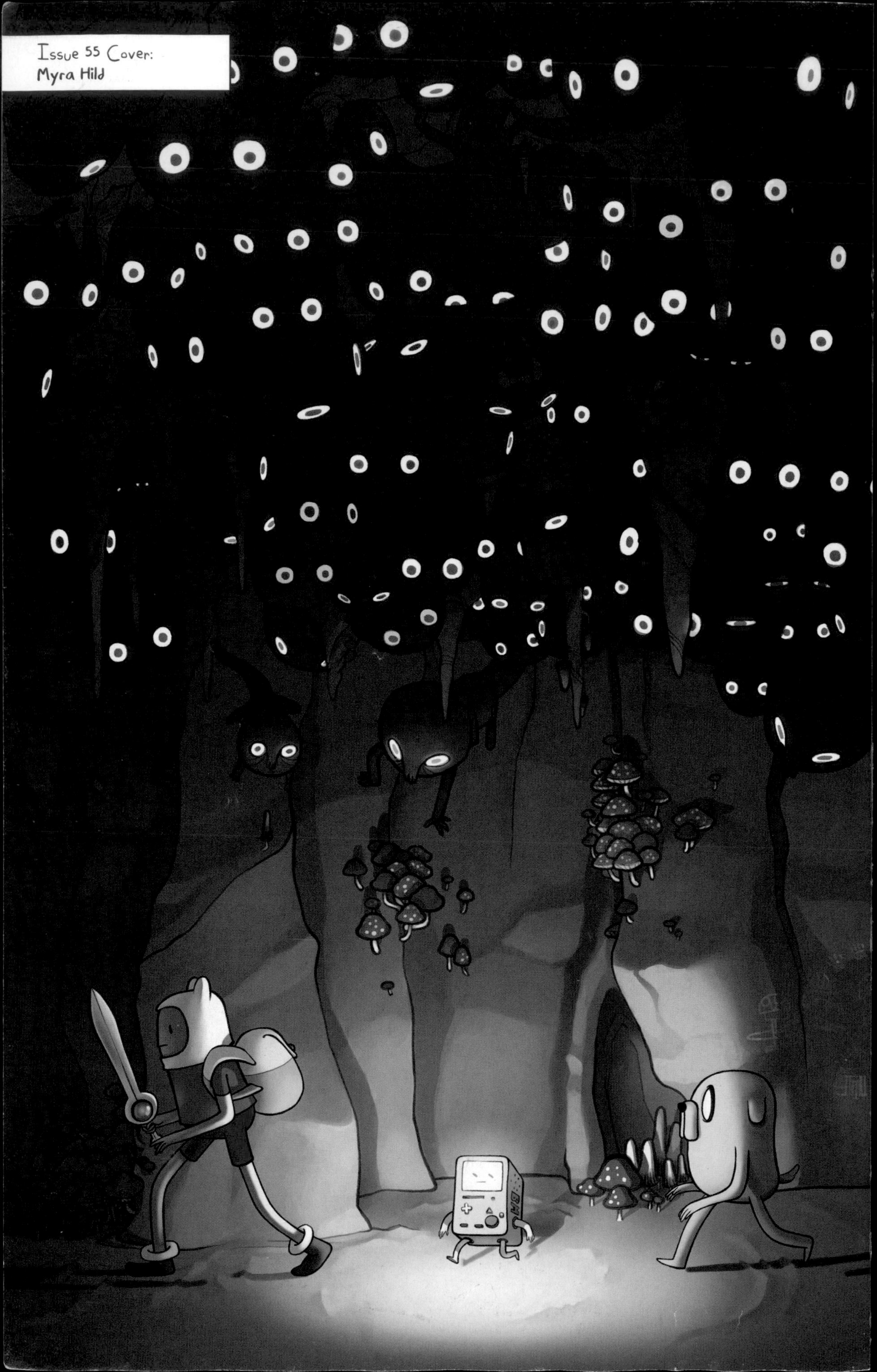

Issue 55 Subscription Cover:
**Sarah Searle**

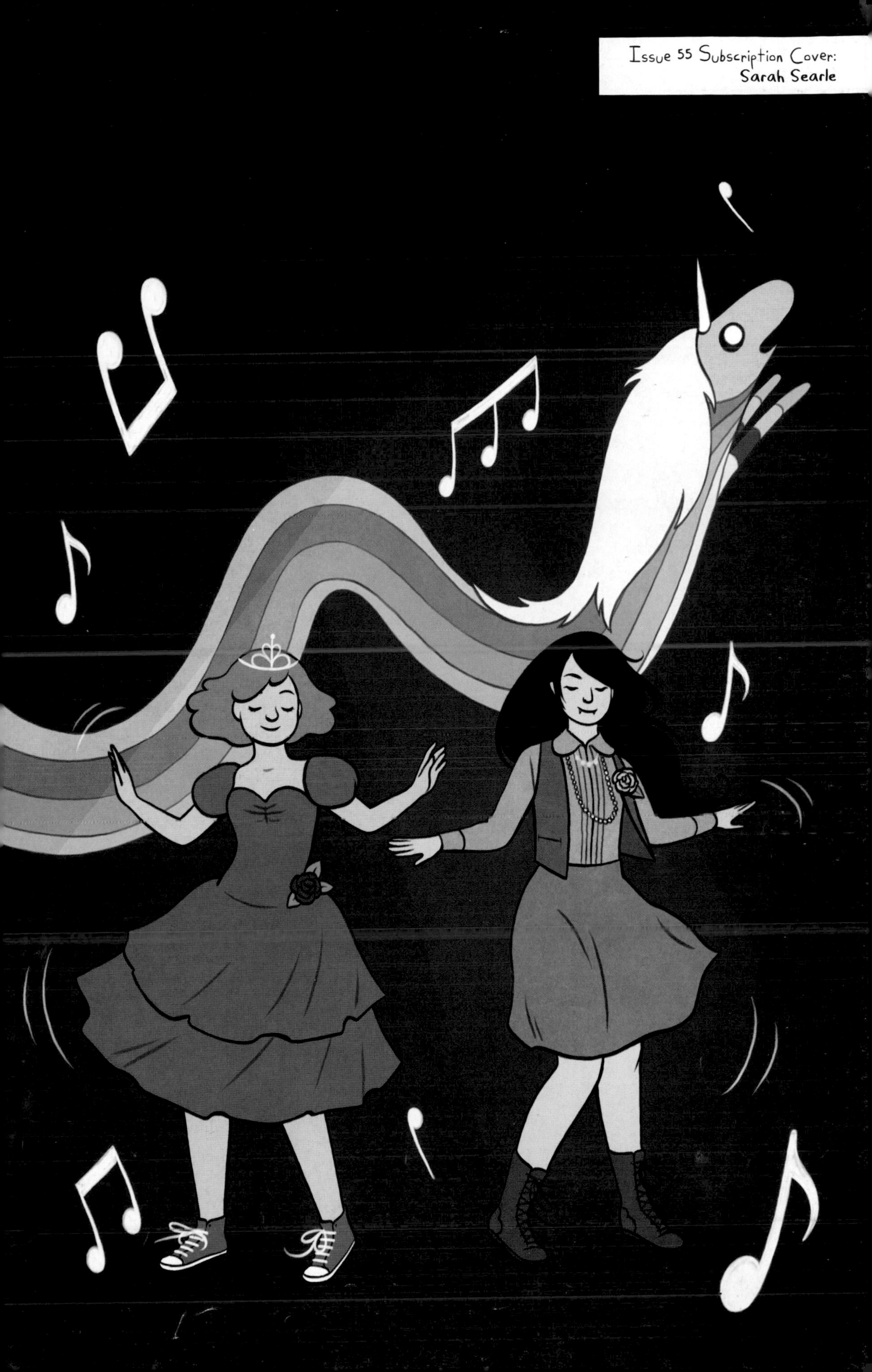

Issue 56 Cover:
Bree Lundberg

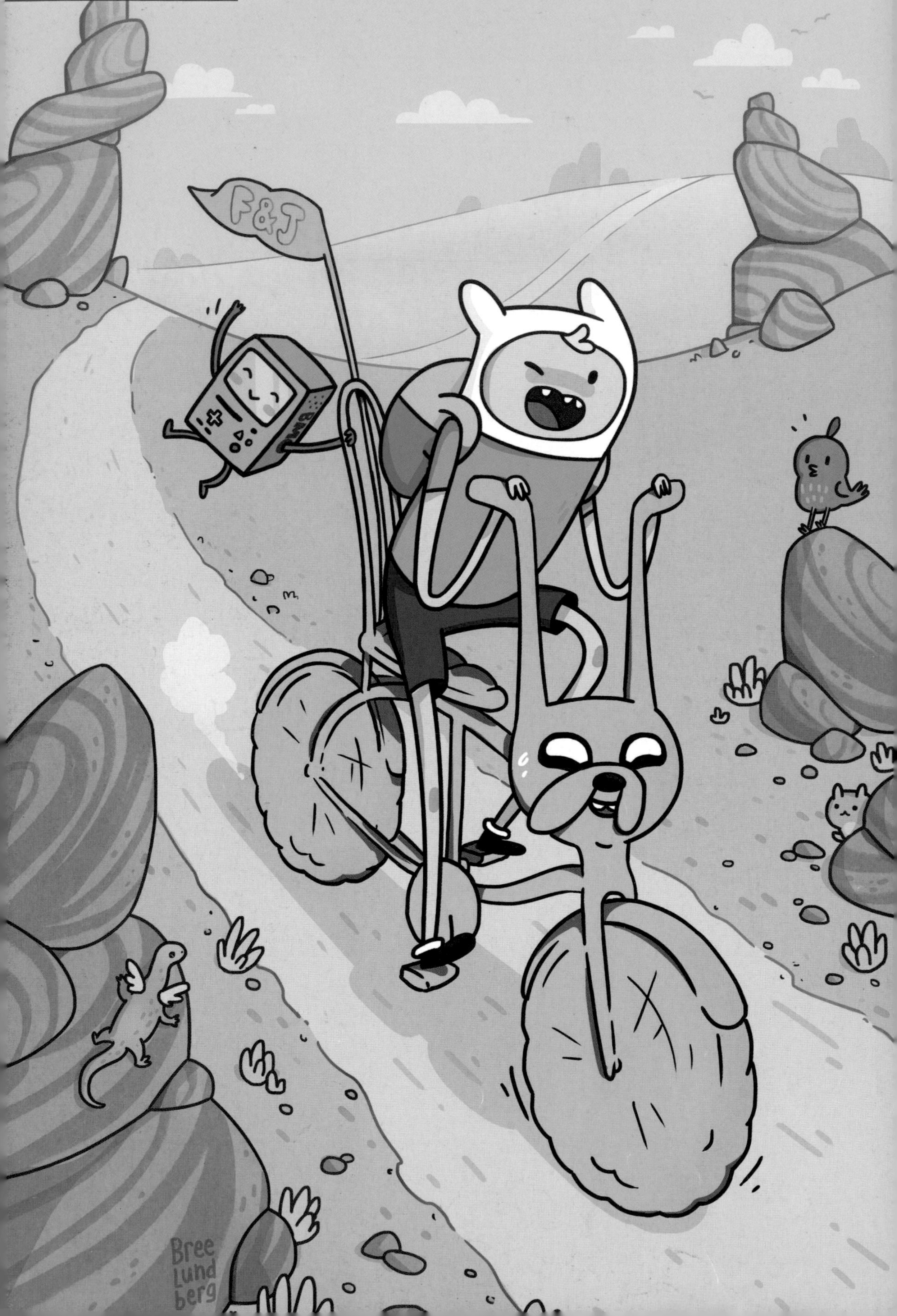
F&J
BMO
Bree
Lund
berg

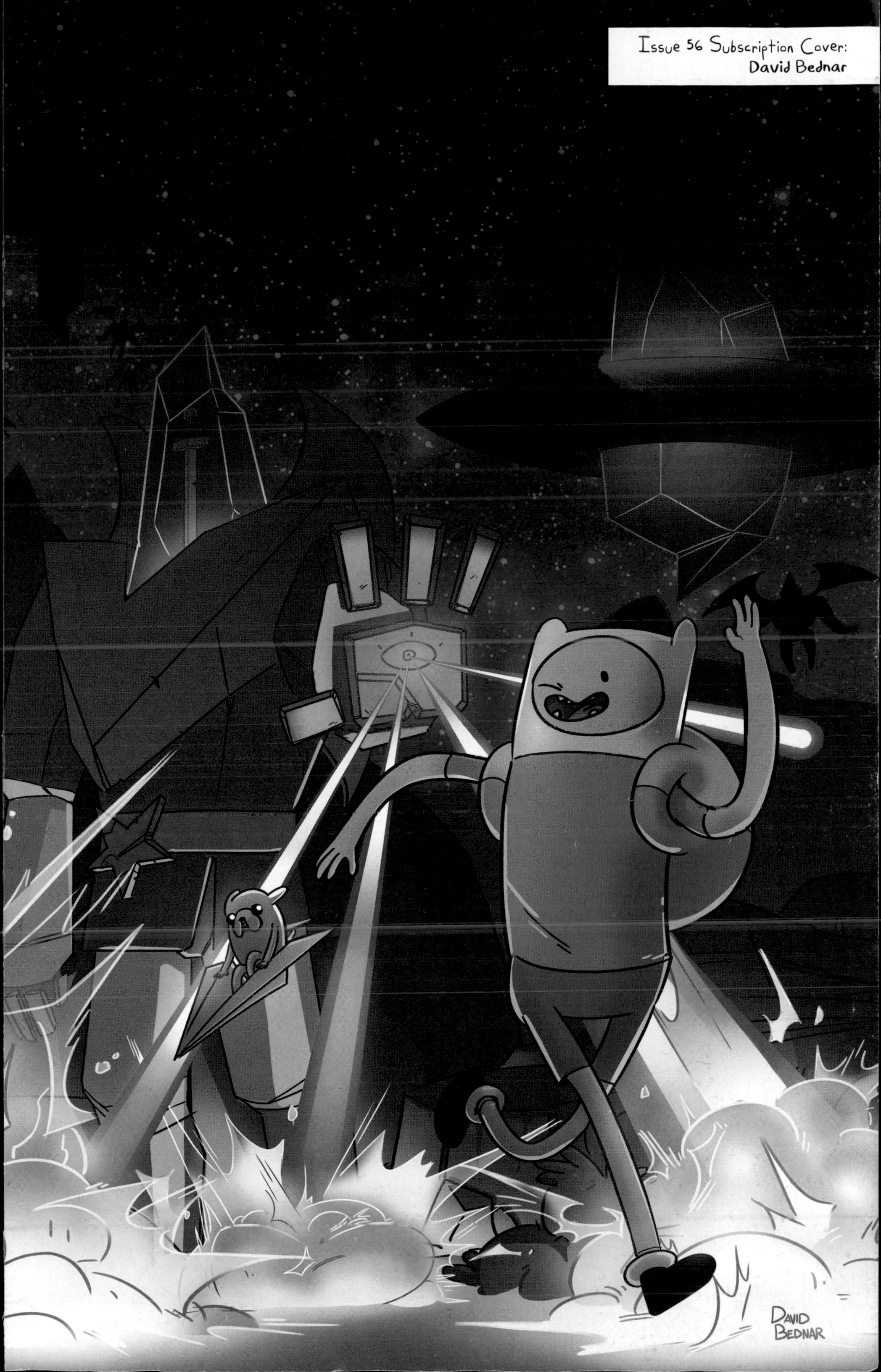
DAVID
BEDNAR

Issue 56 Subscription Cover:
David Bednar

Issue 57 Cover:
Shannon Wright

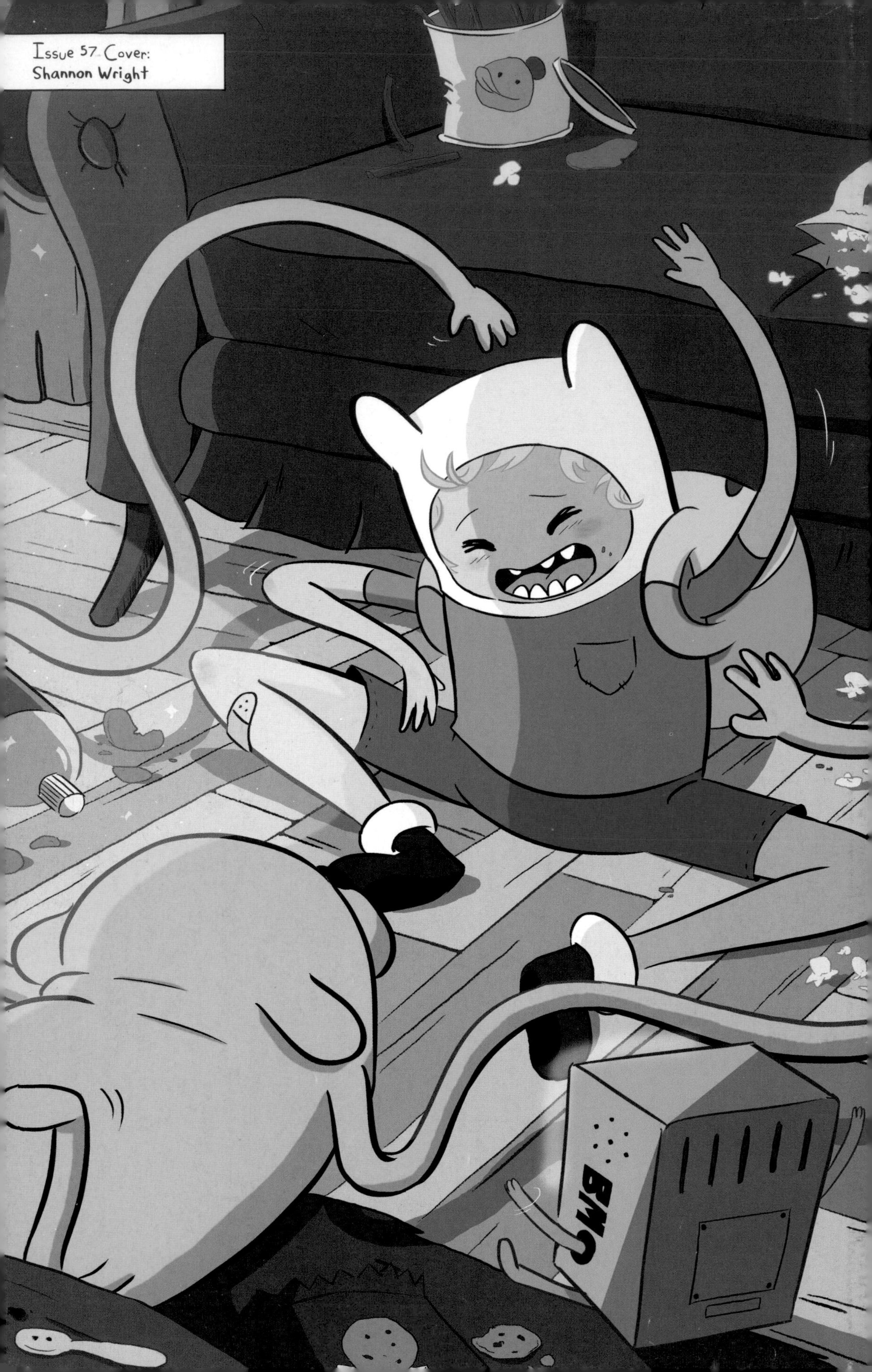
BMO

Issue 57 Subscription Cover:
Siobhan Keenan

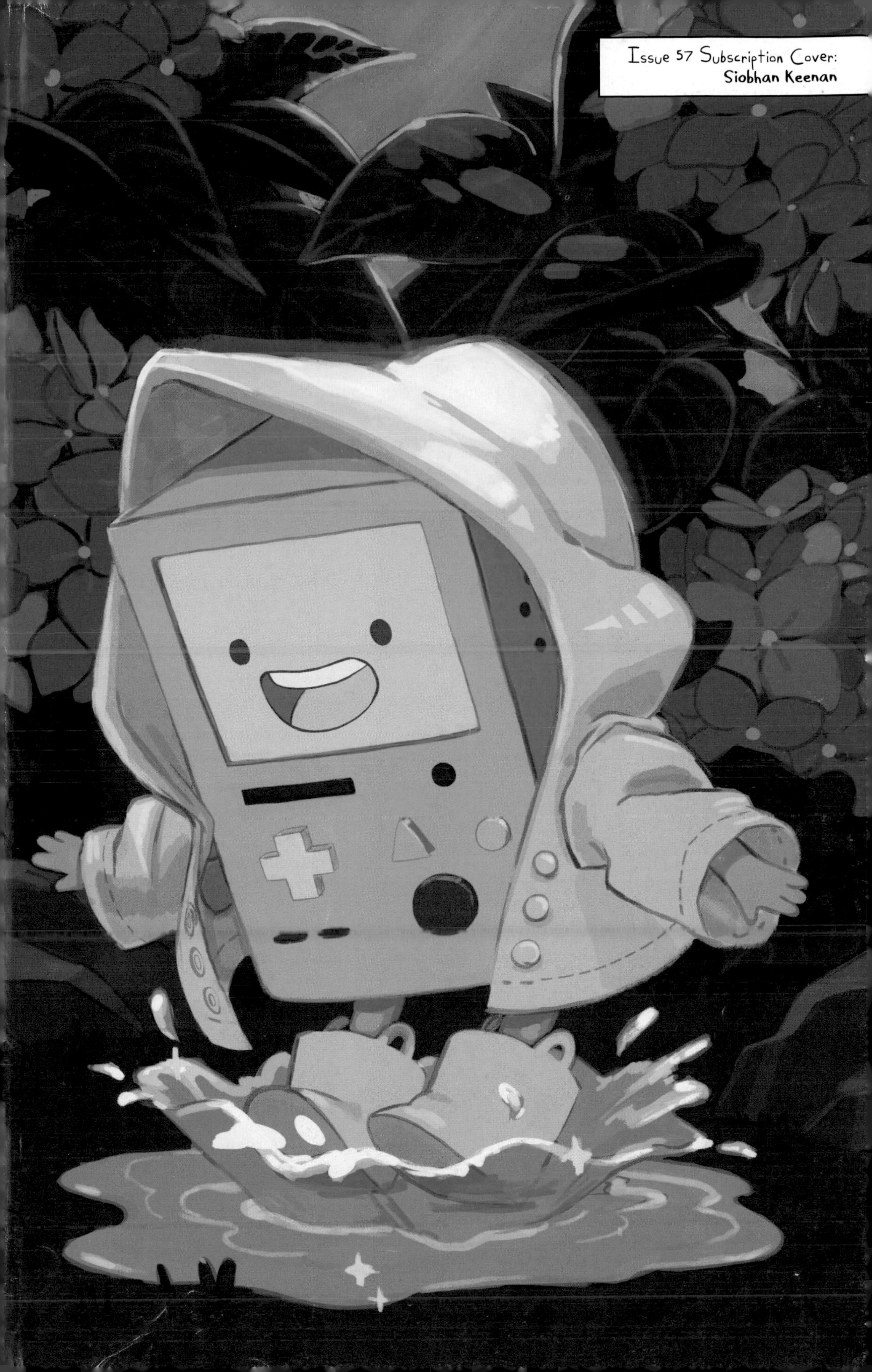

# DISCOVER
# EXPLOSIVE NEW WORLDS